Praise for Lorrie Moore's

ℬIRDS OF AMERICA

"A nest of tales that captures the eternal, hummingbird flutter of the human heart.... A volume in which everything comes together: the author's mordant Dorothy Parker wit, the Joycean epiphanies, the Flannery O'Connor–esque moments of clarity and grace."
—*The Atlanta Journal-Constitution*

"These new stories sparkle; they are keenly and poignantly mindful of the idioms, banalities and canards of contemporary American society, and they hum with Moore's earmark droll and incisive banter, her astonishing ability to render the intricacy of character in a few sharply focused details."
—*Houston Chronicle*

"Cements [Moore's] reputation as one of our finest writers of fiction."
—*Austin American-Statesman*

"Lorrie Moore has made laughingstocks of all of us. And we're devotedly, blissfully grateful. . . . Moore . . . packs more rambunctious American humor and worldly-wide melancholy into a story than many lesser writers can into an entire novel."
—*Newsday*

"[Moore] uses language to create a kind of carbonated prose: sentences with pop and fizz, with an effervescence of imagination that continually surprises."
—*The Dallas Morning News*

"Bats, flamingos, crows, performing ducks and bird feeders crop up in every story, but the real subject is human nature and the myriad ways Moore's characters flock together or fly apart in the face of change, stasis or grief. . . . Gorgeous. . . . Rarely has a writer achieved such consistency, humor and compassion."
—*Seattle Post-Intelligencer*

Lorrie Moore

$\mathscr{B}$IRDS OF AMERICA

Lorrie Moore is the author of the story collections
Self-Help, *Like Life*, and *Birds of America*, and the nov-
els *Who Will Run the Frog Hospital?*, *Anagrams*, and
A Gate at the Stairs. Her work has appeared in *The
New Yorker*, *The Best American Short Stories*, and *Prize
Stories: The O. Henry Awards*. She is a professor of
English at the University of Wisconsin in Madison.

BIRDS OF AMERICA

Stories

Lorrie Moore

VINTAGE CONTEMPORARIES
Vintage Books
A Division of Random House, Inc.
New York

FIRST VINTAGE CONTEMPORARIES EDITION, JANUARY 2010

Eleven of these stories were originally published in slightly different form in the following:

Elle: "Agnes of Iowa"; *Harper's*: "What You Want to Do Fine" (originally titled "Lucky Ducks"); *The New York Times*: "Four Calling Birds, Three French Hens" (originally titled "If Only Bert Were Here"); *The New Yorker*: "Beautiful Grade," "Charades," "Community Life," "Dance in America," "People Like That Are the Only People Here," "Which Is More Than I Can Say About Some People," and "Willing"; *The Paris Review*: "Terrific Mother."

Grateful acknowledgment is made to the following for permission to reprint previously published material:

Alfred A. Knopf, Inc.: Excerpt from "Syrinx" from *A Silence Opens* by Amy Clampitt, copyright © 1993 by Amy Clampitt. Reprinted by permission of Alfred A. Knopf, Inc.; *W. W. Norton & Company, Inc.*: Excerpt from "The Meaning of Birds" from *Indistinguishable from the Darkness* by Charlie Smith, copyright © 1990 by Charlie Smith. Reprinted by permission of W. W. Norton & Company, Inc.

The Library of Congress has cataloged the Knopf edition as follows:
Moore, Lorrie.
Birds of America by Lorrie Moore.—1st ed.
p. cm.
1. United States—Social life and customs—20th century—Fiction.
PS3565.O6225B57 1999
813'.54—dc21
98-6144 CIP

Vintage ISBN: 978-0-307-47496-4

Book design by Dorothy S. Baker

www.vintagebooks.com

Printed in the United States of America
20 19 18 17 16 15 14 13 12

This book is for my sister and for my parents

and for Benjamin

CONTENTS

ACKNOWLEDGMENTS

For their greatly appreciated and timely generosity I wish to thank the Ingram Merrill Foundation, the University of Wisconsin Graduate Research Committee, and the Dane County Cultural Affairs Commission. I also wish to thank, as ever, Melanie Jackson and Victoria Wilson for their abiding patience and skill. My gratitude also goes to the various editors who saw some of these stories early (and into light): Pat Towers, George Plimpton, Mike Levitas, Barbara Jones, Bill Buford, and Alice Quinn.

Birds of America

. . . it is not news that we live in a world
Where beauty is unexplainable
And suddenly ruined
And has its own routines. We are often far
From home in a dark town, and our griefs
Are difficult to translate into a language
Understood by others.

CHARLIE SMITH
"The Meaning of Birds"

Is it *o-ka-lee*
Or *con-ka-ree*, is it really *jug jug*,
Is it *cuckoo* for that matter?—
Much less whether a bird's call
Means anything in
Particular, or at all.

AMY CLAMPITT
"Syrinx"

WILLING

How can I live my life without committing an
act with a giant scissors?

—JOYCE CAROL OATES,
"An Interior Monologue"

In her last picture, the camera had lingered at the hip, the
naked hip, and even though it wasn't her hip, she acquired a
reputation for being willing.

"You have the body," studio heads told her over lunch at
Chasen's.

She looked away. "Habeas corpus," she said, not smiling.

"Pardon me?" A hip that knew Latin. Christ.

"Nothing," she said. They smiled at her and dropped
names. Scorsese, Brando. Work was all playtime to them, playtime with gel in their hair. At times, she felt bad that it *wasn't*
her hip. It should have been her hip. A mediocre picture, a
picture queasy with pornography: these, she knew, eroticized
the unavailable. The doctored and false. The stand-in. Unwit-
tingly, she had participated. Let a hip come between. A false,
unavailable, anonymous hip. She herself was true as a goddamn
dairy product; available as lunch whenever.

But she was pushing forty.

She began to linger in juice bars. Sit for entire afternoons in places called I Love Juicy or Orange-U-Sweet. She drank juice and, outside, smoked a cigarette now and then. She'd been taken seriously—once—she knew that. Projects were discussed: Nina. Portia. Mother Courage with makeup. Now her hands trembled too much, even drinking juice, *especially* drinking juice, a Vantage wobbling between her fingers like a compass dial. She was sent scripts in which she was supposed to say lines she would never say, not wear clothes she would never not wear. She began to get obscene phone calls, and postcards signed, "Oh yeah, baby." Her boyfriend, a director with a growing reputation for expensive flops, a man who twice a week glowered at her Fancy Sunburst guppy and told it to get a job, became a Catholic and went back to his wife.

"Just when we were working out the bumps and chops and rocks," she said. Then she wept.

"I know," he said. "I know."

And so she left Hollywood. Phoned her agent and apologized. Went home to Chicago, rented a room by the week at the Days Inn, drank sherry, and grew a little plump. She let her life get dull—dull, but with Hostess cakes. There were moments bristling with deadness, when she looked out at her life and went *"What?"* Or worse, feeling interrupted and tired, "Wha—?" It had taken on the shape of a terrible mistake. She hadn't been given the proper tools to make a real life with, she decided, that was it. She'd been given a can of gravy and a hairbrush and told, "There you go." She'd stood there for years, blinking and befuddled, brushing the can with the brush.

Still, she was a minor movie star, once nominated for a major award. Mail came to her indirectly. A notice. A bill. A Thanksgiving card. But there was never a party, a dinner, an opening, an iced tea. One of the problems with people in Chicago, she remembered, was that they were never lonely at the same time. Their sadnesses occurred in isolation, lurched and spazzed, sent them spinning fizzily back into empty, padded corners, disconnected and alone.

She watched cable and ordered in a lot from a pizza place. A life of obscurity and radical calm. She rented a piano and practiced scales. She invested in the stock market. She wrote down her dreams in the morning to locate clues as to what to trade. *Disney,* her dreams said once. *St. Jude's Medical.* She made a little extra money. She got obsessed. The words *cash cow* nestled in the side of her mouth like a cud. She tried to be original—not a good thing with stocks—and she began to lose. When a stock went down, she bought more of it, to catch it on the way back up. She got confused. She took to staring out the window at Lake Michigan, the rippled slate of it like a blackboard gone bad.

"Sidra, *what* are you doing there?" shrieked her friend Tommy long distance over the phone. "Where are you? You're living in some state that borders on North Dakota!" He was a screenwriter in Santa Monica and once, a long time ago and depressed on Ecstasy, they had slept together. He was gay, but they had liked each other very much.

"Maybe I'll get married," she said. She didn't mind Chicago. She thought of it as a cross between London and Queens, with a dash of Cleveland.

"Oh, *please,*" he shrieked again. "What are you *really* doing?"

"Listening to seashore and self-esteem tapes," she said. She blew air into the mouth of the phone.

"Sounds like dust on the needle," he said. "Maybe you should get the squawking crickets tape. Have you *heard* the squawking crickets tape?"

"I got a bad perm today," she said. "When I was only halfway through with the rod part, the building the salon's in had a blackout. There were men drilling out front who'd struck a cable."

"How awful for you," he said. She could hear him tap his fingers. He had made himself the make-believe author of a make-believe book of essays called *One Man's Opinion,* and when he was bored or inspired, he quoted from it. "I was once in a rock band called Bad Perm," he said instead.

"Get out." She laughed.

His voice went hushed and worried. "What *are* you *doing* there?" he asked again.

Her room was a corner room where a piano was allowed. It was L-shaped, like a life veering off suddenly to become something else. It had a couch and two maple dressers and was never as neat as she might have wanted. She always had the DO NOT DISTURB sign on when the maids came by, and so things got a little out of hand. Wispy motes of dust and hair the size of small heads bumped around in the corners. Smudge began to darken the moldings and cloud the mirrors. The bathroom faucet dripped, and, too tired to phone anyone, she tied a string around the end of it, guiding the drip quietly into the drain, so it wouldn't bother her anymore. Her only plant, facing east in the window, hung over the popcorn popper and dried to a brown crunch. On the ledge, a jack-o'-lantern she had carved for Halloween had rotted, melted, froze, and now looked like a collapsed basketball—one she might have been saving for sentimental reasons, one from the *big game*! The man who brought her room service each morning—two poached eggs and a pot of coffee—reported her to the assistant manager, and she received a written warning slid under the door.

On Fridays, she visited her parents in Elmhurst. It was still hard for her father to look her in the eyes. He was seventy now. Ten years ago, he had gone to the first movie she had ever been in, saw her remove her clothes and dive into a pool. The movie was rated PG, but he never went to another one. Her mother went to all of them and searched later for encouraging things to say. Even something small. She refused to lie. "I liked the way you said the line about leaving home, your eyes wide and your hands fussing with your dress buttons," she wrote. "That red dress was so becoming. You should wear bright colors!"

"My father takes naps a lot when I visit," she said to Tommy.

"Naps?"

"I embarrass him. He thinks I'm a whore hippie. A hippie whore."

"That's ridiculous. As I said in *One Man's Opinion*, you're the most sexually conservative person I know."

"Yeah, well."

Her mother always greeted her warmly, puddle-eyed. These days, she was reading thin paperback books by a man named Robert Valleys, a man who said that after observing all the suffering in the world—war, starvation, greed—he had discovered the cure: hugs.

Hugs, hugs, hugs, hugs, hugs.

Her mother believed him. She squeezed so long and hard that Sidra, like an infant or a lover, became lost in the feel and smell of her—her sweet, dry skin, the gray peach fuzz on her neck. "I'm so glad you left that den of iniquity," her mother said softly.

But Sidra still got calls from the den. At night, sometimes, the director phoned from a phone booth, desiring to be forgiven as well as to direct. "I think of all the things you might be thinking, and I say, 'Oh, Christ.' I mean, do you think the things I sometimes think you do?"

"Of course," said Sidra. "Of course I think those things."

"*Of course!* *Of course* is a term that has no place in this conversation!"

When Tommy phoned, she often felt a pleasure so sudden and flooding, it startled her.

"God, I'm so glad it's you!"

"You have no right to abandon American filmmaking this way!" he would say affectionately, and she would laugh loudly, for minutes without stopping. She was starting to have two speeds: Coma and Hysteria. Two meals: breakfast and popcorn. Two friends: Charlotte Peveril and Tommy. She could hear the clink of his bourbon glass. "You are too gifted a person to be living in a state that borders on North Dakota."

"Iowa."

"Holy bejesus, it's worse than I thought. I'll bet they say that there. I'll bet they say 'Bejesus.' "

"I live downtown. They don't say that here."

"Are you anywhere near Champaign-Urbana?"

"No."

"I went there once. I thought from its name that it would be a different kind of place. I kept saying to myself, 'Champagne, ur*bah* na, *champagne,* ur*bah* na! Champagne! Urbana!' " He sighed. "It was just this thing in the middle of a field. I went to a Chinese restaurant there and ordered my entire dinner with *extra* MSG."

"I'm in Chicago. It's not so bad."

"Not so bad. There are no movie people there. Sidra, what about your *acting talent*?"

"I have no acting talent."

"Hello?"

"You heard me."

"I'm not sure. For a minute there, I thought maybe you had that dizziness thing again, that inner-ear imbalance."

"Talent. I don't have *talent*. I have willingness. What *talent*?" As a kid, she had always told the raunchiest jokes. As an adult, she could rip open a bone and speak out of it. Simple, clear. There was never anything to stop her. Why was there never anything to stop her? "I can stretch out the neck of a sweater to point at a freckle on my shoulder. Anyone who didn't get enough attention in nursery school can do that. Talent is something else."

"Excuse me, okay? I'm only a screenwriter. But someone's got you thinking you went from serious actress to aging bimbo.

That's ridiculous. You just have to weather things a little out here. Besides. I think willing yourself to do a thing is brave, and the very essence of talent."

Sidra looked at her hands, already chapped and honeycombed with bad weather, bad soap, bad life. She needed to listen to the crickets tape. "But I *don't* will myself," she said. "I'm just already willing."

She began to go to blues bars at night. Sometimes she called Charlotte Peveril, her one friend left from high school.

"Siddy, how are you?" In Chicago, Sidra was thought of as a hillbilly name. But in L.A., people had thought it was beautiful and assumed she'd made it up.

"I'm fine. Let's go get drunk and listen to music."

Sometimes she just went by herself.

"Don't I know you from the movies?" a man might ask at one of the breaks, smiling, leering in a twinkly way.

"Maybe," she'd say, and he would look suddenly panicked and back away.

One night, a handsome man in a poncho, a bad poncho—though was there such a thing as a good poncho? asked Charlotte—sat down next to her with an extra glass of beer. "You look like you should be in the movies," he said. Sidra nodded wearily. "But I don't go to the movies. So if you *were* in the movies, I would never have gotten to set my eyes on you."

She turned her gaze from his poncho to her sherry, then back. Perhaps he had spent some time in Mexico or Peru. "What do you do?"

"I'm an auto mechanic." He looked at her carefully. "My name's Walter. Walt." He pushed the second beer her way. "The drinks here are okay as long as you don't ask them to mix anything. Just don't ask them to mix anything!"

She picked it up and took a sip. There was something about him she liked: something earthy beneath the act. In L.A., beneath the act you got nougat or Styrofoam. Or glass. Sidra's mouth was lined with sherry. Walt's lips shone with beer. "What's the last movie you saw?" she asked him.

"The last movie I saw. Let's see." He was thinking, but she could tell he wasn't good at it. She watched with curiosity the folded-in mouth, the tilted head: at last, a guy who didn't go to the movies. His eyes rolled back like the casters on a clerk's chair, searching. "You know what I saw?"

"No. What?" She was getting drunk.

"It was this cartoon movie." Animation. She felt relieved. At least it wasn't one of those bad art films starring what's-her-name. "A man is asleep, having a dream about a beautiful little country full of little people." Walt sat back, looked around the room, as if that were all.

"*And?*" She was going to have to push and pull with this guy.

" 'And?' " he repeated. He leaned forward again. "And one day the people realize that they are only creatures in this man's dream. Dream people! And if the man wakes up, they will no longer exist!"

Now she hoped he wouldn't go on. She had changed her mind a little.

"So they all get together at a town meeting and devise a plan," he continued. Perhaps the band would be back soon. "They will burst into the man's bedroom and bring him back to a padded, insulated room in the town—the town of his own dream—and there they will keep watch over him to make sure he stays asleep. And they do just that. Forever and ever, everyone guarding him carefully, but apprehensively, making sure he never wakes up." He smiled. "I forget what the name of it was."

"And he never wakes up."

"Nope." He grinned at her. She liked him. She could tell he could tell. He took a sip of his beer. He looked around the bar, then back at her. "Is this a great country or what?" he said.

She smiled at him, with longing. "Where do you live," she asked, "and how do I get there?"

"I met a man," she told Tommy on the phone. "His name is Walter."

"A forced relationship. You're in a state of stress—you're in a *syndrome,* I can tell. You're going to force this romance. What does he do?"

"Something with cars." She sighed. "I want to sleep with someone. When I'm sleeping with someone, I'm less obsessed with the mail."

"But perhaps you should just be alone, be by yourself for a while."

"Like you've ever been alone," said Sidra. "I mean, have you *ever* been alone?"

"I've been alone."

"Yeah, and for how long?"

"Hours," said Tommy. He sighed. "At least it felt like hours."

"Right," she said, "so don't go lecturing me about inner resources."

"Okay. So I sold the mineral rights to my body years ago, but, hey, at least *I* got good money for mine."

"I got some money," said Sidra. "I got some."

Walter leaned her against his parked car. His mouth was slightly lopsided, paisley-shaped, his lips anneloid and full, and he kissed her hard. There was something numb and on hold in her. There were small dark pits of annihilation she discovered in her heart, in the loosening fist of it, and she threw herself into them, falling. She went home with him, slept with him. She told him who she was. A minor movie star once nominated

for a major award. She told him she lived at the Days Inn. He
had been there once, to the top, for a drink. But he did not seem
to know her name.

"Never thought I'd sleep with a movie star," he did say.
"I suppose that's every man's dream." He laughed—lightly,
nervously.

"Just don't wake up," she said. Then she pulled the covers
to her chin.

"Or change the dream," he added seriously. "I mean, in the
movie I saw, everything is fine until the sleeping guy begins to
dream about something else. I don't think he wills it or anything; it just happens."

"You didn't tell me about that part."

"That's right," he said. "You see, the guy starts dreaming
about flamingos and then all the little people turn into flamingos and fly away."

"Really?" said Sidra.

"I *think* it was flamingos. I'm not too expert with birds."

"You're *not?*" She was trying to tease him, but it came out
wrong, like a lizard with a little hat on.

"To tell you the truth, I really don't think I ever saw a single movie you were in."

"Good." She was drifting, indifferent, no longer paying
attention.

He hitched his arm behind his head, wrist to nape. His
chest heaved up and down. "I think I may of *heard* of you,
though."

Django Reinhardt was on the radio. She listened, carefully.
"Astonishing sounds came from that man's hands," Sidra
murmured.

Walter tried to kiss her, tried to get her attention back. He
wasn't that interested in music, though at times he tried to be.
" 'Astonishing sounds'?" he said. "Like this?" He cupped his
palms together, making little pops and suction noises.

"Yeah," she murmured. But she was elsewhere, letting a dry wind sweep across the plain of her to sleep. "Like that."

He began to realize, soon, that she did not respect him. A bug could sense it. A doorknob could figure it out. She never quite took him seriously. She would talk about films and film directors, then look at him and say, "Oh, never mind." She was part of some other world. A world she no longer liked.

And now she was somewhere else. Another world she no longer liked.

But she was willing. Willing to give it a whirl. Once in a while, though she tried not to, she asked him about children, about having children, about turning kith to kin. How did he feel about all that? It seemed to her that if she were ever going to have a life of children and lawn mowers and grass clippings, it would be best to have it with someone who was not demeaned or trivialized by discussions of them. Did he like those big fertilized lawns? How about a nice rock garden? How did he feel deep down about those combination storm windows with the built-in screens?

"Yeah, I like them all right," he said, and she would nod slyly and drink a little too much. She would try then not to think too strenuously about her *whole life.* She would try to live life one day at a time, like an alcoholic—drink, don't drink, drink. Perhaps she should take drugs.

"I always thought someday I would have a little girl and name her after my grandmother." Sidra sighed, peered wistfully into her sherry.

"What was your grandmother's name?"

Sidra looked at his paisley mouth. "Grandma. Her name was Grandma." Walter laughed in a honking sort of way. "Oh, thank you," murmured Sidra. "Thank you for laughing."

Walter had a subscription to *AutoWeek.* He flipped through

it in bed. He also liked to read repair manuals for new cars, particularly the Toyotas. He knew a lot about control panels, light-up panels, side panels.

"You're so obviously wrong for each other," said Charlotte over tapas at a tapas bar.

"Hey, please," said Sidra. "I think my taste's a little subtler than that." The thing with tapas bars was that you just kept stuffing things into your mouth. "Obviously wrong is just the beginning. That's where I *always* begin. At obviously wrong." In theory, she liked the idea of mismatched couples, the wrangling and retangling, like a comedy by Shakespeare.

"I can't imagine you with someone like him. He's just not special." Charlotte had met him only once. But she had heard of him from a girlfriend of hers. He had slept around, she'd said. "Into the pudding" is how she phrased it, and there were some boring stories. "Just don't let him humiliate you. Don't mistake a lack of sophistication for sweetness," she added.

"I'm supposed to wait around for someone special, while every other girl in this town gets to have a life?"

"I don't know, Sidra."

It was true. Men could be with whomever they pleased. But women had to date better, kinder, richer, and bright, bright, bright, or else people got embarrassed. It suggested sexual things. "I'm a very average person," she said desperately, somehow detecting that Charlotte already knew that, knew the deep, dark, wildly obvious secret of that, and how it made Sidra slightly pathetic, unseemly—*inferior,* when you got right down to it. Charlotte studied Sidra's face, headlights caught in the stare of a deer. Guns don't kill people, thought Sidra fizzily. Deer kill people.

"Maybe it's that we all used to envy you so much," Charlotte said a little bitterly. "You were so talented. You got all the lead parts in the plays. You were everyone's dream of what *they* wanted."

Sidra poked around at the appetizer in front of her, gardening it like a patch of land. She was unequal to anyone's wistfulness. She had made too little of her life. Its loneliness shamed her like a crime. "Envy," said Sidra. "That's a lot like hate, isn't it." But Charlotte didn't say anything. Probably she wanted Sidra to change the subject. Sidra stuffed her mouth full of feta cheese and onions, and looked up. "Well, all I can say is, I'm glad to be back." A piece of feta dropped from her lips.

Charlotte looked down at it and smiled. "I know what you mean," she said. She opened her mouth wide and let all the food inside fall out onto the table.

Charlotte could be funny like that. Sidra had forgotten that about her.

Walter had found some of her old movies in the video-rental place. She had a key. She went over one night and discovered him asleep in front of *Recluse with Roommate*. It was about a woman named Rose who rarely went out, because when she did, she was afraid of people. They seemed like alien life-forms—soulless, joyless, speaking asyntactically. Rose quickly became loosened from reality. Walter had it freeze-framed at the funny part, where Rose phones the psych ward to have them come take her away, but they refuse. She lay down next to him and tried to sleep, too, but began to cry a little. He stirred. "What's wrong?" he asked.

"Nothing. You fell asleep. Watching me."

"I was tired," he said.

"I guess so."

"Let me kiss you. Let me find your panels." His eyes were closed. She could be anybody.

"Did you like the beginning part of the movie?" This need in her was new. Frightening. It made her hair curl. When had she ever needed so much?

"It was okay," he said.

. . .

"So what is this guy, a race-car driver?" asked Tommy.

"No, he's a mechanic."

"Ugh! Quit him like a music lesson!"

"Like *a music lesson*? What is this, *Similes from the Middle Class? One Man's Opinion?*" She was irritated.

"Sidra. This is not right! You need to go out with someone really smart for a change."

"I've been out with smart. I've been out with someone who had two Ph.D.'s. We spent all of our time in bed with the light on, proofreading his vita." She sighed. "Every little thing he'd ever done, every little, little, little. I mean, have you ever seen a vita?"

Tommy sighed, too. He had heard this story of Sidra's before. "Yes," he said. "I thought Patti LuPone was great."

"Besides," she said. "Who says he's not smart?"

The Japanese cars were the most interesting. Though the Americans were getting sexier, trying to keep up with them. *Those Japs!*

"Let's talk about my world," she said.

"What world?"

"Well, something *I'm* interested in. Something where there's something in it for me."

"Okay." He turned and dimmed the lights, romantically. "Got a stock tip for you," he said.

She was horrified, dispirited, interested.

He told her the name of a company somebody at work invested in. AutVis.

"What is it?"

"I don't know. But some guy at work said buy this week. They're going to make some announcement. If I had money, I'd buy."

She bought, the very next morning. A thousand shares. By the afternoon, the stock had plummeted 10 percent; by the following morning, 50. She watched the ticker tape go by on the bottom of the TV news channel. She had become the major stockholder. The major stockholder of a dying company! Soon they were going to be calling her, wearily, to ask what she wanted done with the forklift.

"You're a neater eater than I am," Walter said to her over dinner at the Palmer House.

She looked at him darkly. "What the hell were you thinking of, recommending that stock?" she asked. "How could you be such an irresponsible idiot?" She saw it now, how their life would be together. She would yell; then he would yell. He would have an affair; then she would have an affair. And then they would be gone and gone, and they would live in that gone.

"I got the name wrong," he said. "Sorry."

"You what?"

"It wasn't AutVis. It was AutDrive. I kept thinking it was vis for vision."

" 'Vis for vision,' " she repeated.

"I'm not that good with names," confessed Walter. "I do better with concepts."

" 'Concepts,' " she repeated as well.

The concept of anger. The concept of bills. The concept of flightless, dodo love.

Outside, there was a watery gust from the direction of the lake. "Chicago," said Walter. "The Windy City. Is this the Windy City or what?" He looked at her hopefully, which made her despise him more.

She shook her head. "I don't even know why we're together," she said. "I mean, why are we even together?"

He looked at her hard. "I can't answer that for you," he yelled. He took two steps back, away from her. "You've got to answer that for yourself!" And he hailed his own cab, got in, and rode away.

She walked back to the Days Inn alone. She played scales soundlessly, on the tops of the piano keys, her thin-jointed fingers lifting and falling quietly like the tines of a music box or the legs of a spider. When she tired, she turned on the television, moved through the channels, and discovered an old movie she'd been in, a love story—murder mystery called *Finishing Touches*. It was the kind of performance she had become, briefly, known for: a patched-together intimacy with the audience, half cartoon, half revelation; a cross between shyness and derision. She had not given a damn back then, sort of like now, only then it had been a style, a way of being, not a diagnosis or demise.

Perhaps she should have a baby.

In the morning, she went to visit her parents in Elmhurst. For winter, they had plastic-wrapped their home—the windows, the doors—so that it looked like a piece of avant-garde art. "Saves on heating bills," they said.

They had taken to discussing her in front of her. "It was a movie, Don. It was a movie about adventure. Nudity can be art."

"That's not how I saw it! That's not how I saw it at all!" said her father, red-faced, leaving the room. Naptime.

"How are you doing?" asked her mother, with what seemed like concern but was really an opening for something else. She had made tea.

"I'm okay, really," said Sidra. Everything she said about herself now sounded like a lie. If she was bad, it sounded like a lie; if she was fine—also a lie.

Her mother fiddled with a spoon. "I was envious of you." Her mother sighed. "I was always so envious of you! My own daughter!" She was shrieking it, saying it softly at first and then shrieking. It was exactly like Sidra's childhood: just when she thought life had become simple again, her mother gave her a new portion of the world to organize.

"I have to go," said Sidra. She had only just gotten there, but she wanted to go. She didn't want to visit her parents anymore. She didn't want to look at their lives.

She went back to the Days Inn and phoned Tommy. She and Tommy understood each other. "I *get* you," he used to say. His childhood had been full of sisters. He'd spent large portions of it drawing pictures of women in bathing suits—Miss Kenya from Nairobi!—and then asking one of the sisters to pick the most beautiful. If he disagreed, he asked another sister.

The connection was bad, and suddenly she felt too tired. "Darling, are you okay?" he said faintly.

"I'm okay."

"I think I'm hard of hearing," he said.

"I think I'm hard of talking," she said. "I'll phone you tomorrow."

She phoned Walter instead. "I need to see you," she said.

"Oh, really?" he said skeptically, and then added, with a sweetness he seemed to have plucked expertly from the air like a fly, "Is this a great country or what?"

She felt grateful to be with him again. "Let's never be apart," she whispered, rubbing his stomach. He had the physical inclinations of a dog: he liked stomach, ears, excited greetings.

"Fine by me," he said.

"Tomorrow, let's go out to dinner somewhere really expensive. My treat."

"Uh," said Walter, "tomorrow's no good."

"Oh."

"How about Sunday?"

"What's wrong with tomorrow?"

"I've got. Well, I've gotta work and I'll be tired, first of all."

"What's second of all?"

"I'm getting together with this woman I know."

"Oh?"

"It's no big deal. It's nothing. It's not a date or anything."

"Who is she?"

"Someone whose car I fixed. Loose mountings in the exhaust system. She wants to get together and talk about it some more. She wants to know about catalytic converters. You know, women are afraid of getting taken advantage of."

"Really!"

"Yeah, well, so Sunday would be better."

"Is she attractive?"

Walter scrinched up his face and made a sound of unenthusiasm. "Enh," he said, and placed his hand laterally in the air, rotating it up and down a little.

Before he left in the morning, she said, "Just don't sleep with her."

"*Sidra,*" he said, scolding her for lack of trust or for attempted supervision—she wasn't sure which.

That night, he didn't come home. She phoned and phoned and then drank a six-pack and fell asleep. In the morning, she phoned again. Finally, at eleven o'clock, he answered.

She hung up.

At 11:30, her phone rang. "Hi," he said cheerfully. He was in a good mood.

"So where were you all night?" asked Sidra. This was what she had become. She felt shorter and squatter and badly coiffed.

There was some silence. "What do you mean?" he said cautiously.

"You know what I mean."

More silence. "Look, I didn't call this morning to get into a heavy conversation."

"Well, then," said Sidra, "you certainly called the wrong number." She slammed down the phone.

She spent the day trembling and sad. She felt like a cross

between Anna Karenina and Amy Liverhaus, who used to shout from the fourth-grade cloakroom, "I just don't feel *appreciated.*" She walked over to Marshall Field's to buy new makeup. "You're much more of a cream beige than an ivory," said the young woman working the cosmetics counter.

But Sidra clutched at the ivory. "People are always telling me that," she said, "and it makes me very cross."

She phoned him later that night and he was there. "We need to talk," she said.

"I want my key back," he said.

"Look. Can you just come over here so that we can talk?"

He arrived bearing flowers—white roses and irises. They seemed wilted and ironic; she leaned them against the wall in a dry glass, no water.

"All right, I admit it," he said. "I went out on a date. But I'm not saying I slept with her."

She could feel, suddenly, the promiscuity in him. It was a heat, a creature, a tenant twin. "I already know you slept with her."

"How can you know that?"

"Get a life! What am I, an idiot?" She glared at him and tried not to cry. She hadn't loved him enough and he had sensed it. She hadn't really loved him at all, not really.

But she had liked him a lot!

So it still seemed unfair. A bone in her opened up, gleaming and pale, and she held it to the light and spoke from it. "I want to know one thing." She paused, not really for effect, but it had one. "Did you have oral sex?"

He looked stunned. "What kind of question is that? I don't have to answer a question like that."

"*You don't have to answer a question like that.* You don't have any rights here!" she began to yell. She was dehydrated. "You're the one who did this. Now I want the truth. I just want to know. Yes or no!"

He threw his gloves across the room.

"Yes or no," she said.

He flung himself onto the couch, pounded the cushion with his fist, placed an arm up over his eyes.

"Yes or no," she repeated.

He breathed deeply into his shirtsleeve.

"Yes or no."

"Yes," he said.

She sat down on the piano bench. Something dark and coagulated moved through her, up from the feet. Something light and breathing fled through her head, the house of her plastic-wrapped and burned down to tar. She heard him give a moan, and some fleeing hope in her, surrounded but alive on the roof, said perhaps he would beg her forgiveness. Promise to be a new man. She might find him attractive as a new, begging man. Though at some point, he would have to stop begging. He would just have to be normal. And then she would dislike him again.

He stayed on the sofa, did not move to comfort or be comforted, and the darkness in her cleaned her out, hollowed her like acid or a wind.

"I don't know what to do," she said, something palsied in her voice. She felt cheated of all the simple things—the radical calm of obscurity, of routine, of blah domestic bliss. "I don't want to go back to L.A.," she said. She began to stroke the tops of the piano keys, pushing against one and finding it broken—thudding and pitchless, shiny and mocking like an opened bone. She hated, hated her life. Perhaps she had always hated it.

He sat up on the sofa, looked distraught and false—his face badly arranged. He should practice in a mirror, she thought. He did not know how to break up with a movie actress. It was boys' rules: don't break up with a movie actress. Not in Chicago. If *she* left *him,* he would be better able to explain it, to himself, in the future, to anyone who asked. His voice shifted into something meant to sound imploring. "I know" was what he said, in a tone approximating hope, faith, some charity or other. "I know you might not *want* to."

"For your own good," he was saying. "Might be willing . . ." he was saying. But she was already turning into something else, a bird—a flamingo, a hawk, a flamingo-hawk—and was flying up and away, toward the filmy pane of the window, then back again, circling, meanly, with a squint.

He began, suddenly, to cry—loudly at first, with lots of *oh*s, then tiredly, as if from a deep sleep, his face buried in the poncho he'd thrown over the couch arm, his body sinking into the plush of the cushions—a man held hostage by the anxious cast of his dream.

"What can I do?" he asked.

But his dream had now changed, and she was gone, gone out the window, gone, gone.

WHICH IS MORE THAN I CAN SAY
ABOUT SOME PEOPLE

It was a fear greater than death, according to the magazines. Death was number four. After mutilation, three, and divorce, two. Number one, the real fear, the one death could not even approach, was public speaking. Abby Mallon knew this too well. Which is why she had liked her job at American Scholastic Tests: she got to work with words in a private way. The speech she made was done in the back, alone, like little shoes cobbled by an elf: spider is to web as weaver is to *blank*. That one was hers. She was proud of that.

Also, *blank* is to heartache as forest is to bench.

But then one day the supervisor and the AST district coordinator called her upstairs. She was good, they said, but perhaps she had become *too* good, too *creative,* they suggested, and gave her a promotion out of the composing room and into the high school auditoriums of America. She would have to travel and give speeches, tell high school faculty how to prepare students for

the entrance exams, meet separately with the juniors and
seniors and answer their questions unswervingly, with authority and grace. "You may have a vacation first," they said, and
handed her a check.

"Thank you," she said doubtfully. In her life, she had been
given the gift of solitude, a knack for it, but now it would be of
no professional use. She would have to become a people person.

"A *peeper* person?" queried her mother on the phone from
Pittsburgh.

"*People,*" said Abby.

"Oh, those," said her mother, and she sighed the sigh of
death, though she was strong as a brick.

Of all Abby's fanciful ideas for self-improvement (the inspira-
tional video, the breathing exercises, the hypnosis class), the
Blarney Stone, with its whoring barter of eloquence for love—
O GIFT OF GAB, read the T-shirts—was perhaps the most
extreme. Perhaps. There had been, after all, her marriage to
Bob, her boyfriend of many years, after her dog, Randolph, had
died of kidney failure and marriage to Bob seemed the only way
to overcome her grief. Of course, she had always admired the
idea of marriage, the citizenship and public speech of it, the
innocence rebestowed, and Bob was big and comforting. But he
didn't have a lot to say. He was not a verbal man. Rage gave
him syntax—but it just wasn't enough! Soon Abby had begun
to keep him as a kind of pet, while she quietly looked for dis-
tractions of depth and consequence. She looked for words. She
looked for ways with words. She worked hard to befriend a lyricist from New York—a tepid, fair-haired, violet-eyed bachelor—she and most of the doctors' wives and arts administrators
in town. He was newly arrived, owned no car, and wore the
same tan blazer every day. "Water, water everywhere but not a
drop to drink," said the bachelor lyricist once, listening wanly
to the female chirp of his phone messages. In his apartment,

there were no novels or bookcases. There was one chair, as well as a large television set, the phone machine, a rhyming dictionary continuously renewed from the library, and a coffee table. Women brought him meals, professional introductions, jingle commissions, and cash grants. In return, he brought them small piebald stones from the beach, or a pretty weed from the park. He would stand behind the coffee table and recite his own songs, then step back and wait fearfully to be seduced. To be lunged at and devoured by the female form was, he believed, something akin to applause. Sometimes he would produce a rented lute and say, "Here, I've just composed a melody to go with my Creation verse. Sing along with me."

And Abby would stare at him and say, "But I don't know the tune. I haven't heard it yet. You just made it up, you said."

Oh, the vexations endured by a man of poesy! He stood paralyzed behind the coffee table, and when Abby did at last step forward, just to touch him, to take his pulse, perhaps, *to capture one of his arms in an invisible blood-pressure cuff*! he crumpled and shrank. "Please don't think I'm some kind of emotional Epstein-Barr," he said, quoting from other arguments he'd had with women. "I'm not indifferent or dispassionate. I'm calm. I'm romantic, but I'm calm. I have appetites, but I'm very calm about them."

When she went back to her husband—"Honey, you're home!" Bob exclaimed—she lasted only a week. Shouldn't it have lasted longer—the mix of loneliness and lust and habit she always felt with Bob, the mix that was surely love, for it so often felt like love, how could it not be love, surely nature intended it to be, surely nature with its hurricanes and hail was counting on this to suffice? Bob smiled at her and said nothing. And the next day, she booked a flight to Ireland.

How her mother became part of the trip, Abby still couldn't exactly recall. It had something to do with a stick shift: how

Abby had never learned to drive one. "In my day and age," said her mother, "everyone learned. We all learned. Women had skills. They knew how to cook and sew. Now women have no skills."

The stick shifts were half the rental price of the automatics.

"If you're looking for a driver," hinted her mother, "I can still see the road."

"That's good," said Abby.

"And your sister Theda's spending the summer at your aunt's camp again." Theda had Down's syndrome, and the family adored her. Every time Abby visited, Theda would shout, "Look at you!" and throw her arms around her in a terrific hug. "Theda's, of course, sweet as ever," said her mother, "which is more than I can say about some people."

"That's probably true."

"I'd like to see Ireland while I can. Your father, when he was alive, never wanted to. I'm Irish, you know."

"I know. One-sixteenth."

"That's right. Of course, your father was Scottish, which is a totally different thing."

Abby sighed. "It seems to me that *Japanese* would be a totally different thing."

"*Japanese?*" hooted her mother. "Japanese is close."

And so in the middle of June, they landed at the Dublin airport together. "We're going to go all around this island, every last peninsula," said Mrs. Mallon in the airport parking lot, revving the engine of their rented Ford Fiesta, "because that's just the kind of crazy Yuppies we are."

Abby felt sick from the flight; and sitting on what should be the driver's side but without a steering wheel suddenly seemed emblematic of something.

Her mother lurched out of the parking lot and headed for the nearest roundabout, crossing into the other lane only twice.

"I'll get the hang of this," she said. She pushed her glasses far-ther up on her nose and Abby could see for the first time that her mother's eyes were milky with age. Her steering was jerky and her foot jumped around on the floor, trying to find the clutch. Perhaps this had been a mistake.

"Go straight, Mom," said Abby, looking at her map.

They zigged and zagged to the north, up and away from Dublin, planning to return to it at the end, but now heading toward Drogheda, Abby snatching up the guidebook and then the map again and then the guidebook, and Mrs. Mallon shout-ing, "What?" or "Left?" or "This can't be right; let me see that thing." The Irish countryside opened up before them, its pas-toral patchwork and stone walls and its chimney aroma of turf fires like some other century, its small stands of trees, abutting fields populated with wildflowers and sheep dung and cut sod and cows with ear tags, beautiful as women. Perhaps fairy folk lived in the trees! Abby saw immediately that to live amid the magic feel of this place would be necessarily to believe in magic. To live here would make you superstitious, warm-hearted with secrets, unrealistic. If you were literal, or practi-cal, you would have to move—or you would have to drink.

They drove uncertainly past signs to places unmarked on the map. They felt lost—but not in an uncharming way. The old narrow roads with their white side markers reminded Abby of the vacations the family had taken when she was little, the cow-country car trips through New England or Virginia—in those days before there were interstates, or plastic cups, or a populace depressed by asphalt and french fries. Ireland was a trip into the past of America. It was years behind, unmarred, like a story or a dream or a clear creek. I'm a child again, Abby thought. I'm back. And just as when she was a child, she sud-denly had to go to the bathroom.

"I have to go to the bathroom," she said. To their left was a sign that said ROAD WORKS AHEAD, and underneath it some-one had scrawled, "No, it doesn't."

Mrs. Mallon veered the car over to the left and slammed on the brakes. There were some black-faced sheep haunch-marked in bright blue and munching grass near the road.

"Here?" asked Abby.

"I don't want to waste time stopping somewhere else and having to buy something. You can go behind that wall."

"Thanks," said Abby, groping in her pocketbook for Kleenex. She missed her own apartment. She missed her neighborhood. She missed the plentiful U-Pump-Itt's, where, she often said, at least they spelled *pump* right! She got out and hiked back down the road a little way. On one of the family road trips thirty years ago, when she and Theda had had to go to the bathroom, their father had stopped the car and told them to "go to the bathroom in the woods." They had wandered through the woods for twenty minutes, looking for the bathroom, before they came back out to tell him that they hadn't been able to find it. Her father had looked perplexed, then amused, and then angry—his usual pattern.

Now Abby struggled over a short stone wall and hid, squatting, eyeing the sheep warily. She was spacey with jet lag, and when she got back to the car, she realized she'd left the guidebook back on a stone and had to turn around and retrieve it.

"There," she said, getting back in the car.

Mrs. Mallon shifted into gear. "I always feel that if people would just be like animals and excrete here and there rather than in a single agreed-upon spot, we wouldn't have any pollution."

Abby nodded. "That's brilliant, Mom."

"Is it?"

They stopped briefly at an English manor house, to see the natural world cut up into moldings and rugs, wool and wood captive and squared, the earth stolen and embalmed and shellacked. Abby wanted to leave. "Let's leave," she whispered.

"What is it with you?" complained her mother. From there,

they visited a neolithic passage grave, its floor plan like a birth in reverse, its narrow stone corridor spilling into a high, round room. They took off their sunglasses and studied the Celtic curlicues. "Older than the pyramids," announced the guide, though he failed to address its most important feature, Abby felt: its deadly maternal metaphor.

"Are you still too nervous to cross the border to Northern Ireland?" asked Mrs. Mallon.

"Uh-huh." Abby bit at her thumbnail, tearing the end of it off like a tiny twig.

"Oh, come on," said her mother. "Get a grip."

And so they crossed the border into the North, past the flak-jacketed soldiers patrolling the neighborhoods and barbed wire of Newry, young men holding automatic weapons and walking backward, block after block, their partners across the street, walking forward, on the watch. Helicopters flapped above. "This is a little scary," said Abby.

"It's all show," said Mrs. Mallon breezily.

"It's a scary show."

"If you get scared easily."

Which was quickly becoming the theme of their trip— Abby could see that already. That Abby had no courage and her mother did. And that it had forever been that way.

"You scare too easily," said her mother. "You always did. When you were a child, you wouldn't go into a house unless you were reassured there were no balloons in it."

"I didn't like balloons."

"And you were scared on the plane coming over," said her mother.

Abby grew defensive. "Only when the flight attendant said there was no coffee because the percolator was broken. Didn't you find that alarming? And then after all that slamming, they still couldn't get one of the overhead bins shut." Abby remembered this like a distant, bitter memory, though it had only been yesterday. The plane had taken off with a terrible shudder, and when it proceeded with the rattle of an old subway car, particularly over Greenland, the flight attendant had gotten on the address system to announce there was nothing to worry about, especially when you think about "how heavy air really is."

Now her mother thought she was Tarzan. "I want to go on that rope bridge I saw in the guidebook," she said.

On page 98 in the guidebook was a photograph of a rope-and-board bridge slung high between two cliffs. It was supposed to be for fishermen, but tourists were allowed, though they were cautioned about strong winds.

"Why do you want to go on the rope bridge?" asked Abby.

"*Why?*" replied her mother, who then seemed stuck and fell silent.

For the next two days, they drove east and to the north, skirting Belfast, along the coastline, past old windmills and sheep farms, and up out onto vertiginous cliffs that looked out toward Scotland, a pale sliver on the sea. They stayed at a tiny stucco bed-and-breakfast, one with a thatched roof like Cleopatra bangs. They slept lumpily, and in the morning in the breakfast room with its large front window, they ate their cereal and rashers and black and white pudding in an exhausted way, going through the motions of good guesthood—"Yes, the troubles," they agreed, for who could say for certain whom you were talking to? It wasn't like race-riven America, where you always knew. Abby nodded. Out the window, there was a breeze, but she couldn't hear the faintest rustle of it. She could only see it silently moving the dangling branches of the sun-sequined spruce, just slightly, like objects hanging from a rearview mirror in someone else's car.

She charged the bill to her Visa, tried to lift both bags, and then just lifted her own.

"Good-bye! Thank you!" she and her mother called to their host. Back in the car, briefly, Mrs. Mallon began to sing "Toora-

loora-loora." " 'Over in Killarney, many years ago,' " she war-
bled. Her voice was husky, vibrating, slightly flat, coming in
just under each note like a saucer under a cup.

And so they drove on. The night before, a whole day could
have shape and design. But when it was upon you, it could vanish tragically to air.

They came to the sign for the rope bridge.

"I want to do this," said Mrs. Mallon, and swung the car
sharply right. They crunched into a gravel parking lot and
parked; the bridge was a quarter-mile walk from there. In the
distance, dark clouds roiled like a hemorrhage, and the wind
was picking up. Rain mizzled the windshield.

"I'm going to stay here," said Abby.

"You are?"

"Yeah."

"Whatever," said her mother in a disgusted way, and she
got out, scowling, and trudged down the path to the bridge,
disappearing beyond a curve.

Abby waited, now feeling the true loneliness of this trip.
She realized she missed Bob and his warm, quiet confusion;
how he sat on the rug in front of the fireplace, where her dog,
Randolph, used to sit; sat there beneath the five Christmas
cards they'd received and placed on the mantel—five, including the one from the paperboy—sat there picking at his feet, or
naming all the fruits in his fruit salad, remarking life's great
variety! or asking what was wrong (in his own silent way),
while poking endlessly at a smoldering log. She thought, too,
about poor Randolph, at the vet, with his patchy fur and begging, dying eyes. And she thought about the pale bachelor lyricist, how he had once come to see her, and how he hadn't even
placed enough pressure on the doorbell to make it ring, and so
had stood there waiting on the porch, holding a purple cone-
flower, until she just happened to walk by the front window
and see him standing there. *O poetry!* When she invited him in,
and he gave her the flower and sat down to decry the coded

bloom and doom of all things, decry as well his own unearned deathlessness, how everything hurtles toward oblivion, except words, which assemble themselves in time like molecules in space, for God was an act—an act!—of language, it hadn't seemed silly to her, not really, at least not *that* silly.

The wind was gusting. She looked at her watch, worried now about her mother. She turned on the radio to find a weather report, though the stations all seemed to be playing strange, redone versions of American pop songs from 1970. Every so often, there was a two-minute quiz show—Who is the president of France? Is a tomato a vegetable or a fruit?—questions that the caller rarely if ever answered correctly, which made it quite embarrassing to listen to. Why did they do it? Puzzles, quizzes, game shows. Abby knew from AST that a surprising percentage of those taking the college entrance exams never actually applied to college. People just loved a test. Wasn't that true? People loved to put themselves to one.

Her mother was now knocking on the glass. She was muddy and wet. Abby unlocked the door and pushed it open. "Was it worth it?" Abby asked.

Her mother got in, big and dank and puffing. She started the car without looking at her daughter. "What a bridge," she said finally.

The next day, they made their way along the Antrim coast, through towns bannered with Union Jacks and Scottish hymns, down to Derry with its barbed wire and IRA scrawlings on the city walls—"John Major is a Zionist Jew" ("Hello," said a British officer when they stopped to stare)—and then escaping across bandit country, and once more down across the border into the south, down the Donegal coast, its fishing villages like some old, never-was Cape Cod. Staring out through the windshield, off into the horizon, Abby began to think that all the beauty and ugliness and turbulence one found scattered through nature, one could also find in people themselves, all collected there, all together in a single place. No matter what terror or loveliness the earth could produce—winds, seas—a person could produce the same, lived with the same, lived with all that mixed-up nature swirling inside, every bit. There was nothing as complex in the world—no flower or stone—as a single hello from a human being.

Once in a while, Abby and her mother broke their silences with talk of Mrs. Mallon's job as office manager at a small flashlight company—"I had to totally rearrange our insurance policies. The dental and Major Medical were eating our lunch!"—or with questions about the route signs, or the black dots signifying the auto deaths. But mostly, her mother wanted to talk about Abby's shaky marriage and what she was going to do. "Look, another ruined abbey," she took to saying every time they passed a heap of medieval stones.

"When you going back to Bob?"

"I went back," said Abby. "But then I left again. Oops."

Her mother sighed. "Women of your generation are always hoping for some other kind of romance than the one they have," said Mrs. Mallon. "Aren't they?"

"Who knows?" said Abby. She was starting to feel a little tight-lipped with her mother, crammed into this space together like astronauts. She was starting to have a highly inflamed sense of event: a single word rang and vibrated. The slightest movement could annoy, the breath, the odor. Unlike her sister, Theda, who had always remained sunny and cheerfully intimate with everyone, Abby had always been darker and left to her own devices; she and her mother had never been very close. When Abby was a child, her mother had always repelled her a bit—the oily smell of her hair, her belly button like a worm curled in a pit, the sanitary napkins in the bathroom wastebasket, horrid as a war, then later strewn along the curb by raccoons who would tear them from the trash cans at night. Once at a restaurant, when she was little, Abby had burst into an unlatched ladies' room stall, only to find her mother sitting there in a dazed and unseemly way, peering out at her from the toilet seat like a cuckoo in a clock.

There were things one should never know about another person.

Later, Abby decided that perhaps it hadn't been her mother at all.

Yet now here she and her mother were, sharing the tiniest of cars, reunited in a wheeled and metal womb, sharing small double beds in bed-and-breakfasts, waking up with mouths stale and close upon each other, or backs turned and rocking in angry-seeming humps. *The land of ire!* Talk of Abby's marriage and its possible demise trotted before them on the road like a herd of sheep, insomnia's sheep, and it made Abby want to have a gun.

"I never bothered with conventional romantic fluff," said Mrs. Mallon. "I wasn't the type. I always worked, and I was practical, put myself forward, and got things done and over with. If I liked a man, I asked him out myself. That's how I met your father. I asked him out. I even proposed the marriage."

"I know."

"And then I stayed with him until the day he died. Actually, three days after. He was a good man." She paused. "Which is more than I can say about some people."

Abby didn't say anything.

"Bob's a good man," added Mrs. Mallon.

"I didn't say he wasn't."

There was silence again between them now as the countryside once more unfolded its quilt of greens, the old roads triggering memories as if it were a land she had traveled long ago, its mix of luck and unluck like her own past; it seemed stuck in time, like a daydream or a book. Up close the mountains were craggy, scabby with rock and green, like a buck's antlers trying to lose their fuzz. But distance filled the gaps with moss. Wasn't that the truth? Abby sat quietly, glugging Ballygowan water from a plastic bottle and popping Extra Strong Mints. Perhaps she should turn on the radio, listen to one of the call-in quizzes or to the news. But then her mother would take over, fiddle and retune. Her mother was always searching for country music, songs with the words *devil woman*. She loved those.

"Promise me one thing," said Mrs. Mallon.

"What?" said Abby.

"That you'll try with Bob."

At what price? Abby wanted to yell, but she and her mother were too old for that now.

Mrs. Mallon continued, thoughtfully, with the sort of pseudowisdom she donned now that she was sixty. "Once you're with a man, you have to sit still with him. As scary as it seems. You have to be brave and learn to reap the benefits of inertia," and here she gunned the motor to pass a tractor on a curve. LOOSE CHIPPINGS said the sign. HIDDEN DIP. But Abby's mother drove as if these were mere cocktail party chatter. A sign ahead showed six black dots.

"Yeah," said Abby, clutching the dashboard. "Dad was inert. Dad was inert, except that once every three years he jumped up and socked somebody in the mouth."

"That's not true."

"It's basically true."

In Killybegs, they followed the signs for Donegal City. "You women today," Mrs. Mallon said. "You expect too much."

"If it's Tuesday, this must be Sligo," said Abby. She had taken to making up stupid jokes. "What do you call a bus with a soccer team on it?"

"What?" They passed a family of gypsies, camped next to a mountain of car batteries they hoped to sell.

"A football coach." Sometimes Abby laughed raucously,

and sometimes not at all. Sometimes she just shrugged. She was waiting for the Blarney Stone. That was all she'd come here for, so everything else she could endure.

They stopped at a bookshop to get a better map and inquire, perhaps, as to a bathroom. Inside, there were four customers: two priests reading golf books, and a mother with her tiny son, who traipsed after her along the shelves, begging, "Please, Mummy, just a wee book, Mummy. Please just a wee book." There was no better map. There was no bathroom. "Sorry," the clerk said, and one of the priests glanced up quickly. Abby and her mother went next door to look at the Kinsale smocks and wool sweaters—tiny cardigans that young Irish children, on sweltering summer days of seventy-one degrees, wore on the beach, over their bathing suits. "So cute," said Abby, and the two of them wandered through the store, touching things. In the back by the wool caps, Abby's mother found a marionette hanging from a ceiling hook and began to play with it a little, waving its arms to the store music, which was a Beethoven concerto. Abby went to pay for a smock, ask about a bathroom or a good pub, and when she came back, her mother was still there, transfixed, conducting the concerto with the puppet. Her face was arranged in girlish joy, luminous, as Abby rarely saw it. When the concerto was over, Abby handed her a bag. "Here," she said, "I bought you a smock."

Mrs. Mallon let go of the marionette, and her face darkened. "I never had a real childhood," she said, taking the bag and looking off into the middle distance. "Being the oldest, I was always my mother's confidante. I always had to act grownup and responsible. Which wasn't my natural nature." Abby steered her toward the door. "And then when I really was grown up, there was Theda, who needed all my time, and your father of course, with his demands. But then there was you. You I liked. You I could leave alone."

"I bought you a smock," Abby said again.

They used the bathroom at O'Hara's pub, bought a single

mineral water and split it, then went on to the Drumcliff cemetery to see the dead Yeatses. Then they sped on toward Sligo
City to find a room, and the next day were up and out to Knock
to watch lame women, sick women, women who wanted to get
pregnant ("Knocked up," said Abby) rub their rosaries on the
original stones of the shrine. They drove down to Clifden,
around Connemara, to Galway and Limerick—"There once
were two gals from America, one named Abby and her mother
named Erica. . . ." They sang, minstrel speed demons around
the Ring of Kerry, its palm trees and blue and pink hydrangea
like a set from an operetta. "Playgirls of the Western World!"
exclaimed her mother. They came to rest, at dark, near Ballylickey, in a bed-and-breakfast, a former hunting lodge, in a glen
just off the ring. They ate a late supper of toddies and a soda
bread their hostess called "Curranty Dick."

"Don't I know it," said Mrs. Mallon. Which depressed
Abby, like a tacky fixture in a room, and so she excused herself
and went upstairs, to bed.

It was the next day, through Ballylickey, Bantry, Skibbereen,
and Cork, that they entered Blarney. At the castle, the line to
kiss the stone was long, hot, and frightening. It jammed the
tiny winding stairs of the castle's suffocating left tower, and
people pressed themselves against the dark wall to make room
for others who had lost their nerve and were coming back
down.

"This is ridiculous," said Abby. But by the time they'd
reached the top, her annoyance had turned to anxiety. To kiss
the stone, she saw, people had to lie on their backs out over a
parapet, stretching their necks out to place their lips on the
underside of a supporting wall where the stone was laid. A
strange-looking leprechaunish man was squatting at the side of
the stone, supposedly to help people arch back, but he seemed
to be holding them too loosely, a careless and sadistic glint in

his eyes, and some people were changing their minds and going back downstairs, fearful and inarticulate as ever.

"I don't think I can do this," said Abby hesitantly, tying her dark raincoat more tightly around her.

"Of course you can," said her mother. "You've come all this way. This is why you came." Now that they were at the top of the castle, the line seemed to be moving quickly. Abby looked back, and around, and the view was green and rich, and breathtaking, like a photo soaked in dyes.

"Next!" she heard the leprechaun shouting.

Ahead of them, a German woman was struggling to get back up from where the leprechaun had left her. She wiped her mouth and made a face. "That vuz awfhul," she grumbled.

Panic seized Abby. "You know what? I don't want to do this," she said again to her mother. There were only two people ahead of them in line. One of them was now getting down on his back, clutching the iron supports and inching his hands down, arching at the neck and waist to reach the stone, exposing his white throat. His wife stood above him, taking his picture.

"But you came all this way! Don't be a ninny!" Her mother was bullying her again. It never gave her courage; in fact, it deprived her of courage. But it gave her bitterness and impulsiveness, which could look like the same thing.

"Next," said the leprechaun nastily. He hated these people; one could see that. One could see he half-hoped they would go crashing down off the ledge into a heap of raincoats, limbs, and traveler's checks.

"Go on," said Mrs. Mallon.

"I can't," Abby whined. Her mother was nudging and the leprechaun was frowning. "I can't. You go."

"No. Come on. Think of it as a test." Her mother gave her a scowl, unhinged by something lunatic in it. "You work with tests. And in school, you always did well on them."

"For tests, you have to study."

"You studied!"

"I didn't study the right thing."

"Oh, Abby."

"I can't," Abby whispered. "I just don't think I can." She breathed deeply and moved quickly. "Oh—okay." She threw her hat down and fell to the stone floor fast, to get it over with.

"Move back, move back," droned the leprechaun, like a train conductor.

She could feel now no more space behind her back; from her waist up, she was out over air and hanging on only by her clenched hands and the iron rails. She bent her head as far back as she could, but it wasn't far enough.

"Lower," said the leprechaun.

She slid her hands down farther, as if she were doing a trick on a jungle gym. Still, she couldn't see the stone itself, only the castle wall.

"Lower," said the leprechaun.

She slid her hands even lower, bent her head back, her chin skyward, could feel the vertebrae of her throat pressing out against the skin, and this time she could see the stone. It was about the size of a microwave oven and was covered with moisture and dirt and lipstick marks in the shape of lips—lavender, apricot, red. It seemed very unhygienic for a public event, filthy and wet, and so now instead of giving it a big smack, she blew a peck at it, then shouted, "Okay, help me up, please," and the leprechaun helped her back up.

Abby stood and brushed herself off. Her raincoat was covered with whitish mud. "Eeyuhh," she said. But she had done it! At least sort of. She put her hat back on. She tipped the leprechaun a pound. She didn't know how she felt. She felt nothing. Finally, these dares one made oneself commit didn't change a thing. They were all a construction of wish and string and distance.

"Now my turn," said her mother with a kind of reluctant

determination, handing Abby her sunglasses, and as her mother got down stiffly, inching her way toward the stone, Abby suddenly saw something she'd never seen before: her mother was terrified. For all her bullying and bravado, her mother was proceeding, and proceeding badly, through a great storm of terror in her brain. As her mother tried to inch herself back toward the stone, Abby, now privy to her bare face, saw that this fierce bonfire of a woman had gone twitchy and melancholic—it was a ruse, all her formidable display. She was only trying to prove something, trying pointlessly to defy and overcome her fears—instead of just learning to live with them, since, hell, you were living with them anyway. "Mom, you okay?" Mrs. Mallon's face was in a grimace, her mouth open and bared. The former auburn of her hair had descended, Abby saw, to her teeth, which she'd let rust with years of coffee and tea.

Now the leprechaun was having to hold her more than he had the other people. "Lower, now lower."

"Oh, God, not any lower," cried Mrs. Mallon.

"You're almost there."

"I don't see it."

"There you got it?" He loosened his grip and let her slip farther.

"Yes," she said. She let out a puckering, spitting sound. But then when she struggled to come back up, she seemed to be stuck. Her legs thrashed out before her; her shoes loosened from her feet; her skirt rode up, revealing the brown tops of her panty hose. She was bent too strangely, from the hips, it seemed, and she was plump and didn't have the stomach muscles to lift herself back up. The leprechaun seemed to be having difficulty.

"Can someone here help me?"

"Oh my God," said Abby, and she and another man in line immediately squatted next to Mrs. Mallon to help her. She was heavy, stiff with fright, and when they had finally lifted her and gotten her sitting, then standing again, she seemed stricken and pale.

A guard near the staircase volunteered to escort her down. "Would you like that, Mom?" and Mrs. Mallon simply nodded.

"You get in front of us," the guard said to Abby in the singsong accent of County Cork, "just in case she falls." And Abby got in front, her coat taking the updraft and spreading to either side as she circled slowly down into the dungeon-dark of the stairwell, into the black like a bat new to its wings.

In a square in the center of town, an evangelist was waving a Bible and shouting about "the brevity of life," how it was a thing grabbed by one hand and then gone, escaped through the fingers. "God's word is quick!" he called out.

"Let's go over there," said Abby, and she took her mother to a place called Brady's Public House for a restorative Guinness. "Are you okay?" Abby kept asking. They still had no place to stay that night, and though it remained light quite late, and the inns stayed open until ten, she imagined the two of them temporarily homeless, sleeping under the stars, snacking on slugs. Stars the size of Chicago! Dew like a pixie bath beneath them! They would lick it from their arms.

"I'm fine," she said, waving Abby's questions away. "What a stone!"

"Mom," said Abby, frowning, for she was now wondering about a few things. "When you went across that rope bridge, did you do that okay?"

Mrs. Mallon sighed. "Well, I got the idea of it," she said huffily. "But there were some gusts of wind that caused it to buck a little, and though some people thought that was fun, I had to get down and crawl back. You'll recall there was a little rain."

"You crawled back on your hands and knees?"

"Well, yes," she admitted. "There was a nice Belgian man who helped me." She felt unmasked, no doubt, before her daughter and now gulped at her Guinness.

Abby tried to take a cheerful tone, switching the subject a little, and it reminded her of Theda, Theda somehow living in her voice, her larynx suddenly a summer camp for the cheerful and slow. "Well, look at you!" said Abby. "Do you feel eloquent and confident, now that you've kissed the stone?"

"Not really." Mrs. Mallon shrugged.

Now that they had kissed it, or sort of, would they become self-conscious? What would they end up talking about?

Movies, probably. Just as they always had at home. Movies with scenery, movies with songs.

"How about you?" asked Mrs. Mallon.

"Well," said Abby, "mostly I feel like we've probably caught strep throat. And yet, and yet . . ." Here she sat up and leaned forward. No tests, or radio quizzes, or ungodly speeches, or songs brain-dead with biography, or kooky prayers, or shouts, or prolix conversations that with drink and too much time always revealed how stupid and mean even the best people were, just simply this: "A toast. I feel a toast coming on."

"You do?"

"Yes, I do." No one had toasted Abby and Bob at their little wedding, and that's what had been wrong, she believed now. No toast. There had been only thirty guests and they had simply eaten the ham canapes and gone home. How could a marriage go right? It wasn't that such ceremonies were important in and of themselves. They were nothing. They were zeros. But they were zeros as placeholders; they held numbers and equations intact. And once you underwent them, you could move on, know the empty power of their blessing, and not spend time missing them.

From here on in, she would believe in toasts. One was collecting itself now, in her head, in a kind of hesitant philately.

She gazed over at her mother and took a deep breath. Perhaps her mother had never shown Abby affection, not really, but she had given her a knack for solitude, with its terrible lurches outward, and its smooth glide back to peace. Abby would toast her for that. It was really the world that was one's brutal mother, the one that nursed and neglected you, and your own mother was only your sibling in that world. Abby lifted her glass. "May the worst always be behind you. May the sun daily warm your arms. . . ." She looked down at her cocktail napkin for assistance, but there was only a cartoon of a big-chested colleen, two shamrocks over her breasts. Abby looked back up. *God's word is quick!* "May your car always start—" But perhaps God might also begin with tall, slow words; the belly bloat of a fib; the distended tale. "And may you always have a clean shirt," she continued, her voice growing gallant, public and loud, "and a holding roof, healthy children and good cabbages—and may you be with me in my heart, Mother, as you are now, in this place; always and forever—like a flaming light."

There was noise in the pub.

Blank is to childhood as journey is to lips.

"Right," said Mrs. Mallon, looking into her stout in a concentrated, bright-eyed way. She had never been courted before, not once in her entire life, and now she blushed, ears on fire, lifted her pint, and drank.

DANCE IN AMERICA

I tell them dance begins when a moment of hurt combines with a moment of boredom. I tell them it's the body's reaching, bringing air to itself. I tell them that it's the heart's triumph, the victory speech of the feet, the refinement of animal lunge and flight, the purest metaphor of tribe and self. It's life flipping death the bird.

I make this stuff up. But then I feel the stray voltage of my rented charisma, hear the jerry-rigged authority in my voice, and I, too, believe. I'm convinced. The troupe dismantled, the choreography commissions dwindling, my body harder to make limber, to make go, I have come here for two weeks—to Pennsylvania Dutch country, as a "Dancer in the Schools." I visit classes, at colleges and elementary schools, spreading Dance's holy word. My head fills with my own yack. What interior life has accrued in me is depleted fast, emptied out my mouth, as I stand before audiences, answering their fearful, forbidding *German* questions about art and my "whorish dances" (the thrusted hip, the sudden bump and grind before an *attitude*). They ask why everything I make seems so "feministic."

"I think the word is *feministical*," I say. I've grown tired. I burned down my life for a few good pieces, and now this.

With only one night left, I've fled the Quality Inn. (CREAMED CHICKEN ON WAFFLE $3.95 reads the sign out front. How could I leave?) The karaoke in the cocktail lounge has kept me up, all those tipsy and bellowing voices just back from the men's room and urged to the front of the lounge to sing "Sexual Healing" or "Alfie." I've accepted an invitation to stay with my old friend Cal, who teaches anthropology at Burkwell, one of the myriad local colleges. He and his wife own a former frat house they've never bothered to renovate. "It was the only way we could live in a house this big," he says. "Besides, we're perversely fascinated by the wreckage." It is Fastnacht, the lip of Lent, the night when the locals make hot fried dough and eat it in honor of Christ. We are outside, before dinner, walking Cal's dog, Chappers, in the cold.

"The house *is* amazing to look at," I say. "It's beat-up in such an intricate way. Like a Rauschenberg. Like one of those beautiful wind-tattered billboards one sees in the California desert." I'm determined to be agreeable; the house, truth be told, is a shock. Maple seedlings have sprouted up through the dining room floorboards, from where a tree outside has pushed into the foundation. Squirrels the size of collies scrabble in the walls. Paint is chipping everywhere, in scales and blisters and flaps; in the cracked plaster beneath are written the names of women who, in 1972, 1973, and 1974, spent the night during Spring Rush weekend. The kitchen ceiling reads "Sigma power!" and "Wank me with a spoon."

But I haven't seen Cal in twelve years, not since he left for Belgium on a Fulbright, so I must be nice. He seems different to me: shorter, older, cleaner, despite the house. In a burst of candor, he has already confessed that those long years ago, out of friendship for me, he'd been exaggerating his interest in dance. "I didn't get it," he admitted. "I kept trying to figure out the *story*. I'd look at the purple guy who hadn't moved in awhile, and I'd think, So what's the issue with *him*?"

Now Chappers tugs at his leash. "Yeah, the house." Cal sighs. "We did once have a painter give us an estimate, but we were put off by the names of the paints: Myth, Vesper, Snicker-doodle. I didn't want anything called Snickerdoodle in my house."

"What *is* a Snickerdoodle?"

"I think they're hunted in Madagascar."

I leap to join him, to play. "Or eaten in Vienna," I say.

"Or worshiped in L.A." I laugh again for him, and then we watch as Chappers sniffs at the roots of an oak.

"But a myth or a vesper—they're always good," I add.

"Crucial," he says. "But we didn't need paint for that."

Cal's son, Eugene, is seven and has cystic fibrosis. Eugene's whole life is a race with medical research. "It's not that I'm not for the arts," says Cal. "*You're* here; money for the arts brought you here. That's wonderful. It's wonderful to see you after all these years. It's wonderful to fund the arts. *It's* wonderful; you're wonderful. The arts are so nice and wonderful. But really: I say, let's give all the money, every last fucking dime, to science."

Something chokes up in him. There can be optimism in the increments, the bits, the chapters; but I haven't seen him in twelve years and he has had to tell me the whole story, straight from the beginning, and it's the whole story that's just so sad.

"We both carried the gene but never knew," he says. "That's the way it works. The odds are one in twenty, times one in twenty, and then after that, still only one in four. One in sixteen hundred, total. Bingo! We should move to Vegas."

When I first knew Cal, we were in New York, just out of graduate school; he was single, and anxious, and struck me as someone who would never actually marry and have a family, or if he did, would marry someone decorative, someone slight.

But now, twelve years later, his silver-haired wife, Simone, is nothing like that: she is big and fierce and original, joined with him in grief and courage. She storms out of PTA meetings. She glues little sequins to her shoes. English is her third language; she was once a French diplomat to Belgium and to Japan. "I miss the caviar" is all she'll say of it. "I miss the caviar so much." Now, in Pennsylvania Dutchland, she paints satirical oils of long-armed handless people. "The locals," she explains in her French accent, giggling. "But I can't paint hands." She and Eugene have made a studio from one of the wrecked rooms upstairs.

"How is Simone through all this?" I ask.

"She's better than I am," he says. "She had a sister who died young. She expects unhappiness."

"But isn't there hope?" I ask, stuck for words.

Already, Cal says, Eugene has degenerated, grown worse, too much liquid in his lungs. "Stickiness," he calls it. "If he were three, instead of seven, there'd be *more* hope. The researchers are making some strides; they really are."

"He's a great kid," I say. Across the street, there are old Colonial houses with candles lit in each window; it is a Pennsylvania Dutch custom, or left over from Desert Storm, depending on whom you ask.

Cal stops and turns toward me, and the dog comes up and nuzzles him. "It's not just that Eugene's great," he says. "It's not just the precocity or that he's the only child I'll ever have. It's also that he's such a good person. He accepts things. He's very good at understanding everything."

I cannot imagine anything in my life that contains such sorrow as this, such anticipation of missing someone. Cal falls silent, the dog trots before us, and I place my hand lightly in the middle of Cal's back as we walk like that through the cold, empty streets. Up in the sky, Venus and the thinnest paring of sickle moon, like a cup and saucer, like a nose and mouth, have made the Turkish flag in the sky. "Look at that," I say to Cal as we traipse after the dog, the leash taut as a stick.

"Wow," Cal says. "The Turkish flag."

"You're back, you're back!" Eugene shouts from inside, dashing toward the front door as we step up onto the front porch with Chappers. Eugene is in his pajamas already, his body skinny and hunched. His glasses are thick, magnifying, and his eyes, puffed and swimming, seem not to miss a thing. He slides into the front entryway, in his stocking feet, and lands on the floor. He smiles up at me, all charm, like a kid with a crush. He has painted his face with Merthiolate and hopes we'll find that funny.

"Eugene, you look beautiful!" I say.

"No I don't!" he says. "I look *witty.*"

"Where's your mother?" asks Cal, unleashing the dog.

"In the kitchen. Dad, Mom says you have to go up to the attic and bring down one of the pans for dinner." He gets up and chases after Chappers, to tackle him and bring him back.

"We have a couple pots up there to catch leaks," Cal explains, taking off his coat. "But then we end up needing the pots for cooking, so we fetch them back."

"Do you need some help?" I don't know whether I should be with Simone in the kitchen, Cal in the attic, or Eugene on the floor.

"Oh, no. You stay here with Eugene," he says.

"Yeah. Stay here with me." Eugene races back from the dog and grabs my leg. The dog barks excitedly.

"You can show Eugene your video," Cal suggests as he leaves the room.

"Show me your dance video," he says to me in a singsong. "Show me, show me."

"Do we have time?"

"We have fifteen minutes," he says with great authority. I go upstairs and dig it out of my bag, then come back down. We plug it into the VCR and nestle on the couch together. He huddles close, cold in the drafty house, and I extend my long sweater around him like a shawl. I try to explain a few things, in a grown-up way, how this dance came to be, how movement, repeated, breaks through all resistance into a kind of stratosphere: from recalcitrance to ecstasy; from shoe to bird. The tape is one made earlier in the week. It is a demonstration with fourth graders. They each had to invent a character, then design a mask. They came up with various creatures: Miss Ninja Peacock. Mr. Bicycle Spoke Head. Evil Snowman. Saber-toothed Mom: "Half-girl-half-man-half-cat." Then I arranged the kids in a phalanx and led them, with their masks on, in an improvised dance to Kenny Loggins's "This Is It."

He watches, rapt. His brown hair hangs in strings in his face, and he chews on it. "There's Tommy Crowell," he says. He knows the fourth graders as if they were royalty. When it is over, he looks up at me, smiling, but businesslike. His gaze behind his glasses is brilliant and direct. "That was really a wonderful dance," he says. He sounds like an agent.

"Do you really think so?"

"Absolutely," he says. "It's colorful and has lots of fun, interesting steps."

"Will you be my agent?" I ask.

He scowls, unsure. "I don't know. Is the agent the person who drives the car?"

"Dinner's ready!" Simone calls from two rooms away, the "Wank me with a spoon" room.

"Coming!" shouts Eugene, and he leaps off the couch and slides into the dining room, falling sideways into his chair. "*Whoo,*" he says, out of breath. "I almost didn't make it."

"Here," says Cal. He places a goblet of pills at Eugene's place setting.

Eugene makes a face, but in the chair, he gets up on his knees, leans forward, glass of water in one hand, and begins the arduous activity of taking all the pills.

I sit in the chair opposite him and place my napkin in my lap.

Simone has made a soup with hard-boiled eggs in it (a regional recipe, she explains), as well as Peking duck, which is ropy and sweet. Cal keeps passing around the basket of bread, anxiously, talking about how modern man has only been around for 45,000 years and probably the bread hasn't changed much since then.

"Forty-five thousand years?" says Simone. "That's all? That can't be. I feel like we've been *married* for that long."

There are people who talk with their hands. Then there are people who talk with their arms. Then there are people who talk with their arms over their head. These are the ones I like best. Simone is one of those.

"Nope, that's it," says Cal, chewing. "Forty-five thousand. Though for about two hundred thousand years before that, early man was going through all kinds of anatomical changes to get where we are today. It was a *very* exciting time." He pauses, a little breathlessly. "I wish I could have been there."

"Ha!" exclaims Simone.

"Think of the parties," I say.

"Right," says Simone. " 'Joe, how've you been? Your head's so *big* now, and, well, what is this crazy thing you're doing with your thumb?' A lot like the parties in Soda Springs, Idaho."

"Simone used to be married to someone in Soda Springs, Idaho," Cal says to me.

"You're kidding!" I say.

"Oh, it was very brief," she says. "He was ridiculous. I got rid of him after about six months. Supposedly, he went off and killed himself." She smiles at me impishly.

"Who killed himself?" asks Eugene. He has swallowed all the pills but one.

"Mommy's first husband," says Cal.

"Why did he kill himself?" Eugene is staring at the middle of the table, trying to think about this.

"Eugene, you've lived with your mother for seven years now, and you don't know why someone close to her would want to kill himself?" Simone and Cal look straight across at each other and laugh brightly.

Eugene smiles in an abbreviated and vague way. He understands this is his parents' joke, but he doesn't like or get it. He is bothered they have turned his serious inquiry into a casual laugh. He wants information! But now, instead, he just digs into the duck, poking and looking.

Simone asks about the school visits. What am I finding? Are people nice to me? What is my life like back home? Am I married?

"I'm not married," I say.

"But you and Patrick are still together, aren't you?" Cal says in a concerned way.

"Uh, no. We broke up."

"You broke up?" Cal puts his fork down.

"Yes," I say, sighing.

"Gee, I thought you guys would never break up!" he says in a genuinely flabbergasted tone.

"*Really?*" I find this reassuring somehow, that my relationship at least looked good from the outside, at least to someone.

"Well, not *really*," admits Cal. "Actually, I thought you guys would break up long ago."

"Oh," I say.

"So *you* could marry her?" says the amazing Eugene to his father, and we all laugh loudly, pour more wine into glasses, and hide our faces in them.

"The thing to remember about love affairs," says Simone, "is that they are all like having raccoons in your chimney."

"Oh, not the raccoon story," groans Cal.

"Yes! The raccoons!" cries Eugene.

I'm sawing at my duck.

"We have raccoons sometimes in our chimney," explains Simone.

"Hmmm," I say, not surprised.

"And once we tried to smoke them out. We lit a fire, knowing they were there, but we hoped that the smoke would cause them to scurry out the top and never come back. Instead, they caught on fire and came crashing down into our living room, all charred and in flames and running madly around until they dropped dead." Simone swallows some wine. "Love affairs are like that," she says. "They all are like that."

I'm confused. I glance up at the light, an old brass octopus of a chandelier. All I can think of is how Patrick said, when he left, fed up with my "selfishness," that if I were worried about staying on alone at the lake house, with its squirrels and call girl–style lamps, I should just rent the place out—perhaps to a nice lesbian couple like myself.

But Eugene, across from me, nods enthusiastically, looks pleased. He's heard the raccoon story before and likes it. Once again, it's been told right, with flames and gore.

Now there is salad, which we pick and tear at like crows. Afterward, we gaze upon the bowl of fruit at the center of the table, lazily pick a few grapes off their stems. We sip hot tea that Cal brings in from the kitchen. We sip until it's cool, and then until it's gone. Already the time is ten o'clock.

"Dance time, dance time!" says Eugene when we're through. Every night, before bed, they all go out into the living room and dance until Eugene is tired and falls asleep on the sofa. Then they carry him upstairs and tuck him in.

He comes over to my chair and takes my hand, leads me out into the living room.

"What music shall we dance to?" I ask.

"You choose," he says, and leads me to the shelf where they

keep their compact discs. Perhaps there is some Stravinsky. Perhaps *Petrouchka*, with its rousing salute to Shrovetide.

"Will you come see me tomorrow when you visit the fourth graders?" he asks as I'm looking through the selection. Too much Joan Baez. Too much Mahler. "I'm in room one oh four," he says. "When you visit the fourth graders, you can just stop by my classroom and wave to me from the door. I sit between the bulletin board and the window."

"Sure!" I say, not knowing that, in a rush, I will forget, and that I'll be on the plane home already, leafing through some inane airline magazine, before I remember that I forgot to do it. "Look," I say, finding a Kenny Loggins disc. It has the song he heard earlier, the one from the video. "Let's play this."

"Goody," he says. "Mom! Dad! Come on!"

"All right, Eugenie-boy," says Cal, coming in from the dining room. Simone is behind him.

"I'm Mercury, I'm Neptune, now I'm Pluto so far away," says Eugene, dashing around the room, making up his own dance.

"They're doing the planets in school," says Simone.

"Yes," says Eugene. "We're doing the planets!"

"And which planet," I ask him, "do you think is the most interesting?" Mars, with its canals? Saturn, with its rings?

Eugene stands still, looks at me thoughtfully, solemnly. "Earth, of course," he says.

Cal laughs. "Well, that's the right answer!"

"This is it!" sings Kenny Loggins. "This is it!" We make a phalanx and march, strut, slide to the music. We crouch, move backward, then burst forward again. We're aiming to create the mildewy, resinous sweat smell of dance, the parsed, repeated movement. Cal and Simone are into it. They jiggle and link arms. "This is it!" In the middle of the song, Eugene suddenly sits down to rest on the sofa, watching the grown-ups. Like the best dancers and audiences in the world, he is determined not to cough until the end.

"Come here, honey," I say, going to him. I am thinking not only of my own body here, that unbeguilable, broken basket, that stiff meringue. I am not, Patrick, thinking only of myself, my lost troupe, my empty bed. I am thinking of the dancing body's magnificent and ostentatious scorn. This is how we offer ourselves, enter heaven, enter speaking: we say with motion, in space, This is what life's done so far down here; this is all and what and everything it's managed—this body, these bodies, that body—so what do you think, Heaven? What do you fucking think?

"Stand next to me," I say, and Eugene does, looking up at me with his orange warrior face. We step in place: knees up, knees down. Knees up, knees down. Dip-glide-slide. Dip-glide-slide. "This is it!" "This is it!" Then we go wild and fling our limbs to the sky.

COMMUNITY LIFE

When Olena was a little girl, she had called them lie-berries—
a fibbing fruit, a story store—and now she had a job in one. She
had originally wanted to teach English literature, but when
she failed to warm to the graduate study of it, its french-fried
theories—a vocabulary of arson!—she'd transferred to library
school, where everyone was taught to take care of books, ten-
derly, as if they were dishes or dolls.

She had learned to read at an early age. Her parents, newly
settled in Vermont from Tirgu Mures in Transylvania, were
anxious that their daughter learn to speak English, to blend in
with the community in a way they felt they probably never
would, and so every Saturday they took her to the children's
section of the Rutland library and let her spend time with the
librarian, who chose books for her and sometimes even read a
page or two out loud, though there was a sign that said PLEASE
BE QUIET BOYS AND GIRLS. No comma.

Which made it seem to Olena that only the boys had to be
quiet. She and the librarian could do whatever they wanted.

She had loved the librarian.

And when Olena's Romanian began to recede altogether, and in its stead bloomed a slow, rich English-speaking voice, not unlike the librarian's, too womanly for a little girl, the other children on her street became even more afraid of her. *"Dracula!"* they shouted. *"Transylvaniess!"* they shrieked, and ran. "You'll have a new name now," her father told her the first day of first grade. He had already changed their last name from Todorescu to Resnick. His shop was called "Resnick's Furs." "From here on in, you will no longer be Olena. You will have a nice American name: Nell."

"You make to say ze name," her mother said. "When ze teacher tell you *Olena,* you say, *'No, Nell.'* Say *Nell.*"

"Nell," said Olena. But when she got to school, the teacher, sensing something dreamy and outcast in her, clasped her hand and exclaimed, "Olena! What a beautiful name!" Olena's heart filled with gratitude and surprise, and she fell in close to the teacher's hip, adoring and mute.

From there on in, only her parents, in their throaty Romanian accents, ever called her Nell, her secret, jaunty American self existing only for them.

"Nell, how are ze ozer children at ze school?"

"Nell, please to tell us what you do."

Years later, when they were killed in a car crash on the Farm to Market Road, and the Nell-that-never-lived died with them, Olena, numbly rearranging the letters of her own name on the envelopes of the sympathy cards she received, discovered what the letters spelled: *Olena; Alone.* It was a body walled in the cellar of her, a whiff and forecast of doom like an early, rotten spring—and she longed for the Nell-that-never-lived's return. She wished to start over again, to be someone living coltishly in the world, not someone hidden away, behind books, with a carefully learned voice and a sad past.

She missed her mother the most.

. . .

The library Olena worked in was one of the most prestigious university libraries in the Midwest. It housed a large collection of rare and foreign books, and she had driven across several states to get there, squinting through the splattered tempera of insects on the windshield, watching for the dark tail of a possible tornado, and getting sick, painfully, in Indiana, in the rest rooms of the dead-Hoosier service plazas along I-80. The ladies' rooms there had had electric eyes for the toilets, the sinks, the hand dryers, and she'd set them all off by staggering in and out of the stalls or leaning into the sinks. "You the only one in here?" asked a cleaning woman. "You the only one in here making this racket?" Olena had smiled, a dog's smile; in the yellowish light, everything seemed tragic and ridiculous and unable to stop. The flatness of the terrain gave her vertigo, she decided, that was it. The land was windswept; there were no smells. In Vermont, she had felt cradled by mountains. Now, here, she would have to be brave.

But she had no memory of how to be brave. Here, it seemed, she had no memories at all. Nothing triggered them. And once in a while, when she gave voice to the fleeting edge of one, it seemed like something she was making up.

She first met Nick at the library in May. She was temporarily positioned at the reference desk, hauled out from her ordinary task as supervisor of foreign cataloging, to replace someone who was ill. Nick was researching statistics on municipal campaign spending in the state. "Haven't stepped into a library since I was eighteen," he said. He looked at least forty.

She showed him where he might look. "Try looking here," she said, writing down the names of indexes to state records, but he kept looking at *her*. "Or here."

"I'm managing a county board seat campaign," he said. "The election's not until the fall, but I'm trying to get a jump on things." His hair was a coppery brown, threaded through with silver. There was something animated in his eyes, like pond life. "I just wanted to get some comparison figures. Will you have a cup of coffee with me?"

"I don't think so," she said.

But he came back the next day and asked her again.

The coffee shop near campus was hot and noisy, crowded with students, and Nick loudly ordered espresso for them both. She usually didn't like espresso, its gritty, cigarish taste. But there was in the air that kind of distortion that bent you a little; it caused your usual self to grow slippery, to wander off and shop, to get blurry, bleed, bevel with possibility. She drank the espresso fast, with determination and a sense of adventure. "I guess I'll have a second," she said, and wiped her mouth with a napkin.

"I'll get it," said Nick, and when he came back, he told her some more about the campaign he was running. "It's important to get the endorsements of the neighborhood associations," he said. He ran a bratwurst and frozen yogurt stand called Please Squeeze and Bratwursts. He had gotten to know a lot of people that way. "I feel alive and relevant, living my life like this," he said. "I don't feel like I've sold out."

"Sold out to what?" she asked.

He smiled. "I can tell you're not from around here," he said. He raked his hand through the various metals of his hair. "*Selling out.* Like doing something you really never wanted to do, and getting paid too much for it."

"Oh," she said.

"When I was a kid, my father said to me, 'Sometimes in life, son, you're going to find you have to do things you don't want to do,' and I looked him right in the eye and said, 'No fucking way.' " Olena laughed. "I mean, you probably always wanted to be a librarian, right?"

She looked at all the crooked diagonals of his face and

couldn't tell whether he was serious. "Me?" she said. "I first went to graduate school to be an English professor." She sighed, switched elbows, sinking her chin into her other hand. "I did try," she said. "I read Derrida. I read Lacan. I read *Reading Lacan*. I read 'Reading *Reading Lacan*'—and that's when I applied to library school."

"I don't know who Lacan is," he said.

"He's, well—you see? That's why I like libraries: No whos or whys. Just 'where is it?' "

"And *where* are you from?" he asked, his face briefly animated by his own clever change of subject. "Originally." There was, it seemed, a way of spotting those not native to the town. It was a college town, attractive and dull, and it hurried the transients along—the students, gypsies, visiting scholars and comics—with a motion not unlike peristalsis.

"Vermont," she said.

"Vermont!" Nick exclaimed, as if this were exotic, which made her glad she hadn't said something like Transylvania. He leaned toward her, confidentially. "I have to tell you: I own one chair from Ethan Allen Furniture."

"You do?" She smiled. "I won't tell anyone."

"Before that, however, I was in prison, and didn't own a stick."

"Really?" she asked. She sat back. Was he telling the truth? As a girl, she'd been very gullible, but she had always learned more that way.

"I went to school here," he said. "In the sixties. I bombed a warehouse where the military was storing research supplies. I got twelve years." He paused, searching her eyes to see how she was doing with this, how *he* was doing with it. Then he fetched back his gaze, like a piece of jewelry he'd merely wanted to show her, quick. "There wasn't supposed to be anyone there; we'd checked it all out in advance. But this poor asshole named Lawrence Sperry—Larry Sperry! Christ, can you imagine having a name like that?"

"Sure," said Olena.

Nick looked at her suspiciously. "He was in there, working late. He lost a leg and an eye in the explosion. I got the federal pen in Winford. Attempted murder."

The thick coffee coated his lips. He had been looking steadily at her, but now he looked away.

"Would you like a bun?" asked Olena. "I'm going to go get a bun." She stood, but he turned and gazed up at her with such disbelief that she sat back down again, sloppily, sidesaddle. She twisted forward, leaned into the table. "I'm sorry. Is that all true, what you just said? Did that really happen to you?"

"*What?*" His mouth fell open. "You think I'd make that up?"

"It's just that, well, I work around a lot of literature," she said.

" 'Literature,' " he repeated.

She touched his hand. She didn't know what else to do. "Can I cook dinner for you some night? Tonight?"

There was a blaze in his eye, a concentrated seeing. He seemed for a moment able to look right into her, know her in a way that was uncluttered by actually knowing her. He seemed to have no information or misinformation, only a kind of pho- tography, factless but true.

"Yes," he said, "you can."

Which was how he came to spend the evening beneath the cheap stained-glass lamp of her dining room, its barroom red, its Schlitz-Tiffany light, and then to spend the night, and not leave.

Olena had never lived with a man before. "Except my father," she said, and Nick studied her eyes, the streak of blankness in them, when she said it. Though she had dated two different boys in college, they were the kind who liked to leave early, to eat breakfast without her at smoky greasy spoons, to sit at the counter with the large men in the blue windbreakers, read the paper, get their cups refilled.

She had never been with anyone who stayed. Anyone who'd moved in his box of tapes, his Ethan Allen chair.

Anyone who'd had lease problems at his old place.

"I'm trying to bring this thing together," he said, holding her in the middle of the afternoon. "My life, the campaign, my thing with you: I'm trying to get all my birds to land in the same yard." Out the window, there was an afternoon moon, like a golf ball, pocked and stuck. She looked at the calcified egg of it, its coin face, its blue neighborhood of nothing. Then she looked at him. There was the pond life again in his eyes, and in the rest of his face a hesitant, warm stillness.

"Do you like making love to me?" she asked, at night, during a thunderstorm.

"Of course. Why do you ask?"

"Are you satisfied with me?"

He turned toward her, kissed her. "Yes," he said. "I don't need a show."

She was quiet for a long time. "People are giving shows?"

The rain and wind rushed down the gutters, snapped the branches of the weak trees in the side yard.

He had her inexperience and self-esteem in mind. At the movies, at the beginning, he whispered, "Twentieth Century–Fox. Baby, that's you." During a slapstick part, in a library where card catalogs were upended and scattered wildly through the air, she broke into a pale, cold sweat, and he moved toward her, hid her head in his chest, saying, "Don't look, don't look." At the end, they would sit through the long credits—gaffer, best boy, key grip. "That's what *we* need to get," he said. "A grip."

"Yes," she said. "Also a *negative cutter.*"

Other times, he encouraged her to walk around the house naked. "If you got it, do it." He smiled, paused, feigned confusion. "If you do it, have it. If you flaunt it, do it."

"If you have it, got it," she added.

"If you say it, mean it." And he pulled her toward him like a dancing partner with soft shoes and the smiling mouth of love. But too often she lay awake, wondering. There was something missing. Something wasn't happening to her, or was it to him? All through the summer, the thunderstorms set the sky on fire while she lay there, listening for the train sound of a tornado, which never came—though the lightning ripped open the night and lit the trees like things too suddenly remembered, then left them indecipherable again in the dark.

"You're not feeling anything, are you?" he finally said. "What is wrong?"

"I'm not sure," she said cryptically. "The rainstorms are so loud in this part of the world." The wind from a storm blew through the screens and sometimes caused the door to the bedroom to slam shut. "I don't like a door to slam," she whispered. "It makes me think someone is mad."

At the library, there were Romanian books coming in—Olena was to skim them, read them just enough to proffer a brief description for the catalog listing. It dismayed her that her Romanian was so weak, that it had seemed almost to vanish, a mere handkerchief in a stairwell, and that now, daily, another book arrived to reprimand her.

She missed her mother the most.

On her lunch break, she went to Nick's stand for a frozen yogurt. He looked tired, bedraggled, his hair like sprockets. "You want the Sperry Cherry or the Lemon Bomber?" he asked. These were his joke names, the ones he threatened really to use someday.

"How about apple?" she said.

He cut up an apple and arranged it in a paper dish. He squeezed yogurt from a chrome machine. "There's a fund-raiser tonight for the Teetlebaum campaign."

"Oh," she said. She had been to these fund-raisers before. At first she had liked them, glimpsing corners of the city she would never have seen otherwise, Nick leading her out into them, Nick knowing everyone, so that it seemed her life filled with possibility, with homefulness. But finally, she felt, such events were too full of dreary, glad-handing people speaking incessantly of their camping trips out west. They never really spoke *to* you. They spoke toward you. They spoke at you. They spoke near you, on you. They believed themselves crucial to the welfare of the community. But they seldom went to libraries. They didn't read books. "At least they're *contributers to the community*," said Nick. "At least they're not sucking the blood of it."

"Lapping," she said.

"What?"

"Gnashing and lapping. Not sucking."

He looked at her in a doubtful, worried way. "I looked it up once," she said.

"Whatever." He scowled. "At least they care. At least they're trying to give something back."

"I'd rather live in Russia," she said.

"I'll be back around ten or so," he said.

"You don't want me to come?" Truth was she disliked Ken Teetlebaum. Perhaps Nick had figured this out. Though he had the support of the local leftover Left, there was something fatuous and vain about Ken. He tended to do little isometric leg exercises while you were talking to him. Often he took out a Woolworth photo of himself and showed it to people. "Look at this," he'd say. "This was back when I had long hair, can you believe it?" And people would look and see a handsome teenaged boy who bore only a slight resemblance to the puffy Ken Teetlebaum of today. "Don't I look like Eric Clapton?"

"Eric Clapton would never have sat in a Woolworth photo booth like some high school girl," Olena had said once, in the caustic blurt that sometimes afflicts the shy. Ken had looked at her in a laughing, hurt sort of way, and after that he stopped showing the photo around when she was present.

"You can come, if you want to." Nick reached up, smoothed his hair, and looked handsome again. "Meet me there."

The fund-raiser was in the upstairs room of a local restaurant called Dutch's. She paid ten dollars, went in, and ate a lot of raw cauliflower and hummus before she saw Nick back in a far corner, talking to a woman in jeans and a brown blazer. She was the sort of woman that Nick might twist around to look at in restaurants: fiery auburn hair cut bluntly in a pageboy. She had a pretty face, but the hair was too severe, too separate and tended to. Olena herself had long, disorganized hair, and she wore it pulled back messily in a clip. When she reached up to wave to Nick, and he looked away without acknowledging her, back toward the auburn pageboy, Olena kept her hand up and moved it back, to fuss with the clip. She would never fit in here, she thought. Not among these jolly, activist-clerk types. She preferred the quiet poet-clerks of the library. They were delicate and territorial, intellectual, and physically unwell. They sat around at work, thinking up Tom Swifties: *I have to go to the hardware store, he said wrenchingly.*

Would you like a soda? he asked spritely.

They spent weekends at the Mayo Clinic. "An amusement park for hypochondriacs," said a cataloger named Sarah. "A cross between Lourdes and *The New Price Is Right,*" said someone else named George. These were the people she liked: the kind you couldn't really live with.

She turned to head toward the ladies' room and bumped into Ken. He gave her a hug hello, and then whispered in her ear, "You live with Nick. Help us think of an issue. I need another issue."

"I'll get you one at the issue store," she said, and pulled away as someone approached him with a heartily extended hand and a false, booming "Here's the man of the hour." In the bathroom, she stared at her own reflection: in an attempt at extroversion, she had worn a tunic with large slices of watermelon depicted on the front. What had she been thinking of?

She went into the stall and slid the bolt shut. She read the graffiti on the back of the door. *Anita loves David S.* Or: *Christ + Diane W.* It was good to see that even in a town like this, people could love one another.

"Who were you talking to?" she asked him later at home.

"Who? What do you mean?"

"The one with the plasticine hair."

"Oh, Erin? She does look like she does something to her hair. It looks like she hennas it."

"It looks like she tacks it against the wall and stands underneath it."

"She's head of the Bayre Corners Neighborhood Association. Come September, we're really going to need her endorsement."

Olena sighed, looked away.

"It's the democratic process," said Nick.

"I'd rather have a king and queen," she said.

The following Friday, the night of the Fish Fry Fund-raiser at the Labor Temple, was the night Nick slept with Erin of the Bayre Corners Neighborhood Association. He arrived back home at seven in the morning and confessed to Olena, who, when Nick hadn't come home, had downed half a packet of Dramamine to get to sleep.

"I'm sorry," he said, his head in his hands. "It's a sixties thing."

"A sixties thing?" She was fuzzy, zonked from the Dramamine.

"You get all involved in a political event, and you find yourself sleeping together. She's from that era, too. It's also that, I don't know, she just seems to really care about her community. She's got this reaching, expressive side to her. I got caught up in that." He was sitting down, leaning forward on his knees, talking to his shoes. The electric fan was blowing on him, moving his hair gently, like weeds in water.

"A sixties thing?" Olena repeated. "A sixties thing, what is that—like 'Easy to Be Hard'?" It was the song she remembered best. But now something switched off in her. The bones in her chest hurt. Even the room seemed changed—brighter and awful. Everything had fled, run away to become something else. She started to perspire under her arms and her face grew hot. "You're a murderer," she said. "That's finally what you are. That's finally what you'll always be." She began to weep so loudly that Nick got up, closed the windows. Then he sat down and held her—who else was there to hold her?—and she held him back.

He bought her a large garnet ring, a cough drop set in brass. He did the dishes ten straight days in a row. She had a tendency to go to bed right after supper and sleep, heavily, needing the escape. She had become afraid of going out—restaurants, stores, the tension in her shoulders, the fear gripping her face when she was there, as if people knew she was a foreigner and a fool—and for fifteen additional days he did the cooking and shopping. His car was always parked on the outside of the driveway, and hers was always in first, close, blocked in, as if to indicate who most belonged to the community, to the world, and who most belonged tucked in away from it, in a house. Perhaps in bed. Perhaps asleep.

"You need more life around you," said Nick, cradling her, though she'd gone stiff and still. His face was plaintive and suntanned, the notes and varnish of a violin. "You need a greater sense of life around you." Outside, there was the old rot smell of rain coming.

"How have you managed to get a suntan when there's been so much rain?" she asked.

"It's summer," he said. "I work outside, remember?"

"There are no sleeve marks," she said. "Where are you going?"

She had become afraid of the community. It was her enemy. Other people, other women.

She had, without realizing it at the time, learned to follow Nick's gaze, learned to learn his lust, and when she did go out, to work at least, his desires remained memorized within her. She looked at the attractive women he would look at. She turned to inspect the face of every pageboy haircut she saw from behind and passed in her car. She looked at them furtively or squarely—it didn't matter. She appraised their eyes and mouths and wondered about their bodies. She had become him: she longed for these women. But she was also herself, and so she despised them. She lusted after them, but she also wanted to beat them up.

A rapist.

She had become a rapist, driving to work in a car.

But for a while, it was the only way she could be.

She began to wear his clothes—a shirt, a pair of socks—to keep him next to her, to try to understand why he had done what he'd done. And in this new empathy, in this pants role, like an opera, she thought she understood what it was to make love to a woman, to open the hidden underside of her, like secret food, to thrust yourself up in her, her arch and thrash, like a puppet, to watch her later when she got up and walked around without you, oblivious to the injury you'd surely done her. How could you not love her, gratefully, marveling? She was so mysterious, so recovered, an unshared thought enlivening her eyes; you wanted to follow her forever.

A man in love. That was a man in love. So different from a woman.

A woman cleaned up the kitchen. A woman gave and hid, gave and hid, like someone with a May basket.

She made an appointment with a doctor. Her insurance covered her only if she went to the university hospital, and so she made an appointment there.

"I've made a doctor's appointment," she said to Nick, but he had the water running in the tub and didn't hear her. "To find out if there's anything wrong with me."

When he got out, he approached her, nothing on but a towel, pulled her close to his chest, and lowered her to the floor, right there in the hall by the bathroom door. Something was swooping, back and forth in an arc above her. May Day, May Day. She froze.

"What was that?" She pushed him away.

"What?" He rolled over on his back and looked. Something was flying around in the stairwell—a bird. "A bat," he said.

"Oh my God," cried Olena.

"The heat can bring them out in these old rental houses," he said, stood, rewrapped his towel. "Do you have a tennis racket?"

She showed him where it was. "I've only played tennis once," she said. "Do you want to play tennis sometime?" But he proceeded to stalk the bat in the dark stairwell.

"Now don't get hysterical," he said.

"I'm already hysterical."

"Don't get— There!" he shouted, and she heard the *thwack* of the racket against the wall, and the soft drop of the bat to the landing.

She suddenly felt sick. "Did you have to kill it?" she said.

"What did you want me to do?"

"I don't know. Capture it. Rough it up a little." She felt guilty, as if her own loathing had brought about its death. "What kind of bat is it?" She tiptoed up to look, to try to glimpse its monkey face, its cat teeth, its pterodactyl wings veined like beet leaves. "What kind? Is it a fruit bat?"

"Looks pretty straight to me," said Nick. With his fist, he tapped Olena's arm lightly, teasingly.

"Will you stop?"

"Though it *was* doing this whole astrology thing—I don't know. Maybe it's a zodiac bat."

"Maybe it's a brown bat. It's not a vampire bat, is it?"

"I think you have to go to South America for those," he said. "Take your platform shoes!"

She sank down on the steps, pulled her robe tighter. She felt for the light switch and flicked it on. The bat, she could now see, was small and light-colored, its wings folded in like a packed tent, a mouse with backpacking equipment. It had a sweet face, like a deer, though blood drizzled from its head. It reminded her of a cat she'd seen once as a child, shot with a BB in the eye.

"I can't look anymore," she said, and went back upstairs.

Nick appeared a half hour later, standing in the doorway. She was in bed, a book propped in her lap—a biography of a French feminist, which she was reading for the hairdo information.

"I had lunch with Erin today," he said.

She stared at the page. Snoods. Turbans and snoods. You could go for days in a snood. "Why?"

"A lot of different reasons. For Ken, mostly. She's still head of the neighborhood association, and he needs her endorsement. I just wanted to let you know. Listen, you've gotta cut me some slack."

She grew hot in the face again. "I've cut you some slack," she said. "I've cut you a whole forest of slack. The whole global slack forest has been cut for you." She closed the book. "I don't know why you cavort with these people. They're nothing but a bunch of clerks."

He'd been trying to look pleasant, but now he winced a little. "Oh, I see," he said. "Miss High-Minded. You whose father made his living off furs. Furs!" He took two steps toward her, then turned and paced back again. "I can't believe I'm living with someone who grew up on the proceeds of tortured animals!"

She was quiet. This lunge at moral fastidiousness was something she'd noticed a lot in the people around here. They were not good people. They were not kind. They played around and lied to their spouses. But they recycled their newspapers!

"Don't drag my father into this."

"Look, I've spent years of my life working for peace and free expression. I've been in prison already. I've lived in a cage! I don't need to live in another one."

"You and your free expression! You who can't listen to me for two minutes!"

"Listen to you what?"

"Listen to me when I"—and here she bit her lip a little— "when I tell you that these people you care about, this hateful Erin what's-her-name, they're just small, awful, nothing people."

"So they don't *read enough books*," he said slowly. "Who the fuck cares."

The next day he was off to a meeting with Ken at the Senior Citizens Association. The host from *Jeopardy!* was going to be there, and Ken wanted to shake a few hands, sign up volunteers. The host from *Jeopardy!* was going to give a talk.

"I don't get it," Olena said.

"I know." He sighed, the pond life treading water in his

eyes. "But, well—it's the American way." He grabbed up his keys, and the look that quickly passed over his face told her this: she wasn't pretty enough.

"I hate America," she said.

Nonetheless, he called her at the library during a break. She'd been sitting in the back with Sarah, thinking up Tom Swifties, her brain ready to bleed from the ears, when the phone rang. "You should see this," he said. "Some old geezer raises his hand, I call on him, and he stands up, and the first thing he says is, 'I had my hand raised for ten whole minutes and you kept passing over me. I don't like to be passed over. You can't just pass over a guy like me, not at my age.' "

She laughed, as he wanted her to.

This hot dog's awful, she said frankly.

"To appeal to the doctors, Ken's got all these signs up that say 'Teetlebaum for tort reform.' "

"Sounds like a Wallace Stevens poem," she said.

"I don't know what I expected. But the swirl of this whole event has not felt right."

She's a real dog, he said cattily.

She was quiet, deciding to let him do the work of this call.

"Do you realize that Ken's entire softball team just wrote a letter to *The Star,* calling him a loudmouth and a cheat?"

"Well," she said, "what can you expect from a bunch of grown men who pitch underhand?"

There was some silence. "I care about us," he said finally. "I just want you to know that."

"Okay," she said.

"I know I'm just a pain in the ass to you," he said. "But you're an inspiration to me, you are."

I like a good sled dog, she said huskily.

"Thank you for just—for saying that," she said.

"I just sometimes wish you'd get involved in the community, help out with the campaign. Give of yourself. Connect a little with something."

· · ·

At the hospital, she got up on the table and pulled the paper gown tightly around her, her feet in the stirrups. The doctor took a plastic speculum out of a drawer. "Anything particular seem to be the problem today?" asked the doctor.

"I just want you to look and tell me if there's anything wrong," said Olena.

The doctor studied her carefully. "There's a class of medical students outside. Do you mind if they come in?"

"Excuse me?"

"You know this is a teaching hospital," she said. "We hope that our patients won't mind contributing to the education of our medical students by allowing them in during an examination. It's a way of contributing to the larger medical community, if you will. But it's totally up to you. You can say no."

Olena clutched at her paper gown. *There's never been an accident, she said recklessly.* "How many of them are there?"

The doctor smiled quickly. "Seven," she said. "Like dwarfs."

"They'll come in and do what?"

The doctor was growing impatient and looked at her watch. "They'll participate in the examination. It's a learning visit."

Olena sank back down on the table. She didn't feel that she could offer herself up this way. *You're only average, he said meanly.*

"All right," she said. "Okay."

Take a bow, he said sternly.

The doctor opened up the doorway and called a short way down the corridor. "Class?"

They were young, more than half of them men, and they gathered around the examination table in a horseshoe shape, looking slightly ashamed, sorry for her, no doubt, the way art students sometimes felt sorry for the shivering model they were about to draw. The doctor pulled up a stool between Olena's feet and inserted the plastic speculum, the stiff, widening arms of it uncomfortable, embarrassing. "Today we will be doing a routine pelvic examination," she announced loudly, and then she got up again, went to a drawer, and passed out rubber gloves to everyone.

Olena went a little blind. A white light, starting at the center, spread to the black edges of her sight. One by one, the hands of the students entered her, or pressed on her abdomen, felt hungrily, innocently, for something to learn from her, in her.

She missed her mother the most.

"Next," the doctor was saying. And then again. "All right. Next?"

Olena missed her mother the most.

But it was her father's face that suddenly loomed before her now, his face at night in the doorway of her bedroom, coming to check on her before he went to bed, his bewildered face, horrified to find her lying there beneath the covers, touching herself and gasping, his whispered "Nell? Are you okay?" and then his vanishing, closing the door loudly, to leave her there, finally forever; to die and leave her there feeling only her own sorrow and disgrace, which she would live in like a coat.

There were rubber fingers in her, moving, wriggling around, but not like the others. She sat up abruptly and the young student withdrew his hand, moved away. "He didn't do it right," she said to the doctor. She pointed at the student. "He didn't do it correctly!"

"All right, then," said the doctor, looking at Olena with concern and alarm. "All right. You may all leave," she said to the students.

The doctor herself found nothing. "You are perfectly normal," she said. But she suggested that Olena take vitamin B and listen quietly to music in the evening.

Olena staggered out through the hospital parking lot, not finding her car at first. When she found it, she strapped herself in tightly, as if she were something wild—an animal or a star.

She drove back to the library and sat at her desk. Everyone had gone home already. In the margins of her notepad she wrote, "Alone as a book, alone as a desk, alone as a library, alone as a pencil, alone as a catalog, alone as a number, alone as a notepad." Then she, too, left, went home, made herself tea. She felt separate from her body, felt herself dragging it up the stairs like a big handbag, its leathery hollowness something you could cut up and give away or stick things in. She lay between the sheets of her bed, sweating, perhaps from the tea. The world felt over to her, used up, off to one side. There were no more names to live by.

One should live closer. She had lost her place, as in a book. One should live closer to where one's parents were buried.

Waiting for Nick's return, she felt herself grow dizzy, float up toward the ceiling, look down on the handbag. Tomorrow, she would get an organ donor's card, an eye donor's card, as many cards as she could get. She would show them all to Nick. "Nick! Look at my cards!"

And when he didn't come home, she remained awake through the long night, through the muffled thud of a bird hurling itself against the window, through the thunder leaving and approaching like a voice, through the Frankenstein light of the storm. Over her house, in lieu of stars, she felt the bright heads of her mother and father, searching for her, their eyes beaming down from the sky.

Oh, there you are, they said. *Oh, there you are.*

But then they went away again, and she lay waiting, fist in her spine, for the grace and fatigue that would come, surely it must come, of having given so much to the world.

AGNES OF IOWA

Her mother had given her the name Agnes, believing that a good-looking woman was even more striking when her name was a homely one. Her mother was named Cyrena, and was beautiful to match, but had always imagined her life would have been more interesting, that she herself would have had a more dramatic, arresting effect on the world and not ended up in Cassell, Iowa, if she had been named Enid or Hagar or Maude. And so she named her first daughter Agnes, and when Agnes turned out not to be attractive at all, but puffy and prone to a rash between her eyebrows, her hair a flat and bilious hue, her mother backpedaled and named her second daughter Linnea Elise (who turned out to be a lovely, sleepy child with excellent bones, a sweet, full mouth, and a rubbery mole above her lip that later in life could be removed without difficulty, everyone was sure).

Agnes herself had always been a bit at odds with her name. There was a brief period in her life, in her mid-twenties, when she had tried to pass it off as French—she had put in the accent grave and encouraged people to call her "On-yez." This was when she was living in New York City, and often getting together with her cousin, a painter who took her to parties in TriBeCa lofts or at beach houses or at mansions on lakes upstate. She would meet a lot of not very bright rich people who found the pronunciation of her name intriguing. It was the rest of her they were unclear on. "On-yez, where are you from, dear?" asked a black-slacked, frosted-haired woman whose skin was papery and melanomic with suntan. "Originally." She eyed Agnes's outfit as if it might be what in fact it was: a couple of blue things purchased in a department store in Cedar Rapids.

"Where am I from?" Agnes said it softly. "Iowa." She had a tendency not to speak up.

"Where?" The woman scowled, bewildered.

"Iowa," Agnes repeated loudly.

The woman in black touched Agnes's wrist and leaned in confidentially. She moved her mouth in a concerned and exaggerated way, like a facial exercise. "No, dear," she said. *"Here* we say *O-hi-o."*

That had been in Agnes's mishmash decade, after college. She had lived improvisationally then, getting this job or that, in restaurants or offices, taking a class or two, not thinking too far ahead, negotiating the precariousness and subway flus and scrimping for an occasional manicure or a play. Such a life required much exaggerated self-esteem. It engaged gross quantities of hope and despair and set them wildly side by side, like a Third World country of the heart. Her days grew messy with contradictions. When she went for walks, for her health, cinders would spot her cheeks and soot would settle in the furled leaf of each ear. Her shoes became unspeakable. Her blouses darkened in a breeze, and a blast of bus exhaust might linger in her hair for hours. Finally, her old asthma returned and, with a hacking, incessant cough, she gave up. "I feel like I've got five years to live," she told people, "so I'm moving back to Iowa so that it'll feel like fifty."

When she packed up to leave, she knew she was saying good-bye to something important, which was not that bad, in a way, because it meant that at least you had said hello to it to begin with, which most people in Cassell, Iowa, she felt, could not claim to have done.

A year and a half later, she married a boyish man twelve years her senior, a Cassell realtor named Joe, and together they bought a house on a little street called Birch Court. She taught a night class at the Arts Hall and did volunteer work on the Transportation Commission in town. It was life like a glass of water: half-empty, half-full. Half-full. Half-full. Oops: half-empty. Over the years, she and Joe tried to have a baby, but one night at dinner, looking at each other in a lonely way over the meat loaf, they realized with shock that they probably never would. Nonetheless, after six years, they still tried, vandalizing what romance was left in their marriage.

"Honey," she would whisper at night when he was reading under the reading lamp and she had already put her book away and curled toward him, wanting to place the red scarf over the lamp shade but knowing it would annoy him and so not doing it. "Do you want to make love? It would be a good time of month."

And Joe would groan. Or he would yawn. Or he would already be asleep. Once, after a long, hard day, he said, "I'm sorry, Agnes. I guess I'm just not in the mood."

She grew exasperated. "You think *I'm* in the mood?" she said. "I don't want to do this any more than you do," and he looked at her in a disgusted way, and it was two weeks after that that they had the sad dawning over the meat loaf.

At the Arts Hall, formerly the Grange Hall, Agnes taught the Great Books class, but taught it loosely, with cookies. She let her students turn in poems and plays and stories that they themselves had written; she let them use the class as their own little time to be creative. Someone once even brought in a sculpture: an electric one with blinking lights.

After class, she sometimes met with students individually. She recommended things for them to write about or read or consider in their next project. She smiled and asked if things were going well in their lives. She took an interest.

"You should be stricter," said Willard Stauffbacher, the head of the Instruction Department; he was a short, balding musician who liked to tape on his door pictures of famous people he thought he looked like. Every third Monday, he conducted the monthly departmental meeting—aptly named, Agnes liked to joke, since she did indeed depart mental. "Just because it's a night course doesn't mean you shouldn't impart standards," Stauffbacher said in a scolding way. "If it's piffle, use the word *piffle*. If it's meaningless, write *meaningless* across the top of every page." He had once taught at an elementary school and once at a prison. "I feel like I do all the real work around here," he added. He had posted near his office a sign that read RULES FOR THE MUSIC ROOM:

I will stay in my seat unless [sic] permission to move.
I will sit up straight.
I will listen to directions.
I will not bother my neighbor.
I will not talk when Mr. Stauffbacher is talking.
I will be polite to others.
I will sing as well as I can.

Agnes stayed after one night with Christa, the only black student in her class. She liked Christa a lot—Christa was smart and funny, and Agnes sometimes liked to stay after with her to chat. Tonight, Agnes had decided to talk Christa out of writing about vampires all the time.

"Why don't you write about that thing you told me about that time?" Agnes suggested.

Christa looked at her skeptically. "What thing?"

"The time in your childhood, during the Chicago riots, walking with your mother through the police barricades."

"Man, I lived that. Why should I want to write about it?"

Agnes sighed. Maybe Christa had a point. "It's just that I'm no help to you with this vampire stuff," Agnes said. "It's formulaic, genre fiction."

"You would be of more help to me with *my childhood?*"

"Well, with more serious stories, yes."

Christa stood up, perturbed. She grabbed back her vampire story. "You with all your Alice Walker and Zora Hurston. I'm just not interested in that anymore. I've done that already. I read those books years ago."

"Christa, please don't be annoyed." *Please do not talk when Mr. Stauffbacher is talking.*

"You've got this agenda for me."

"Really, I don't at all," said Agnes. "It's just that—you know what it is? It's that I'm just sick of these vampires. They're so roaming and repeating."

"If you were black, what you're saying might have a different spin. But the fact is, you're not," Christa said, and picked up her coat and strode out—though ten seconds later, she gamely stuck her head back in and said, "See you next week."

"We need a visiting writer who's black," Agnes said in the next depart mental meeting. "We've never had one." They were looking at their budget, and the readings this year were pitted against Dance Instruction, a program headed up by a redhead named Evergreen.

"The Joffrey is just so much central casting," said Evergreen, apropos of nothing. As a vacuum cleaner can start to pull up the actual thread of a carpet, her brains had been sucked dry by too much yoga. No one paid much attention to her.

"Perhaps we can get Harold Raferson in Chicago," Agnes suggested.

"We've already got somebody for the visiting writer slot," said Stauffbacher coyly. "An Afrikaner from Johannesburg."

"What?" said Agnes. Was he serious? Even Evergreen barked out a laugh.

"W. S. Beyerbach. The university's bringing him in. We pay our five hundred dollars and we get him out here for a day and a half."

"Who?" asked Evergreen.

"This has already been decided?" asked Agnes.

"Yup." Stauffbacher looked accusingly at Agnes. "I've done a lot of work to arrange for this. *I've* done all the work!"

"Do less," said Evergreen.

When Agnes first met Joe, they'd fallen madly upon each other. They'd kissed in restaurants; they'd groped, under coats, at the movies. At his little house, they'd made love on the porch, or the landing of the staircase, against the wall in the hall by the door to the attic, filled with too much desire to make their way to a real room.

Now they struggled self-consciously for atmosphere, something they'd never needed before. She prepared the bedroom carefully. She played quiet music and concentrated. She lit candles—as if she were in church, praying for the deceased. She donned a filmy gown. She took hot baths and entered the bedroom in nothing but a towel, a wild fishlike creature of moist, perfumed heat. In the nightstand drawer she still kept the charts a doctor once told her to keep, still placed an X on any date she and Joe actually had sex. But she could never show these to her doctor; not now. It pained Agnes to see them. She and Joe looked like worse than bad shots. She and Joe looked like idiots. She and Joe looked dead.

Frantic candlelight flickered on the ceiling like a puppet show. While she waited for Joe to come out of the bathroom, Agnes lay back on the bed and thought about her week, the bloody politics of it, how she was not very good at politics. Once, before he was elected, she had gone to a rally for Bill Clinton, but when he was late and had kept the crowd waiting for over an hour, and when the sun got hot and bees began landing on people's heads, when everyone's feet hurt and tiny children began to cry and a state assemblyman stepped forward to announce that Clinton had stopped at a Dairy Queen in Des Moines and that was why he was late—Dairy Queen!—she had grown angry and resentful and apolitical in her own sweet-starved thirst and she'd joined in with some other people who had started to chant, "Do us a favor, tell us the flavor."

Through college she had been a feminist—basically: she shaved her legs, *but just not often enough,* she liked to say. She signed day-care petitions, and petitions for Planned Parenthood. And although she had never been very aggressive with men, she felt strongly that she knew the difference between feminism and Sadie Hawkins Day—which some people, she believed, did not.

"Agnes, are we out of toothpaste or is this it—oh, okay, I see."

And once, in New York, she had quixotically organized the ladies' room line at the Brooks Atkinson Theatre. Because the play was going to start any minute and the line was still twenty women long, she had gotten six women to walk across the lobby with her to the men's room. "Everybody out of there?" she'd called in timidly, allowing the men to finish up first, which took awhile, especially with other men coming up impatiently and cutting ahead in line. Later, at intermission, she saw how it should have been done. Two elderly black women, with greater expertise in civil rights, stepped very confidently into the men's room and called out, "Don't mind us, boys. We're coming on in. Don't mind us."

"Are you okay?" asked Joe, smiling. He was already beside her. He smelled sweet, of soap and minty teeth, like a child.

"I think so," she said, and turned toward him in the bordello light of their room. He had never acquired the look of maturity anchored in sorrow that burnished so many men's faces. His own sadness in life—a childhood of beatings, a dying mother—was like quicksand, and he had to stay away from it entirely. He permitted no unhappy memories spoken aloud. He stuck with the same mild cheerfulness he'd honed successfully as a boy, and it made him seem fatuous—even, she knew, to himself. Probably it hurt his business a little.

"Your mind's wandering," he said, letting his own eyes close.

"I know." She yawned, moved her legs onto his for warmth, and in this way, with the candles burning into their tins, she and Joe fell asleep.

The spring arrived cool and humid. Bulbs cracked and sprouted, shot up their green periscopes, and on April first, the Arts Hall offered a joke lecture by T. S. Eliot, visiting scholar. "The Cruelest Month," it was called. "You don't find that funny?" asked Stauffbacher.

April fourth was the reception for W. S. Beyerbach. There was to be a dinner afterward, and then Beyerbach was to visit Agnes's Great Books class. She had assigned his second collection of sonnets, spare and elegant things with sighing and diaphanous politics. The next afternoon there was to be a reading.

Agnes had not been invited to the dinner, and when she asked about this, in a mildly forlorn way, Stauffbacher shrugged, as if it were totally out of his hands. I'm a *published poet*, Agnes wanted to say. She *had* published a poem once—in *The Gizzard Review*, but still!

"It was Edie Canterton's list," Stauffbacher said. "I had nothing to do with it."

She went to the reception anyway, annoyed, and when she planted herself like a splayed and storm-torn tree near the cheese, she could actually feel the crackers she was eating forming a bad paste in her mouth and she became afraid to smile. When she finally introduced herself to W. S. Beyerbach, she stumbled on her own name and actually pronounced it "On-yez."

"On-yez," repeated Beyerbach in a quiet Englishy voice. Condescending, she thought. His hair was blond and white, like a palomino, and his eyes were blue and scornful as mints. She could see he was a withheld man; although some might say *shy,* she decided it was *withheld:* a lack of generosity. Passive-aggressive. It was causing the people around him to squirm and blurt things nervously. He would simply nod, the smile on his face faint and vaguely pharmaceutical. Everything about him was tight and coiled as a door spring. From living in *that country,* thought Agnes. How could he live in that country?

Stauffbacher was trying to talk heartily about the mayor. Something about his old progressive ideas, and the forthcoming convention center. Agnes thought of her own meetings on the Transportation Commission, of the mayor's leash law for cats, of his new squadron of meter maids and bicycle police, of a councilman the mayor once slugged in a bar. "Now, of course, the mayor's become a fascist," said Agnes in a voice that sounded strangely loud, bright with anger.

Silence fell all around. Edie Canterton stopped stirring the punch. Agnes looked about her. "Oh," she said. "Are we not supposed to use *that word* in this room?" Beyerbach's expression went blank. Agnes's face burned in confusion.

Stauffbacher appeared pained, then stricken. "More cheese, anyone?" he asked, holding up the silver tray.

. . .

After everyone left for dinner, she went by herself to the Dunk 'N Dine across the street. She ordered the California BLT and a cup of coffee, and looked over Beyerbach's work again: dozens of images of broken, rotten bodies, of the body's mutinies and betrayals, of the body's strange housekeeping and illicit pets. At the front of the book was a dedication—*To DFB (1970–1989).* Who could that be? A political activist, maybe. Perhaps it was the young woman referred to often in his poems, "a woman who had thrown aside the unseasonal dress of hope," only to look for it again "in the blood-blooming shrubs." Perhaps if Agnes got a chance, she would ask him. Why not? A book was a public thing, and its dedication was part of it. If it was too personal a question for him, *tough.* She would find the right time, she decided. She paid the check, put on her jacket, and crossed the street to the Arts Hall, to meet Beyerbach by the front door. She would wait for the moment, then seize it.

He was already at the front door when she arrived. He greeted her with a stiff smile and a soft "Hello, Onyez," an accent that made her own voice ring coarse and country-western.

She smiled and then blurted, "I have a question to ask you." To her own ears, she sounded like Johnny Cash.

Beyerbach said nothing, only held the door open for her and then followed her into the building.

She continued as they stepped slowly up the stairs. "May I ask to whom your book is dedicated?"

At the top of the stairs, they turned left down the long corridor. She could feel his steely reserve, his lip-biting, his shyness no doubt garbed and rationalized with snobbery, but so much snobbery to handle all that shyness, he could not possibly be a meaningful critic of his country. She was angry with him. *How can you live in that country?* she again wanted to say, although she remembered when someone had once said that to her—a Danish man on Agnes's senior trip abroad to Copenhagen. It had been during the Vietnam War and the man had stared meanly, righteously. "The United States—how can you live in that country?" the man had asked. Agnes had shrugged. "A lot of my stuff is there," she'd said, and it was then that she first felt all the dark love and shame that came from the pure accident of home, the deep and arbitrary place that happened to be yours.

"It's dedicated to my son," Beyerbach said finally.

He would not look at her, but stared straight ahead along the corridor floor. Now Agnes's shoes sounded very loud.

"You lost a son," she said.

"Yes," he said. He looked away, at the passing wall, past Stauffbacher's bulletin board, past the men's room, the women's room, some sternness in him broken, and when he turned back, she could see his eyes filling with water, his face a plethora, reddened with unbearable pressure.

"I'm so sorry," Agnes said.

Side by side now, their footsteps echoed down the corridor toward her classroom; all the anxieties she felt with this mournfully quiet man now mimicked the anxieties of love. What should she say? It must be the most unendurable thing to lose a child. Shouldn't he say something of this? It was his turn to say something.

But he would not. And when they finally reached her classroom, she turned to him in the doorway and, taking a package from her purse, said simply, in a reassuring way, "We always have cookies in class."

Now he beamed at her with such relief that she knew she had for once said the right thing. It filled her with affection for him. Perhaps, she thought, that was where affection began: in an unlikely phrase, in a moment of someone's having unexpectedly but at last said the right thing. *We always have cookies in class.*

She introduced him with a bit of flourish and biography. Positions held, universities attended. The students raised their hands and asked him about apartheid, about shantytowns and

homelands, and he answered succinctly, after long sniffs and
pauses, only once referring to a question as "unanswerably fey,"
causing the student to squirm and fish around in her purse for
something, nothing, Kleenex perhaps. Beyerbach did not seem
to notice. He went on, spoke of censorship, how a person must
work hard not to internalize a government's program of censorship, since that is what a government would like best, for *you* to
do it *yourself,* and how he was not sure he had not succumbed.
Afterward, a few students stayed and shook his hand, formally,
awkwardly, then left. Christa was the last. She, too, shook his
hand and then started chatting amiably. They knew someone
in common—Harold Raferson in Chicago!—and as Agnes
quickly wiped the seminar table to clear it of cookie crumbs,
she tried to listen, but couldn't really hear. She made a small
pile of crumbs and swept them into one hand.

"Good night" sang out Christa when she left.

"Good night, Christa," said Agnes, brushing the crumbs
into the wastebasket.

Now she stood with Beyerbach in the empty classroom.
"Thank you so much," she said in a hushed way. "I'm sure they
all got quite a lot out of that. I'm very sure they did."

He said nothing, but smiled at her gently.

She shifted her weight from one leg to the other. "Would
you like to go somewhere and get a drink?" she asked. She was
standing close to him, looking up into his face. He was tall, she
saw now. His shoulders weren't broad, but he had a youthful
straightness to his carriage. She briefly touched his sleeve. His
suitcoat was corduroy and bore the faint odor of clove. This was
the first time in her life that she had ever asked a man out for a
drink.

He made no move to step away from her, but actually
seemed to lean toward her a bit. She could feel his dry breath,
see up close the variously hued spokes of his irises, the grays
and yellows in the blue. There was a sprinkling of small freckles near his hairline. He smiled, then looked at the clock on the

wall. "I would love to, really, but I have to get back to the hotel to make a phone call at ten-fifteen." He looked a little disappointed—not a lot, thought Agnes, but certainly a little.

"Oh, well," she said. She flicked off the lights and in the dark he carefully helped her on with her jacket. They stepped out of the room and walked together in silence, back down the corridor to the front entrance of the hall. Outside on the steps, the night was balmy and scented with rain. "Will you be all right walking back to your hotel?" she asked. "Or—"

"Oh, yes, thank you. It's just around the corner."

"Right. That's right. Well, my car's parked way over there. So I guess I'll see you tomorrow afternoon at your reading."

"Yes," he said. "I shall look forward to that."

"Yes," she said. "So shall I."

The reading was in the large meeting room at the Arts Hall and was from the sonnet book she had already read, but it was nice to hear the poems again, in his hushed, pained tenor. She sat in the back row, her green raincoat sprawled beneath her on the seat like a leaf. She leaned forward, onto the seat ahead of her, her back an angled stem, her chin on double fists, and she listened like that for some time. At one point, she closed her eyes, but the image of him before her, standing straight as a compass needle, remained caught there beneath her lids, like a burn or a speck or a message from the mind.

Afterward, moving away from the lectern, Beyerbach spotted her and waved, but Stauffbacher, like a tugboat with a task, took his arm and steered him elsewhere, over toward the side table with the little plastic cups of warm Pepsi. We are both men, the gesture seemed to say. We both have *bach* in our names. Agnes put on her green coat. She went over toward the Pepsi table and stood. She drank a warm Pepsi, then placed the empty cup back on the table. Beyerbach finally turned toward her and smiled familiarly. She thrust out her hand. "It was a wonderful reading," she said. "I'm very glad I got the chance to meet you." She gripped his long, slender palm and locked thumbs. She could feel the bones in him.

"Thank you," he said. He looked at her coat in a worried way. "You're leaving?"

She looked down at her coat. "I'm afraid I have to get going home." She wasn't sure whether she really had to or not. But she'd put on the coat, and it now seemed an awkward thing to take off.

"Oh," he murmured, gazing at her intently. "Well, all best wishes to you, Onyez."

"Excuse me?" There was some clattering near the lectern.

"All best to you," he said, something retreating in his expression.

Stauffbacher suddenly appeared at her side, scowling at her green coat, as if it were incomprehensible.

"Yes," said Agnes, stepping backward, then forward again to shake Beyerbach's hand once more; it was a beautiful hand, like an old and expensive piece of wood. "Same to you," she said. Then she turned and fled.

For several nights, she did not sleep well. She placed her face directly into her pillow, then turned it some for air, then flipped over to her back and opened her eyes, staring at the far end of the room through the stark angle of the door frame toward the tiny light from the bathroom which illumined the hallway, faintly, as if someone had just been there.

For several days, she thought perhaps he might have left her a note with the secretary, or that he might send her one from an airport somewhere. She thought that the inadequacy of their good-bye would haunt him, too, and that he might send her a postcard as elaboration.

But he did not. Briefly, she thought about writing him a letter, on Arts Hall stationery, which for money reasons was no longer the stationery, but photocopies of the stationery. She knew he had flown to the West Coast, then off to Tokyo, then Sydney, then back to Johannesburg, and if she posted it now, perhaps he would receive it when he arrived. She could tell him once more how interesting it had been to meet him. She could enclose her poem from *The Gizzard Review*. She had read in the newspaper an article about bereavement—and if she were her own mother, she could send him that, too.

Thank God, thank God, she was not her mother.

Spring settled firmly in Cassell with a spate of thundershowers. The perennials—the myrtle and grape hyacinths—blossomed around town in a kind of civic blue, and the warming air brought forth an occasional mosquito or fly. The Transportation Commission meetings were dreary and long, too often held over the dinner hour, and when Agnes got home, she would replay them for Joe, sometimes bursting into tears over the parts about the photoradar or the widening interstate.

When her mother called, Agnes got off the phone fast. When her sister called about her mother, Agnes got off the phone even faster. Joe rubbed her shoulders and spoke to her of carports, of curb appeal, of asbestos-wrapped pipes.

At the Arts Hall, she taught and fretted and continued to receive the usual memos from the secretary, written on the usual scrap paper—except that the scrap paper this time, for a while, consisted of the extra posters for the Beyerbach reading. She would get a long disquisition on policies and procedures concerning summer registration, and she would turn it over and there would be his face—sad and pompous in the photograph. She would get a simple phone message—"Your husband called. Please phone him at the office"—and on the back would be the ripped center of Beyerbach's nose, one minty eye, an elbowish chin. Eventually, there were no more, and the scrap paper moved on to old contest announcements, grant deadlines, Easter concert notices.

At night, she and Joe did yoga to a yoga show on TV. It was part of their effort not to become their parents, though marriage, they knew, held that hazard. The functional disenchantment, the sweet habit of each other had begun to put lines around her mouth, lines that looked like quotation marks—as if everything she said had already been said before. Sometimes their old cat, Madeline, a fat and pampered calico reaping the benefits of life with a childless couple during their childbearing years, came and plopped herself down with them, between them. She was accustomed to much nestling and appreciation and drips from the faucet, though sometimes she would vanish outside, and they would not see her for days, only to spy her later, in the yard, dirty and matted, chomping a vole or eating old snow.

For Memorial Day weekend, Agnes flew with Joe to New York, to show him the city for the first time. "A place," she said, "where if you're not white and not born there, you're not automatically a story." She had grown annoyed with Iowa, the pathetic thirdhand manner in which the large issues and conversations of the world were encountered, the oblique and tired way history situated itself there—if ever. She longed to be a citizen of the globe!

They roller-skated in Central Park. They looked in the Lord & Taylor windows. They went to the Joffrey. They went to a hair salon on Fifty-seventh Street and there she had her hair dyed red. They sat in the window booths of coffee shops and got coffee refills and ate pie.

"So much seems the same," she said to Joe. "When I lived

here, everyone was hustling for money. The rich were. The poor were. But everyone tried hard to be funny. Everywhere you went—a store, a manicure place—someone was telling a joke. A *good* one." She remembered it had made any given day seem bearable, that impulse toward a joke. It had been a determined sort of humor, an intensity mirroring the intensity of the city, and it seemed to embrace and alleviate the hard sadness of people having used one another and marred the earth the way they had. "It was like brains having sex. It was like every brain was a sex maniac." She looked down at her pie. "People really worked at it, the laughing," she said. "People need to laugh."

"They do," said Joe. He took a swig of coffee, his lips out over the cup in a fleshy flower. He was afraid she might cry—she was getting that look again—and if she did, he would feel guilty and lost and sorry for her that her life was not here anymore, but in a far and boring place now with him. He set the cup down and tried to smile. "They sure do," he said. And he looked out the window at the rickety taxis, the oystery garbage and tubercular air, seven pounds of chicken giblets dumped on the curb in front of the restaurant where they were. He turned back to her and made the face of a clown.

"What are you doing?" she asked.

"It's a clown face."

"What do you mean, 'a clown face'?" Someone behind her was singing "I Love New York," and for the first time she noticed the strange irresolution of the tune.

"A regular clown face is what I mean."

"It didn't look like that."

"No? What did it look like?"

"You want me to do the face?"

"Yeah, do the face."

She looked at Joe. Every arrangement in life carried with it the sadness, the sentimental shadow, of its not being something else, but only itself: she attempted the face—a look of such monstrous emptiness and stupidity that Joe burst out in a howling sort of laughter, like a dog, and then so did she, air exploding through her nose in a snort, her head thrown forward, then back, then forward again, setting loose a fit of coughing.

"Are you okay?" asked Joe, and she nodded. Out of politeness, he looked away, outside, where it had suddenly started to rain. Across the street, two people had planted themselves under the window ledge of a Gap store, trying to stay dry, waiting out the downpour, their figures dark and scarecrowish against the lit window display. When he turned back to his wife—his sad young wife—to point this out to her, to show her what was funny to a man firmly in the grip of middle age, she was still bent sideways in her seat, so that her face fell below the line of the table, and he could only see the curve of her heaving back, the fuzzy penumbra of her thin spring sweater, and the garish top of her bright, new, and terrible hair.

CHARADES

It's fitting that Christmas should degenerate to this, its barest bones. The family has begun to seem to Therese like a pack of thespians anyway; everyone arrives, performs for one another, catches early flights out, to Logan or O'Hare. Probably it's appropriate that a party game should literally appear and insert itself in the guise of a holiday tradition (which it isn't). Usually, no one in Therese's family expresses much genuine feeling anyway; everyone aims instead—though gamely!—for enactments.

Each year now, the stage is a new one—their aging parents, in their restless old age, buying and selling town houses, moving steadily southward from Maine. The real estate is Therese's mother's idea. Since he's retired, Therese's father has focused more on bird feeders; he is learning how to build them. "Who knows what he'll do next?" Her mother sighs. "He'll probably start carving designs into the side of the house."

This year, they are in Bethesda, Maryland, near where Andrew, Therese's brother, lives. Andrew works as an electrical engineer and is married to a sweet, pretty, part-time private detective named Pam. Pam is pixie-haired and smiley. Who would ever suspect her of discreetly gathering confidences and facts for one's adversaries? She freezes hams. She makes Jell-O salad days in advance. She and Andrew are the parents of a one-and-a-half-year-old named Winnie, who already reads.

Reads the reading videos on TV, but reads.

Everyone has divided into teams, four and four, and written the names of famous people, songs, films, plays, books on scraps of wrapping paper torn off the gifts hours earlier. It is another few hours until Therese and her husband Ray's flight, at 4:30, from National Airport. "Yes," says Therese, "I guess we'll have to forgo the 'Averell Harriman: Statesman for All Seasons' exhibit."

"I don't know why you couldn't catch a later flight," says Therese's sister, Ann. She is scowling. Ann is the youngest, and ten years younger than Therese, who is the oldest, but lately Ann's voice has taken up a prissy and matronly scolding that startles Therese. "Four-thirty," says Ann, pursing her lips and propping her feet up on the chair next to her. "That's a little ridiculous. You're missing dinner." Her shoes are pointy and Victorian-looking. They are green suede—a cross between a courtesan's and Peter Pan's.

The teams are divided in such a way that Therese and Ray and her parents are on one team, Andrew and Pam, Ann and Tad, Ann's fiancé, on the other. Tad is slender and red-haired, a marketing rep for Neutrogena. He and Ann have just become engaged. After nearly a decade of casting about in love and work, Ann is now going to law school and planning her summer wedding. Since Therese worked for years as a public defender and is currently, through a fluky political appointment, a county circuit court judge, she has assumed that Ann's decision to be a lawyer is a kind of sororal affirmation, that it will some-how mean the two of them will have new things in common, that Ann will have questions for her, observations, forensic things to say. But this seems not to be so. Ann appears instead to be preoccupied with trying to hire bands and caterers, and to rent a large room in a restaurant. "Ugh," said Therese sympathetically. "Doesn't it make you want to elope?" Therese and Ray were married at the courthouse, with the file clerks as witnesses.

Ann shrugged. "I'm trying to figure out how to get everybody from the church to the restaurant in a way that won't wrinkle their outfits and spoil the pictures."

"Really?" asked Therese. "You are?"

The titles are put in two big salad bowls, each team receiving the other's bowl of titles. Therese's father goes first. "All right! Everyone ready!" He has always been witty, competitive, tense; games have usually brought out the best and worst in him. These days, however, he seems anxious and elderly. There is a pain in his eyes, something sad and unfocused that sometimes stabs at them—the fear of a misspent life, or an uncertainty as to where he's left the keys. He signals that his assigned name is a famous person. No one could remember how to signal that and so the family has invented one: a quick pompous posture, hands on hips, chin in air. Mustering up a sense of drama, Therese's father does this well.

"Famous person!" Everyone shouts it, though of course there is someone who shouts "Idiot" to be witty. This time, it is Therese's mother.

"Idiot!" she shouts. "Village idiot!"

But Therese's father has continued signaling the syllables, ignoring his wife, slapping the fingers of his right hand hard on his left sleeve. The famous person has three names. He is doing the first name, first syllable. He takes out a dollar bill and points to it.

"George Washington," shouts Ray.

"George Washington Carver!" shouts Therese. Therese's father shakes his head angrily, turning the dollar around and pointing at it violently. It bothers him not to be able to control the discourse.

"Dollar bill," says Therese's mother.

"Bill!" says Therese. At this, her father begins nodding and pointing at her psychotically. *Yes, yes, yes.* Now he makes stretching motions with his hands. "Bill, Billy, William," says Therese, and her father points wildly at her again. "William," she says. "William Kennedy Smith."

"Yes!" shouts her father, clapping his hands and throwing his head back as if to praise the ceiling.

"William Kennedy Smith?" Ann is scowling again. "How did you get that from just William?"

"He's been in the news." Therese shrugs. She does not know how to explain Ann's sourness. Perhaps it has something to do with Ann's struggles in law school, or with Therese's being a circuit court judge, or with the diamond on Ann's finger, which is so huge that it seems, to Therese, unkind to wear it around their mother's, which is, when one gets right down to it, a chip. Earlier this morning, Ann told Therese that she is going to take Tad's name, as well. "You're going to call yourself Tad?" Therese asked, but Ann was not amused. Ann's sense of humor was never that flexible, though she used to like a good sight gag.

Ann officiously explained the name change: "Because I believe a family is like a team, and everyone on the team should have the same name, like a color. I believe a spouse should be a team player."

Therese no longer has any idea who Ann is. She liked her better when Ann was eight, with her blue pencil case, and a strange, loping run that came from having one leg a quarter of an inch longer than the other. Ann was more attractive as a child. She was awkward and inquiring. She was cute. Or so she seemed to Therese, who was mostly in high school and college, slightly depressed and studying too much, destroying her already-bad eyes, so that now she wore glasses so thick her eyes swam in a cloudy way behind them. This morning, when she'd stood listening to Ann talk about team players, Therese had smiled and nodded, but she felt preached at, as if she were a messy, wayward hippie. She wanted to grab her sister, throw herself upon her, embrace her, shut her up. She tried to understand Ann's dark and worried nuptial words, but instead she found herself recalling the pratfalls she used to perform for Ann—Therese could take a fall straight on the face—in order to make Ann laugh.

Ann's voice was going on now. "When you sit too long, the bodices bunch up. . . ."

Therese mentally measured the length of her body in front of her and wondered if she could do it. Of course she could. Of course. But *would* she? And then suddenly, she knew she would. She let her hip twist and fell straight forward, her arm at an angle, her mouth in a whoop. She had learned to do this in drama club when she was fifteen. She hadn't been pretty, and it was a means of getting the boys' attention. She landed with a thud.

"You still do that?" asked Ann with incredulity and disgust. "You're a judge and you still *do* that?"

"Sort of," said Therese from the floor. She felt around for her glasses.

Now it is the team player herself standing up to give clues to her team. She looks at the name on her scrap of paper and makes a slight face. "I need a consultation," she says in a vaguely repelled way that perhaps she imagines is sophisticated. She takes the scrap of wrapping paper over to Therese's team. "What is this?" Ann asks. There in Ray's handwriting is a misspelled *Arachnophobia*.

"It's a movie," says Ray apologetically. "Did I spell it wrong?"

"I think you did, honey," says Therese, leaning in to look at it. "You got some of the *o*'s and *a*'s mixed up." Ray is dyslexic. When the roofing business slows in the winter months, instead of staying in with a book, or going to psychotherapy, he drives to cheap matinees of bad movies—"flicks," he calls them, or "cliffs" when he's making fun of himself. Ray misspells every-thing. Is it *input* or *imput?* Is it *averse, adverse,* or *adversed? Stock* or *stalk? Carrot* or *karate?* His roofing business has a reputation for being reasonable, but a bit slipshod and second-rate. Nonetheless, Therese thinks he is great. He is never conde-scending. He cooks infinite dishes with chicken. He is ardent and capable and claims almost every night in his husbandly way to find Therese the sexiest woman he's ever known. Therese likes that. She is also having an affair with a young assistant DA in the prosecutor's office, but it is a limited thing—like taking her gloves off, clapping her hands, and putting the gloves back on again. It is quiet and undiscoverable. It is nothing, except that it is sex with a man who is not dyslexic, and once in a while, Jesus Christ, she needs that.

Ann is acting out *Arachnophobia,* the whole concept, rather than working syllable by syllable. She stares into her fiancé's eyes, wiggling her fingers about and then jumping away in a fright, but Tad doesn't get it, though he does look a little alarmed. Ann waves her Christmas-manicured nails at him more furiously. One of the nails has a little Santa Claus painted on it. Ann's black hair is cut severely in sharp, expensive lines, and her long, drapey clothes hang from her shoulders, as if still on a hanger. She looks starved and rich and enraged. Everything seems struggled toward and forced, a little cartoonish, like the green shoes, which may be why her fiancé suddenly shouts out, "Little Miss Muffett!" Ann turns now instead to Andrew, motioning at him encouragingly, as if to punish Tad. The awk-ward lope of her childhood has taken on a chiropracticed slink. Therese turns back toward her own team, toward her father, who is still muttering something about William Kennedy Smith. "A woman shouldn't be in a bar at three o'clock in the morning, that's all there is to it."

"Dad, that's ludicrous," whispers Therese, not wanting to interrupt the game. "Bars are open to everyone. Public Accom-modations Law."

"I'm not talking about the cold legalities," he says chastisingly. He has never liked lawyers, and is baffled by his daughters. "I'm talking about a long-understood *moral code*." Her father is of that Victorian sensibility that deep down respects prostitutes more than it does women in general.

" 'Long-understood moral code'?" Therese looks at him gently. "Dad, you're seventy-five years old. Things change."

"*Arachnophobia!*" Andrew shouts, and he and Ann rush together and do high fives.

Therese's father makes a quick little spitting sound, then crosses his legs and looks the other way. Therese looks over at her mother and her mother is smiling at her conspiratorially, behind Therese's father's back, making little donkey ears with her fingers, her sign for when she thinks he's being a jackass.

"All right, forget the William Kennedy Smith. Doll, your turn," says Therese's father to her mother. Therese's mother gets up slowly but bends gleefully to pick up the scrap of paper. She looks at it, walks to the center of the room, and shoves the paper scrap in her pocket. She faces the other team and makes the sign for a famous person.

"Wrong team, Mom," says Therese, and her mother says "Oops," and turns around. She repeats the famous person stance.

"Famous person," says Ray encouragingly. Therese's mother nods. She pauses for a bit to think. Then she spins around, throws her arms up into the air, collapses forward onto the floor, then backward, hitting her head on the stereo.

"Marjorie, what are you doing?" asks Therese's father. Her mother is lying there on the floor, laughing.

"Are you okay?" Therese asks. Her mother nods, still laughing quietly.

"Fall," says Ray. "Dizziness. Dizzy Gillespie."

Therese's mother shakes her head.

"Epilepsy," says Therese.

"Explode," says her father, and her mother nods. "Explosion. Bomb. Robert Oppenheimer!"

"That's it." Her mother sighs. She has a little trouble getting back up. She is seventy and her knees are jammed with arthritis.

"You need help, Mom?" Therese asks.

"Yeah, Mom, you need help?" asks Ann, who has risen and walked toward the center of the room, to take charge.

"I'm okay." Therese's mother sighs, with a quiet, slightly faked giggle, and walks stiffly back to her seat.

"That was great, Ma," says Therese.

Her mother smiles proudly. "Well, thank you!"

After that, there are many rounds, and every time Therese's mother gets anything like Dom De Luise or Tom Jones, she does her bomb imitation again, whipping herself into a spastic frenzy and falling, then rising stiffly again to great applause. Pam brings Winnie in from her nap and everyone oohs and aahs at the child's sweet sleep-streaked face. "There she is," coos Aunt Therese. "You want to come see Grandma be a bomb?"

"It's your turn," says Andrew impatiently.

"Mine?" asks Therese.

"I think that's right," says her father.

She gets up, digs into the bowl, unfolds the scrap of wrapping paper. It says "Jekylls Street." "I need a consultation here. Andrew, I think this is your writing."

"Okay," he says, rising, and together they step into the foyer.

"Is this a TV show?" whispers Therese. "I don't watch much TV."

"No," says Andrew with a vague smile.

"What is it?"

He shifts his weight, reluctant to tell her. Perhaps it is because he is married to a detective. Or, more likely, it is because he himself works with Top Secret documents from the Defense Department; he was recently promoted from the just plain Secret ones. As an engineer, he consults, reviews, approves. His eyes are suppressed, annoyed. "It's the name of a street two blocks from here." There's a surly and defensive curve to his mouth.

"But that's not the title of anything famous."

"It's a place. I thought we could do names of places."

"It's not a famous place."

"So?"

"I mean, we all could write down the names of streets in our neighborhoods, near where we work, a road we walked down once on the way to a store—"

"You're the one who said we could do places."

"I did? Well, all right, then, what did I say was the sign for a place? We don't have a sign for places."

"I don't know. You figure it out," he says. A saucy rage is all over him now. Is this from childhood? Is this from hair loss? Once, she and Andrew were close. But now, as with Ann, she has no idea who he is anymore. She has only a theory: an electrical engineer worked over years ago by high school guidance counselors paid by the Pentagon to recruit, train, and militarize all the boys with high math SAT scores. "From M.I.T. to MIA," Andrew once put it himself. "A military-industrial asshole." But she can't find that satirical place in him anymore. Last year, at least, they had joked about their upbringing. "I scarcely remember Dad reading to us," she'd said.

"Sure he read to us," said Andrew. "You don't remember him reading to us? You don't remember him reading to us silently from the *Wall Street Journal*?"

Now she scans his hardening face for a joke, a glimmer, a bit of love. Andrew and Ann have seemed close, and Therese feels a bit wistful, wondering when and how that happened.

She is a little jealous. The only expression she can get from Andrew is a derisive one. He is a traffic cop. She is the speeding flower child.

Don't you know I'm a *judge?* she wants to ask. A judge via a fluke political appointment, sure. A judge with a reputation around the courthouse for light sentencing, true. A judge who is having an affair that mildly tarnishes her character—okay. A softy; an easy touch: but a judge nonetheless.

Instead, she says, "Do you mind if I just pick another one?"

"Fine by me," he says, and strides brusquely back into the living room.

Oh, well, Therese thinks. It is her new mantra. It usually calms her better than *ohm,* which she also tries. *Ohm* is where the heart is. *Ohm* is not here. *Oh, well. Oh, well.* When she was first practicing law, to combat her courtroom stage fright, she would chant to herself, *Everybody loves me. Everybody loves me,* and when that didn't work, she'd switch to *Kill! Kill! Kill!*

"We're doing another one," announces Andrew, and Therese picks another one.

A book and a movie. She opens her palms, prayerlike for a book. She cranks one hand in the air for a movie. She pulls on her ear and points at a lamp. "Sounds like *light,*" Ray says. His expression is open and helpful. "Bite, kite, dite, fight, night—"

Therese signals yes, that's it.

"Night," repeats Ray.

"Tender Is the Night," says her mother.

"Yes!" says Therese, and bends to kiss her mother on the cheek. Her mother smiles exuberantly, her face in a kind of burst; she loves affection, is hungry and grateful for it. When she was younger, she was a frustrated, mean mother, and so she is pleased when her children act as if they don't remember.

It is Andrew's turn. He stands before his own team, staring at the red scrap in his hand. He ponders it, shakes his head, then looks back toward Therese. "This must be yours," he says with a smirk that maybe is a good-natured smirk. Is there such a thing? Therese hopes.

"You need a consultation?" She gets up to look at the writing; it reads, "The Surrey with the Fringe on Top." "Yup, that's mine," she says.

"Come here," he says, and the two of them go back down the corridor toward the foyer again. This time, Therese notices the photographs her parents have hung there. Photographs of their children, of weddings and Winnie, though all the ones of Therese seem to her to be aggressively unflattering, advertising an asymmetry in her expression, or the magnified haziness of her eyes, her hair in a dry, peppery frizz. Vanity surges in her: surely there must have been better pictures! The ones of Andrew, of Ann, of Tad, of Pam and Winnie are sunlit, posed, wholesome, pretty. But the ones of Therese seem slightly disturbed, as if her parents were convinced she is insane.

"We'll stand here by the demented-looking pictures of me," says Therese.

"Ann sent her those," says Andrew.

"Really?" says Therese.

He studies her hair. "Didn't your hair used to be a different color? I don't remember it ever being quite that color. What *is* that color?"

"Why, whatever do you mean?"

"Look," he says, getting back to the game. "I've never heard of this," and he waves the scrap of paper as if it were a gum wrapper.

"You haven't? It's a song: 'Geese and chicks and ducks better scurry, when I take you out in the surrey . . . ' "

"No."

"No?" She keeps going. She looks up at him romantically, yearningly. " 'When I take you out in my surrey, when I take you out in my surrey with the fringe on—' "

"No," Andrew interrupts emphatically.

"Hmm. Well, don't worry. Everyone on your team will know it."

The righteous indignation is returning to his face. "If *I* don't know it, what makes you think *they'll* know it?" Perhaps this is because of his work, the technosecrecy of it. *He* knows; *they* don't.

"They'll know it," Therese says. "I guarantee." She turns to leave.

"Whoa, whoa, whoa," says Andrew. The gray-pink of rage is back in his skin. What has he become? She hasn't a clue. He is successfully top secret. He is classified information. "I'm not doing this," he says. "I refuse."

Therese stares at him. This is the assertiveness he can't exercise on the job. Perhaps here, where he is no longer a cog-though-a-prized cog, he can insist on certain things. The Cold War is over, she wants to say. But what has replaced it is this: children who have turned on one another, now that the gods—or were they only guards?—have fled. "Okay, fine," she says. "I'll make up another."

"We're doing another one," announces Andrew triumphantly as they go back into the living room. He waves the paper scrap. "Have any of you ever even heard of a song called 'The Surrey with the Fringe on Top'?"

"Sure," says Pam, looking at him in a puzzled way. No doubt he seems different to her around the holidays.

"You have?" He seems a bit flummoxed. He looks at Ann. "Have you?"

Ann looks reluctant to break ranks with him but says, quietly, "Yeah."

"Tad, how about you?" he asks.

Tad has been napping off and on, his head thrown back against the sofa, but now he jerks awake. "Uh, yeah," he says.

"Tad's not feeling that well," says Ann.

In desperation, Andrew turns toward the other team. "And you all know it, too?"

"I don't know it," says Ray. He is the only one. He doesn't know a show tune from a chauffeur. In a way, that's what Therese likes about him.

Andrew sits back down, refusing to admit defeat. "Ray didn't know it," he says.

Therese can't think of a song, so she writes "Clarence Thomas" and hands the slip back to Andrew. As he ponders his options, Therese's mother gets up and comes back holding Dixie cups and a bottle of cranberry drink. "Who would like some cranberry juice?" she says, and starts pouring. She hands the cups out carefully to everyone. "We don't have the wineglasses unpacked, so we'll have to make do."

"We'll have to make do" is one of their mother's favorite expressions, acquired during the Depression and made indelible during the war. When they were little, Therese and Andrew used to look at each other and say, "We'll have to make do-do," but when Therese glances over at Andrew now, nothing registers. He has forgotten. He is thinking only of the charade.

Ray sips his a little sloppily, and a drop spills on the chair. Therese hands him a napkin and he dabs at the upholstery with it, but it is Ann who is swiftly up, out to the kitchen, and back with a cold, wet cloth, wiping at Ray's chair in a kind of rebuke.

"Oh, don't worry," her mother is saying.

"I think I've got it," says Ann solemnly.

"I'm doing my clues now," says Andrew impatiently. Therese looks over at Winnie, who, calm and observant in her mother's arms, a pink incontinent Buddha who knows all her letters, seems like the sanest person in the room.

Andrew is making a sweeping gesture with his arm, something meant to include everyone in the room.

"People," says Tad.

"Family," says Pam.

Ann has come back from the kitchen and sits down on the sofa. "Us," she says.

Andrew smiles and nods.

"Us. Thom-us," says Ann. "Clarence Thomas."

"Yes," says Andrew with a clap. "What was the time on that?"

"Thirty seconds," says Tad.

"Well, I guess he's on the tip of everyone's tongue," says Therese's mother.

"I guess so," says Therese.

"It was interesting to see all those black people from Yale," says Therese's mother. "All sitting there in the Senate caucus room. I'll bet their parents were proud."

Ann did not get in to Yale. "What I don't like," she says, "is all these black people who don't like whites. They're so hostile. I see it all the time in law school. Most white people are more than willing to sit down, be friendly and integrated. But it's the blacks who are too angry."

"Imagine that," says Ray.

"Yes. Imagine," says Therese. "Why would they be angry? You know what else I don't like? I don't like all these gay men who have gotten just a little too somber and butch. You know what I mean? They're so funereal and upset these days! Where is the mincing and *high-spiritedness* of yesteryear? Where is the *gayness* in *gay*? It's all so confusing and inconvenient! You can't tell who's who without a goddamn *Playbill*!" She stands up and looks at Ray. It is time to go. She has lost her judicial temperament hours ago. She fears she is going to do another pratfall, only this time she will break something. Already she sees herself carted out on a stretcher, taken toward the airport, and toward home, saying the final words she has to say to her family, has always had to say to her family. Sounds like *could cry*.

"Good-bye!"

"Good-bye!"

"Good-bye!"

"Good-bye!"

"Good-bye!"

"Good-bye!"

"Good-bye!"

But first Ray must do his charade, which is Confucius. "Okay. I'm ready," he says, and begins to wander around the living room in a wild-eyed daze, looking as confused as possible, groping at the bookcases, placing his palm to his brow. And in that moment, Therese thinks how good-looking he is and how kind and strong and how she loves nobody else in the world even half as much.

FOUR CALLING BIRDS,
THREE FRENCH HENS

When the cat died on Veterans Day, his ashes then packed into a cheesy pink-posied tin and placed high upon the mantel, the house seemed lonely and Aileen began to drink. She had lost all her ties to the animal world. She existed now in a solely man-made place: the couch was furless, the carpet dry and unmauled, the kitchen corner where the food dish had been no longer scabby with Mackerel Platter and hazardous for walking.

Oh, Bert!

He had been a beautiful cat.

Her friends interpreted the duration and intensity of her sorrow as a sign of displaced mourning: her grief was for some-thing larger, more appropriate—it was the impending death of her parents; it was the son she and Jack had never had (though wasn't three-year-old Sofie cute as a zipper?); it was this whole Bosnia, Cambodia, Somalia, Dinkins, Giuliani, NAFTA thing.

No, really, it was just Bert, Aileen insisted. It was just her sweet, handsome cat, her buddy of ten years. She had been with him longer than she had with either Jack or Sofie or half her friends, and he was such a smart, funny guy—big and loyal and verbal as a dog.

"What do you mean, *verbal as a dog?*" Jack scowled.

"I swear it," she said.

"Get a grip," said Jack, eyeing her glass of blended malt. Puccini's "Humming Chorus," the Brahms "Alto Rhapsody," and Samuel Barber's Adagio for Strings all murmured in succession from the stereo. He flicked it off. "You've got a daughter. There are holidays ahead. That damn cat wouldn't have shed one tear over you."

"I really don't think that's true," she said a little wildly, perhaps with too much fire and malt in her voice. She now spoke that way sometimes, insisted on things, ventured out on a limb, lived dangerously. She had already—carefully, obediently—stepped through all the stages of bereavement: anger, denial, bargaining, Häagen-Dazs, rage. Anger to rage—who said she wasn't making progress? She made a fist but hid it. She got headaches, mostly prickly ones, but sometimes the zigzag of a migraine made its way into her skull and sat like a cheap, crazy tie in her eye.

"I'm sorry," said Jack. "Maybe he would have. Fund-raisers. Cards and letters. Who can say? You two were close, I know."

She ignored him. "Here," she said, pointing at her drink. "Have a little festive lift!" She sipped at the amber liquor, and it stung her chapped lips.

"Dewar's," said Jack, looking with chagrin at the bottle.

"Well," she said defensively, sitting up straight and buttoning her sweater. "I suppose you're out of sympathy with Dewar's. I suppose you're more of a *Do-ee.*"

"That's right," said Jack disgustedly. "That's right! And tomorrow I'm going to wake up and find I've been edged out by Truman!" He headed angrily up the stairs, while she listened for the final clomp of his steps and the cracking slam of the door.

Poor Jack: perhaps she had put him through too much. Just

last spring, there had been her bunion situation—the limping, the crutch, and the big blue shoe. Then in September, there had been Mimi Andersen's dinner party, where Jack, the only non-smoker, was made to go out on the porch while everyone else stayed inside and lit up. And *then,* there had been Aileen's one-woman performance of "the housework version of *Lysistrata.*" "No Sweepie, No Kissie," Jack had called it. But it had worked. Sort of. For about two weeks. There was, finally, only so much one woman on the vast and wicked stage could do.

"I'm worried about you," said Jack in bed. "I'm being earnest here. And not in the Hemingway sense, either." He screwed up his face. "You see how I'm talking? Things are wacko around here." Their bookcase headboard was so stacked with novels and sad memoirs, it now resembled a library carrel more than a conjugal bed.

"You're fine. I'm fine. Everybody's fine," said Aileen. She tried to find his hand under the covers, then just gave up.

"You're someplace else," he said. "Where are you?"

The birds had become emboldened, slowly reclaiming the yard, filling up the branches, cheeping hungrily in the mornings from the sills and eaves. "What is that *shrieking?*" Aileen asked. The leaves had fallen, but now jays, ravens, and house finches darkened the trees—some of them flying south, some of them staying on, pecking the hardening ground for seeds. Squirrels moved in poking through the old apples that had dropped from the flowering crab. A possum made a home for himself under the porch, thumping and chewing. Raccoons had discovered Sofie's little gym set, and one morning Aileen looked out and saw two of them swinging on the swings. She'd wanted animal life? Here was animal life!

"Not this," she said. "None of this would be happening if Bert were still here." Bert had patrolled the place. Bert had kept things in line.

"Are you talking to me?" asked Jack.

"I guess not," she said.

"What?"

"I think we need to douse this place in repellent."

"You mean, like, bug spray?"

"Bug spray, Bugs Bunny," chanted Sofie. "Bug spray, Bugs Bunny."

"I don't know what I mean," said Aileen.

At her feminist film-critique group, they were still discussing *Cat Man,* a movie done entirely in flashback from the moment a man jumps off the ledge of an apartment building. Instead of being divided into acts or chapters, the movie was divided into floor numbers, in descending order. At the end of the movie, the handsome remembering man lands on his feet.

Oh, Bert!

One of the women in Aileen's group—Lila Conch—was angry at the movie. "I just hated the way anytime a woman character said anything of substance, she also happened to be half-naked."

Aileen sighed. "Actually, I found those parts the most true to life," she said. "They were the parts I liked best."

The group glared at her. "Aileen," said Lila, recrossing her legs. "Go to the kitchen for us, dear, and set up the brownies and tea."

"Seriously?" asked Aileen.

"Uh—yes," said Lila.

Thanksgiving came and went in a mechanical way. Aileen and Jack, with Sofie, went out to a restaurant and ordered different things, as if the three of them were strangers asserting their ornery tastes. Then they drove home. Only Sofie, who had ordered the child's Stuffed Squash, was somehow pleased, sitting in the car seat in back and singing a Thanksgiving song she'd learned at day care. " 'Oh, a turkey's not a pig, you doink / He doesn't says *oink* / He says *gobble, gobble, gobble.* " Their last truly good holiday had been Halloween, when Bert was still alive and they had dressed him up as Jack. They'd then dressed Jack as Bert, Aileen as Sofie, and Sofie as Aileen. "Now, I'm you, Mommy," Sofie had said when Aileen had tied one of her kitchen aprons around her and pressed lipstick onto her mouth. Jack came up and rubbed his Magic Marker whiskers against Aileen, who giggled in her large pink footie pajamas. The only one who wasn't having that much fun was Bert himself, sporting one of Jack's ties, and pawing at it to get it off. When he didn't succeed, he gamely dragged the tie around for a while, trying to ignore it. Then, cross and humiliated, he waddled over to the corner near the piano and lay there, annoyed. Remembering this, a week later—when Bert was dying in an oxygen tent at the vet's, heart failing, fluid around his lungs (though his ears still pricked up when Aileen came to visit him; she wore her usual perfume so he would know her smell, and hand-fed him cat snacks when no one else could get him to eat)—Aileen had felt overwhelmed with sorrow and regret.

"I think you should see someone," said Jack.

"Are we talking a psychiatrist or an affair?"

"An affair, of course." Jack scowled. "An *affair?*"

"I don't know." Aileen shrugged. The whiskey she'd been drinking lately had caused her joints to swell, so that now when she lifted her shoulders, they just kind of stayed like that, stiffly, up around her ears.

Jack rubbed her upper arm, as if he either loved her or was wiping something off on her sleeve. Which could it be? "Life is a long journey across a wide country," he said. "Sometimes the weather's good. Sometimes it's bad. Sometimes it's so bad, your car goes off the road."

"Really."

"Just go talk to someone," he said. "Our health plan will cover part."

"Okay," she said. "Okay. Just—no more metaphors."

She got recommendations, made lists and appointments, conducted interviews.

"I have a death-of-a-pet situation," she said. "How long does it take for you to do those?"

"I beg your pardon?"

"How long will it take you to get me over the death of my cat, and how much do you charge for it?"

Each of the psychiatrists, in turn, with their slightly different outfits, and slightly different potted plants, looked shocked.

"Look," Aileen said. "Forget Prozac. Forget Freud's abandonment of the seduction theory. Forget Jeffrey Masson—or is it *Jackie* Mason? The only thing that's going to revolutionize *this* profession is Bidding the Job!"

"I'm afraid we don't work that way," she was told again and again—until finally, at last, she found someone who did.

"I specialize in Christmas," said the psychotherapist, a man named Sidney Poe, who wore an argyle sweater vest, a crisp bow tie, shiny black oxfords, and no socks. "Christmas specials. You feel better by Christmas, or your last session's free."

"I like the sound of that," said Aileen. It was already December first. "I like the sound of that a lot."

"Good," he said, giving her a smile that, she had to admit, looked crooked and unsound. "Now, what are we dealing with here, a cat or a dog?"

"A cat," she said.

"Whoa-boy." He wrote something down, muttered, looked dismayed.

"Can I ask you a question first?" asked Aileen.

"Certainly," he said.

"Do you offer Christmas specials because of the high suicide rates around Christmas?"

" 'The high suicide rates around Christmas,' " he repeated in an amused and condescending way. "It's a myth, the high suicide rates around Christmas. It's the *homicide* rate that's high. Holiday homicide. All that time the family suddenly gets to spend together, and then *bam*, that *eggnog*."

She went to Sidney Poe on Thursdays—"Advent Thursdays," she called them. She sat before him with a box of designer Kleenex on her lap, recalling Bert's finer qualities and golden moments, his great sense of humor and witty high jinks. "He used to try to talk on the phone, when *I* was on the phone. And once, when I was looking for my keys, I said aloud, " 'Where're my keys?' and he came running into the room, thinking I'd said, Where's my *kitty*?"

Only once did she actually have to slap Sidney awake— lightly. Mostly, she could just clap her hands once and call his name—*Sid!*—and he would jerk upright in his psychiatrist's chair, staring wide.

"In the intensive care unit at the animal hospital," Aileen continued, "I saw a cat who'd been shot in the spine with a BB. I saw dogs recovering from jaw surgery. I saw a retriever who'd had a hip replacement come out into the lobby dragging a little cart behind him. He was so happy to see his owner. He dragged himself toward her and she knelt down and spread her arms wide to greet him. She sang out to him and cried. It was the animal version of *Porgy and Bess*." She paused for a minute. "It made me wonder what was going on in this country. It made me think we should ask ourselves, What in hell's going on?"

"I'm afraid we're over our time," said Sidney.

The next week, she went to the mall first. She wandered in and out of the stores with their thick tinsel and treacly Muzak Christmas carols. Everywhere she went, there were little cat

Christmas books, cat Christmas cards, cat Christmas wrapping paper. She hated these cats. There were boring, dopey, caricatured, interchangeable—not a patch on Bert.

"I had great hopes for Bert," she said later to Sidney. "They gave him all the procedures, all the medications—but the drugs knocked his kidneys out. When the doctor suggested putting him to sleep, I said, 'Isn't there anything else we can do?' and you know what the doctor said? He said, 'Yes. An autopsy.' A thousand dollars later and he says, 'Yes. An autopsy.'"

"Eeeeyew," said Sid.

"A cashectomy," said Aileen. "They gave poor Bert a cashectomy!" And here she began to cry, thinking of the sweet, dire look on Bert's face in the oxygen tent, the bandaged tube in his paw, the wet fog in his eyes. It was not an animal's way to die like that, but she had subjected him to the full medical treatment, signed him up for all that metallic and fluorescent voodoo, not knowing what else to do.

"Tell me about Sofie."

Aileen sighed. Sofie was adorable. Sofie was terrific. "She's fine. She's great." Except Sofie was getting little notes sent home with her from day care. "Today, Sofie gave the teacher the finger—except it was her index finger." Or "Today, Sofie drew a mustache on her face." Or "Today, Sofie demanded to be called 'Walter.'"

"Really."

"Our last really good holiday was Halloween. I took her trick-or-treating around the neighborhood, and she was so cute. It was only by the end of the night that she began to catch on to the whole concept of it. Most of the time, she was so excited, she'd ring the bell, and when someone came to the door, she'd thrust out her bag and say, 'Look! I've got treats for you!'"

Aileen had stood waiting, down off the porches, on the sidewalk, in her big pink footie pajamas. She'd let Sofie do the talking. "I'm my mommy and my mommy's me," Sofie explained.

"I see," said the neighbors. And then they'd call and wave from the doorway. "Hello, Aileen! How are you doing?"

"We've got to focus on Christmas here," said Sidney.

"Yes," said Aileen despairingly. "We've only got one more week."

On the Thursday before Christmas, she felt flooded with memories: the field mice, the day trips, the long naps together. "He had limited notes to communicate his needs," she said. "He had his 'food' mew, and I'd follow him to his dish. He had his 'out' mew, and I'd follow him to the door. He had his 'brush' mew, and I'd go with him to the cupboard where his brush was kept. And then he had his existential mew, where I'd follow him vaguely around the house as he wandered in and out of rooms, not knowing exactly what or why."

Sidney's eyes began to well. "I can see why you miss him," he said.

"You can?"

"Of course! But that's all I can leave you with."

"The Christmas special's up?"

"I'm afraid so," he said, standing. He reached to shake her hand. "Call me after the holiday and let me know how you feel."

"All right," she said sadly. "I will."

She went home, poured herself a drink, stood by the mantel. She picked up the pink-posied tin and shook it, afraid she might hear the muffled banging of bones, but she heard nothing. "Are you sure it's even him?" Jack asked. "With animals, they probably do mass incinerations. One scoop for cats, two for dogs."

"*Please*," she said. At least she had not buried Bert in the local pet cemetery, with its intricate gravestones and maudlin inscriptions—*Beloved Rexie: I'll be joining you soon*. Or, *In memory of Muffin, who taught me to love.*

"I got the very last Christmas tree," said Jack. "It was leaning against the shed wall, with a broken high heel, and a cigarette dangling from its mouth. I thought I'd bring it home and feed it soup."

At least she had sought something more tasteful than the cemetery, sought the appropriate occasion to return him to earth and sky, get him down off the fireplace and out of the house in a meaningful way, though she'd yet to find the right day. She had let him stay on the mantel and had mourned him deeply—it was only proper. You couldn't pretend you had lost nothing. A good cat had died—you had to begin there, not let your blood freeze over. If your heart turned away at this, it would turn away at something greater, then more and more until your heart stayed averted, immobile, your imagination redistributed away from the world and back only toward the bad maps of yourself, the sour pools of your own pulse, your own tiny, mean, and pointless wants. Stop here! Begin here! Begin with Bert!

Here's to Bert!

Early Christmas morning, she woke Sofie and dressed her warmly in her snowsuit. There was a light snow on the ground and a wind blew powdery gusts around the yard. "We're going to say good-bye to Bert," said Aileen.

"Oh, Bert!" said Sofie, and she began to cry.

"No, it'll be happy!" said Aileen, feeling the pink-posied tin in her jacket pocket. "He wants to go out. Do you remember how he used to want to go out? How he would mee-ow at the door and then we would let him go?"

"Mee-ow, mee-ow," said Sofie.

"Right," said Aileen. "So that's what we're going to do now."

"Will he be with Santa Claus?"

"Yes! He'll be with Santa Claus!"

They stepped outside, down off the porch steps. Aileen pried open the tin. Inside, there was a small plastic bag and she tore that open. Inside was Bert: a pebbly ash like the sand and ground shells of a beach. Summer in December! What was Christmas if not a giant mixed metaphor? What was it about if not the mystery of interspecies love—God's for man! Love had sought a chasm to leap across and landed itself right here: the Holy Ghost among the barn animals, the teacher's pet sent to be adored and then to die. Aileen and Sofie each seized a fistful of Bert and ran around the yard, letting wind take the ash and scatter it. Chickadees flew from the trees. Frightened squirrels headed for the yard next door. In freeing Bert, perhaps they would become him a little: banish the interlopers, police the borders, then go back inside and play with the decorations, claw at the gift wrap, eat the big headless bird.

"Merry Christmas to Bert!" Sofie shouted. The tin was now empty.

"Yes, Merry Christmas to Bert!" said Aileen. She shoved the tin back into her pocket. Then she and Sofie raced back into the house, to get warm.

Jack was in the kitchen, standing by the stove, still in his pajamas. He was pouring orange juice and heating buns.

"Daddy, Merry Christmas to Bert!" Sofie popped open the snaps of her snowsuit.

"Yes," said Jack, turning. "Merry Christmas to Bert!" He handed Sofie some juice, then Aileen. But before she drank hers, Aileen waited for him to say something else. He cleared his throat and stepped forward. He raised his glass. His large quizzical smile said, This is a very weird family. But instead, he exclaimed, "Merry Christmas to everyone in the whole wide world!" and let it go at that.

BEAUTIFUL GRADE

It's a chilly night, bitter inside and out. After a grisly month-long court proceeding, Bill's good friend Albert has become single again—and characteristically curatorial: Albert has invited his friends over to his sublet to celebrate New Year's Eve and watch his nuptial and postnuptial videos, which Albert has hauled down from the bookcase and proffered with ironic wonder and glee. At each of his three weddings, Albert's elderly mother had videotaped the ceremony, and at the crucial moment in the vows, each time, Albert's face turns impishly from his bride, looks straight into his mother's camera, and says, "I do. I swear I do." The divorce proceedings, by contrast, are mute, herky-jerky, and badly lit ("A clerk," says Albert): there are wan smiles, business suits, the waving of a pen.

At the end, Albert's guests clap. Bill puts his fingers in his mouth and whistles shrilly (not every man can do this; Bill himself didn't learn until college, though already that was thirty years ago; three decades of ear-piercing whistling—

youth shall not be wasted on the young). Albert nods, snaps the tapes back into their plastic cases, turns on the lights, and sighs.

"No more weddings," Albert announces. "No more divorces. No more wasting time. From here on in, I'm just going to go out there, find a woman I really don't like very much, and give her a house."

Bill, divorced only once, is here tonight with Debbie, a woman who is too young for him: at least that is what he knows is said, though the next time it is said to his face, Bill will shout, "I beg your pardon!" Maybe not shout. Maybe squeak. Squeak with a dash of begging. Then he'll just hurl himself to the ground and plead for a quick stoning. For now, this second, however, he will pretend to a braver, more evolved heart, explaining to anyone who might ask how much easier it would be to venture out still with his ex-wife, someone his own age, but no, not Bill, not big brave Bill: Bill has entered something complex, spiritually biracial, politically tricky, and, truth be told, physically demanding. Youth will not be wasted on the young.

Who the hell is that?

She looks fourteen!

You can't be serious!

Bill has had to drink more than usual. He has had to admit to himself that on his own, without any wine, he doesn't have a shred of the courage necessary for this romance.

("Not to pry, Bill, or ply you with feminist considerations, but, excuse me—you're dating a twenty-five-year-old?"

"Twenty-four," he says. "But you were close!")

His women friends have yelled at him—or sort of yelled. It's really been more of a cross between sighing and giggling. "Don't be cruel," Bill has had to say.

Albert has been kinder, more delicate, in tone if not in substance. "*Some* people might consider your involvement with this girl a misuse of your charm," he said slowly.

"But I've worked hard for this charm," said Bill. "Believe me, I started from scratch. Can't I do with it what I want?"

Albert sized up Bill's weight loss and slight tan, the sprinkle of freckles like berry seeds across Bill's arms, the summer whites worn way past Labor Day in the law school's cavernous, crowded lecture halls, and he said, "Well then, *some* people might think it a mishandling of your position." He paused, put his arm around Bill. "But hey, I think it has made you look very—tennisy."

Bill shoved his hands in his pockets. "You mean the whole kindness of strangers thing?"

Albert took his arm back. "What are you talking about?" he asked, and then his face fell in a kind of melting, concerned way. "Oh, you poor thing," he said. "You poor, poor thing."

Bill has protested, obfuscated, gone into hiding. But he is too tired to keep Debbie in the closet anymore. The body has only so many weeks of stage fright in it before it simply gives up and just goes out onstage. Moreover, this semester Debbie is no longer taking either of his Constitutional Law classes. She is no longer, between weekly lectures, at home in his bed, with a rented movie, saying things that are supposed to make him laugh, things like "Open up, doll. Is that drool?" and "Don't you dare think I'm doing this for a good grade. I'm doing this for a *beautiful* grade." Debbie no longer performs her remarks at him, which he misses a little, all that effort and desire. "If I'm just a passing fancy, then I want to pass fancy," she once said. Also, "Law school: It's the film school of the nineties."

Debbie is no longer a student of his in any way, so at last their appearance together is only unattractive and self-conscious-making but not illegal. Bill can show up with her for dinner. He can live in the present, his newly favorite tense.

But he must remember who is here at this party, people for whom history, acquired knowledge, the accumulation of days and years is everything—or is this simply the convenient shorthand of his own paranoia? There is Albert, with his videos; Albert's old friend Brigitte, a Berlin-born political scientist; Stanley Mix, off every other semester to fly to Japan and study the zoological effects of radiation at Hiroshima and Nagasaki; Stanley's wife, Roberta, a travel agent and obsessive tabulator of Stanley's frequent flyer miles (Bill has often admired her posters: STEP BACK IN TIME, COME TO ARGENTINA says the one on her door); Lina, a pretty visiting Serb teaching in Slavic Studies; and Lina's doctor husband, Jack, a Texan who five years ago in Yugoslavia put Dallas dirt under the laboring Lina's hospital bed so that his son could be "born on Texan soil." ("But the boy is a total *sairb*," Lina says of her son, rolling her lovely *r*'s. "Just don't tell Jack.")

Lina.

Lina, Lina.

Bill is a little taken with Lina.

"You are with Debbie because somewhere in your pahst ease some pretty leetle girl who went away from you," Lina said to him once on the phone.

"Or, how about because everyone else I know is married."

"Ha!" she said. "You only believe they are married."

Which sounded, to Bill, like the late-night, adult version of *Peter Pan*—no Mary Martin, no songs, just a lot of wishing and thinking lovely thoughts; then afterward all the participants throw themselves out the window.

And never, never land?

Marriage, Bill thinks: *it*'s the film school of the nineties.

Truth be told, Bill is a little afraid of suicide. Taking one's life, he thinks, has too many glitzy things to offer: a real edge on the narrative (albeit retrospectively), a disproportionate philosophical advantage (though again, retrospectively), the last word, the final cut, the parting shot. Most importantly, it gets you the hell out of there, wherever it is you are, and he can see how such a thing might happen in a weak but brilliant moment, one you might just regret later while looking down from the depthless sky or up through two sandy anthills and some weeds.

Still, Lina is the one he finds himself thinking about, and carefully dressing for in the morning—removing all dry-cleaning tags and matching his socks.

Albert leads them all into the dining room and everyone drifts around the large teak table, studying the busily constructed salads at each place setting—salads, which, with their knobs of cheese, jutting chives, and little folios of frisée, resemble small Easter hats.

"Do we wear these or eat them?" asks Jack. In his mouth is a piece of gray chewing gum like a rat's brain.

"I admire gay people," Bill's voice booms. "To have the courage to love whom you want to love in the face of all bigotry."

"Relax," Debbie murmurs, nudging him. "It's only salad."

Albert indicates in a general way where they should sit, alternating male, female, like the names of hurricanes, though such seating leaves all the couples split and far apart, on New Year's Eve no less, as Bill suspects Albert wants it.

"Don't sit next to him—he bites," says Bill to Lina as she takes a place next to Albert.

"Six degrees of separation," says Debbie. "Do you believe that thing about how everyone is separated by only six people?"

"Oh, *we*'re separated by at least six, aren't we, darling?" says Lina to her husband.

"At least."

"No, I mean by *only* six," says Debbie. "I mean strangers." But no one is listening to her.

"This is a political New Year's Eve," says Albert. "We're here to protest the new year, protest the old; generally get a

petition going to Father Time. But also eat: in China it's the
Year of the Pig."

"Ah, one of those years of the Pig," says Stanley. "I love
those."

Bill puts salt on his salad, then looks up apologetically. "I
salt everything," he says, "so it can't get away."

Albert brings out salmon steaks and distributes them with
Brigitte's help. Ever since Albert was denied promotion to full-
professor rank, his articles on Flannery O'Connor ("A Good
Man Really *Is* Hard to Find," "Everything That Rises *Must
Indeed* Converge," and "The Totemic South: The Violent *Actually Do* Bear It Away!") failing to meet with collegial acclaim,
he has become determined to serve others, passing out the
notices and memoranda, arranging the punch and cookies at
various receptions. He has not yet become very good at it, however, but the effort touches and endears. Now everyone sits with
their hands in their laps, leaning back when plates are set before
them. When Albert sits down, they begin to eat.

"You know, in Yugoslavia," says Jack, chewing, "a person
goes to school for four years to become a waiter. Four years of
waiter school."

"Typical Yugoslavians," adds Lina. "They have to go to
school for four years to learn how to serve someone."

"I'll bet they do it well," Bill says stupidly. Everyone
ignores him, for which he is grateful. His fish smells fishier
than the others—he is sure of it. Perhaps he has been poisoned.

"Did you hear about that poor Japanese foreign student
who stopped to ask directions and was shot because he was
thought to be an intruder?" This is Debbie, dear Debbie. How
did she land on this?

"Oh, God, I know. Wasn't that terrible?" says Brigitte.

"A shooting like that really makes a lot of sense, too," says

Bill, "when you think about how the Japanese are particularly known for their street crime." Lina chortles and Bill pokes at his fish a little.

"I guess the man thought the student was going to come in and reprogram his computer," says Jack, and everyone laughs.

"Now is that racist?" asks Bill.

"Is it?"

"Maybe."

"I don't think so."

"Not in any real way."

"It's just us."

"What's that supposed to mean?"

"Would anyone like more food?"

"So Stanley," says Lina. "How is the research going?"

Is this absent querying or pointed interrogation? Bill can't tell. The last time they were all together, they got into a terrible discussion about World War II. World War II is not necessarily a good topic of conversation generally, and among the eight of them, it became a total hash. Stanley yelled, Lina threatened to leave, and Brigitte broke down over dessert: "I was a little girl; I was there," Brigitte said of Berlin.

Lina, whose three uncles, she'd once told Bill, had been bayoneted by Nazis, sighed and looked off at the wallpaper— wide pale stripes like pajamas. It was impossible to eat.

Brigitte looked accusingly at everyone, her face swelling like a baked apple. Tears leaked out of her eyes. "They did not have to bomb like that. Not like that. They did not have to bomb so much," and then she began to sob, then choke back sobs, and then just choke.

It had been a shock to Bill. For years, Brigitte had been the subject of his skeptical, private jokes with Albert. They would make up fake titles for her books on European history: *That Kooky Führer* and *Hitler: What a Nutroll!* But that evening, Brigitte's tears were so bitter and full, after so many years, that it haunted and startled him. What did it mean to cry like that—*at dinner?* He had never known a war in that way or ever, really. He had never even known a dinner in that way.

"Fine," says Stanley to Lina. "Great, really. I'm going back next month. The small-head-size data is the most interesting and conclusive thus far." He chews his fish. "If I got paid by the word, I'd be a rich man." He has the supple, overconfident voice of a panelist from the Texaco Opera Quiz.

"Jack here gets paid by the word," says Bill, "and that word is *Next?*" Perhaps Bill could adroitly switch the subject away from nuclear devastation and steer it toward national health plans. Would that be an improvement? He remembers once asking Lina what kind of medicine Jack practiced. "Oh, he's a gynecological surgeon," she said dismissively. "Something to do with things dropping into the vagina." She gave a shudder. "I don't like to think about it."

Things dropping into the vagina. The word *things* had for some reason made Bill think of tables and chairs, or, even more glamorously, pianos and chandeliers, and he has now come to see Jack as a kind of professional mover: the Allied Van Lines of the OB-GYN set.

"After all this time, Bill is still skeptical about doctors," Jack now says.

"I can see that," says Stanley.

"I once had the wrong tonsil removed," says Bill.

"Are you finding a difference between Hiroshima and Nagasaki?" persists Lina.

Stanley turns and looks at her. "That's interesting that you should ask that. You know, Hiroshima was a uranium bomb and Nagasaki a plutonium. And the fact is, we're finding more damaging results from the uranium."

Lina gasps and puts down her fork. She turns and looks in an alarmed way at Stanley, studying, it seems, the condition of his face, the green-brown shrapnel of his dried acne cysts, like lentils buried in the skin.

"They used two different kinds of bombs?" she says.

"That's right," says Stanley.

"You mean, all along, right from the start, this was just an experiment? They designed it explicitly right from the beginning, as *something to study*?" Blood has rushed to her face.

Stanley grows a little defensive. He is, after all, one of the studiers. He shifts in his chair. "There are some very good books written on the subject. If you don't understand what happened regarding Japan during World War Two, you would be well advised to read a couple of them."

"Oh, I see. Then we could have a better conversation," says Lina. She turns away from Stanley and looks at Albert.

"Children, children," murmurs Albert.

"World War Two," says Debbie. "Wasn't that the war to end all wars?"

"No, that was World War One," says Bill. "By World War Two, they weren't making any promises."

Stanley will not relent. He turns to Lina again. "I have to say, I'm surprised to see a Serbian, in a matter of foreign policy, attempting to take the moral high ground," he says.

"Stanley, I used to like you," says Lina. "Remember when you were a nice guy? I do."

"I do, too," says Bill. "There was that whole smiling, handing-out-money thing he used to do."

Bill feels inclined to rescue Lina. This year, she has been through a lot. Just last spring, the local radio station put her on a talk show and made her answer questions about Bosnia. In attempting to explain what was going on in the former Yugoslavia, she said, "You have to think about what it might mean for Europe to have a nationalist, Islamic state," and "Those fascist Croats," and "It's all very complicated." The next day, students boycotted her classes and picketed her office with signs that read GENOCIDE IS NOT 'COMPLICATED' and REPENT, IMPERIALIST. Lina had phoned Bill at his office. "You're a lawyer. They're hounding me. Aren't these students breaking a law? Surely, Bill, they are breaking a law."

"Not really," said Bill. "And believe me, you wouldn't want to live in a country where they were."

"Can't I get a motion to strike? What is that? I like the way it sounds."

"That's used in pleadings or in court. That's not what you want."

"No, I guess not. From them, I just want no more motion. Plus, I want to strike them. There's nothing you can do?"

"They have their rights."

"They understand nothing," she said.

"Are you okay?"

"No. I banged up the fender parking my car, I was so upset. The headlight fell out, and even though I took it into the car place, they couldn't salvage it."

"You've gotta keep those things packed in ice, I think."

"These *cheeldren,* good God, have no conception of the world. I am well known as a pacifist and resister; I was the one last year in Belgrade, buying gasoline out of Coke bottles, hiding a boy from the draft, helping to organize the protests and the radio broadcasts and the rock concerts. Not them. I was the one standing there with the crowd, clapping and chanting beneath Milosevic's window: 'Don't count on us.' " Here Lina's voice fell into a deep Slavic singsong. "Don't count on us. Don't count on us." She paused dramatically. "We had T-shirts and posters. That was no small thing."

" 'Don't count on us?' " said Bill. "I don't mean to sound skeptical, but as a political slogan, it seems, I don't know, a little . . ." Lame. It lacked even the pouty energy and determination of "Hell no, we won't go." Perhaps some obscenity would have helped. "Don't fucking count on us, motherfucker." That would have been better. Certainly a better T-shirt.

"It was all very successful," said Lina indignantly.

"But how exactly do you measure success?" asked Bill. "I mean, it took time, but, you'll forgive me, we *stopped* the war in Vietnam."

"Oh, you are all so obsessed with your Vietnam," said Lina.

The next time Bill saw her, it was on her birthday, and she'd had three and a half whiskeys. She exclaimed loudly about the beauty of the cake, and then, taking a deep breath, she dropped her head too close to the candles and set her hair spectacularly on fire.

What does time measure but itself? What can it assess but the mere deposit and registration of itself within a thing?

A large bowl of peas and onions is passed around the table. They've already dispensed with the O. J. Simpson jokes— the knock-knock one and the one about the sunglasses. They've banned all the others, though Bill is now asked his opinion regarding search and seizure. Ever since he began living in the present tense, Bill sees the Constitution as a blessedly changing thing. He does not feel current behavior should be made necessarily to conform to old law. He feels personally, for instance, that he'd throw away a few First Amendment privileges—abortion protest, say, and all telemarketing, perhaps some pornography (though not Miss April 1965—never!)—in exchange for gutting the Second Amendment. The Founding Fathers were revolutionaries, after all. They would be with him on this, he feels. They would be for making the whole thing up as you go along, reacting to things as they happened, like a great, wild performance piece. "There's nothing sacred about the Constitution; it's just another figmentary contract: it's a palimpsest you can write and write and write on. But then whatever is there when you get pulled over are the rules for then. For now." Bill believes in free speech. He believes in expensive speech. He doesn't believe in shouting "Fire" in a crowded movie theater, but he does believe in shouting "Fie!" and has done it twice himself—both times at *Forrest Gump.* "I'm a big believer in the Rules for Now. Also, Promises for Now, Things to Do for Now, and the ever-handy This Will Do for Now."

Brigitte glares at him. "Such moral excellence," she says. "Yes," agrees Roberta, who has been quiet all evening, probably figuring out airfare upgrades for Stanley. "How attractive."

"I'm talking theoretical," says Bill. "I believe in common sense. In theory. Theoretical common sense." He feels suddenly cornered and misunderstood. He wishes he weren't constantly asked to pronounce on real-life legal matters. He has never even tried an actual case except once, when he was just out of law school. He'd had a small practice then in the basement of an old sandstone schoolhouse in St. Paul, and the sign inside the building directory said WILLIAM D. BELMONT, ATTORNEY-AT-LAW: ONE LEVEL DOWN. It always broke his heart a little, that *one level down.* The only case he ever took to trial was an armed robbery and concealed weapon case, and he had panicked. He dressed in the exact same beiges and browns as the bailiffs—a subliminal strategy he felt would give him an edge, make him seem at least as much a part of the court "family" as the prosecutor. But by the close of the afternoon, his nerves were shot. He looked too desperately at the jury (who, once in the deliberation room, and in the time it took to order the pizza and wolf it down, voted unanimously to convict). He'd looked imploringly at all their little faces and said, "Ladies and gentlemen, if my client's not innocent, I'll eat my shorts."

At the end of his practice, he had taken to showing up at other people's office parties—not a good sign in life.

Now, equipped with a more advanced degree, like the other people here, Bill has a field of scholarly, hypothetical expertise, plus a small working knowledge of budgets and parking and E-mail. He doesn't mind the E-mail, has more or less gotten used to it, its vaguely smutty Etch-A-Sketch, though once he found himself lost in the Internet and before he knew it had written his name across some bulletin board on which the only other name was "Stud Boy." Mostly, however, his professional life has been safe and uneventful. Although he is bothered by faculty meetings and by the word *text*—every time he hears it, he feels he should just give up, go off and wear a powdered wig somewhere—it intrigues Bill to belong to academe, with its international hodgepodge and asexual attire, a place where to think and speak *as if* one has lived is always preferable to the alternatives. Such a value cuts down on regrets. And Bill is cutting down. He is determined to cut down. Once, he was called in by the head of the law school and admonished for skipping so many faculty meetings. "It's costing you about a thousand dollars in raises every year," said the dean.

"Really?" replied Bill, "Well, if that's all, it's worth every dime."

"Eat, eat," says Albert. He is bringing in the baked potatoes and dessert cheeses. Things are a little out of whack. *Is a dinner party a paradigm of society or a vicious pantomime of the family?* It is already 10:30. Brigitte has gotten up again to help him. They return with sour cream, chives, grappa and cognac. Debbie looks across the table at Bill and smiles warmly. Bill smiles back. At least he thinks he does.

This taboo regarding age is to make us believe that life is long and actually improves us, that we are wiser, better, more knowledgeable later on than early. It is a myth concocted to keep the young from learning what we really are and despising and murdering us. We keep them sweet-breathed, unequipped, suggesting to them that there is something more than regret and decrepitude up ahead.

Bill is still writing an essay in his head, one of theoretical common sense, though perhaps he is just drinking too much and it is not an essay at all but the simple metabolism of sugar. But this is what he knows right now, with dinner winding up and midnight looming like a death gong: life's embrace is quick and busy, and everywhere in it people are equally lacking and well-meaning and nuts. *Why not admit history's powers to*

*divide and destroy? Why attach ourselves to the age-old stories in the
belief that they are truer than the new ones? By living in the past, you
always know what comes next, and that robs you of surprises. It
exhausts and warps the mind. We are lucky simply to be alive together;
why get differentiating and judgmental about who is here among us?
Thank God there is anyone at all.*

"I believe in the present tense," Bill says now, to no one in
particular. "I believe in amnesty." He stops. People are looking
but not speaking. "Or is that just fancy rhetoric?"

"It's not that fancy," says Jack.

"It's fancy," Albert says kindly, ever the host, "without
being schmancy." He brings out more grappa. Everyone drinks
it from the amber, green, and blue of Albert's Depression glass
glasses.

"I mean—" Bill begins, but then he stops, says nothing.
Chilean folk music is playing on the stereo, wistful and melancholy: "Bring me all your old lovers, so I can love you, too," a
woman sings in Spanish.

"What does that mean?" Bill asks, but at this point he may
not actually be speaking out loud. He cannot really tell. He sits
back and listens to the song, translating the sad Spanish. Every
songwriter in their smallest song seems to possess some monu-
mental grief clarified and dignified by melody, Bill thinks. His
own sadnesses, on the other hand, slosh about in his life in a
low-key way, formless and self-consuming. *Modest* is how he
sometimes likes to see it. No one is modest anymore. Everyone
exalts their disappointments. They do ceremonious battle with
everything; they demand receipts and take their presents
back—all the unhappy things that life awkwardly, stupidly,
without thinking, without bothering even to get to know them
a little or to ask around! has given them. They bring it all back
for an exchange.

As has he, hasn't he?

·   ·   ·

The young were sent to earth to amuse the old. Why not be amused?

Debbie comes over and sits next to him. "You're looking very rumpled and miffed," she says quietly. Bill only nods. What can he say? She adds, "Rumpled and miffed—doesn't that sound like a law firm?"

Bill nods again. "One in a Hans Christian Andersen story," he says. "Perhaps the one the Ugly Duckling hired to sue his parents."

"Or the one that the Little Mermaid retained to stick it to the Prince," says Debbie, a bit pointedly, Bill thinks—who can tell? Her girlish voice, out of sheer terror, perhaps, has lately adorned itself with dreamy and snippy mannerisms. Probably Bill has single-handedly aged her beyond her years.

Jack has stood and is heading for the foyer. Lina follows.

"Lina, you're leaving?" asks Bill with too much feeling in his voice. He sees that Debbie, casting her eyes downward, has noted it.

"Yes, we have a little tradition at home, so we can't stay for midnight." Lina shrugs a bit nonchalantly, then picks up her red wool scarf and lassoes her neck with it, a loose noose. Jack holds her coat up behind her, and she slides her arms into the satin lining.

It's sex, Bill thinks. They make love at the stroke of midnight.

"A tradition?" asks Stanley.

"Uh, yes," Lina says dismissively. "Just a little contemplation of the upcoming year is all. I hope you all have a happy rest of the New Year Eve."

Lina always leaves the apostrophe *s* out of New Year's Eve, Bill notes, oddly enchanted. And why *should* New Year's Eve have an apostrophe *s*? It shouldn't. Christmas Eve doesn't. Logically—

"They have sex at the stroke of midnight," says Albert after they leave.

"I knew it!" shouts Bill.

"Sex at the stroke of midnight?" asks Roberta.

"I myself usually save that for Lincoln's Birthday," says Bill.

"It's a local New Year's tradition apparently," says Albert.

"I've lived here twenty years and I've never heard of it," says Stanley.

"Neither have I," says Roberta.

"Nor I," says Brigitte.

"Me, neither," says Bill.

"Well, we'll all have to do something equally compelling," says Debbie.

Bill's head spins to look at her. The bodice of her black velvet dress is snowy with napkin lint. Her face is flushed from drink. What does she mean? She means nothing at all.

"Black-eyed peas!" cries Albert. And he dashes into the kitchen and brings out an iron pot of warm, pasty, black-dotted beans and six spoons.

"Now this is a tradition I know," says Stanley, and he takes one of the spoons and digs in.

Albert moves around the room with his pot. "You can't eat until the stroke of midnight. The peas have to be the first thing you consume in the New Year and then you'll have good luck all year long."

Brigitte takes a spoon and looks at her watch. "We've got five minutes."

"What'll we do?" asks Stanley. He is holding his spoonful of peas like a lollipop, and they are starting to slide.

"We'll contemplate our fruitful work and great accomplishments." Albert sighs. "Though, of course, when you think about Gandhi, or Pasteur, or someone like Martin Luther King, Jr., dead at thirty-nine, it sure makes you wonder what you've done with your life."

"We've done some things," says Bill.

"Yes? Like what?" asks Albert.

"We've . . ." And here Bill stops for a moment. "We've . . . had some excellent meals. We've . . . bought some nice shirts. We've gotten a good trade-in or two on our cars—I think I'm going to go kill myself now."

"I'll join you," says Albert. "Knives are in the drawer by the sink."

"How about the vacuum cleaner?"

"Vacuum cleaner in the back closet."

"Vacuum cleaner?" hoots Roberta. But no one explains or goes anywhere. Everyone just sits.

"Peas poised!" Stanley suddenly shouts. They all get up and stand in a horseshoe around the hearth with its new birch logs and bright but smoky fire. They lift their mounded spoons and eye the mantel clock with its ancient minute hand jerking toward midnight.

"Happy New Year," says Albert finally, after some silence, and lifts his spoon in salute.

"Amen," says Stanley.

"Amen," says Roberta.

"Amen," say Debbie and Brigitte.

"Ditto," says Bill, his mouth full, but indicating with his spoon.

Then they all hug quickly—"Gotcha!" says Bill with each hug—and begin looking for their coats.

"You always seem more interested in other women than in me," Debbie says when they are back at his house after a silent ride home, Debbie driving. "Last month it was Lina. And the month before that it was . . . it was Lina again." She stops for a minute. "I'm sorry to be so selfish and pathetic." She begins to cry, and as she does, something cracks open in her and Bill sees straight through to her heart. It is a good heart. It has had nice parents and good friends, lived only during peacetime, and been kind to animals. She looks up at him. "I mean, I'm romantic and passionate. I believe if you're in love, that's enough. I believe love conquers all."

Bill nods sympathetically, from a great distance.

"But I don't want to get into one of these feeble, one-sided, patched-together relationships—no matter how much I care for you."

"Whatever happened to love conquers all, just four seconds ago?"

Debbie pauses. "I'm older now," she says.

"You kids. You grow up so fast."

Then there is a long silence between them, the second in this new New Year. Finally, Debbie says, "Don't you know that Lina's having an affair with Albert? Can't you see they're in love?"

Something in Bill drops, squares off, makes a neat little knot. "No, I didn't see." He feels the sickened sensation he has sometimes felt after killing a housefly and finding blood in it.

"You yourself had suggested they might be lovers."

"I did? Not seriously. Really? I did?"

"But Bill, hadn't you heard? I mean, it's all over campus."

Actually, he had heard some rumors; he had even said, "Hope so" and once "May God bless their joyous union." But he hadn't meant or believed any of it. Such rumors seemed ham-handed, literal, unlikely. And yet wasn't reality always cheesy and unreliable just like that; wasn't fate literal in exactly that way? He thinks of the severed, crossed fingers found perfectly survived in the wreckage of a local plane crash last year. Such fate was contrary and dense, like a dumb secretary, failing to understand the overall gestalt and desire of the wish. He prefers a deeper, cleverer, even tardy fate, like that of a girl he knew once in law school who, years before, had been raped, shot, and left for dead but then had crawled ten hours out of the woods to the highway with a .22 bullet in her head and flagged a car. That's when you knew that life was making something up to you, that the narrative was apologizing. That's when you knew

God had glanced up from his knitting, perhaps even risen from his freaking wicker rocker, and staggered at last to the window to look.

Debbie studies Bill, worried and sympathetic. "You're just not happy in this relationship, are you?" she says.

These terms! This talk! Bill is not good at this; she is better at it than he; she is probably better at everything than he: at least she has not used the word *text*.

"Just don't use the word *text*," he warns.

Debbie is quiet. "You're just not happy with your life," she says.

"I suppose I'm not." *Don't count on us. Don't count on us, motherfucker.*

"A small bit of happiness is not so hard, you know. You could manage it. It's pretty much open-book. It's basically a take-home."

Suddenly, sadness is devouring him. The black-eyed peas! Why aren't they working? Debbie's face flickers and tenses. All her eye makeup has washed away, her eyes bare and round as lightbulbs. "You were always a tough grader," she says. "Whatever happened to grading on a curve?"

"I don't know," he says. "Whatever happened to that?"

Her eyelids lower and she falls soundlessly across his lap, her hair in a golden pinwheel about her head. He can feel the firm watery press of her breasts against his thigh.

How can he assess his life so harshly and ungratefully, when he is here with her, when she is so deeply kind, and a whole new year is upon them like a long, cheap buffet? How could he be so strict and mean?

"I've changed my mind," he says. "I'm happy. I'm bursting."

"You are not," she says, but she turns her face upward and smiles hopefully, like something brief and floral and in need of heat.

"I am," he insists, but looks away, to think, to think of anything else at all, to think of his ex-wife—*Bring me all your old lovers, so I can love you, too*—still living in St. Paul with his daughter, who in five years will be Debbie's age. He believes that he was happy once then, for a long time, for a while. "We are this far from a divorce," his wife had said bitterly at the end. And if she had spread her arms wide, they might have been able to find a way back, the blinking, intermittent wit of her like a lighthouse to him, but no: she had held her index finger and her thumb up close to her face in a mean pinch of salt. Still, before he left, their marriage a spluttering but modest ruin, only two affairs and a dozen sharp words between them, they'd come home from the small humiliations they would endure at work, separately and alone, and they'd turn them somehow into desire. At the very end, they'd taken walks together in the cool wintry light that sometimes claimed those last days of August—the air chill, leaves already dropping in wind and scuttling along the sidewalk, the neighborhood planted with ocher mums, even the toughest weeds in bridal flower, the hydrangea blooms gone green and drunk with their own juice. Who would not try to be happy?

And just as he had then on those walks, he remembers now how, as a boy in Duluth, he'd once imagined a monster, a demon, chasing him home from school. It was one particular winter: Christmas was past, the snow was dirty and crusted, his father was overseas, and his young sister, Lily, home from the hospital's iron lung, lay dying of polio in her bed upstairs at home. His parents had always—discreetly, they probably felt, though also recklessly and maybe guiltily, too—enjoyed their daughter more than their serious older boy. Perhaps it was a surprise even to themselves. But Bill, in studying their looks and words, had discerned it, though in response he had never known what to do. How could he make himself more enjoyable? With his father away, he wrote long boring letters with everything spelled correctly. "Dear Dad, How are you? I am fine." But he didn't mail them. He saved them up, tied them in a string, and when his father came home, he gave him the packet. His father said "Thank you," tucked the letters in his coat, and never mentioned them again. Instead, every day for a year, his father went upstairs and wept for Lily.

Once, when she'd still been pretty and well, Bill went through an entire day repeating everything Lily said, until she cried in torment and his mother slapped him hard against the eye.

Lily had been enjoyed. They enjoyed her. Who could blame them? Enjoyable girl! Enjoyable joy! But Bill could not attain such a thing, either side of it, for himself. He glimpsed it all from behind some atmosphere, from across some green and scalloped sea—"Dear Dad, How are you? I am fine"—as if it were a planet that sometimes sparkled into view, or a tropical island painted in hot, picture-book shades of orange.

But deep in his private January boyhood, he knew, there were colors that were true: the late-afternoon light was bluish and dark, the bruised tundra of the snowbanks scary and silver and cold. Stepping slowly at first, the hulking monster-man, the demon-man, red and giant, with a single wing growing out of its back, would begin to chase Bill. It chased him faster and faster, up and down every tiny hill to home, casting long shadows that would occasionally, briefly, fall upon them both like a net. While the church bells chimed their four o'clock hymn, the monster-man would fly in a loping, wonky way, lunging and leaping and skittering across the ice toward Bill's heels. Bill rounded a corner. The demon leapt over a bin of road salt. Bill cut across a path. The demon followed. And the terror of it all—as Bill flung himself onto his own front porch and into the unlocked and darkened house, slamming the door, sinking back against it, sliding down onto the doormat, safe at last among the clutter of boots and shoes but still gasping the wide lucky gasps of his great and narrow escape—was thrilling to him in a world that had already, and with such indifferent skill, forsaken all its charms.

WHAT YOU WANT TO DO FINE

Mack has moved so much in his life that every phone number
he comes across seems to him to be one he's had before. "I swear
this used to be *my* number," he says, putting the car into park
and pointing at the guidebook: 923-7368. The built-in
cadence of a phone number always hits him the same personal
way: like something familiar but lost, somehting momentous
yet insignificant—like an act of love with a girl he used to date.

"Just call," says Quilty. They are off Route 55, at the first
McDonald's outside of Chicago. They are on a vacation, a road
trip, a "pile stuff in and go" kind of thing. Quilty has been
singing movie themes all afternoon, has gotten fixated on "To
Sir with Love," and he and Mack now seemed destined to make
each other crazy: Mack passing buses too quickly while fumbling for more gum (chewing the sugar out fast, stick by stick),
and Quilty, hunched over the glove compartment, in some pur-
ple-faced strain of emotion brought on by the line "Those
schoolgirl days of telling tales and biting nails are gone." "I

would be a genius now," Quilty has said three times already, "if only I'd memorized Shakespeare instead of Lulu."

"If only," says Mack. Mack himself would be a genius now if only he had been born a completely different person. But what could you do? He'd read in a magazine once that geniuses were born only to women over thirty; his own mother had been twenty-nine. Damn! So fucking close!

"Let's just get a hotel reservation someplace and take a bath-oil bath," Quilty says now. "And don't dicker. You're always burning up time trying to get a bargain."

"That's so wrong?"

Quilty grimaces. "I don't like what comes after 'dicker.' "

"What is that?"

Quilty sighs. "*Dickest.* I mean, really: it's not a contest!" Quilty turns to feel for Guapo, his Seeing Eye dog, a chocolate Lab too often left panting in the backseat of the car while they stop for coffee. "Good dog, good dog, yes." A "bath-oil bath" is Quilty's idea of how to end a good day as well as a bad. "Tomorrow, we'll head south, along the Mississippi, then to New Orleans, and then back up to the ducks at the Peabody Hotel at the end. Does that sound okay?"

"If that's what you want to do, fine," says Mack.

They had met only two years ago at the Tapston, Indiana, Sobriety Society. Because he was new in town, recently up from some stupid quickie job painting high-voltage towers in the south of the state, and suddenly in need of a lawyer, Mack phoned Quilty the next day. "I was wondering if we could strike a deal," Mack had said. "One old drunk to another."

"Perhaps," said Quilty. He may have been blind and a recovering drinker, but with the help of his secretary, Martha, he had worked up a decent legal practice and did not give his services away for free. Good barter, however, he liked. It made life easier for a blind man. He was, after all, a practical person. Beneath all his eccentricities, he possessed a streak of pragmatism so sharp and deep that others mistook it for sanity.

"I got myself into a predicament," Mack explained. He told Quilty how difficult it was being a housepainter, new in town to boot, and how some of these damn finicky housewives could never be satisfied with what was true professional work, and how, well, he had a lawsuit on his hands. "I'm being sued for sloppy house painting, Mr. Stein. But the only way I can pay you is in more house painting. Do you have a house that needs painting?"

"Bad house painting as both the accusation and the retainer?" Quilty hooted. He loved a good hoot—it brought Guapo to his side. "That's like telling me you're wanted for counterfeiting but you can pay me in cash."

"I'm sorry," said Mack.

"It's all right," Quilty said. He took Mack's case, got him out of it as best he could—"the greatest art in the world," Quilty told the judge at the settlement hearing, "has been known to mumble at the edges"—then had Mack paint his house a clear, compensatory, cornflower blue. Or was it, suggested a neighbor, in certain streaky spots *delphinium?* At lunchtime, Quilty came home from his office up the street and stopped in the driveway, Guapo heeled at his feet, Mack above them on the ladder humming some mournful Appalachian love song, or a jazzed-up version of "Taps." Why "Taps"? "It's the town we live in," Mack would later explain, "and it's the sound of your cane."

Day is done. Gone the sun.

"How we doing there, Mack?" asked Quilty. His dark hair was long and bristly as rope, and he often pulled on it while speaking. "The neighbors tell me my bushes are all blue."

"A little dripping couldn't be avoided," Mack said unhappily. He never used tarps, the way other painters did. He didn't even own any.

"Well, doesn't offend me," said Quilty, tapping meaning-fully at his sunglasses.

But afterward, painting the side dormer, Mack kept hearing Quilty inside, on the phone with a friend, snorting in a loud horselaugh: "Hey, what do *I* know? *I* have blue bushes!"

Or "I'm having the shrubs dyed blue: the nouveau riche—look out—will always be with you."

When the house was almost finished, and oak leaves began to accumulate on the ground in gold-and-ruby piles the color of pears, and the evenings settled in quickly and disappeared into that long solvent that was the beginning of a winter night, Mack began to linger and stall—over coffee and tea, into dinner, then over coffee and tea again. He liked to watch Quilty move deftly about the kitchen, refusing Mack's help, fixing simple things—pasta, peas, salads, bread and butter. Mack liked talking with him about the Sobriety Society meetings, swapping stories about those few great benders that sat in their memories like gorgeous songs and those others that had just plain wrecked their lives. He watched Quilty's face as fatigue or fondness spilled and rippled across it. Quilty had been born blind and had never acquired the guise and camouflage of the sighted; his face remained unclenched, untrained, a clean canvas, transparent as a baby's gas, clear to the bottom of him. In a face so unguarded and unguarding, one saw one's own innocent self—and one sometimes recoiled.

But Mack found he could not go away—not entirely. Not really. He helped Quilty with his long hair, brushing it back for him and gathering it in a leather tie. He brought Quilty gifts lifted from secondhand stores downtown. A geography book in Braille. A sweater with a coffee stain on the arm—was that too mean? Cork coasters for Quilty's endless cups of tea.

"I am gratefully beholden, my dear," Quilty had said each time, speaking, as he sometimes did, like a goddamn Victorian valentine and touching Mack's sleeve. "You are the kindest man I've ever had in my house."

And perhaps because what Quilty knew best were touch and words, or perhaps because Mack had gone through a pig's life of everything tearing at his feelings, or maybe because the earth had tilted into shadow and cold and the whole damned future seemed dipped in that bad ink, one night in the living room, after a kiss that took only Mack by surprise, and even then only slightly, Mack and Quilty became lovers.

Still, there were times it completely baffled Mack. How had he gotten here? What soft punch in the mouth had sent him reeling to this new place?

Uncertainty makes for shyness, and shyness, Quilty kept saying, is what keeps the world together. Or, rather, is what *used* to keep the world together, used to keep it from going mad with chaos. Now—now!—was a different story.

A different story? "I don't like stories," said Mack. "I like food. I like car keys." He paused. "I like pretzels."

"Okaaaay," said Quilty, tracing the outline of his own shoulder and then Mack's.

"You do this a lot, don't you?" asked Mack.

"Do what? Upgrade in the handyman department?"

"Bring into your bed some big straight guy you think's a little dumb."

"I never do that. Never have." He cocked his head to one side. "Before." With his flat almond-shaped fingertips, he played Mack's arm like a keyboard. "Never before. You are my big sexual experiment."

"But you see, you're *my* big sexual experiment," insisted Mack. In his life before Quilty, he could never have imagined being in bed with a skinny naked guy wearing sunglasses. "So how can that be?"

"Honey, it *bes*."

"But someone's got to be in charge. How can both of us survive on some big experimental adventure? Someone's got to be steering the ship."

"Oh, the ship be damned. We'll be fine. We are in this

thing together. It's luck. It's God's will. It's synchronicity! Serendipity! Kismet! Camelot! Annie, honey, Get Your Fucking Gun!" Quilty was squealing.

"My ex-wife's name is Annie," said Mack.

"I know, I know. That's why I said it," said Quilty, trying now not to sigh. "Think of it this way: the blind leading the straight. It can work. It's not impossible."

In the mornings, the phone rang too much, and it sometimes annoyed Mack. Where were the pretzels and the car keys when you really needed them? He could see that Quilty knew the exact arm's distance to the receiver, picking it up in one swift pluck. "Are you *sans* or *avec?*" Quilty's friends would ask. They spoke loudly and theatrically—as if to a deaf person—and Mack could always hear.

"*Avec,*" Quilty would say.

"Oooooh," they would coo. "And how *is* Mr. Avec today?"

"You should move your stuff in here," Quilty finally said to Mack one night.

"Is that what you want?" Mack found himself deferring in ways that were unfamiliar to him. He had never slept with a man before, that was probably it—though years ago there had been those nights when Annie'd put on so much makeup and leather, her gender seemed up for grabs: it had been oddly attractive to Mack, self-sufficient; it hadn't required him and so he'd wanted to get close, to get next to it, to learn it, make it need him, take it away, make it die. Those had been strange, bold nights, a starkness between them that was more like an ancient bone-deep brawl than a marriage. But ultimately, it all remained unreadable for him, though reading, he felt, was not a natural thing and should not be done to people. In general, people were not road maps. People were not hieroglyphs or books. They were not stories. A person was a collection of accidents. A person was an infinite pile of rocks with things growing underneath. In general, when you felt a longing for love, you took a woman and possessed her gingerly and not too hopefully until you finally let go, slept, woke up, and she eluded you once more. Then you started over. Or not.

Nothing about Quilty, however, seemed elusive.

"Is that what I want? Of course it's what I want. Aren't I a walking pamphlet for desire?" asked Quilty. "In Braille, of course, but still. Check it out. Move in. Take me."

"Okay," said Mack.

Mack had had a child with Annie, their boy, Lou, and just before the end, Mack had tried to think up words to say to Annie, to salvage things. He'd said "okay" a lot. He did not know how to raise a child, a toothless, trickless child, but he knew he had to protect it from the world a little; you could not just hand it over and let the world go at it. "There's something that with time grows between people," he said once, in an attempt to keep them together, keep Lou. If he lost Lou, he believed, it would wreck his life completely. "Something that grows whether you like it or not."

"Gunk," Annie said.

"What?"

"Gunk!" she shouted. "Gunk grows between people!"

He slammed the door, went drinking with his friends. The bar they all went to—Teem's Pub—quickly grew smoky and dull. Someone, Bob Bacon, maybe, suggested going to Visions and Sights, a strip joint out near the interstate. But Mack was already missing his wife. "Why would I want to go to a place like that," Mack said loudly to his friends, "when I've got a beautiful wife at home?"

"Well, then," Bob said, "let's go to *your* house."

"Okay," he said. "Okay."

And when they got there, Annie was already gone. She had packed fast, taken Lou, and fled.

Now it is two and a half years since Annie left, and here Mack is with Quilty, traveling: their plan is to head through Chicago and St. Louis and then south along the Mississippi. They will check into bed-and-breakfasts, tour the historic sights, like spouses. They have decided on this trip now in October in part because Mack is recuperating from a small procedure. He has had a small benign cyst razored from "an intimate place."

"The bathroom?" asked Quilty that first day after the surgery, and reached to feel Mack's thick black stitches, then sighed. "What's the unsexiest thing we can do for the next two weeks?"

"Go on a trip," Mack suggested.

Quilty hummed contentedly. He found the insides of Mack's wrists, where the veins were stiff cords, and caressed them with his thumbs. "Married men are always the best," he said. "They're so grateful and butch."

"Give me a break," said Mack.

The next day, they bought quart bottles of mineral water and packets of saltines, and drove out of town, out the speedway, with the Resurrection Park cemetery on one side and the Sunset Memories Park cemetery on the other—a route the cabbies called "the Bone Zone." When he'd first arrived in Tapston, Mack drove a cab for a week, and he'd gotten to know the layout of the town fast. "I'm in the Bone Zone," he used to have to say into the radio mouthpiece. "I'm in the Bone Zone." But he'd hated that damn phrase and hated waiting at the airport, all the lousy tips and heavy suitcases. And the names of things in Tapston—apartment buildings called Crestview Manor, treeless subdivisions called Arbor Valley, the cemeteries undisguised as Sunset Memories and Resurrection Park—all gave him the creeps. *Resurrection Park!* Jesus Christ. Every damn Hoosier twisted words right to death.

But cruising out the Bone Zone for a road trip in Quilty's car jazzed them both. They could once again escape all the unfortunateness of this town and its alarming resting places. "Farewell, you ole stiffs," Mack said.

"Good-bye, all my clients," cried Quilty when they passed

the county jail. "Good-bye, good-bye!" Then he sank back blissfully in his seat as Mack sped the car toward the interstate, out into farm country, silver-topped silos gleaming like space-ships, the air grassy and thick with hog.

"I'd like to make a reservation for a double room, if possi-ble," Mack now shouts over the noise of the interstate traffic. He looks and sees Quilty getting out of the car, leaving Guapo, feeling and tapping his way with his cane, toward the entrance to McDonald's.

"Yes, a double room," says Mack. He looks over his shoul-der, keeping an eye on Quilty. "American Express? Yes." He fumbles through Quilty's wallet, reads the number out loud. He turns again and sees Quilty ordering a soda but not finding his wallet, since he'd given it to Mack for the call. Mack sees Quilty tuck his cane under his arm and pat all his pockets, find-ing nothing there but a red Howe Caverns handker-chief.

"You want the number on the card? Three one one two . . ."

Quilty now turns to leave, without a soda, and heads for the door. But he chooses the wrong door. He wanders into the Play-land by mistake, and Mack can see him thrashing around with his cane amid the plastic cheeseburgers and the french fry swings, lit up at night for the kids. There is no exit from the Playland except back through the restaurant, but Quilty obvi-ously doesn't know this and first taps, then bangs his cane against the forest of garish obstacles.

". . . eight one zero zero six," repeats the reservations clerk on the phone.

By the time Mack can get to him, Quilty is collapsed on a ceramic chicken breast. "Good night, Louise. I thought you'd left me," Quilty says. "I swear, from here on in, I'll do whatever you want. I've glimpsed the abyss, and, by God, it's full of big treacherous pieces of patio furniture."

"We've got a room," says Mack.

"Fantastic. Can we also get a soda?" Mack lets Quilty take his elbow and then walks Quilty back inside, where they order

Pepsis and a single apple pie the size of an eyeglass pouch—to split in the car, like children.

"Have a nice day," says the boy at the counter.

"Thanks for the advice," says Quilty.

They have brought along the game Trivial Pursuit, and at night Quilty likes to play. Though Mack complies—if that's what you want to do, fine—he thinks it's a dumb game. If you don't know the answer, you feel stupid. And if you do know the answer, you feel just as stupid. *More* stupid. What are you doing with that stupid bit of information in your brain? Mack would prefer to lie in the room and stare at the ceiling, thinking about Chicago, thinking about their day. "Name four American state capitals named after presidents," he reads sleepily from a card. He would rather try to understand the paintings he has seen that afternoon, and has almost understood: the Halloween hues of the Lautrecs; the chalky ones of Puvis de Chavannes; the sweet finger paints of the Vuillards and Bonnards, all crowded with window light and commodes. Mack had listened to the buzzing voice coming from Quilty's headphones, but he hadn't gotten his own headphones. Let a blind man be described to! Mack had his own eyes. But finally, overwhelmed by poor Quilty's inability either to see or touch the paintings, he had led Quilty downstairs to the statuary, and when no one was looking, he'd placed Quilty's hands upon the naked marble figure of a woman. "Ah," Quilty had said, feeling the nose and lips, and then he grew quiet and respectful at her shoulders, at her breasts, and hips, and when he got down past the thighs and knees to her feet, Quilty laughed out loud. Feet! These he knew best. These he liked.

Afterward, they went to a club to hear a skit called "Kuwait Until Dark."

"Lincoln, Jackson, Madison, Jefferson City," says Quilty.

"Do you think we will have a war?" He seems to have grown impatient with the game. "You were in the service once. Do you think this is it? The big George Bush showdown?"

"Nah," says Mack. He had been in the army only during peacetime. He'd been stationed in Texas, then in Germany. He'd been with Annie: those were good years. Only a little crying. Only a little drinking. Later, he'd been in the reserves, but the reserves were never called up—everyone knew that. Until now. "Probably it's just a sales demo for the weapons."

"Well, they'll go off, then," says Quilty. "Won't they? If it's a demonstration, things will be demonstrated."

Mack picks another card. "In the song 'They Call the Wind Maria,' what do they call the rain?"

"It's Mar-eye-a, not Maria," says Quilty.

"It's Mar-eye-a?" asks Mack. "Really?"

"Really," says Quilty. There is something wicked and scolding that comes over Quilty's face in this game. "It's your turn." He thrusts out his hand. "Now give me the card so you don't cheat."

Mack hands him the card. "Mar-eye-a," says Mack. The song is almost coming back to him—he recalls it from somewhere. Maybe Annie used to sing it. "They call the wind Mar-eye-a. They call the rain . . . Okay. I think it's coming. . . ." He presses his fingers to his temples, squinting and thinking. "They call the wind Mar-eye-ah. They call the rain . . . Okay. Don't tell me. They call the rain . . . Pariah!"

"Pariah?" Quilty guffaws.

"Okay, then," says Mack, exasperated. "Heavy. They call the rain Heavy Rain." He reaches aggressively for his minibar juice. Next time, he's just going to look quickly at the back of the card.

"Don't you want to know the right answer?"

"No."

"Okay, I'll just go on to the next card." He picks one up,

pretending to read. "It says here, 'Darling, is there life on Mars? Yes or no.' "

Mack has gone back to thinking about the paintings. "I say no," he says absently.

"Hmmm," says Quilty, putting the card down. "I think the answer is yes. Look at it this way: they're sure there are ice crystals. And where there is ice, there is water. And where there is water, there is waterfront property. And where there is waterfront property, there are Jews!" He claps his hands and sinks back onto the acrylic quilting of the bedspread. "Where are you?" he asks finally, waving his arms out in the air.

"I'm here," says Mack. "I'm right here." But he doesn't move.

"You're here? Well, good. At least you're not at my cousin Esther's Martian lake house with her appalling husband, Howard. Though sometimes I wonder how they're doing. How are they? They never come to visit. I frighten them so much." He pauses. "Can I ask you a question?"

"Okay."

"What do I look like?"

Mack hesitates. "Brown eyes, brown eyebrows, and brown hair."

"That's it?"

"Okay. Brown teeth, too."

"Really!"

"Sorry," says Mack. "I'm a little tired."

Hannibal is like all the river towns that have tried recently to spruce themselves up, make antique shops and bed-and-breakfasts from the shoreline mansions. It saddens Mack. There is still a despondent grandeur to these houses, but it radiates out, in a kind of shrug, onto a drab economy of tidbit tourism and health-care facilities. A hundred years of flight and rehab lie on the place like rain. Heavy rain! The few barges that still push this far upriver seem quaint and ridiculous. But Quilty wants to hear what all the signs say—the Mark Twain Diner, the Tom 'n Huck Motel; it amuses him. They take the tour of Sam Clemens's houses, of Mr. Clemens's office, of the little jail. They get on a tiny train Quilty calls "Too, Too Twain," which tours the area and makes the place seem even more spritely and hopeless. Quilty feels along the wide boards of the whitewashed fence. "This is modern paint," he says.

"Latex," says Mack.

"Oooh, talk to me, talk to me, baby."

"Will you stop?"

"Okay. All right."

"Pretty dog," a large woman in a violet dress says to them in the Tom Sawyer Diner. The diner is situated next to a parking lot and a mock-up of the legendary fence, and it serves BLTs in red plastic baskets with stiff wax paper and fries. Quilty has ordered his usual glass of milk.

"Thank you," says Quilty to the woman, who then stops to pet Guapo before heading for her car in the parking lot. Quilty looks suddenly annoyed. "*He* gets all the compliments, and *I* have to say thank you."

"You want a compliment?" asks Mack, disgusted. "Okay. You're pretty, too," says Mack.

"*Am* I? Well, how will I ever know, if everyone just keeps complimenting my dog!"

"I can't believe you're jealous of your goddamn dog. Here," Mack says. "I refuse to talk to someone with a milk mustache." He hands Quilty a napkin, touching the folded edge of it to his cheek.

Quilty takes it and wipes his mouth. "Just when we were getting so good at being boring together," he says. He reaches over and pats Mack's arm, then reaches up and roughly pets his head. Mack's hair is thin and swept back, and Quilty swipes at it from behind.

"Ow," says Mack.

"I keep forgetting your hair is so Irish and sensitive," he said. "We've gotta get you some good tough Jew hair."

"Great," says Mack. He is growing tired of this, tired of them. They've been on these trips too many times before. They've visited Mother Goose's grave in Boston. They've visited the battlefield at Saratoga. They've visited Arlington. "Too many cemeteries!" said Mack. "It's the goddamn Bone Zone wherever we go!" They visited the Lincoln Memorial ("I imagine it's like a big marble Oz," said Quilty. "Abraham Oz. A much better name, don't you think?"). Right next door, they visited the Vietnam War Memorial, mind-numbing in its bloodless catalog of blood, Mack preferring instead the alternative monument, the buddy statue put up by the vets, something that wanted less to be art than to be human. "It's about the guys, not just the *names of the guys*," he said. "*Guys* died there. A list didn't die there." But Quilty, who had spent an hour feeling for friends who'd died in '68 and '70, had sighed in a vaguely disgusted, condescending way.

"You're missing it totally," he said. "A list did die. An incredible heartbreaking list."

"Sorry I'm not such an intellectual," said Mack.

"You're jealous because I was feeling around for other men."

"Yeah. I'm jealous. I'm jealous I'm not up there. I'm jealous because—stupid me—I waited until peacetime to enlist."

Quilty sighed. "I almost went. But I had a high draft number. Plus, guess what? Flat feet!"

At that, they both broke, feebly, into loud, exhausted laughter, like two tense lunatics, right there by the wall, until someone in a uniform asked them to leave: other people were trying to pray.

Trying to go someplace without cemeteries, they once flew to Key West, ate a lot of conch chowder and went to Audubon's house, which wasn't Audubon's house at all, but a place where Audubon had stayed once or something, shooting the birds he then painted. "He shot them?" Mack kept asking. "He shot the damn birds?"

"Revolting," said Quilty loudly. "The poor birds. From now on, I'm going to give all my money to the *Autobahn* Society. Let's make those Mercedes go fast, fast, fast!"

To prevent Mack's drinking in despair, they later found an AA meeting and dropped in, made friends and confessed to them, though not exactly in that order. The following day, new pals in tow, they strolled through Hemingway's house in feather boas—"just to taunt Papa."

"Before he wrote about them," said Quilty, pretending to read the guidebook out loud, "Hemingway shot his characters. It was considered an unusual but not unheard-of creative method. Still, even within literary circles, it is not that widely discussed."

The next morning, at the request of a sweet old man named Chuck, they went to an AIDS memorial service. They sat next to Chuck and held his hand. Walt Whitman poems were read. Cello suites were played so exquisitely that people fell forward onto their own knees, collapsed by the beauty of grief. After the benediction, everyone got solemnly into their cars and drove slowly to the grave site. No matter how Mack and Quilty tried to avoid cemeteries, there they were again. A boneyard had its own insistent call: like rocks to sailors, or sailors to other sailors. "This is all too intense," whispered Mack in the middle of a prayer; at the grave site, Mack had positioned them farther off from the mourners than Quilty knew. "This is supposed to be our vacation. When this prayer is over, let's go to the beach and eat cupcakes." Which is what they did, letting Guapo run up and down the sand, chasing gulls, while the two of them lay there on a towel, the sea air blasting their faces.

Now, on this trip, Mack is in a hurry. He wants to leave the chipping white brick of Hannibal, the trees and huckleberries, the local cars all parked in the lot of some Tony's Lounge. He wants to get on to St. Louis, to Memphis, to New Orleans, then back. He wants to be done with touring, this mobile life they embark on too often, like old ladies testing out their new, sturdy shoes. He wants his stitches removed.

"I hope there won't be scars," he says.

"Scars?" says Quilty in that screechy mockery he sometimes puts on. "I can't believe I'm with someone who's worried about having a good-looking dick."

"Here is your question. What American playwright was imprisoned for her work?"

"*Her* work. Aha. Lillian Hellman? I doubt it. Thornton Wilder—"

"Mae West," blurts out Mack.

"Don't do that! I hadn't answered yet!"

"What does it matter?"

"It matters to me!"

There is only a week left.

"In St. Louis"—Quilty pretends again, his old shtick, to read from the guidebook as they take the bumpy ride to the top of the arch—"there is the famous gateway, or 'arch,' built by the McDonald Corporation. Holy Jesus, America, get down on your knees!"

"I am, I am."

"Actually, that's true. I heard someone talking about it downstairs. This thing was built by a company named McDonald. A golden arch of gray stone. That is the gateway to the West. At sunset very golden. Very arch."

"Whaddyaknow." Gray stone again. There's no getting away from it.

"Describe the view to me," says Quilty when they get out at the top.

Mack looks out through the windows. "Adequate," he says.

"I said describe, not *rate.*"

"Midwestern. Aerial. Green and brown."

Quilty sighs. "I don't think blind men should date deaf-mutes until the how-to book has been written."

Mack is getting hungry. "Are you hungry?"

"It's too stressful!" adds Quilty. "No, I'm not hungry." They make the mistake of going to the aquarium, instead of to an early dinner, which causes every sea creature to look delicious to Mack. Quilty makes the tour with a group led by a cute schoolteacherish guide named Judy, but Mack ventures off on his own. He feels like a dog set loose among schoolchildren: Here are his friends! The elegant nautilus, the electric eel, the stingray with its wavy cape and idiot grin, silently shrieking against the glass—or is it feeding?

When is a thing shrieking and when is it feeding—and why can't Mack tell?

It is the wrong hour of the day, the wrong hour of life, to be around sea creatures. Shrieking or feeding. Breaded or fried. There is a song Mack's aunt used to sing to him when he was little: "I am a man upon the land. I am a Silkie on the sea." And he thinks of this now, this song about a half man, half seal or bird—what was it? It was a creature who comes back to fetch his child—his child by a woman on the land. But the woman's new husband is a hunter, a good shot, and kills him when he tries to escape back to the sea with the child. Perhaps that was best, in the end. Still the song was sad. Stolen love, lost love, amphibious doom—all the transactions of Mack's own life: I am a Silkie on the sea. "My life is lucky and rich," he used to tell himself when he was painting high-voltage towers in Kentucky and the electric field on those ladders stood the hairs of his arms on end. Lucky and Rich! They sounded like springer spaniels, or two unsavory uncles. Uncle Lucky! Uncle Rich!

I am a man upon the land, he thinks. But here at sea, what am I? Shrieking or feeding?

Quilty comes up behind him, with Guapo. "Let's go to dinner," he says.

"Thank you," says Mack.

After dinner, they lie in their motel bed and kiss. "Ah, dear, yes," murmurs Quilty, his "dears" and "my dears" like sweet compresses in the heat, and then there are no more words. Mack pushes close, his cool belly warming. His heart thumps against Quilty's like a water balloon shifting and thrusting its liquid from side to side. There is something comforting, thinks Mack, in embracing someone the same size as you. Something exhilarating, even: having your chins over each other's shoulders, your feet touching, your heads pressed ear-to-ear. Plus he likes—he loves—Quilty's mouth on him. A man's full mouth. There is always something a little desperate and diligent about Quilty, poised there with his lips big and searching and his wild unshaded eyes like the creatures of the aquarium, captive yet wandering free in their enclosures. With the two of them kissing like this—*exculpatory, specificity, rubric*—words are foreign money. There is only the soft punch in the mouth, the shrieking and feeding both, which fills Mack's ears with light. This, he thinks, this is how a blind man sees. This is how a fish walks. This is how rocks sing. There is nothing at all like a man's strong kiss: apologies to the women of Kentucky.

They eat breakfast at a place called Mama's that advertises "throwed rolls."

"What are those?" asks Quilty. They turn out merely to be warm buttermilk rolls thrown at the clientele by the waiters. Mack's roll hits him squarely in the chest, where he continues to clutch it, in shock. "Don't worry," says the waiter to Quilty. "Won't throw one at you, a blind man, but just maybe at your dawg."

"Good God," says Quilty. "Let's get out of here."

On the way out, by the door, Mack stops to read the

missing-child posters. He does not look at the girls. He looks at the boys: Graham, age eight; Eric, age five. So that's what five looks like, thinks Mack. Lou will be five next week.

Mack takes the slow southerly roads. He and Quilty are like birds, reclaiming the summer that left them six weeks before in the north. "I'll bet in Tapston they've all got salt spats on their boots already," says Mack. "Bet they've got ice chunks in their tires." Quilty hates winter, Mack knows. The frozen air makes things untouchable, unsmellable. When the weather warms, the world comes back. "The sun smells like fire," Quilty says, and smiles. Past the bleached doormat of old wheat fields, the land grows greener. There is cotton harvested as far north as Missouri, the fields spread out like bolts of dotted swiss, and Mack and Quilty stop on the shoulder once, get out to pick a blossom, peel back the wet bud, feel the cotton slowly dry. "See what you miss, being a Yankee," says Mack.

"Missing is all I do," says Quilty.

They come upon a caravan of Jeeps and Hummers painted beige and headed south for a ship that no doubt will take them from one gulf to another. Mack whistles. "Holy shit," he says.

"What?"

"Right now, there're about two hundred army vehicles in front of us, freshly painted desert beige."

"I can't bear it," says Quilty. "There's going to be a war."

"I could have sworn there wouldn't be. I could have sworn there was just going to be a television show."

"I'll bet there's a war." They drive to Cooter along with the Jeeps, then swing off to Heloise to look at the river. It is still the same slow mongoose brown, lacking beauty of some kind

Mack can't quite name. The river seems to him like a big ticky dog that doesn't know its own filth and keeps following your car along on the side as you drive.

They get out of the car to stretch. Mack lights a cigarette, thinking of the Jeeps and the Saudi desert. "So there it is. Brown and more brown. Guess that's all there is to a river."

"You're so . . . *Peggy Lee*," says Quilty. "How about a little Jerome Kern? It don't plant taters. It don't plant cotton. It just keeps rolling along."

Mack knows the song but doesn't even look at Quilty.

"Smell the mud and humidity of it," says Quilty, breathing deeply.

"I do. Great humidity," says Mack. He feels weary. He also feels sick of trying, tired of living, and scared of dying. If Quilty wants musical comedy, there it is: musical comedy. Mack drags on his cigarette. The prospect of a war has seized his brain. It engages some old, ongoing terror in him. As a former soldier, he still believes in armies. But he believes in armies at rest, armies relaxing, armies shopping at the PX, armies eating supper in the mess hall. But armies as TV-network football teams? The quick beginning of the quick end.

"I hear the other side doesn't even have socks," says Quilty when they are back in the car, thinking of the war. "Or rather, they have *some* socks, but they don't all match."

"Probably the military's been waiting for this for years. Something to ace—at last."

"Thank God you're not still in the reserves. They're calling up all the reserves." Quilty reaches up under Mack's shirt and rubs his back. "Young people have been coming into my office all month to have their wills drawn up."

Mack was in the reserves only a year before he was thrown out for drunkenness on one of the retreats.

"The reserves used to be one big camping trip," Mack says.

"Well, now it's a camping trip gone awry. A camping trip

with aspirations. A *big* hot camping trip. Kamp with a *K*. These kids coming in for wills: you should hear the shock in their voices."

Mack drives slowly, dreamy with worry. "How you doing back there, Miss Daisy?" Quilty calls over his shoulder to Guapo. Outside of Memphis, on the Arkansas side, they stop at a Denny's, next to a warehouse of dinettes, and they let Guapo out to run again.

Dinettes, thinks Mack. That's just what this world needs: a warehouse of dinettes.

"I once tried to write a book," says Quilty, seated cozily in his booth, eating an omelette.

"Oh, yeah?"

"Yeah. I had these paragraphs that were so huge, they went on for pages. Sentences that were also just enormous—two or three pages long. I had to shrink things down, I was told."

Mack smiles. "How about words? Did you use big words, too?"

"Huge words. And to top it off, I began the whole thing with a letter I razored off a billboard." He pauses. "That's a joke."

"I get it."

"There *was* a book, though. I was going to call it *Dating My Sofa: A Blind Man's Guide to Life.*"

Mack is quiet. There is always too much talking on these trips.

"Let's hit Memphis on the way back," says Quilty irritably. "For now, let's head straight to New Orleans."

"That's what you want to do? Fine." Mack has no great fondness for Memphis. Once, as a boy, he'd been chased by a bee there, down a street that was long and narrow and lined on one side with parked cars. He'd ducked into a phone booth, but the bee waited for him, and Mack ended up stepping out after twenty minutes and getting stung anyway. It wasn't true what they said about bees. They were not all that busy. They had time. They could wait. It was a myth, that stuff about busy as a bee.

"That way, coming back," adds Quilty, "we can take our time and hit the Peabody when the ducks are out. I want to do the whole duck thing."

"Sure," says Mack. "The duck thing is the thing." On the way out of Denny's, Mack pulls slightly away from Quilty to look at another missing-child poster. A boy named Seth, age five. The world—one cannot drive fast or far enough away from it—is coming at him in daggers.

"What are you looking at?"

"Nothing," says Mack, then adds absently, "a boy."

"Really?" says Quilty.

Mack drives fast down through the small towns of the Delta: Eudora, Eupora, Tallula—the poorest ones with names like Hollywood, Banks, Rich. In each of them, a Baptist church is nestled up against a bait shop or a Tina's Touch of Class Cocktails. The strawy weeds are tall as people, and the cotton puffs here are planted in soils grown sandy, near shacks and burned-out cars, a cottonseed-oil factory towering over the fields, the closest hamburger at a Hardee's four miles away. Sometimes the cotton fields look like snow. Mack notices the broken-down signs: EAT MAID-RITE EATS or CAN'T BEAT DICK'S MEAT. They are both innocent and old, that peculiar mix, like a baby that looks like a grandmother, or a grandmother that looks like a girl. He and Quilty eat lunch and dinner at places that serve hush puppies and batter-fried pickles; it reminds Mack of his aunt's cooking. The air thickens and grows warm. Sinclair brontosauruses and old-style Coke signs protrude from the road stops and gas stations, and then, closer to Baton Rouge, antique stores sell the same kinds of old Coke signs.

"Recycling," says Mack.

"Everyone's recycling," says Quilty.

"Someone told me once"—Mack is thinking of Annie

now—"that we are all made from stars, that every atom in our bodies was at one time the atom of a star."

"And you believed them?" Quilty hoots.

"Fuck you," says Mack.

"I mean, in between, we were probably also some cheese at a sorority tea. Our ancestral relationship to stars!" says Quilty, now far away, making his point before some judge. "It's the biological equivalent of hearsay."

They stay in an antebellum mansion with a canopy bed. They sit beneath the canopy and play Trivial Pursuit.

Mack once again reads aloud his own questions. "Who was George Bush referring to when reminiscing: 'We've had some triumphs; we've made some mistakes; we've had some sex'?"

Mack stares. The canopy bed looks psychotic. Out the window he sees a sign across the street that says SPACE FOR LEASE AT ABSOLUTELY YOGURT. Next to it, a large white woman is hitting a small black dog with a shopping bag. What is wrong with this country? He turns the card over and looks. "Ronald Reagan," he says. He has taken to cheating like this.

"Is that your answer?" asks Quilty.

"Yes."

"Well, you're probably right," says Quilty, who often knows the answer before Mack has read it to him. Mack stares at the bed again, its canopy like the headdress the Duchess wore in *Alice in Wonderland.* His aunt would sometimes read that book to him, and it always made him feel queasy and confused.

On the nightstand, there are sachets of peach and apricot pits, the sickly sweet smell of a cancer ward. Everything here now in this room reminds him of his aunt.

"What former Pittsburgh Pirates slugger was the only player inducted into the Baseball Hall of Fame in 1988?" Mack reads. It is Quilty's turn.

"I've landed on the damn *sports* category?"

"Yup. What's your answer?"

"Linda Ronstadt. She was in *The Pirates of Penzance.* I know it went to Pittsburgh. I'm just not sure about the Hall of Fame part."

Mack is quiet.

"Am I right?"

"No."

"Well, you never used to do that—land me on those sports questions. Now you're getting difficult."

"Yup," says Mack.

The next morning, they go to a Coca-Cola museum, which the South seems to be full of. "You'd think Coca-Cola was a national treasure," Mack says.

"It's not?" says Quilty.

Individual states, Georgia and Mississippi and whichever else, are all competing for claims: first served here, first bottled there—first thirst, first burst—it is one big corporate battle of the bands. There is a strange kind of refuge from this to be found in driving through yet another cemetery, this one at Vicksburg, and so they do it, but quickly, keeping the trip moving so they will not feel, as they might have in Tapston, the irretrievable loss of each afternoon, the encroaching darkness, each improvised day over with at last—only to start up again, in the morning, oppressively identical, a checker in a game of checkers, or a joke in a book of jokes.

"They seem to have all this organized by state," says Mack, looking out over the Vicksburg grounds, the rolling green dotted as if with aspirins. He looks back at the park map, which he has spread over the steering wheel. Here he is: back in the Bone Zone.

"Well, let's go to the Indiana part," says Quilty, "and praise the Hoosier dead."

"Okay," says Mack, and when he comes upon a single small stone that says *Indiana*—not the proper section at all—he slows down and says, "Here's the section," so that Quilty can roll down the window and shout, "Praise the Hoosier dead!" There are kindnesses one can perform for a blind man more easily than for the sighted.

Guapo barks and Mack lets loose with an incongruous rebel yell.

"Whose side are you on?" scolds Quilty, rolling his window back up. "Let's get out of here. It's too hot."

They drive some distance out of the park and then stop at the Civil War Museum they saw advertised the day before.

"Is this a fifty?" Quilty whispers, thrusting a bill toward Mack as they approach the entrance cashier.

"No, it's a twenty."

"Find me a fifty. Is this a fifty?"

"Yeah, that's a fifty."

Quilty thrusts the fifty toward the cashier. "Excuse me," he says in a loud voice. "Do you have change for a great American general?"

"Do believe I do," says the cashier, who chuckles a bit, taking the fifty and lifting up the drawer to his register. "You Yankees are always liking to do that."

Inside, the place is dark and cool and lined with glass display cases and mannequins in uniforms. There are photographs of soldiers and nurses and "President and Mrs. Davis." Because almost everything is behind glass and cannot be touched, Quilty grows bored. " 'The city of Vicksburg,' " Mack reads aloud, " 'forced to surrender to Grant on the Fourth of July, refused to celebrate Independence Day again until 1971.' "

"When no one cared anymore," adds Quilty. "I like a place with a strong sense of grudge—which they, of course, call 'a keen acquaintance with history.' " He clears his throat. "But let's get on to New Orleans. I also like a place that doesn't give a shit."

In a restaurant overlooking the river, they eat yet more hush puppies and catfish. Guapo, unleashed, runs up and down the riverbank like a mad creature.

In the dusk, they head south, toward the Natchez Trace, through Port Gibson: "TOO BEAUTIFUL TO BURN"— ULYSSES S. GRANT, says the WELCOME sign. Quilty is dozing. It is getting dark, and the road isn't wide, but Mack passes all the slow-moving cars: an old VW bus (northern winters have eliminated these in Tapston), a red pickup piled with hay, a Plymouth Duster full of deaf people signing in a fantastic dance of hands. The light is on inside the Duster, and Mack pulls up alongside, watching. Everyone is talking at once—fingers flying, chopping, stretching the air, twining, pointing, touching. It is astonishing and beautiful. If only Quilty weren't blind, thinks Mack. If only Quilty weren't blind, he would really like being deaf.

There are, in New Orleans, all manner of oysters Rockefeller. There is the kind with the spinach chopped long and coarse like seaweed, scabs of bacon in a patch on top. Then there is the kind with the spinach moussed to a bright lime and dolloped onto the shell like algae. There is the kind with spinach leaves laid limply off the edge like socks. There is the kind with cheese. There is the kind without. There is even the kind with tofu.

"Whatever happened to clams casino?" asks Mack. "I used to get those in Kentucky. Those were great."

"Shellfish from a landlocked place? Never a great idea, my dear," says Quilty. "Stick with Nawlins. A city no longer known for its prostitutes quickly becomes known for its excellent food. Think about it. There's Paris. There's here. A city currently known for its prostitutes—Las Vegas, Amsterdam, Washington, D.C.—is seldom a good food city."

"You should write a travel book." Was Mack being sarcastic? Mack himself couldn't say.

"That's what *Dating My Sofa* was going to be. A kind of armchair travel book. For the blind."

"I thought *Dating My Sofa* was going to be a novel."

"Before it was a novel, it was going to be a travel book."

They leave behind the wrought-iron cornstalk fence of their little inn for a walk through the Quarter. Soon they are at the
wharf, and with little else to do, they step aboard a glittering
paddle wheeler for a Plantation River cruise. Quilty trips on a
slightly raised plank on the ramp. "You know, I find this city
neither big nor easy," he says. The tour is supposed to be beer
and sun and a little jazz band, but there is also a stop at Chal-
mette, the site of the Battle of New Orleans, so that people can
get off and traipse through the cemetery.

Mack takes Quilty to a seat in the sun, then sits beside him.
Guapo lifts his head and smells the swampy air. "No more
cemeteries," says Mack, and Quilty readily agrees, though Mack
also wonders whether, when they get there, they will be able to
resist. It seems hard for them, when presented with all that
toothy geometry of stone and bone, not to rush right up and say
hi. The two of them are ill-suited to life; no doubt that is it. In
feeling peculiar, homeless, cursed, and tired, they have become
way too friendly. They no longer have any standards at all.

"All the graves are on stilts here anyway," says Mack. "The
sea level and all." The calliope starts up and the paddle wheel
begins to revolve. Mack tips his head back to rest it against the
seat and look at the sky all streaked with stringy clouds, bird
blue cracked fuzzily with white. To the right, the clouds have
more shape and against the blue look like the figures of a
Wedgwood dish. What a fine fucking bowl beneath which they
have all been caught and asked to swim out their days! "Look at
it this way," people used to say to Mack. "Things could be
worse"—a bumper sticker for a goldfish or a bug. And it wasn't
wrong—it just wasn't the point.

He falls asleep, and by the time the boat returns to the
wharf, ten thousand anesthesiologists have invaded the town.

There are buses and crowds. "Uh-oh. Look out. A medical convention," says Mack to Quilty. "Watch your step." At a turquoise kiosk near the pier, he spots more missing-children posters. He half-expects to see himself and Quilty posted up there, two more lost boys in America. Instead, there is a heart-breaking nine-year-old named Charlie. There is a three-year-old named Kyle. There is also the same kid from Denny's up north: Seth, age five.

"Are they cute?" asks Quilty.

"Who?" says Mack.

"All those nice young doctors," says Quilty. "Are they good-looking?"

"Hell if I know," says Mack.

"Oh, don't give me that," says Quilty. "You forget to whom you are speaking, my dear. I can *feel* you looking around."

Mack says nothing for a while. Not until after he's led Quilty over to a café for some chicory coffee and a beignet, which he feeds pieces of to Guapo. The people at the table next to them, in some kind of morbid theatrical contest, are reading aloud obituaries from the *Times-Picayune*. "This town's wacko," says Mack. Back at the hotel, someone in the next room is playing "The Star-Spangled Banner" on the kazoo.

They speed out the next day—across the incandescent olive milk of the swamps, leafless, burned trees jutting from them like crosses. "You're going too fast," says Quilty. "You're driving like goddamn Sean Penn!" Mack, following no particular route, heads out toward the salt marshes: grebes, blackbirds, sherbet-winged flamingos fly in low over the feathery bulrushes. It is all pretty, in its bleak way. Lone cattle are loose and munching cordgrass amid the oil rigs.

"Which way are we going?"

He suddenly swings north toward Memphis. "North. Memphis." All he can think of now is getting back.

"What are you thinking of?"

"Nothing."

"What are you looking at?"

"Nothing. Scenery."

"Hot bods?"

"Yeah. Just saw a great cow," says Mack. "And a not-bad possum."

When they are finally checked into the Peabody Hotel, it is already late afternoon. Their room is a little stuffy and lit in a strange, golden way. Mack flops on the bed.

Quilty, beginning to perspire, takes his jacket off and throws it on the floor. "Y'know: what is wrong with you?" he asks.

"What do you mean, *me*? What is wrong with *you*?"

"You're so distracted and weird."

"We're traveling. I'm sight-seeing. I'm tired. Sorry if I seem distant."

" 'Sight-seeing.' That's nice! How about me? Yoo-hoo!"

Mack sighs. When he goes on the attack like this, Quilty tends to head in five miserable directions at once. He has a brief nervous breakdown and shouts from every shattered corner of it, then afterward pulls himself together and apologizes. It is all a bit familiar. Mack closes his eyes, to sail away from him. He floats off and, trying not to think of Lou, briefly thinks of Annie, though the sudden blood rush that stiffens him pulls at his stitches and snaps him awake. He sits up. He kicks off his shoes and socks and looks at his pickled toes: slugs in a box.

Quilty is cross-legged on the floor, trying to do some deep-breathing exercises. He is trying to get chi to his meridians—or something like that. "You think I don't know you're attracted to half the people you see?" Quilty is saying. "You think I'm stupid or something? You don't think I feel your head turn and your gaze stop everywhere we go?"

"What?"

"You're too much," Quilty finally says to Mack.

"*I'm* too much? You are! You're so damn nervous and territorial," Mack says.

"I have a highly inflamed sense of yard," says Quilty. He has given up on the exercises. "Blind people do. I don't want you sticking your hitchhiker's thumb out over the property line. It's a betrayal and an eyesore to the community!"

"What community? What are you talking about?"

"All you sighted people are alike. You think we're Mr. Magoo! You think I'm not as aware as some guy who paints water towers and's got cysts on his dick?"

Mack shakes his head. He sits up and starts to put his shoes back on. "You really go for the juggler, don't you?" he says.

"Juggler?" Quilty howls. "*Juggler?* No, obviously, I go for the clowns."

Mack is puzzled. Quilty's head is tilted in that hyperalert way that says nothing in the room will get past him. "Juggler," Mack says. "Isn't that the word? What is the word?"

"A juggler," says Quilty, slowly for the jury, "is someone who juggles."

Mack's chest tightens around a small emptied space. He feels his own crappy luck returning like a curse. "You don't even like me, do you?" he says.

"Like you? Is that what you're really asking?"

"I'm not sure," says Mack. He looks around the hotel room. Not this, not any room with Quilty in it would ever be his home.

"Let me tell you a story," says Quilty.

"I don't like stories," Mack says.

It now seems to have cost Mack so much to be here. In his mind—a memory or a premonition, which is it, his mind does not distinguish—he sees himself returning not just to Tapston but to Kentucky or to Illinois, wherever it is Annie lives now, and stealing back his own-blooded boy, whom he loves, and who is his, and running fast with him toward a car, putting him in and driving off. It would be the proper thing, in a way. Other men have done it.

Quilty's story goes like this: "A woman came to my office

once very early on in my practice. Her case was a simple divorce that she made complicated by greed and stubbornness, and she worked up quite a bill. When she got the bill, she phoned me, shouting and saying angry things. I said, 'Look, we'll work out a payment plan. One hundred dollars a month. How does that sound?' I was reasonable. My practice was new and struggling. Still, she refused to pay a cent. I had to take out a loan to pay my secretary, and I never forgot that. So, five years later, that very same woman's doctor phones me. She's got bone cancer, the doctor says, and I'm one of the only German Jews in town and might have the same blood type for a marrow transfusion for her. Would I consider it, at least consider having a blood test? I said, 'Absolutely not,' and hung up. The doctor called back. He begged me, but I hung up again. A month later, the woman died."

"What's your point?" says Mack. Quilty's voice is flying apart now.

"That that is the truth about me," he says. "Don't you see—"

"Yes, *I* fucking see. I am the one here who does the seeing! Me and Guapo."

He pauses for a long time. "I don't forgive anybody anything. That is the point."

"Y'know what? This whole thing is such a crock," says Mack, but his voice is thin and diffident, and he finishes putting on his shoes, but without socks, and then grabs up his coat.

Downstairs, the clock says quarter to five, and a crowd is gathering to watch the ducks. A red carpet has already been rolled out from the elevator to the fountain, and this makes the ducks excited, anxious for the evening ritual, their clipped wings fluttering. Mack takes a table in the back and orders a double whiskey with ice. He drinks it fast—it freezes and burns in that great old way: it has been too long. He orders another. The pianist on the other side of the lobby is playing

"Street of Dreams": "Love laughs at a king/Kings don't mean a thing" the man sings, and it seems to Mack the most beautiful song in the world. Men everywhere are about to die for reasons they don't know and wouldn't like if they did—but here is a song to do it by, so that life, in its mad spasms, might not demolish so much this time.

The ducks drink and dive in the fountain.

Probably Mack is already drunk as a horse.

Near the Union Avenue door is a young woman mime, juggling Coke bottles. People waiting for the ducks have gathered to watch. Even in her white pancake makeup, she is attractive. Her red hair is bright as a daylily and beneath her black leotards her legs are taut as an archer's bow.

Go for the juggler, thinks Mack. His head hurts, but his throat and lungs are hot and clear.

Out of the corner of his eye, he suddenly notices Quilty and Guapo, stepping slow and unsure, making their way around the far edge of the crowd. Their expressions are lonely and distraught, even Guapo's. Mack looks back at the fountain. Soon Guapo will find him—but Mack is not going to move until then, needing the ceremony of Quilty's effort. He knows Quilty will devise some conciliatory gift. He will come up and touch Mack and whisper, "Come back, don't be angry, you know this is how the two of us get."

But for now, Mack will just watch the ducks, watch them summoned by their caretaker, an old uniformed black man who blows a silver whistle and wields a long rod, signaling the ducks out of the water, out onto the carpet in a line. They haven't had a thing to say about it, these ducks, thinks Mack, haven't done a thing to deserve it, but there they are, God's lilies, year-round in a giant hotel, someone caring for them the rest of their lives. All the other birds of the world—the mange-hollowed hawks, the lordless hens, the dumb clucks—will live punishing, unblessed lives, winging it north, south, here, there, searching for a place of rest. But not these. Not these *rich,*

lucky ducks! graced with rug and stairs, upstairs and down, roof
to pool to penthouse, always steered, guided, welcomed toward
those golden elevator doors like a heaven's mouth, and though
it isn't really a heaven's mouth, it is maybe the lip of all there is.

Mack sighs. Why must he always take the measure of his
own stupid suffering? Why must he always look around and
compare his own against others'?

Because God wants people to.

Even if you're comparing yourself to ducks?

Especially if you're comparing yourself to ducks.

He feels his own head shrink with the hate that is love with
no place to go. He will do it: he will go back and get Lou if it
kills him. A million soldiers are getting ready to die for less.
He will find Annie; maybe it won't be that hard. And at first,
he will ask her nicely. But then he will do what a father must: a
boy is a father's. Sons love their fathers like nothing else. Mack
read that once in a magazine.

Yet the more he imagines finding Lou, the more greatly he
suspects that the whole mad task will indeed kill him. He
sees—as if again in a vision (of what he must prevent or of what
he cannot prevent, who knew with visions?)—the death of
himself and the sorrow of his boy. He sees the wound in his own
back, his eyes turning from fish-gray jellies to the plus and
minus signs of a comic-book corpse. He sees Lou scratched and
crawling back toward a house, the starry sky Mack's mocking
sparkled shroud.

But he will do it anyway, or what is he? Pond scum envying
the ducks.

All is well. Safely rest. God is nigh.

As the birds walk up the red carpet, quacking and honking
fussily, a pack of pleased Miss Americas, Mack watches them
pause and look up, satisfied but quizzical, into the burst of
lights from the tourists' cameras, the hollywood explosion of

them along the runner. The birds weave a little, stop, then proceed again, seeming uncertain why anyone would want to take these pictures, flash a light, be there at all, why any of this should be happening, though, by God, and sometimes surely not by God, it happened every day.

Quilty, at the edge of the crowd, holds up his fingers, giving each person he passes the peace sign and saying, "Peace." He comes close to Mack.

"Peace," he says.

"People don't say that anymore," says Mack.

"Well, they should," says Quilty. His nostrils have begun to flare, in that way that always signals a sob. He sinks to the floor and grabs Mack's feet. Quilty's gestures of contrition are like comets: infrequent and brilliant, but with a lot of space garbage. "No more war!" Quilty cries. "No more devastation!"

For the moment, it is only Quilty who is devastated. People are looking. "You're upstaging the ducks," says Mack.

Quilty pulls himself up via Mack's trousers. "Have pity," he says.

This is Quilty's audition ritual: whenever he feels it is time for it, he calls upon himself to audition for love. He has no script, no reliable sense of stage, just a faceful of his heart's own greasepaint and a relentless need for applause.

"Okay, okay," says Mack, and as the elevator closes on the dozen birds and their bowing trainer, everybody in the hotel lounge claps.

"Thank you," murmurs Quilty. "You are too kind, too kind."

REAL ESTATE

And yet of course these trinkets are endearing . . .
   —"Glitter and Be Gay"

It must be, Ruth thought, that she was going to die in the spring. She felt such inexplicable desolation then, such sludge in the heart, felt the season's mockery, all that chartreuse humidity in her throat like a gag. How else to explain such a feeling? She could almost burst—could one burst with joylessness? What she was feeling was too strange, too contrary, too isolated for a mere emotion. It had to be a premonition—one of being finally whisked away after much boring flailing and flapping and the pained, purposeless work that constituted life. And in spring, no less: a premonition of death. A rehearsal. A secretary's call to remind of the appointment.

Of course, it had always been in the spring that she discovered her husband's affairs. But the last one was years ago, and what did she care about all that now? There had been a parade of flings—in the end, they'd made her laugh: Ha! Ha! Ha! Ha! Ha! Ha! Ha! Ha! Ha! Ha! Ha! Ha! Ha! Ha! Ha! Ha!
Ha! Ha! Ha! Ha! Ha! Ha! Ha! Ha! Ha! Ha! Ha! Ha!
Ha! Ha! Ha! Ha! Ha! Ha! Ha! Ha! Ha! Ha! Ha! Ha! Ha!

Ha! Ha! Ha! Ha! Ha! Ha! Ha! Ha! Ha! Ha! Ha! Ha! Ha! Ha!
Ha! Ha! Ha! Ha! Ha! Ha! Ha! Ha! Ha! Ha! Ha! Ha! Ha! Ha!
Ha! Ha! Ha! Ha! Ha! Ha! Ha! Ha! Ha! Ha! Ha! Ha! Ha! Ha!
Ha! Ha! Ha! Ha! Ha! Ha! Ha! Ha! Ha! Ha! Ha! Ha! Ha! Ha!
Ha! Ha! Ha! Ha! Ha! Ha! Ha! Ha! Ha! Ha! Ha! Ha! Ha! Ha!
Ha! Ha! Ha! Ha! Ha! Ha! Ha! Ha! Ha! Ha! Ha! Ha! Ha! Ha!
Ha! Ha! Ha! Ha! Ha! Ha! Ha! Ha! Ha! Ha! Ha! Ha! Ha! Ha!
Ha! Ha! Ha! Ha! Ha! Ha! Ha! Ha! Ha! Ha! Ha! Ha! Ha! Ha!
Ha! Ha! Ha! Ha! Ha! Ha! Ha! Ha! Ha! Ha! Ha! Ha! Ha! Ha!
Ha! Ha! Ha! Ha! Ha! Ha! Ha! Ha! Ha! Ha! Ha! Ha! Ha! Ha!
Ha! Ha! Ha! Ha! Ha! Ha! Ha! Ha! Ha! Ha! Ha! Ha! Ha! Ha!
Ha! Ha! Ha! Ha! Ha! Ha! Ha! Ha! Ha! Ha! Ha! Ha! Ha! Ha!
Ha! Ha! Ha! Ha! Ha! Ha! Ha! Ha! Ha! Ha! Ha! Ha! Ha! Ha!
Ha! Ha! Ha! Ha! Ha! Ha! Ha! Ha! Ha! Ha! Ha! Ha! Ha! Ha!
Ha! Ha! Ha! Ha! Ha! Ha! Ha! Ha! Ha! Ha! Ha! Ha! Ha! Ha!
Ha! Ha! Ha! Ha! Ha! Ha! Ha! Ha! Ha! Ha! Ha! Ha! Ha! Ha!
Ha! Ha! Ha! Ha! Ha! Ha! Ha! Ha! Ha! Ha! Ha! Ha! Ha! Ha!
Ha! Ha! Ha! Ha! Ha! Ha! Ha! Ha! Ha! Ha! Ha! Ha! Ha! Ha!
Ha! Ha! Ha! Ha! Ha! Ha! Ha! Ha! Ha! Ha! Ha! Ha! Ha! Ha!
Ha! Ha! Ha! Ha! Ha! Ha! Ha! Ha! Ha! Ha! Ha! Ha! Ha! Ha!
Ha! Ha! Ha! Ha! Ha! Ha! Ha! Ha! Ha! Ha! Ha! Ha! Ha! Ha!
Ha! Ha! Ha! Ha! Ha! Ha! Ha! Ha! Ha! Ha! Ha! Ha! Ha! Ha!
Ha! Ha! Ha! Ha! Ha! Ha! Ha! Ha! Ha! Ha! Ha! Ha! Ha! Ha!
Ha! Ha! Ha! Ha! Ha! Ha! Ha! Ha! Ha! Ha! Ha! Ha! Ha! Ha!
Ha! Ha! Ha! Ha! Ha! Ha! Ha! Ha! Ha! Ha! Ha! Ha! Ha! Ha!
Ha! Ha! Ha! Ha! Ha! Ha! Ha! Ha! Ha! Ha! Ha! Ha! Ha! Ha!
Ha! Ha! Ha! Ha! Ha! Ha! Ha! Ha! Ha! Ha! Ha! Ha! Ha! Ha!
Ha! Ha! Ha! Ha! Ha! Ha! Ha! Ha! Ha! Ha! Ha! Ha! Ha! Ha!
Ha! Ha! Ha! Ha! Ha! Ha! Ha! Ha! Ha! Ha! Ha! Ha! Ha! Ha!
Ha! Ha! Ha! Ha! Ha! Ha! Ha! Ha! Ha! Ha! Ha! Ha! Ha! Ha!
Ha! Ha! Ha! Ha! Ha! Ha! Ha! Ha! Ha! Ha! Ha! Ha! Ha! Ha!

Ha! Ha! Ha! Ha! Ha! Ha! Ha! Ha! Ha! Ha! Ha! Ha! Ha! Ha!
Ha! Ha! Ha! Ha! Ha! Ha! Ha! Ha! Ha! Ha! Ha! Ha! Ha! Ha!
Ha! Ha! Ha! Ha! Ha! Ha! Ha! Ha! Ha! Ha! Ha! Ha! Ha! Ha!
Ha! Ha! Ha! Ha! Ha! Ha! Ha! Ha! Ha! Ha! Ha! Ha! Ha! Ha!
Ha! Ha! Ha! Ha! Ha! Ha! Ha! Ha! Ha! Ha! Ha! Ha! Ha! Ha!
Ha! Ha! Ha! Ha! Ha! Ha! Ha! Ha! Ha! Ha! Ha! Ha! Ha! Ha!
Ha! Ha! Ha! Ha! Ha! Ha! Ha! Ha! Ha! Ha! Ha! Ha! Ha! Ha!
Ha! Ha! Ha! Ha! Ha! Ha! Ha! Ha! Ha! Ha! Ha! Ha! Ha! Ha!
Ha! Ha! Ha! Ha! Ha! Ha! Ha! Ha! Ha! Ha! Ha! Ha! Ha! Ha!
Ha! Ha! Ha! Ha! Ha! Ha! Ha! Ha! Ha! Ha! Ha! Ha! Ha! Ha!
Ha! Ha! Ha! Ha! Ha! Ha! Ha! Ha! Ha! Ha! Ha! Ha! Ha! Ha!
Ha! Ha! Ha! Ha! Ha! Ha! Ha! Ha! Ha! Ha! Ha! Ha! Ha! Ha!
Ha! Ha! Ha! Ha! Ha! Ha! Ha! Ha! Ha! Ha! Ha! Ha! Ha! Ha!
Ha! Ha! Ha! Ha! Ha! Ha! Ha! Ha! Ha! Ha! Ha! Ha! Ha! Ha!
Ha! Ha! Ha! Ha! Ha! Ha! Ha! Ha! Ha! Ha! Ha! Ha! Ha! Ha!
Ha! Ha! Ha! Ha! Ha! Ha! Ha! Ha! Ha! Ha! Ha! Ha! Ha! Ha!
Ha! Ha! Ha! Ha! Ha! Ha! Ha! Ha! Ha! Ha! Ha! Ha! Ha! Ha!
Ha! Ha! Ha! Ha! Ha! Ha! Ha! Ha! Ha! Ha! Ha! Ha! Ha! Ha!
Ha! Ha! Ha! Ha! Ha! Ha! Ha! Ha! Ha! Ha! Ha! Ha! Ha! Ha!
Ha! Ha! Ha! Ha! Ha! Ha! Ha! Ha! Ha! Ha! Ha! Ha! Ha! Ha!
Ha! Ha! Ha! Ha! Ha! Ha! Ha! Ha! Ha! Ha! Ha! Ha! Ha! Ha!
Ha! Ha! Ha! Ha! Ha! Ha! Ha! Ha! Ha! Ha! Ha! Ha! Ha! Ha!
Ha! Ha! Ha! Ha! Ha! Ha! Ha! Ha! Ha! Ha! Ha! Ha! Ha! Ha!
Ha! Ha! Ha! Ha! Ha! Ha! Ha! Ha! Ha! Ha! Ha! Ha! Ha! Ha!
Ha! Ha! Ha! Ha! Ha! Ha! Ha! Ha! Ha! Ha! Ha! Ha! Ha! Ha!
Ha! Ha! Ha! Ha! Ha! Ha! Ha! Ha! Ha! Ha! Ha! Ha! Ha! Ha!
Ha! Ha! Ha! Ha! Ha! Ha! Ha! Ha! Ha! Ha! Ha! Ha! Ha! Ha!
Ha! Ha! Ha! Ha! Ha! Ha! Ha! Ha! Ha! Ha! Ha! Ha! Ha! Ha!
Ha! Ha! Ha! Ha! Ha! Ha! Ha! Ha! Ha! Ha! Ha! Ha! Ha! Ha!
Ha! Ha! Ha! Ha! Ha! Ha! Ha! Ha! Ha! Ha! Ha! Ha! Ha! Ha!
Ha! Ha! Ha!

Holding fast to her little patch of marital ground, she'd watched as his lovers floated through like ballerinas, or dande-

lion down, all of them sudden and fleeting, as if they were cal-
endar girls ripped monthly by the same mysterious calendar-
ripping wind that hurried time along in old movies. Hello!
Good-bye! Ha! Ha! Ha! What did Ruth care now? Those girls
were over and gone. The key to marriage, she concluded, was
just not to take the thing too personally.

"You *assume* they're over and gone," said her friend Carla,
who, in Ruth's living room, was working on both her inner
child and her inner thighs, getting rid of the child but in touch
with the thighs; Ruth couldn't keep it straight. Carla sometimes came over and did her exercises in the middle of Ruth's
Afghan rug. Carla liked to blurt out things and then say,
"Ooops, did I say that?" Or sometimes: "You know what? Life
is short. Dumpy, too, so you've got to do your best: no Empire
waists." She lay on her back and did breathing exercises and
encouraged Ruth to do the same. "I can't. I'll just fall asleep,"
said Ruth, though she suspected she wouldn't really.

Carla shrugged. "If you fall asleep, great. It's a beauty nap.
If you almost do but don't actually, it's meditation."

"*That's* meditation?"

"That's meditation."

Two years ago, when Ruth was going through chemo—the
oncologist in Chicago had set Ruth's five-year survival chances
at fifty-fifty; how mean not to lie and say sixty-forty!—Carla
had brought over lasagnas, which lasted in their various shrinking incarnations in Ruth's refrigerator for weeks. "Try not to
think of roadkill when you reheat," Carla said. She also brought
over sage and rosemary soaps, which looked like slabs of butter
with twigs in them. She brought Ruth a book to read, a collection of stories entitled *Trust Me,* and she had, on the jacket,
crossed out the author's name and written in her own: Carla
McGraw. Carla was a friend. Who had many friends these days?

"I do assume," Ruth said. "I have to." Terence's last affair,
two springs ago, had ended badly. He'd told Ruth he had a
meeting that would go on rather late, until ten or so, but then

he arrived home, damp and disheveled, at 7:30. "The meeting's been canceled," he said, and went directly upstairs, where she could hear him sobbing in the bathroom. He cried for almost an hour, and as she listened to him, her heart filled up with pity and a deep, sisterly love. At all the funerals for love, love had its neat trick of making you mourn it so much, it reappeared. Popped right up from the casket. Or, if it didn't reappear itself, it sent a relative of startling resemblance, a thin and charming twin, which you took back home with you to fatten and cradle, nuzzle and scold.

Oh, the rich torment that was life. She just didn't investigate Terence's activities anymore. No steaming open credit-card statements, no "accidentally" picking up the phone extension. As the doctor who diagnosed her now fully remissioned cancer once said to her, "The only way to know absolutely everything in life is via an autopsy."

Nuptial forensics. Ruth would let her marriage live. No mercy killing, no autopsy. She would let it live! Ha! She would settle, as a person must, for not knowing everything: ignorance as mystery; mystery as faith; faith as food; food as sex; sex as love; love as hate; hate as transcendence. Was this a religion or some weird kind of math?

Or was this, in fact, just spring?

Certain things helped: the occasional Winston (convinced, as Ruth was, despite the one lung, the lip blisters, and the keloidal track across her ribs, that at the end she would regret the cigarettes she hadn't smoked more than the ones she had; besides, she no longer coughed much at all, let alone so hard that her retinas detached); pots of lobelia ("Excuse me, gotta go," she had said more than once to a loquacious store clerk, "I've got some new lobelia sitting in a steaming hot car"); plus a long, scenic search for a new house.

"A move . . . yes. A move will be good. We've soiled the

nest, in many respects," her husband had said, in the circuitous syntax and ponderous Louisiana drawl that, like so much else about him, had once made her misty with desire and now drove her nuts with scorn. "Think about it, honey," he'd said after the reconciliation, the first remission, and the initial reconnaissance through the realtors—after her feelings had gone well beyond rage into sarcasm and carcinoma. "We should probably consider leaving this home entirely behind. Depending on what you want to do—or, of course. If you have another home in mind, I'm practically certain I'd be amenable. We would want to discuss it, however, or anything else you might be thinking of. I myself—though it may be presumptuous of me, I realize—but then, hey: it wouldn't be the first time, now would it? I myself was thinking that, if you were inclined—"

"Terence!" Ruth clapped her hands twice, sharply. "Speak more quickly! I don't have long to live!" They'd been married for twenty-three years. Marriage, she felt, was a fine arrangement generally, except that one never got it generally. One got it very, very specifically. "And, please," she added, "don't be fooled by the euphemisms of realtors. This was never a home, darling. This is a *house.*"

In this way—a wedding of emotionally handicapped parking spaces, an arduously tatted lace of property and irritation— they'd managed to stay married. He was not such a bad guy!—just a handsome country boy, disbelieving of his own luck, which came to him imperfectly but continually, like crackers from a cookie jar. She had counted on him to make money—was that so wrong?—and he had made some, in used-car dealerships and computer software stock. With its sweet, urgent beginnings, and grateful, hand-holding end, marriage was always its worst in the middle: it was always a muddle, a ruin, an unnavigable field. But it was not, she felt, a total wasteland. In her own marriage there was one sweet little recurrent season, one tiny nameless room, that suited and consoled her. She would lie in Terence's arms and he would be quiet and his quietness would restore her. There was music. There was peace. That was all. There were no words in it. But that tiny spot—like any season, or moon, or theater set; like a cake in a rotary display—invariably spun out of reach and view, and the quarreling would resume and she would have to wait a long time for the cake to come round again.

Of course, their daughter, Mitzy, adored Terence—the hot, lucky fire of him. In Ruth, on the other hand, Mitzy seemed to sense only the chill spirit of a woman getting by. But what was a person in Ruth's position *supposed* to do, except rebuild herself, from the ground up, as an iceberg? Ruth wanted to know! And so, in the strange, warm dissolutions that came over her these May nights silently before sleep, a pointillist's breaking up of the body and self and of the very room, a gentle fracturing to bubbles and black dotted swiss, Ruth began, again, to foresee her own death.

At first, looking at other houses on Sunday afternoons—wandering across other people's floors and carpets, opening the closets to look at other people's shoes—gave Ruth a thrill. The tacky photos on the potter's piano. The dean with no doorknobs. The orthodontist with thirty built-in cubbyholes for his thirty tennis shoes. Wallpaper peeling like birch skin. Assorted stained, scuffed floors and misaligned moldings. The Dacron carpets. The trashy magazines on the coffee table. And those economy snacks! People had pretzel boxes the size of bookcases. And no bookcases. What would they do with a book? Just put it in the pretzel box! Ruth took an unseemly interest in the faulty angles of a staircase landing, or the contents of a room: the ceramic pinecone lamps, the wedding photo of the dogs. Was the town that boring that this was now what amused her? What was so intriguing to her about all this home owning thrown open to the marketplace? The airing of the family vault? The peek into the grave? Ruth hired a realtor. Stepping into a house, hunting out its little spaces, surveying its ceiling stains and roof rot exhilarated her. It amazed her that there was always something wrong with a house, and after awhile, her amazement became a kind of pleasure; it was pleasing that there should always be something wrong. It made the house seem more natural that way.

But soon she backed off. "I could never buy a house that had that magazine on the coffee table," she said once. A kind of fear overtook her. "I don't like that neo-Georgian thing," she said now, before the realtor, Kit, had even turned off the car, forcing Kit to back out again from the driveway. "I'm sorry, but when I look at it," Ruth added, "my eye feels disorganized, and my heart just empties right out."

"I care about you, Ruth," said Kit, who was terrified of losing clients and so worked hard to hide the fact that she had the patience of a gnat. "Our motto is 'We Care,' and that is just so true: We really, really care, Ruth. We care about you. We care about your feelings and desires. We want you to be happy. So, here we are driving along. Driving toward a thing, then driving past. You want a house, Ruth, or shall we just go to the goddamn movies?"

"You think I'm being unrealistic."

"Aw, I get enough realism as it is. Realism's overrated. I mean it about the movies."

"You do?"

"Sure!" And so that once, Ruth went to the movies with her realtor. It was a preseason matinee of *Forrest Gump*, which made her teary with weariness, hurt, and bone-thinning boredom. "Such a career-ender for poor Tom Hanks. Mark my words," Ruth whispered to her realtor, candy wrappers floating down in the dark toward her shoes. "Thank God we bought toffees. What would we do without these toffees?"

. . .

Eventually, not even a month later, in Kit's white Cabriolet, the top down, the wind whipping everyone's hair in an unsightly way, Ruth and Terence took a final tour of the suburbanized cornfields on the periphery of town and found a house. It was the original ancient four-square farmhouse in the center of a 1979 subdivision. A man-made pond had been dug into the former field that edged the side yard. A wishing well full of wildflowers stood in the front yard.

"This is it," Terence said, gesturing toward the house.

"It is?" said Ruth. She tried to study it with an open mind—its porch and dormers angled as if by a Cubist, its chimney crumbling on one side, its cedar shingles ornately leprous with old green paint. "If one of us kisses it, will it turn into a house?" The dispiriting white ranches and split-levels lined up on either side at least possessed a geometry she understood.

"It needs a lot of work," admitted Kit.

"Yes," said Ruth. Even the FOR SALE sign had sprouted a shock of dandelions at its base. "Unlike chocolates, houses are predictable: you always know you're getting rot and decay and a long, tough mortgage. Eat them or put them back in the box—you can't do either without a lawsuit or an ordinance hearing."

"I don't know what you're talking about," said Terence. He took Ruth aside.

"This is it," he hissed. "This is our dream house."

"*Dream* house?" All the dreams she'd been having were about death—its blurry pixilation, its movement through a dark, soft sleep to a hard, bright end.

"I'm surprised you can't see it," said Terence, visibly frustrated.

She squinted again toward the soffits, the Picasso porch,

the roof mottled with moss and soot. She studied the geese and the goose poop, moist, mashed cigars of which littered the stony shore of the pond. "Ah, maybe," she said. "Maybe yes. I think I'm beginning to see it. Who owns it again?"

"A Canadian. He's been renting it out. It's a nice neighborhood. Near a nature conservatory and the zoo."

"The zoo?"

Ruth thought about this. They would have to hire a lot of people, of course. It would be like running a company to get this thing back in shape, bossing everybody around, monitoring the loans and payments. She sighed. Such entrepreneurial spirit did not run in her family. It was not native to her. She came from a long line of teachers and ministers—employees. Hopeless people. People with faith but no hope. There was not one successful small business anywhere in her genes. "I'm starting to see the whole thing," she said.

On the other side of town, where other people lived, a man named Noel and a woman named Nitchka were in an apartment, in the kitchen, having a discussion about music. The woman said, "So you know nothing at all? Not a single song?"

"I don't think so," said Noel. Why was this a problem for her? It wasn't a problem for him. So he didn't know any songs. He had always been willing to let her know more than he did; it didn't bother him, until it bothered her.

"Noel, what kind of upbringing did you have, anyway?" He knew she felt he had been deprived and that he should feel angry about it. But he did! He did feel angry about it! "Didn't your parents ever sing songs to you?" she asked. "Can't you even sing one single song by heart? Sing a song. Just any song."

"Like what?"

"If there was a gun to your head, what song would you sing?"

"I don't know!" he shouted, and threw a chair across the room. They hadn't had sex in two months.

"Is it that you don't even know the *name* of a song?"

At night, every night, they just lay there with their magazines and Tylenol PM and then, often with the lights still on, were whisked quickly down into their own separate worlds of sleep—his filled with lots of whirling trees and antique flying machines and bouquets of ferns. He had no idea why.

"I know the name of a song," he said.

"What song?"

" 'Open the Door, Richard.' "

"What kind of song is that?"

It was a song his friend Richard's mother would sing when he was twelve and he and Richard were locked in the bedroom, flipping madly through magazines: *Breasts and the Rest, Tight Tushies,* and *Lollapalooza Ladies.* But it was a real song, which still existed—though you couldn't find those magazines anymore. Noel had looked.

"See? I know a song that you don't!" he exclaimed.

"Is this a song of spiritual significance to you?"

"Yup, it really is." He picked up a rubber band from the counter, stretched it between his fingers, and released it. It hit her in the chin. "Sorry. That was an accident," he said.

"Something is deeply missing in you!" Nitchka shouted, and stormed out of the apartment for a walk.

Noel sank back against the refrigerator. He could see his own reflection in the window over the sink. It was dim and translucent, and a long twisted cobweb outside, caught on the eaves, swung back and forth across his face like a noose. He looked crazy and ill—but with just a smidgen of charisma! "If there was a gun to your head," he said to the reflection, "what song would you sing?"

.   .   .

Ruth wondered whether she really needed a project this badly. A diversion. A resurrection. An undertaking. Their daughter, Mitzy, grown and gone—was the whole empty nest thing such a crisis that they would devote the rest of their days to this mortician's delight? Was it that horribly, echoey quiet and nothing-nothing not to have Mitzy and her struggles furnishing their lives? Was it so bad no longer to have a daughter's frustrated artistic temperament bleeding daily on the carpet of their brains? Mitzy, dear Mitzy, was a dancer. All those ballet and tap lessons as a child—she wasn't supposed to have taken them seriously! They had been intended as middle-class irony and window dressing—you weren't actually supposed to *become* a dancer. But Mitzy had. Despite that she was the fattest in the troupe every time, never belonging, rejected from every important company, until one day a young director saw how beautifully, soulfully she danced—"How beautifully the fat girl dances!"—and ushered her past the corps, set her center stage, and made her a star. Now she traveled the world over and was the darling of the critics. "Size fourteen, yet!" crowed one reviewer. "It is a miracle to see!" She had become a triumph of feet over heft, spirit over matter, matter over doesn't-matter, a figure of immortality, a big fat angel really, and she had "many, many homosexual fans," as Terence put it. As a result, she now rarely came home. Ruth sometimes got postcards, but Ruth hated postcards—so careless and cheap, especially from this new angel of dance writing to her own sick mother. But that was the way with children.

Once, over a year and a half ago, Mitzy had come home, but it was only for two weeks—during Ruth's chemotherapy. Mitzy was, as usual, in a state of crisis. "Sure they like my work," she wailed as Ruth adjusted that first itchy acrylic wig, the one that used to scare people. "But do they like *me*?" Mitzy was an only child, so it was natural that her first bout of sibling rivalry would be with her own work. When Ruth suggested as much, Mitzy gave her a withering look accompanied by a snorting noise, and after that, with a cocked eyebrow and a wince of a gaze, Mitzy began monopolizing the telephone with moving and travel plans. "You seem to be doing *extremely well,* Mom," she said, looking over her shoulder, jotting things down. Then she'd fled.

At first Terence, even more than she, seemed enlivened by the prospect of new real estate. The simplest discussion—of doorjambs or gutters—made his blood move around his face and neck like a lava lamp. Roof-shingle samples—rough, grainy squares of sepia, rose, and gray—lit his eyes up like love. He brought home doorknob catalogs and phoned a plasterer or two. After a while, however, she could see him tire and retreat, recoil even—another fling flung. "My God, Terence. Don't quit on me now. This is just like the Rollerblades!" He had last fall gone through a Rollerblade period.

"I'm way too busy," he said.

And before Ruth knew it, the entire house project—its purchase and renovation—had been turned over to her.

First Ruth had to try to sell their current house. She decided to try something called a "fosbo." FOSBO: a "For Sale by Owner." She put ads in papers, bought a sign for the front yard, and planted violet and coral impatiens in the flower beds for the horticulturally unsuspecting, those with no knowledge of perennials. Gorgeous yard! Mature plantings! She worked up a little flyer describing the moldings and light fixtures, all "original to the house." Someone came by to look and sniff. He fingered one of the ripped window shades. *"Original to the house?"* he said.

"All right, you're out of here," she said. To subsequent prospective buyers, she abandoned any sales pitch and went for candor. "I admit, this bathroom's got mildew. And look at this *stupid* little hallway. This is why we're moving! We hate this house." She soon hired back her Forrest Gump realtor, who, at the open house, played Vivaldi on the stereo and baked banana bread, selling the place in two hours.

The night after they closed on both houses, having sat silently through the two proceedings, like deaf-mutes being had, the mysterious Canadian once more absent and represented only by a purple-suited realtor named Flo, Ruth and Terence stood in their empty new house and ate take-out Chinese straight from the cartons. Their furniture was sitting in a truck, which was parked in a supermarket parking lot on the east side of town, and it all would be delivered the next day. For now, they stood at the bare front window of their large, echoey new dining room. A small lit candle on the floor cast their shadows up on the ceiling, gloomy and fat. Wind rattled the panes and the boiler in the cellar burst on in small, frightening explosions. The radiators hissed and smelled like cats, burning off dust as they heated up, vibrating the cobwebs in the ceiling corners above them. The entire frame of the house groaned and rumbled. There was scampering in the walls. The sound of foot-steps—or something like footsteps—thudded softly in the attic, two floors above them.

"We've bought a haunted house," said Ruth. Terence's mouth was full of hot cabbagey egg roll. "A ghost!" she continued. "Just a little extra protein. Just a little amino-acid bonus." It was what her own father had always said when he found a small green worm in his bowl of blueberries.

"The house is settling," said Terence.

"It's had a hundred and ten years to settle; you would think it had gotten it done with by now."

"Settling goes on and on," said Terence.

"We would know," said Ruth.

He looked at her, then dug into the container of lo mein.

A scrabbling sound came from the front porch. Terence chewed, swallowed, then walked over to turn the light on, but the light didn't come on. "Was this disclosed?" he shouted.

"It's probably just the lightbulb."

"All new lightbulbs were just put in, Flo said." He opened the front door. "The light's broken, and it should have been disclosed." He was holding a flashlight with one hand and unscrewing the front light with the other. Behind the light fixture gleamed three pairs of masked eyes. Dark raccoon feces were mounded up in the crawl space between the ceiling and the roof.

"What the *hell*?" shouted Terence, backing away.

"This house is *infested*!" said Ruth. She put down her food. "How did those creatures get up there?"

She felt a twinge in her one lung. "How does anything get anywhere—that's what I want to know." She had only ever been the lightest of smokers, never in a high-risk category, but now every pinch, prick, tick, or tock in her ribs, every glitch in the material world anywhere made her want to light up and puff.

"Oh, God, the stench."

"Shouldn't the inspector have found this?"

"Inspectors! Obviously, they're useless. What this place needed was an MRI."

"Ah, geeze. This is the worst."

Every house is a grave, thought Ruth. All that life-stealing fuss and preparation. Which made moving from a house a resurrection—or an exodus of ghouls, depending on your point of view—and made moving *to* a house (yet another house!) the darkest of follies and desires. At best, it was a restlessness come falsely to rest. But the inevitable rot and demolition, from which the soul eventually had to flee (to live in the sky or disperse itself among the trees?), would necessarily make a person stupid with unhappiness.

Oh, well!

After their furniture arrived and was positioned almost exactly the way it had been in their old house, Ruth began to call a lot of people to come measure, inspect, capture, cart away, clean, spray, bring samples, provide estimates and bids, and sometimes they did come, though once people had gotten a deposit, they often disappeared entirely. Machines began to answer instead of humans and sometimes phone numbers announced themselves disconnected altogether. "We're sorry. The number you have reached . . ."

The windows of the new house were huge—dusty, but bright because of their size—and because the shade shop had not yet delivered the shades, the entire neighborhood of spiffy middle management could peer into Ruth and Terence's bedroom. For one long, bewildering day, Ruth took to waving, and only sometimes did people wave back. More often, they just squinted and stared. The next day, Ruth taped bedsheets up to the windows with masking tape, but invariably the sheets fell off after ten minutes. When she bathed, she had to crawl naked out of the bathroom down the hall and into the bedroom and then into the closet to put her clothes on. Or sometimes she just lay there on the bathroom floor and wriggled into things. It was all so very hard.

In their new backyard, crows the size of suitcases cawed and bounced in the branches of the pear tree. Carpenter ants—like shiny pieces of a child's game—swarmed the porch steps. Ruth made even more phone calls, and finally a man with a mottled, bulbous nose and a clean white van with a cockroach painted on it came and doused the ants with poison.

"It just looks like a fire extinguisher, what you're using," said Ruth, watching.

"Ho no, ma'am. Way stronger than that." He wheezed. His

nose was knobby as a pickle. He looked underneath the porch and then back up at Ruth. "There's a whole lot of dying going on in there," he said.

"There's nothing you can do about the crows?" Ruth asked.

"Not me, but you could get a gun and shoot 'em yourself," he said. "It's not legal, but if your house were one hundred yards down that way, it would be. If it were one hundred yards down that way, you could bag twenty crows a day. Since you're where you are, within the town limits, you're going to have to do it at night, with a silencer. Catch 'em live in the morning with nets and corn, then at sunset, take 'em out behind the garage and put 'em out of your misery."

"Nets?" said Ruth.

She called many people. She collected more guesstimates and advice. A guy named Noel from a lawn company advised her to forget about the crows, worry about the squirrels. She should plant her tulips deeper, and with a lot of red pepper, so that squirrels would not dig them up. "Look at all these squirrels!" he said, pointing to the garage roof and to all the weedy flower beds. "And how about some ground cover in here, by the porch, some lilies by the well, and some sunflowers in the side yard?"

"Let me think about it," said Ruth. "I would like to keep some of these violets," she said, indicating the pleasant-looking leaves throughout the irises.

"Those aren't violets. That's a weed. That's a very common, tough little weed."

"I always thought those were violets."

"Nope."

"Things can really overtake a place, can't they? This planet's just one big divisive cutthroat competition of growing. I mean, they look like violets, don't they? The leaves, I mean."

Noel shrugged. "Not to me. Not really."

How could she keep any of it straight? There was spirea and

there was false spirea—she forgot which was which. "Which is the spirea again?" she asked. Noel pointed to the bridal-wreath hedge, which was joyously blooming from left to right, from sun to shade, and in two weeks would sag and brown in the same direction. "Ah, marriage," she said aloud.

"Pardon?" said Noel.

"Are you married?" she asked.

He gave her a tired little smile and said, "No. Trying to make it happen with a girlfriend, but no, not married."

"That's probably better," said Ruth.

"How about this vegetable garden?" he asked nervously.

"It's just a lot of grass with a rhubarb in it," said Ruth. "I'd like to dig the whole thing up and plant roses—unless you think it's bad luck to replace food with flowers. Vanity before the Lord, or something."

"It's up to you," he said.

She called him back that night. He personally, no machine, answered the phone. "I've been thinking about the sunflowers," she said.

"Who is this?" he said.

"Ruth. Ruth Aikins."

"Oh, say, Ruth. Ruth! Hi!"

"Hi," she said in a worried way. He sounded as if he'd been drinking.

"Now what about those sunflowers?" he asked. "I'd like to plant those sunflowers real soon, you know that? Here's why: my girlfriend's talking again about leaving me, and I've just been diagnosed with lymphoma. So I'd like to see some sunflowers come up end of August."

"Oh, my God. Life stinks!" cried Ruth.

"Yup. So I'd like to see some sunflowers. End of summer, I'd like something to look forward to."

"What kind of girlfriend talks about leaving her beau at a time like this?"

"I don't know."

"I mean—good riddance. On the other hand, you know what you should do? You should make yourself a good cup of tea and sit down and write her a letter. You're going to need someone to care for you through all this. Don't let her call all the shots. Let her understand the implications of her behavior and her responsibilities to you. I know whereof I speak."

Ruth was about to explain further, when Noel cleared his throat hotly. "I don't think it's such a great idea for you to go get personal and advising. I mean, look. *Ruth,* is it? You see, I don't even know your name, Ruth. I know a lot of Ruths. You could be goddamned anyone. Ruth this, Ruth that, Ruth who knows. As a matter of fact, the lymphoma thing I just made up, because I thought you were a totally different Ruth." And with that, he hung up.

She put out cages for the squirrels—the squirrels who gnawed the hyacinth bulbs, giving their smooth surfaces runs like stockings, the squirrels who utterly devoured the crocuses. From the back porch, she watched each squirrel thrash around in the cage for an hour, hurling itself against the cage bars and rubbing bald spots into its head, before she finally took pity and drove each one to a faraway quarry to set it free. The quarry was a spot that Terence had recommended as "a beautiful seclusion, a rodent Eden, a hillside of oaks above a running brook." Such poetry: probably he'd gotten laid there once. Talk about your rodent Eden! In actuality, the place was a depressing little gravel gully, with a trickle of brown water running through it, a tiny crew of scrub oaks manning the nearby incline. It was the kind of place where the squirrel mafia would have dumped their offed squirrels.

She lifted the trapdoor and watched each animal scurry off toward the hillside. Did they know what they were doing?

Would they join their friends, or would every last one of them find their way back to the hollow walls of her house and set up shop again?

The bats—bats!—arrived the following week, one afternoon during a loud, dark thundershower, like a horror movie. They flew back and forth in the stairwells, then hung upside down from the picture-frame molding in the dining room, where they discreetly defecated, leaving clumps of shiny black guano pasted to the wall.

Ruth phoned her husband at his office but only got his voice mail, so she then phoned Carla, who came dashing over with a tennis racket, a butterfly net, and a push broom, all with ribbons tied around their handles. "These are my housewarming presents," she said.

"They're swooping again! Look out! They're swooping!"

"Let me at those sons of bitches," Carla said.

From her fetal position on the floor, Ruth looked up at her. "What did I ever do to get such a great friend as you?"

Carla stopped. Her face was flushed with affection, her cheeks blotched with pink. "You think so?" A bat dive-bombed her hair. The old wives' tale—that bats got caught in your hair—seemed truer to Ruth than the new wives' tale—that bats getting caught in your hair was just an old wives' tale. Bats possessed curiosity and arrogance. They were little social scientists. They got close to hair—to investigate, measure, and interview. And when something got close—a moth to a flame, a woman to a house, a woman to a grave, a sick woman to a fresh, wide-open grave like a bed—it could fall in and get caught.

"You gotta stuff your dormer eaves with steel wool," said Carla.

"Hey. Ain't it the truth," said Ruth.

They buried the whacked bats in tabbouleh containers, in the side yard: everything just tabbouleh in the end.

.   .   .

With the crows in mind, Ruth started to go with Carla to the shooting range. The geese, Carla said, were not that big a problem. The geese could be discouraged simply by shaking up the eggs in their nests. Carla was practical. She had a heart the shape of an ax. She brought over a canoe and paddled Ruth out into the cattails to find the goose nests, and there she took each goose egg and shook it furiously. "If you just take and toss the egg," explained Carla, "the damn goose will lay another one. This way, you kill the gosling, and the goose never knows. It sits there warming the damn eggnog until the winter comes, and the goose then just leaves, heartbroken, and never comes back. With the crows, however, you just have to blow their brains out."

At the shooting range, they paid a man with a green metal money box twenty dollars for an hour of shooting. They got several cans of diet Coke, which they bought from a vending machine outside near the rest rooms, and which they set at their feet, at their heels, just behind them. They each had pistols, Ruth's from World War I, Carla's from World War II, which they had bought in an antique-gun store. "Anyone could shoot birds with a shotgun," Carla had said. "Let's be unique."

"That's never really been a big ambition of mine," said Ruth.

They were the only ones there at the range and stood fifty yards from three brown sacks of hay with red circles painted on them. They fired at the circles—one! two! three!—then turned, squatted, set their guns back down, and sipped their Cokes. The noise was astonishing, bursting through the fields around them, echoing off the small hills and back out of the sky, mocking and retaliatory. "My Lord!" Ruth exclaimed. Her gun felt hard and unaimable. "I don't think I'm doing this right," she said. She had expected a pistol to seem light and natural—a seamless extension of her angry feral self. But instead, it felt heavy and huge and so unnaturally loud, she never wanted to fire such a thing again.

But she did. Only twice did she see her hay sack buckle. Mostly, she seemed to be firing too high, into the trees behind the targets, perhaps hitting squirrels—perhaps the very squirrels she had caught in her have-a-heart cage, now set free and shot dead with her have-a-house gun. "It's all too much," said Ruth. "I can't possibly be doing this right. It's way too complicated and mean."

"You've forgotten about the damn crows," said Carla. "Don't forget them."

"That's right," said Ruth, and she picked up the gun again. "Crows." Then she lowered her gun. "But won't I just be shooting them at close range, after I catch them in nets?"

"Maybe," said Carla. "But maybe not."

When Nitchka finally left him, she first watched her favorite TV show, then turned off the television, lifted up her CD player and her now-unhooked VCR, and stopped to poise herself dramatically in the front hall. "You know, you haven't a clue what the human experience is even about," she said.

"This song and dance again," he said. "Are you taking it on the road?" She set her things down outside in the hall so she could slam the door loudly and leave him—leave him, he imagined, for some new, handsome man she had met at work. Dumped for Hunks. That was the title of his life. In heaven, just to spite her, that would be the name of his goddamn band.

He drank a lot that week, and on Friday, his boss, McCarthy, called to say Noel was fired. "You think we can run a lawn store this way?" he said.

"If there was a gun to your head," said Noel, "what song would you sing?"

"Get help," said McCarthy. "That's all I have to say." Then there was a dial tone.

Noel began to collect unemployment, getting to the office just before it closed. He began to sleep in the days and stay up late at night. He got turned around. He went out at midnight for walks, feeling insomniac and mocked by the dark snore of the neighborhood. Rage circled and built in him, like a saxophone solo. He began to venture into other parts of town. Sidewalks appeared, then disappeared again. The moon shone on one side and then on the other. Once, he brought duct tape with him and a ski mask. Another time, he brought duct tape, a ski mask, and a gun one of his stepfathers had given him when he was twenty. If you carefully taped a window from the outside, it could be broken quietly: the glass would stick to the tape and cave gently outward.

"I'm not going to hurt you," he said. He turned on the light in the bedroom. He taped the woman's mouth first, then the man's. He made them get out of bed and stand over by the dresser. "I'm going to take your TV set," said Noel. "And I'm going to take your VCR. But before I do, I want you to sing me a song. I'm a music lover, and I want you to sing me one song, any song. By heart. You first," he said to the man. He pressed the gun to his head. "One song." He pulled the duct tape gently off the man's mouth.

"Any song?" repeated the man. He tried to look into the eyeholes of Noel's ski mask, but Noel turned abruptly and stared at the olive gray glass of the TV.

"Yeah," said Noel. "Any song."

"Okay." The man began. " 'O beautiful for spacious skies, for amber waves of grain . . .' " His voice was deep and sure. " '. . . for purple mountain majesties . . .' " Noel turned back and studied the man carefully. He seemed to know it all by heart. How had he learned it all by heart? "You want *all* the verses?" the man stopped and asked, a bit too proudly, Noel thought, for someone who had a gun aimed his way.

"Nah, that's enough," Noel said irritably. "Now you," he said to the woman. He pulled the duct tape off her mouth. Her upper lip was moistly pink, raw from the adhesive. He glanced down at the tape and saw the spiky glisten of little mustache hairs. She began immediately, anxiously, to sing. " 'You are my lucky star. I'm lucky where you are/Two lovely eyes at me that were—' "

"What kind of song is this?"

She nervously ignored him, kept on: " '. . . beaming, gleaming, I was starstruck.' " She began to sway a little, move her hands up and down. She cleared her throat and modulated upward, a light, chirpy warble, though her face was stretched wide with fright, like heated wax. " 'You're all my lucky charms. I'm lucky in your arms. . . .' " Here her hands fluttered up to her heart.

"All right, that's enough. I'm taking the VCR now."

"That's practically the end anyway," said the woman.

At the next house he did, he got a Christmas carol, plus "La Vie en Rose." At the third house, the week following, he got one nursery rhyme, half a school song, and "Memory" from *Cats*. He began to write down the titles and words. At home, looking over his notepad, he realized he was creating a whole new kind of songbook. Still the heart of these songs eluded him. Looking at the words the next day, a good, almost-new VCR at his feet, he could never conjure the tune. And without the tune, the words seemed stupid and half-mad.

To avoid the chaos of the house entirely, Ruth took to going to matinees. First-run movies, second-run—she didn't care. Movies were the ultimate real estate: you stepped in and looked around and almost always bought. She was especially stirred by a movie she saw about a beautiful widow who fell in love with a space alien who had assumed human form—the form of the woman's long lost husband! Eventually, however, the man had to go back to his real home, and an immense and amazing spaceship came to get him, landing in a nearby field. To Ruth, it seemed so sad and true, just like life: someone assumed the form of the great love of your life, only to reveal himself later as an alien who had to get on a spaceship and go back to his planet. Certainly it had been true for Terence. Terence had gotten on a spaceship and gone back long ago. Although, of course, in real life you seldom saw the actual spaceship. Usually, there was just a lot of drinking, mumbling, and some passing out in the family room.

Sometimes on the way back from the movies, she would drive by their old house. They had sold it to an unmemorable young couple, and now, driving past it slowly, eyeing it like a pervert, she began to want it back. It was a good house. They didn't deserve it, that couple: look how ignorant they were—pulling out all those forsythia bushes as if they were weeds.

Or maybe they *were* weeds. She never knew anymore what was good life and what was bad, what was desirable matter and what was antimatter, what was the thing itself and what was the death of the thing: one mimicked the other, and she resented the work of having to distinguish.

Which, again, was the false spirea and which was the true?

The house was hers. If it hadn't been for that damn banana bread, it still would be hers.

Perhaps she could get arrested creeping slowly past in her car like this. She didn't know. But every time she drove by, the house seemed to see her and cry out, It's you! Hello, hello! You're back! So she tried not to do it too often. She would speed up a little, give a fluttery wave, and drive off.

At home, she could not actually net the crows, though their old habitat, the former cornfield that constituted the neighborhood, continued to attract them like an ancestral land or a good life recalled over gin. They hovered in the yards, tormented the cats, and ate the still-wet day-old songbirds right out of their nests. How was she supposed to catch such fiends? She could not. She draped nets in the branches of trees, to snag them, but always a wind caused the nets to twist or drop, or pages of old newspaper blew by and got stuck inside, plastering the nets with op-ed pages and ads. From the vegetable garden now turning flower bed came the persistent oniony smell of those chives not yet smothered by the weed barrier. And the rhubarb, too, kept exploding stubbornly through, no matter how she plucked at it, though each clutch of stalks was paler and more spindly than the last.

She began generally not to feel well. Never a temple, her body had gone from being a home, to being a house, to being a phone booth, to being a kite. Nothing about it gave her proper shelter. She no longer felt housed within it at all. When she went for a stroll or was out in the yard throwing the nets up into the oaks, other people in the neighborhood walked briskly past her. The healthy, the feeling well, when they felt that way, couldn't remember feeling any other, couldn't imagine it. They were niftily in their bodies. They were not only out of the range of sympathy; they were out of the range of mere imagining. Whereas the sick could only think of being otherwise. Their hearts, their every other thought, went out to that well person they hated a little but wanted to be. But the sick were sick. They were not in charge. They had lost their place at the top of the food chain. The feeling well were running the show; which was why the world was such a savage place. From her own porch, she could hear the PA announcements from the zoo. They were opening; they were closing; would someone move their car. She could also hear the elephant, his sad bluesy trumpet, and the Bengal tiger roaring his heartbreak: all that animal unhappiness. The zoo was a terrible place and a terrible place to live near: the pacing ocelot, the polar bear green with fungus, the zebra demented and hungry and eating the fence, the children brought there to taunt the animals with paper cups and their own clean place in the world, the vulture sobbing behind his scowl.

Ruth began staying inside, drinking tea. She felt tightenings, pain and vertigo, but then, was that so new? It seemed her body, so mysterious and apart from her, could only produce illness. Though once, of course, it had produced Mitzy. How had it done that? Mitzy was the only good thing her body had ever been able to grow. She was a real chunk of change that one, a gorgeous george. How had her body done it? How does a body ever do it? Life inhabits life. Birds inhabit trees. Bones sprout bones. Blood gathers and makes new blood.

A miracle of manufacturing.

On one particular afternoon that was too cool for spring, when Ruth was sitting inside drinking tea so hot it skinned her tongue, she heard something. Upstairs, there was the old pacing in the attic that she had come to ignore. But now there was a knock on the door—loud, rhythmic, urgent. There were voices outside.

"Yes?" Ruth called, approaching the entryway, then opening the door.

Before her stood a girl, maybe fourteen or fifteen years old. "We heard there was a party here," said the girl. She had tar black hair and a silver ring through her upper lip. Her eyes looked meek and lost. "Me and Arianna heard down on State Street that there was a party right here at this house."

"There's not," said Ruth. "There's just not." And then she closed the door, firmly.

But looking out the window, Ruth could see more teenagers gathering in front of the house. They collected on the lawn like fruit flies on fruit. Some sat on the front steps. Some roared up on mopeds. Some hopped out of station wagons crowded with more kids just like themselves. One carload of kids poured out of the car, marched right up the front steps, and, without ringing the bell, opened the unlocked door and walked in.

Ruth put her tea down on the bookcase and walked toward the front entryway. *"Excuse* me!" she said, facing the kids in the front hall.

The kids stopped and stared at her. "May I help you?" asked Ruth.

"We're visiting someone who lives here."

"*I* live here."

"We were invited to a party by a *kid* who lives here."

"There is no kid who lives here. And there is no party."

"There's no kid who lives here?"

"No, there isn't."

A voice suddenly came from behind Ruth. A voice more proprietary, a voice from deeper within the house than even she was. "Yes, there is," it said.

Ruth turned and saw standing in the middle of her living room a fifteen-year-old boy dressed entirely in black, his head shaved spottily, his ears, nose, lips, and eyebrows pierced with multiple gold and copper rings. The rim of his left ear held three bronze clips.

"Who are you?" Ruth asked. Her heart flapped and fluttered, like something hit sloppily by a car.

"I'm Tod."

"Tod?"

"People call me Ed."

"Ed?"

"I live here."

"No, you don't. You don't! What do you mean, you live here?"

"I've been living in your attic."

"You have?" Ruth felt sweat burst forth from behind the wings of her nose. "You're our ghost? You've been pacing around upstairs?"

"Yeah, he has," said one of the kids at the door.

"But I don't understand." Ruth reached over and plucked a Kleenex from the box on the mail table, and wiped her face with it.

"I ran away from my own home months ago. I have a key to this house from the prior owner, who was a friend. So from time to time, I've been sleeping upstairs in your attic. It's not so bad up there."

"You've been what? You've been living here, going in and out? Don't your parents know where you are?" Ruth asked.

"Look, I'm sorry about this party," said Tod. "I didn't mean for it to get this out of hand. I only invited a few people. I thought you were going away. It was supposed to be a small party. I didn't mean for it to be a big party."

"No," said Ruth. "You don't seem to understand. Big party, little party: you weren't supposed to have a party here at all. You were not even supposed to be *in* this house, let alone invite others to join you."

"But I had the key. I thought, I don't know. I thought it would be all right."

"Give me the key. Right now. Give me the key."

He handed her the key, with a smirk. "I don't know if it'll do you any good. Look." Ruth turned and all the kids at the door held up their own shiny brass keys. "I made copies," said Tod.

Ruth began to shriek. "Get out of here! Get out of here right now! All of you! Not only will I have these locks changed but if you ever set foot in this neighborhood again, I'll have the police on you so fast, you won't know what hit you."

"But we need *some*place to drink, man," said one of the departing boys.

"Go to the damn park!"

"The cops are all over the park," one girl whined.

"Then go to the railroad tracks, like we used to do, for God's sake," she yelled. "Just get the hell out of here." She was shocked by the bourgeois venom and indignation in her own voice. She had, after all, once been a hippie. She had taken a lot of windowpane and preached about the evils of private ownership from a red Orlon blanket on a street corner in Chicago.

Life: what an absurd little story it always made.

"Sorry," said Tod. He touched her arm, and, swinging a cloth satchel over his shoulder, walked toward the front door with the rest of them.

"Get the hell out of here," she said. "Ed."

The geese, the crows, the squirrels, the raccoons, the bats, the ants, the kids: Ruth now went to the firing range with Carla as often as she could. She would stand with her feet apart, both hands grasping the gun, then fire. She concentrated, tried to gather bits of strength in her, crumbs to make a loaf. She had been given way too much to cope with in life. Did God have her mixed up with someone else? Get a Job, she shouted silently to God. Get a real Job. I have never been your true and faithful servant. Then she would pull the trigger. When you told a stupid joke to God and got no response, was it that the joke was too stupid, or not quite stupid enough? She narrowed her eyes. Mostly, she just tried to squint, but then dread closed her eyes entirely. She fired again. Why did she not feel more spirited about this, the way Carla did? Ruth breathed deeply before firing, noting the Amazonian asymmetry of her breath, but in her heart she knew she was a mouse. A mouse bearing firearms, but a mouse nonetheless.

"Maybe I should have an affair," said Carla, who then fired her pistol into the gunnysacked hay. "I've been thinking: maybe you should, too."

Now Ruth fired her own gun, its great storm of sound filling her ears. An affair? The idea of taking her clothes off and being with someone who wasn't a medical specialist just seemed ridiculous. Pointless and terrifying. Why would people do it? "Having an affair is for the young," said Ruth. "It's like taking drugs or jumping off cliffs. Why would you want to jump off a cliff?"

"Oh," said Carla. "You obviously haven't seen some of the cliffs *I've* seen."

Ruth sighed. Perhaps, if she knew a man in town who was friendly and attractive, she might—what? What might she do? She felt the opposite of sexy. She felt busy, managerial, thirsty, crazy; everything, when you got right down to it, was the opposite of sexy. If she knew a man in town, she would—would go on a diet for him! But not Jenny Craig. She'd heard of someone who had died on Jenny Craig. If she had to go on a diet with a fake woman's name on it, she would go on the Betty Crocker diet, her own face ladled right in there with Betty's, in that fat red spoon. Yes, if she knew a man in town, perhaps she would let the excitement of knowing him seize the stem of her brain and energize her days. As long as it was only the stem; as long as the petals were left alone. She needed all her petals.

But she didn't know any men in town. Why didn't she know one?

In mid-June, the house he chose was an old former farmhouse in the middle of a subdivision. It was clearly being renovated— there were ladders and tarps in the yard—and in this careless presentation, it seemed an easy target. Music lovers! he thought. They go for renovation! Besides, in an old house there was always one back window that, having warped into a trape-zoid, had then been sanded and resanded and could be lifted off the frame like a lid. When he worked for the lawn company, he'd worked on many houses like these. Perhaps he'd even been here before, a month ago or so—he wasn't sure. Things looked different at night, and tonight the moon was not as bright as last time, less than full, like the face beneath a low slant hat, like a head scalped at the brow.

Noel looked at the couple. They had started singing "Chattanooga Choo-Choo." Lately, to save time, inspire the singers, and amuse himself, Noel had been requesting duets. "Wait a minute," he interrupted. "I wanna write this one down. I've just started to write these things down." And, like a fool, he left them to go into the next room to get a pen and a piece of paper.

"You have a sweet voice," the woman said when he returned. She was standing in front of the nightstand. He was smoothing a creased piece of paper against his chest. "A sweet speaking voice. You must sing well, too."

"Nah, I have a terrible voice," he said. He felt his shirt pocket for a pen. "I was always asked to be quiet when the other children sang. The music teacher in grade school always asked me just to move my lips. 'Glory in eggshell seas,' she would say. 'Just mouth that.' "

"No, no. Your voice is sweet. The timbre is sweet. I can hear it." She took a small step sideways. The man, the husband, stayed where he was. He was wearing a big red sweatshirt and no underwear. His penis hung beneath the shirt hem like a long jewel yam. *Ah, marriage.* The woman, thrusting her hands into the pockets of her nightgown, took another small step. "It's sweet, but with weight."

Noel thought he could hear some people outside calling a dog by clapping their hands. "Bravo," said the owner of the dog, or so it sounded. "Bravo."

"Well, thank you," said Noel, his eyes cast downward.

"Surely your mother must have told you that," she said, but he decided not to answer that one. He turned to write down the words to "Chattanooga Choo-Choo," and with the beginning of the tune edging into his head—*pardon me, boys*—something exploded in the room. Suddenly, he thought he felt the yearning heart of civilization in him, felt at last, oh, Nitchka, what human experience on this planet was all about: its hard fiery center, a quick rudeness in its force; he could feel it catching him, a surprise, like a nail to the brain. A dark violet then light washed over him. Everything went quiet. Music, he saw now, led you steadily into silence. You followed the thread of a song into a sudden sort of sleep. The white paper leapt up in a blinding flash, hot and sharp. The dresser edge caught his cheekbone in a gash, and he seemed no longer to be standing. His shoes slid along the rug. His hands reached up, then down again, then up along the dresser knobs, then flung themselves through the air and back against the floor. His brow, enclosing, then devouring his sight, finally settled dankly against his own sleeve.

Heat drained from his head, like a stone.

A police car pulled up quietly outside, with its lights turned off. There was some distant noise from geese on the pond.

There was no echo after the explosion. It was not like at the range. There had been just a click and a vibrating snap that had flown out before her toward the mask, and then the room roared and went silent, giving back nothing at all.

Terence gasped. "Good God," he said. "I suppose this is just what you've always wanted: a dead man on your bedroom floor."

"What do you mean by that? How can you say such a heartless thing?" Shouldn't her voice have had a quaver in it? Instead, it sounded flat and dry. "Forget being a decent man, Terence. Go for castability. Could you even play a decent man in a movie?"

"Did you have to be such a good shot?" Terence asked. He began to pace.

"I've been practicing," she said. Something immunological surged in her briefly like wine. For a minute, she felt restored and safe—safer than she had in years. How dare anyone come into her bedroom! How much was she expected to take? But then it all left her, wickedly, and she could again feel only her own abandonment and disease. She turned away from Terence and started to cry. "Oh, God, let me die," she finally said. "I am just so tired." Though she could hardly see, she knelt down next to the masked man and pressed his long, strange hands to her own small ones. They were not yet cold—no colder than her own. She thought she could feel herself begin to depart with him, the two of them rising together, translucent as jellyfish, leaving through the air, floating out into a night sky of singing and release, flying until they reached a bright, bright space-ship—a set of teeth on fire in the dark—and, absorbed into the larger light, were taken aboard for home. "And what on earth was all that?" she could hear them both say merrily of their lives, as if their lives were now just odd, noisy, and distant, as in fact they were.

"What have we here?" she heard someone say.

"Look for yourself, I guess," said someone else.

She touched the man's black knit mask. It was pilled with gray, like the dotted swiss of her premonitions, but it was askew, misaligned at the eyes—the soft turkey white of a cheekbone where the eye should be—and it was drenched with water and maroon. She could peel it off to see his face, see who he was, but she didn't dare. She tried to straighten the fabric, tried to find the eyes, then pulled it tightly down and turned away, wiping her hands on her nightgown. Without looking, she patted the dead man's arm. Then she turned and started out of the room. She went down the stairs and ran from the house.

Her crying now came in a stifled and parched way, and her hair fell into her mouth. Her chest ached and all her bones filled with a sharp pulsing. She was ill. She knew. Running barefoot across the lawn, she could feel some chaos in her gut—her intestines no longer curled neat and orderly as a French horn, but heaped carelessly upon one another like a box of vacuum-cleaner parts. The cancer, dismantling as it came, had begun its way back. She felt its poison, its tentacular reach and clutch, as a puppet feels a hand.

"Mitzy, my baby," she said in the dark. "Baby, come home."

Though she would have preferred long ago to have died, fled, gotten it all over with, the body—Jesus, how the body!—took its time. It possessed its own wishes and nostalgias. You could not just turn neatly into light and slip out the window. You couldn't go like that. Within one's own departing but stubborn flesh, there was only the long, sentimental, piecemeal farewell. *Sir? A towel. Is there a towel?* The body, hauling sadnesses, pursued the soul, hobbled after. The body was like a sweet, dim dog trotting lamely toward the gate as you tried slowly to drive off, out the long driveway. *Take me, take me, too,* barked the dog. *Don't go, don't go,* it said, running along the fence, almost keeping pace but not quite, its reflection a shrinking charm in the car mirrors as you trundled past the viburnum, past the pine grove, past the property line, past every last patch of land, straight down the swallowing road, disappearing and disappearing. Until at last it was true: you had disappeared.

PEOPLE LIKE THAT ARE THE ONLY PEOPLE HERE: CANONICAL BABBLING IN PEED ONK

A beginning, an end: there seems to be neither. The whole thing is like a cloud that just lands and everywhere inside it is full of rain. A start: the Mother finds a blood clot in the Baby's diaper. What is the story? Who put this here? It is big and bright, with a broken khaki-colored vein in it. Over the weekend, the Baby had looked listless and spacey, clayey and grim. But today he looks fine—so what is this thing, startling against the white diaper, like a tiny mouse heart packed in snow? Perhaps it belongs to someone else. Perhaps it is something menstrual, something belonging to the Mother or to the Babysitter, something the Baby has found in a wastebasket and for his own demented baby reasons stowed away here. (Babies: they're crazy! What can you do?) In her mind, the Mother takes this away from his body and attaches it to someone else's. There. Doesn't that make more sense?

.   .   .

Still, she phones the clinic at the children's hospital. "Blood in the diaper," she says, and, sounding alarmed and perplexed, the woman on the other end says, "Come in now."

Such pleasingly instant service! Just say "blood." Just say "diaper." Look what you get!

In the examination room, pediatrician, nurse, head resident—all seem less alarmed and perplexed than simply perplexed. At first, stupidly, the Mother is calmed by this. But soon, besides peering and saying "Hmmmm," the pediatrician, nurse, and head resident are all drawing their mouths in, bluish and tight—morning glories sensing noon. They fold their arms across their white-coated chests, unfold them again and jot things down. They order an ultrasound. Bladder and kidneys. "Here's the card. Go downstairs; turn left."

In Radiology, the Baby stands anxiously on the table, naked against the Mother as she holds him still against her legs and waist, the Radiologist's cold scanning disc moving about the Baby's back. The Baby whimpers, looks up at the Mother. *Let's get out of here,* his eyes beg. *Pick me up!* The Radiologist stops, freezes one of the many swirls of oceanic gray, and clicks repeatedly, a single moment within the long, cavernous weather map that is the Baby's insides.

"Are you finding something?" asks the Mother. Last year, her uncle Larry had had a kidney removed for something that turned out to be benign. These imaging machines! They are like dogs, or metal detectors: they find everything, but don't know what they've found. That's where the surgeons come in. They're like the owners of the dogs. "Give me that," they say to the dog. "What the heck is that?"

"The surgeon will speak to you," says the Radiologist.

"Are you finding something?"

"The surgeon will speak to you," the Radiologist says

again. "There seems to be something there, but the surgeon will talk to you about it."

"My uncle once had something on his kidney," says the Mother. "So they removed the kidney and it turned out the something was benign."

The Radiologist smiles a broad, ominous smile. "That's always the way it is," he says. "You don't know exactly what it is until it's in the bucket."

" 'In the bucket,' " the Mother repeats.

The Radiologist's grin grows scarily wider—is that even possible? "That's doctor talk," he says.

"It's very appealing," says the Mother. "It's a very appealing way to talk." Swirls of bile and blood, mustard and maroon in a pail, the colors of an African flag or some exuberant salad bar: *in the bucket*—she imagines it all.

"The Surgeon will see you soon," he says again. He tousles the Baby's ringletty hair. "Cute kid," he says.

"Let's see now," says the Surgeon in one of his examining rooms. He has stepped in, then stepped out, then come back in again. He has crisp, frowning features, sharp bones, and a tennis-in-Bermuda tan. He crosses his blue-cottoned legs. He is wearing clogs.

The Mother knows her own face is a big white dumpling of worry. She is still wearing her long, dark parka, holding the Baby, who has pulled the hood up over her head because he always thinks it's funny to do that. Though on certain windy mornings she would like to think she could look vaguely romantic like this, like some French Lieutenant's Woman of the Prairie, in all of her saner moments she knows she doesn't. Ever. She knows she looks ridiculous—like one of those animals made out of twisted party balloons. She lowers the hood and slips one arm out of the sleeve. The Baby wants to get up and play with the light switch. He fidgets, fusses, and points.

"He's big on lights these days," explains the Mother.

"That's okay," says the Surgeon, nodding toward the light switch. "Let him play with it." The Mother goes and stands by it, and the Baby begins turning the lights off and on, off and on.

"What we have here is a Wilms' tumor," says the Surgeon, suddenly plunged into darkness. He says "tumor" as if it were the most normal thing in the world.

"Wilms'?" repeats the Mother. The room is quickly on fire again with light, then wiped dark again. Among the three of them here, there is a long silence, as if it were suddenly the middle of the night. "Is that apostrophe *s* or *s* apostrophe?" the Mother says finally. She is a writer and a teacher. Spelling can be important—perhaps even at a time like this, though she has never before been at a time like this, so there are barbarisms she could easily commit and not know.

The lights come on: the world is doused and exposed.

"*S* apostrophe," says the Surgeon. "I think." The lights go back out, but the Surgeon continues speaking in the dark. "A malignant tumor on the left kidney."

Wait a minute. Hold on here. The Baby is only a baby, fed on organic applesauce and soy milk—a little prince!—and he was standing so close to her during the ultrasound. How could he have this terrible thing? It must have been *her* kidney. A fifties kidney. A DDT kidney. The Mother clears her throat. "Is it possible it was my kidney on the scan? I mean, I've never heard of a baby with a tumor, and, frankly, I was standing very close." She would make the blood hers, the tumor hers; it would all be some treacherous, farcical mistake.

"No, that's not possible," says the Surgeon. The light goes back on.

"It's not?" says the Mother. Wait until it's *in the bucket,* she thinks. Don't be so sure. *Do we have to wait until it's in the bucket to find out a mistake has been made?*

"We will start with a radical nephrectomy," says the Surgeon, instantly thrown into darkness again. His voice comes from nowhere and everywhere at once. "And then we'll begin with chemotherapy after that. These tumors usually respond very well to chemo."

"I've never heard of a baby having chemo," the Mother says. *Baby* and *Chemo,* she thinks: they should never even appear in the same sentence together, let alone the same life. In her other life, her life before this day, she had been a believer in alternative medicine. Chemotherapy? Unthinkable. Now, suddenly, alternative medicine seems the wacko maiden aunt to the Nice Big Daddy of Conventional Treatment. How quickly the old girl faints and gives way, leaves one just standing there. Chemo? Of course: chemo! Why by all means: chemo. Absolutely! Chemo!

The Baby flicks the switch back on, and the walls reappear, big wedges of light checkered with small framed watercolors of the local lake. The Mother has begun to cry: all of life has led her here, to this moment. After this, there is no more life. There is something else, something stumbling and unlivable, something mechanical, something for robots, but not life. Life has been taken and broken, quickly, like a stick. The room goes dark again, so that the Mother can cry more freely. How can a baby's body be stolen so fast? How much can one heaven-sent and unsuspecting child endure? Why has he not been spared this inconceivable fate?

Perhaps, she thinks, she is being punished: too many baby-sitters too early on. ("Come to Mommy! Come to Mommy-Baby-sitter!" she used to say. But it was a joke!) Her life, perhaps, bore too openly the marks and wigs of deepest drag. Her unmotherly thoughts had all been noted: the panicky hope that his nap would last longer than it did; her occasional desire to kiss him passionately on the mouth (to make out with her baby!); her ongoing complaints about the very vocabulary of motherhood, how it degraded the speaker ("Is this a poopie onesie! Yes, it's a very poopie onesie!"). She had, moreover, on three occasions used the formula bottles as flower vases. She twice let the Baby's ears get fudgy with wax. A few afternoons last month, at snacktime, she placed a bowl of Cheerios on the floor for him to eat, like a dog. She let him play with the Dustbuster. Just once, before he was born, she said, "Healthy? I just want the kid to be rich." A joke, for God's sake! After he was born she announced that her life had become a daily sequence of mind-wrecking chores, the same ones over and over again, like a novel by Mrs. Camus. Another joke! These jokes will kill you! She had told too often, and with too much enjoyment, the story of how the Baby had said "Hi" to his high chair, waved at the lake waves, shouted "Goody-goody-goody" in what seemed to be a Russian accent, pointed at his eyes and said "Ice." And all that nonsensical baby talk: wasn't it a stitch? "Canonical babbling," the language experts called it. He recounted whole stories in it—totally made up, she could tell. He embroidered; he fished; he exaggerated. What a card! To friends, she spoke of his eating habits (carrots yes, tuna no). She mentioned, too much, his sidesplitting giggle. Did she have to be so boring? Did she have no consideration for others, for the intellectual demands and courtesies of human society? Would she not even attempt to be more interesting? It was a crime against the human mind not even to try.

Now her baby, for all these reasons—lack of motherly gratitude, motherly judgment, motherly proportion—will be taken away.

The room is fluorescently ablaze again. The Mother digs around in her parka pocket and comes up with a Kleenex. It is old and thin, like a mashed flower saved from a dance; she dabs it at her eyes and nose.

"The Baby won't suffer as much as you," says the Surgeon.

And who can contradict? Not the Baby, who in his Slavic Betty Boop voice can say only *mama, dada, cheese, ice, bye-bye, outside, boogie-boogie, goody-goody, eddy-eddy,* and *car.* (Who is Eddy? They have no idea.) This will not suffice to express his mortal suffering. Who can say what babies do with their agony and shock? Not they themselves. (Baby talk: isn't it a stitch?) They put it all no place anyone can really see. They are like a different race, a different species: they seem not to experience pain the way *we* do. Yeah, that's it: their nervous systems are not as fully formed, and *they just don't experience pain the way we do.* A tune to keep one humming through the war. "You'll get through it," the Surgeon says.

"How?" asks the Mother. "How does one get through it?"

"You just put your head down and go," says the Surgeon. He picks up his file folder. He is a skilled manual laborer. The tricky emotional stuff is not to his liking. The babies. The babies! What can be said to console the parents about the babies? "I'll go phone the oncologist on duty to let him know," he says, and leaves the room.

"Come here, sweetie," the Mother says to the Baby, who has toddled off toward a gum wrapper on the floor. "We've got to put your jacket on." She picks him up and he reaches for the light switch again. Light, dark. Peekaboo: where's baby? Where did baby go?

At home, she leaves a message—"Urgent! Call me!"—for the Husband on his voice mail. Then she takes the Baby upstairs for his nap, rocks him in the rocker. The Baby waves good-bye to his little bears, then looks toward the window and says, "Bye-bye, outside." He has, lately, the habit of waving good-bye to everything, and now it seems as if he senses an imminent departure, and it breaks her heart to hear him. *Bye-bye!* She sings low and monotonously, like a small appliance, which is how he likes it. He is drowsy, dozy, drifting off. He has grown so much in the last year, he hardly fits in her lap anymore; his limbs dangle off like a pietà. His head rolls slightly inside the crook of her arm. She can feel him falling backward into sleep, his mouth round and open like the sweetest of poppies. All the lullabies in the world, all the melodies threaded through with maternal melancholy now become for her—abandoned as a mother can be by working men and napping babies—the songs of hard, hard grief. Sitting there, bowed and bobbing, the Mother feels the entirety of her love as worry and heartbreak. A quick and irrevocable alchemy: there is no longer one unworried scrap left for happiness. "If you go," she keens low into his soapy neck, into the ranunculus coil of his ear, "we are going with you. We are nothing without you. Without you, we are a heap of rocks. We are gravel and mold. Without you, we are two stumps, with nothing any longer in our hearts. Wherever this takes you, we are following. We will be there. Don't be scared. We are going, too. That is that."

"Take Notes," says the Husband, after coming straight home from work, midafternoon, hearing the news, and saying all the words out loud—*surgery, metastasis, dialysis, transplant*—then collapsing in a chair in tears. "Take notes. We are going to need the money."

"Good God," cries the Mother. Everything inside her suddenly begins to cower and shrink, a thinning of bones. Perhaps this is a soldier's readiness, but it has the whiff of death and defeat. It feels like a heart attack, a failure of will and courage, a power failure: a failure of everything. Her face, when she glimpses it in a mirror, is cold and bloated with shock, her eyes scarlet and shrunk. She has already started to wear sunglasses indoors, like a celebrity widow. From where will her own strength come? From some philosophy? From some frigid little philosophy? She is neither stalwart nor realistic and has trouble with basic concepts, such as the one that says events move in one direction only and do not jump up, turn around, and take themselves back.

The Husband begins too many of his sentences with "What if." He is trying to piece everything together like a train wreck. He is trying to get the train to town.

"We'll just take all the steps, move through all the stages. We'll go where we have to go. We'll hunt; we'll find; we'll pay what we have to pay. What if we can't pay?"

"Sounds like shopping."

"I cannot believe this is happening to our little boy," he says, and starts to sob again. "Why didn't it happen to one of us? It's so unfair. Just last week, my doctor declared me in perfect health: the prostate of a twenty-year-old, the heart of a ten-year-old, the brain of an insect—or whatever it was he said. What a nightmare this is."

What words can be uttered? You turn just slightly and there it is: the death of your child. It is part symbol, part devil, and in your blind spot all along, until, if you are unlucky, it is completely upon you. Then it is a fierce little country abducting you; it holds you squarely inside itself like a cellar room—the best boundaries of you are the boundaries of it. Are there windows? Sometimes aren't there windows?

The Mother is not a shopper. She hates to shop, is generally bad at it, though she does like a good sale. She cannot stroll meaningfully through anger, denial, grief, and acceptance. She goes straight to bargaining and stays there. How much? she calls out to the ceiling, to some makeshift construction of holiness she has desperately, though not uncreatively, assembled in her mind and prayed to; a doubter, never before given to prayer, she must now reap what she has not sown; she must assemble from scratch an entire altar of worship and begging. She tries for noble abstractions, nothing too anthropomorphic, just some Higher Morality, though if this particular Highness looks something like the manager at Marshall Field's, sucking a Frango mint, so be it. Amen. Just tell me what you want, requests the Mother. And how do you want it? More charitable acts? A billion starting now. Charitable thoughts? Harder, but of course! Of course! I'll do the cooking, honey; I'll pay the rent. Just tell me. *Excuse me?* Well, if not to you, to whom do I speak? Hello? To whom do I have to speak around here? A higher-up? A superior? Wait? I can wait. I've got all day. I've got the whole damn day.

The Husband now lies next to her in bed, sighing. "Poor little guy could survive all this, only to be killed in a car crash at the age of sixteen," he says.

The wife, bargaining, considers this. "We'll take the car crash," she says.

"What?"

"Let's Make a Deal! Sixteen Is a Full Life! We'll take the car crash. We'll take the car crash, in front of which Carol Merrill is now standing."

Now the Manager of Marshall Field's reappears. "To take the surprises out is to take the life out of life," he says.

The phone rings. The Husband gets up and leaves the room.

"But I don't want these surprises," says the Mother. "Here! You take these surprises!"

"To know the narrative in advance is to turn yourself into a machine," the Manager continues. "What makes humans human is precisely that they do not know the future. That is why they do the fateful and amusing things they do: who can say how anything will turn out? Therein lies the only hope for redemption, discovery, and—let's be frank—fun, fun, fun! There might be things people will get away with. And not just motel towels. There might be great illicit loves, enduring joy, faith-shaking accidents with farm machinery. But you have to not know in order to see what stories your life's efforts bring you. The mystery is all."

The Mother, though shy, has grown confrontational. "Is this the kind of bogus, random crap they teach at merchandising school? We would like fewer surprises, fewer efforts and mysteries, thank you. K through eight; can we just get K through eight?" It now seems like the luckiest, most beautiful, most musical phrase she's ever heard: K through eight. The very lilt. The very thought.

The Manager continues, trying things out. "I mean, the whole conception of 'the story,' of cause and effect, the whole idea that people have a clue as to how the world works is just a piece of laughable metaphysical colonialism perpetrated upon the wild country of time."

Did they own a gun? The Mother begins looking through drawers.

The Husband comes back into the room and observes her. "Ha! The Great Havoc that is the Puzzle of all Life!" he says of the Marshall Field's management policy. He has just gotten off a conference call with the insurance company and the hospital. The surgery will be Friday. "It's all just some dirty capitalist's idea of a philosophy."

"Maybe it's just a fact of narrative and you really can't politicize it," says the Mother. It is now only the two of them.

"Whose side are you on?"

"I'm on the Baby's side."

"Are you taking notes for this?"

"No."

"You're not?"

"No. I can't. Not this! I write fiction. This isn't fiction."

"Then write nonfiction. Do a piece of journalism. Get two dollars a word."

"Then it has to be true and full of information. I'm not trained. I'm not that skilled. Plus, I have a convenient personal principle about artists not abandoning art. One should never turn one's back on a vivid imagination. Even the whole memoir thing annoys me."

"Well, make things up, but pretend they're real."

"I'm not that insured."

"You're making me nervous."

"Sweetie, darling, I'm not that good. I can't *do this*. I can do—what can I do? I can do quasi-amusing phone dialogue. I can do succinct descriptions of weather. I can do screwball outings with the family pet. Sometimes I can do those. Honey, I only do what I can. I do *the careful ironies of daydream*. I do *the marshy ideas upon which intimate life is built*. But this? Our baby with cancer? I'm sorry. My stop was two stations back. This is irony at its most gaudy and careless. This is a Hieronymus Bosch of facts and figures and blood and graphs. This is a nightmare of narrative slop. This cannot be designed. This cannot even be noted in preparation for a design—"

"We're going to need the money."

"To say nothing of the moral boundaries of pecuniary recompense in a situation such as this—"

"What if the other kidney goes? What if he needs a transplant? Where are the moral boundaries there? What are we going to do, have bake sales?"

"We can sell the house. I hate this house. It makes me crazy."

"And we'll live—where again?"

"The Ronald McDonald place. I hear it's nice. It's the least McDonald's can do."

"You have a keen sense of justice."

"I try. What can I say?" She pauses. "Is all this really happening? I keep thinking that soon it will be over—the life expectancy of a cloud is supposed to be only twelve hours—and then I realize something has occurred that can never ever be over."

The Husband buries his face in his hands: "Our poor baby. How did this happen to him?" He looks over and stares at the bookcase that serves as the nightstand. "And do you think even one of these baby books is any help?" He picks up the Leach, the Spock, the *What to Expect*. "Where in the pages or index of any of these does it say 'chemotherapy' or 'Hickman catheter' or 'renal sarcoma'? Where does it say 'carcinogenesis'? You know what these books are obsessed with? *Holding a fucking spoon.*" He begins hurling the books off the night table and against the far wall.

"Hey," says the Mother, trying to soothe. "Hey, hey, hey." But compared to his stormy roar, her words are those of a backup singer—a Shondell, a Pip—a doo-wop ditty. Books, and now more books, continue to fly.

Take Notes.

Is *fainthearted* one word or two? Student prose has wrecked her spelling.

It's one word. Two words—*Faint Hearted*—what would that be? The name of a drag queen.

Take Notes. In the end, you suffer alone. But at the beginning you suffer with a whole lot of others. When your child has cancer, you are instantly whisked away to another planet: one of bald-headed little boys. Pediatric Oncology. Peed Onk. You wash your hands for thirty seconds in antibacterial soap before you are allowed to enter through the swinging doors. You put paper slippers on your shoes. You keep your voice down. A whole place has been designed and decorated for your nightmare. Here is where your nightmare will occur. We've got a room all ready for you. We have cots. We have refrigerators. "The children are almost entirely boys," says one of the nurses. "No one knows why. It's been documented, but a lot of people out there still don't realize it." The little boys are all from sweet-sounding places—Janesville and Appleton—little heartland towns with giant landfills, agricultural runoff, paper factories, Joe McCarthy's grave (Alone, a site of great toxicity, thinks the Mother. The soil should be tested).

All the bald little boys look like brothers. They wheel their

IVs up and down the single corridor of Peed Onk. Some of the
lively ones, feeling good for a day, ride the lower bars of the IV
while their large, cheerful mothers whiz them along the halls.
Wheee!

The Mother does not feel large and cheerful. In her mind, she is
scathing, acid-tongued, wraith-thin, and chain-smoking out on
a fire escape somewhere. Beneath her lie the gentle undulations
of the Midwest, with all its aspirations to be—to be what? To
be Long Island. How it has succeeded! Strip mall upon strip
mall. Lurid water, poisoned potatoes. The Mother drags deeply,
blowing clouds of smoke out over the disfigured cornfields.
When a baby gets cancer, it seems stupid ever to have given up
smoking. When a baby gets cancer, you think, Whom are we
kidding? Let's all light up. When a baby gets cancer, you think,
Who came up with *this* idea? What celestial abandon gave rise
to *this*? Pour me a drink, so I can refuse to toast.

   The Mother does not know how to be one of these other
mothers, with their blond hair and sweatpants and sneakers and
determined pleasantness. She does not think that she can be
anything similar. She does not feel remotely like them. She
knows, for instance, too many people in Greenwich Village. She
mail-orders oysters and tiramisu from a shop in SoHo. She is
close friends with four actual homosexuals. Her husband is asking her to Take Notes.

   Where do these women get their sweatpants? She will find
out.

   She will start, perhaps, with the costume and work from
there.

   She will live according to the bromides. Take one day at a
time. Take a positive attitude. *Take a hike!* She wishes that
there were more interesting things that were useful and true,
but it seems now that it's only the boring things that are useful
and true. *One day at a time.* And *at least we have our health.* How

ordinary. How obvious. One day at a time. You need a brain for that?

While the Surgeon is fine-boned, regal, and laconic—they have correctly guessed his game to be doubles—there is a bit of the mad, overcaffeinated scientist to the Oncologist. He speaks quickly. He knows a lot of studies and numbers. He can do the math. Good! Someone should be able to do the math! "It's a fast but wimpy tumor," he explains. "It typically metastasizes to the lung." He rattles off some numbers, time frames, risk statistics. Fast but wimpy: the Mother tries to imagine this combination of traits, tries to think and think, and can only come up with Claudia Osk from the fourth grade, who blushed and almost wept when called on in class, but in gym could outrun everyone in the quarter-mile fire-door-to-fence dash. The Mother thinks now of this tumor as Claudia Osk. They are going to get Claudia Osk, make her sorry. All right! Claudia Osk must die. Though it has never been mentioned before, it now seems clear that Claudia Osk should have died long ago. Who was she anyway? So conceited: not letting anyone beat her in a race. Well, hey, hey, hey: don't look now, Claudia!

The Husband nudges her. "Are you listening?"

"The chances of this happening even just to one kidney are one in fifteen thousand. Now given all these other factors, the chances on the second kidney are about one in eight."

"One in eight," says the Husband. "Not bad. As long as it's not one in fifteen thousand."

The Mother studies the trees and fish along the ceiling's edge in the Save the Planet wallpaper border. Save the Planet. Yes! But the windows in this very building don't open and diesel fumes are leaking into the ventilating system, near which, outside, a delivery truck is parked. The air is nauseous and stale.

"Really," the Oncologist is saying, "of all the cancers he could get, this is probably the best."

"We win," says the Mother.

"*Best,* I know, hardly seems the right word. Look, you two probably need to get some rest. We'll see how the surgery and histology go. Then we'll start with chemo the week following. A little light chemo: vincristine and—"

"Vincristine?" interrupts the Mother. "Wine of Christ?"

"The names are strange, I know. The other one we use is actinomycin-D. Sometimes called 'dactinomycin.' People move the *D* around to the front."

"They move the *D* around to the front," repeats the Mother.

"Yup!" the Oncologist says. "I don't know why—they just do!"

"Christ didn't survive his wine," says the Husband.

"But of course he did," says the Oncologist, and nods toward the Baby, who has now found a cupboard full of hospital linens and bandages and is yanking them all out onto the floor. "I'll see you guys tomorrow, after the surgery." And with that, the Oncologist leaves.

"Or, rather, Christ *was* his wine," mumbles the Husband. Everything he knows about the New Testament, he has gleaned from the sound track of *Godspell.* "His blood was the wine. What a great beverage idea."

"A little light chemo. Don't you like that one?" says the Mother. "*Eine kleine* dactinomycin. I'd like to see Mozart write that one up for a big wad o' cash."

"Come here, honey," the Husband says to the Baby, who has now pulled off both his shoes.

"It's bad enough when they refer to medical science as 'an inexact science,'" says the Mother. "But when they start referring to it as 'an art,' I get extremely nervous."

"Yeah. If we wanted art, Doc, we'd go to an art museum." The Husband picks up the Baby. "You're an artist," he says to the Mother, with the taint of accusation in his voice. "They probably think you find creativity reassuring."

The Mother sighs. "I just find it inevitable. Let's go get something to eat." And so they take the elevator to the cafeteria, where there is a high chair, and where, not noticing, they all eat a lot of apples with the price tags still on them.

Because his surgery is not until tomorrow, the Baby likes the hospital. He likes the long corridors, down which he can run. He likes everything on wheels. The flower carts in the lobby! ("Please keep your boy away from the flowers," says the vendor. "We'll buy the whole display," snaps the Mother, adding, "Actual children in a children's hospital—unbelievable, isn't it?") The Baby likes the other little boys. Places to go! People to see! Rooms to wander into! There is Intensive Care. There is the Trauma Unit. The Baby smiles and waves. What a little Cancer Personality! Bandaged citizens smile and wave back. In Peed Onk, there are the bald little boys to play with. Joey, Eric, Tim, Mort, and Tod (Mort! Tod!). There is the four-year-old, Ned, holding his little deflated rubber ball, the one with the intriguing curling hose. The Baby wants to play with it. "It's mine. Leave it alone," says Ned. "Tell the Baby to leave it alone."

"Baby, you've got to share," says the Mother from a chair some feet away.

Suddenly, from down near the Tiny Tim Lounge, comes Ned's mother, large and blond and sweatpanted. "Stop that! Stop it!" she cries out, dashing toward the Baby and Ned and pushing the Baby away. "Don't touch that!" she barks at the Baby, who is only a Baby and bursts into tears because he has never been yelled at like this before.

Ned's mom glares at everyone. "This is drawing fluid from Neddy's liver!" She pats at the rubber thing and starts to cry a little.

"Oh my God," says the Mother. She comforts the Baby, who is also crying. She and Ned, the only dry-eyed people, look at each other. "I'm so sorry," she says to Ned and then to his mother. "I'm so stupid. I thought they were squabbling over a toy."

"It does look like a toy," agrees Ned. He smiles. He is an angel. All the little boys are angels. Total, sweet, bald little angels, and now God is trying to get them back for himself. Who are they, mere mortal women, in the face of this, this powerful and overwhelming and inscrutable thing, God's will? They are the mothers, that's who. You can't have him! they shout every day. You dirty old man! *Get out of here! Hands off!*

"I'm so sorry," says the Mother again. "I didn't know."

Ned's mother smiles vaguely. "Of course you didn't know," she says, and walks back to the Tiny Tim Lounge.

The Tiny Tim Lounge is a little sitting area at the end of the Peed Onk corridor. There are two small sofas, a table, a rocking chair, a television and a VCR. There are various videos: *Speed*, *Dune*, and *Star Wars*. On one of the lounge walls there is a gold plaque with the singer Tiny Tim's name on it: his son was treated once at this hospital and so, five years ago, he donated money for this lounge. It is a cramped little lounge, which, one suspects, would be larger if Tiny Tim's son had actually lived. Instead, he died here, at this hospital and now there is this tiny room which is part gratitude, part generosity, part *fuck-you*.

Sifting through the videocassettes, the Mother wonders what science fiction could begin to compete with the science fiction of cancer itself—a tumor with its differentiated muscle and bone cells, a clump of wild nothing and its mad, ambitious desire to be something: something inside you, instead of you, another organism, but with a monster's architecture, a demon's sabotage and chaos. Think of leukemia, a tumor diabolically taking liquid form, better to swim about incognito in the blood. George Lucas, direct that!

Sitting with the other parents in the Tiny Tim Lounge, the night before the surgery, having put the Baby to bed in his high steel crib two rooms down, the Mother begins to hear the stories: leukemia in kindergarten, sarcomas in Little League, neuroblastomas discovered at summer camp. "Eric slid into third base, but then the scrape didn't heal." The parents pat one another's forearms and speak of other children's hospitals as if they were resorts. "You were at St. Jude's last winter? So were we. What did you think of it? We loved the staff." Jobs have been quit, marriages hacked up, bank accounts ravaged; the parents have seemingly endured the unendurable. They speak not of the *possibility* of comas brought on by the chemo, but of the *number* of them. "He was in his first coma last July," says Ned's mother. "It was a scary time, but we pulled through."

Pulling through is what people do around here. There is a kind of bravery in their lives that isn't bravery at all. It is automatic, unflinching, a mix of man and machine, consuming and unquestionable obligation meeting illness move for move in a giant even-steven game of chess—an unending round of something that looks like shadowboxing, though between love and death, which is the shadow? "Everyone admires us for our courage," says one man. "They have no idea what they're talking about."

I could get out of here, thinks the Mother. I could just get on a bus and go, never come back. Change my name. A kind of witness relocation thing.

"Courage requires options," the man adds.

The Baby might be better off.

"There are options," says a woman with a thick suede headband. "You could give up. You could fall apart."

"No, you can't. Nobody does. I've never seen it," says the man. "Well, not *really* fall apart." Then the lounge falls quiet. Over the VCR someone has taped the fortune from a fortune cookie. "Optimism," it says, "is what allows a teakettle to sing though up to its neck in hot water." Underneath, someone else has taped a clipping from a summer horoscope. "Cancer rules!" it says. Who would tape this up? Somebody's twelve-year-old brother. One of the fathers—Joey's father—gets up and tears them both off, makes a small wad in his fist.

There is some rustling of magazine pages.

The Mother clears her throat. "Tiny Tim forgot the wet bar," she says.

Ned, who is still up, comes out of his room and down the corridor, whose lights dim at nine. Standing next to her chair, he says to the Mother, "Where are you from? What is wrong with your baby?"

In the tiny room that is theirs, she sleeps fitfully in her sweat-pants, occasionally leaping up to check on the Baby. This is what the sweatpants are for: leaping. In case of fire. In case of anything. In case the difference between day and night starts to dissolve, and there is no difference at all, so why pretend? In the cot beside her, the Husband, who has taken a sleeping pill, is snoring loudly, his arms folded about his head in a kind of origami. How could either of them have stayed back at the house, with its empty high chair and empty crib? Occasionally the Baby wakes and cries out, and she bolts up, goes to him, rubs his back, rearranges the linens. The clock on the metal dresser shows that it is five after three. Then twenty to five. And then it is really morning, the beginning of this day, nephrec-tomy day. Will she be glad when it's over, or barely alive, or both? Each day this week has arrived huge, empty, and unknown, like a spaceship, and this one especially is lit a bright gray.

"He'll need to put this on," says John, one of the nurses, bright and early, handing the Mother a thin greenish garment with roses and teddy bears printed on it. A wave of nausea hits her; this smock, she thinks, will soon be splattered with—with what?

The Baby is awake but drowsy. She lifts off his pajamas. "Don't forget, *bubeleh*," she whispers, undressing and dressing him. "We will be with you every moment, every step. When you think you are asleep and floating off far away from everybody, Mommy will still be there." If she hasn't fled on a bus. "Mommy will take care of you. And Daddy, too." She hopes the Baby does not detect her own fear and uncertainty, which she must hide from him, like a limp. He is hungry, not having been allowed to eat, and he is no longer amused by this new place, but worried about its hardships. Oh, my baby, she thinks. And the room starts to swim a little. The Husband comes in to take over. "Take a break," he says to her. "I'll walk him around for five minutes."

She leaves but doesn't know where to go. In the hallway, she is approached by a kind of social worker, a customer-relations person, who had given them a video to watch about the anesthesia: how the parent accompanies the child into the operating room, and how gently, nicely the drugs are administered.

"Did you watch the video?"

"Yes," says the Mother.

"Wasn't it helpful?"

"I don't know," says the Mother.

"Do you have any questions?" asks the video woman. "Do you have any questions?" asked of someone who has recently landed in this fearful, alien place seems to the Mother an absurd and amazing little courtesy. The very specificity of a question would give a lie to the overwhelming strangeness of everything around her.

"Not right now," says the Mother. "Right now, I think I'm just going to go to the bathroom."

When she returns to the Baby's room, everyone is there: the surgeon, the anesthesiologist, all the nurses, the social worker.

In their blue caps and scrubs, they look like a clutch of forget-me-nots, and forget them, who could? The Baby, in his little teddy-bear smock, seems cold and scared. He reaches out and the Mother lifts him from the Husband's arms, rubs his back to warm him.

"Well, it's time!" says the Surgeon, forcing a smile.

"Shall we go?" says the Anesthesiologist.

What follows is a blur of obedience and bright lights. They take an elevator down to a big concrete room, the anteroom, the greenroom, the backstage of the operating room. Lining the walls are long shelves full of blue surgical outfits. "Children often become afraid of the color blue," says one of the nurses. But of course. Of course! "Now, which one of you would like to come into the operating room for the anesthesia?"

"I will," says the Mother.

"Are you sure?" asks the Husband.

"Yup." She kisses the Baby's hair. "Mr. Curlyhead," people keep calling him here, and it seems both rude and nice. Women look admiringly at his long lashes and exclaim, "Always the boys! Always the boys!"

Two surgical nurses put a blue smock and a blue cotton cap on the Mother. The Baby finds this funny and keeps pulling at the cap. "This way," says another nurse, and the Mother follows. "Just put the Baby down on the table."

In the video, the mother holds the baby and fumes are gently waved under the baby's nose until he falls asleep. Now, out of view of camera or social worker, the Anesthesiologist is anxious to get this under way and not let too much gas leak out into the room generally. The occupational hazard of this, his chosen profession, is gas exposure and nerve damage, and it has started to worry him. No doubt he frets about it to his wife every night. Now he turns the gas on and quickly clamps the plastic mouthpiece over the baby's cheeks and lips.

The Baby is startled. The Mother is startled. The Baby starts to scream and redden behind the plastic, but he cannot be heard. He thrashes. "Tell him it's okay," says the nurse to the Mother.

Okay? "It's okay," repeats the Mother, holding his hand, but she knows he can tell it's not okay, because he can see not only that she is still wearing that stupid paper cap but that her words are mechanical and swallowed, and she is biting her lips to keep them from trembling. Panicked, he attempts to sit. He cannot breathe; his arms reach up. *Bye-bye, outside.* And then, quite quickly, his eyes shut; he untenses and has fallen not *into* sleep but aside to sleep, an odd, kidnapping kind of sleep, his terror now hidden someplace deep inside him.

"How did it go?" asks the social worker, waiting in the concrete outer room. The Mother is hysterical. A nurse has ushered her out.

"It wasn't at all like the filmstrip!" she cries. "It wasn't like the filmstrip at all!"

"The filmstrip? You mean the video?" asks the social worker.

"It wasn't like that at all! It was brutal and unforgivable."

"Why that's terrible," she says, her role now no longer misinformational but janitorial, and she touches the Mother's arm, though the Mother shakes it off and goes to find the Husband.

She finds him in the large mulberry Surgery Lounge, where he has been taken and where there is free hot chocolate in small Styrofoam cups. Red cellophane garlands festoon the doorways. She has totally forgotten it is as close to Christmas as this. A pianist in the corner is playing "Carol of the Bells," and it sounds not only unfestive but scary, like the theme from *The Exorcist.*

There is a giant clock on the far wall. It is a kind of porthole into the operating room, a way of assessing the Baby's ordeal: forty-five minutes for the Hickman implant; two and a half hours for the nephrectomy. And then, after that, three months of chemotherapy. The magazine on her lap stays open at a ruby-hued perfume ad.

"Still not taking notes," says the Husband.

"Nope."

"You know, in a way, this is the kind of thing you've *always* written about."

"You are really something, you know that? This is life. This isn't a 'kind of thing.' "

"But this is the kind of thing that fiction is: it's the unlivable life, the strange room tacked onto the house, the extra moon that is circling the earth unbeknownst to science."

"I told you that."

"I'm quoting you."

She looks at her watch, thinking of the Baby. "How long has it been?"

"Not long. Too long. In the end, maybe those're the same things."

"What do you suppose is happening to him right this second?"

Infection? Slipping knives? "I don't know. But you know what? I've gotta go. I've gotta just walk a bit." The Husband gets up, walks around the lounge, then comes back and sits down.

The synapses between the minutes are unswimmable. An hour is thick as fudge. The Mother feels depleted; she is a string of empty tin cans attached by wire, something a goat would sniff and chew, something now and then enlivened by a jolt of electricity.

She hears their names being called over the intercom. "Yes? Yes?" She stands up quickly. Her words have flown out before her, an exhalation of birds. The piano music has stopped. The pianist is gone. She and the Husband approach the main desk, where a man looks up at them and smiles. Before him is a xeroxed list of patients' names. "That's our little boy right there," says the Mother, seeing the Baby's name on the list and pointing at it. "Is there some word? Is everything okay?"

"Yes," says the man. "Your boy is doing fine. They've just finished with the catheter, and they are moving on to the kidney."

"But it's been two hours already! Oh my God, did something go wrong? What happened? What went wrong?"

"Did something go wrong?" The Husband tugs at his collar.

"Not really. It just took longer than they expected. I'm told everything is fine. They wanted you to know."

"Thank you," says the Husband. They turn and walk back toward where they were sitting.

"I'm not going to make it." The Mother sighs, sinking into a fake leather chair shaped somewhat like a baseball mitt. "But before I go, I'm taking half this hospital out with me."

"Do you want some coffee?" asks the Husband.

"I don't know," says the Mother. "No, I guess not. No. Do you?"

"Nah, I don't, either, I guess," he says.

"Would you like part of an orange?"

"Oh, maybe, I guess, if you're having one." She takes an orange from her purse and just sits there peeling its difficult skin, the flesh rupturing beneath her fingers, the juice trickling down her hands, stinging the hangnails. She and the Husband chew and swallow, discreetly spit the seeds into Kleenex, and read from photocopies of the latest medical research, which they begged from the intern. They read, and underline, and sigh and close their eyes, and after some time, the surgery is over. A nurse from Peed Onk comes down to tell them.

"Your little boy's in recovery right now. He's doing well. You can see him in about fifteen minutes."

. . .

How can it be described? How can any of it be described? The trip and the story of the trip are always two different things. The narrator is the one who has stayed home, but then, afterward, presses her mouth upon the traveler's mouth, in order to make the mouth work, to make the mouth say, say, say. One cannot go to a place and speak of it; one cannot both see and say, not really. One can go, and upon returning make a lot of hand motions and indications with the arms. The mouth itself, working at the speed of light, at the eye's instructions, is necessarily struck still; so fast, so much to report, it hangs open and dumb as a gutted bell. All that unsayable life! That's where the narrator comes in. The narrator comes with her kisses and mimicry and tidying up. The narrator comes and makes a slow, fake song of the mouth's eager devastation.

It is a horror and a miracle to see him. He is lying in his crib in his room, tubed up, splayed like a boy on a cross, his arms stiffened into cardboard "no-no's" so that he cannot yank out the tubes. There is the bladder catheter, the nasal-gastric tube, and the Hickman, which, beneath the skin, is plugged into his jugular, then popped out his chest wall and capped with a long plastic cap. There is a large bandage taped over his abdomen. Groggy, on a morphine drip, still he is able to look at her when, maneuvering through all the vinyl wiring, she leans to hold him, and when she does, he begins to cry, but cry silently, without motion or noise. She has never seen a baby cry without motion or noise. It is the crying of an old person: silent, beyond opinion, shattered. In someone so tiny, it is frightening and unnatural. She wants to pick up the Baby and run—out of there, out of there. She wants to whip out a gun: *No-no's, eh? This whole thing is what I call a no-no.* Don't you touch him! she wants to shout at the surgeons and the needle nurses. Not anymore! No more! No more! She would crawl up and lie beside him in the crib if she could. But instead, because of all his intricate wiring, she must lean and cuddle, sing to him, songs of peril and flight: "We gotta get out of this place, if it's the last thing we ever do. We gotta get out of this place . . . there's a better life for me and you."

Very 1967. She was eleven then and impressionable.

The Baby looks at her, pleadingly, his arms splayed out in surrender. To where? Where is there to go? Take me! Take me!

That night, postop night, the Mother and Husband lie afloat in the cot together. A fluorescent lamp near the crib is kept on in the dark. The Baby breathes evenly but thinly in his drugged sleep. The morphine in its first flooding doses apparently makes him feel as if he were falling backward—or so the Mother has been told—and it causes the Baby to jerk, to catch himself over and over, as if he were being dropped from a tree. "Is this right? Isn't there something that should be done?" The nurses come in hourly, different ones—the night shifts seem strangely short and frequent. If the Baby stirs or frets, the nurses give him more morphine through the Hickman catheter, then leave to tend to other patients. The Mother rises to check on him in the low light. There is gurgling from the clear plastic suction tube coming out of his mouth. Brownish clumps have collected in the tube. What is going on? The Mother rings for the nurse. Is it Renée or Sarah or Darcy? She's forgotten.

"What, what is it?" murmurs the Husband, waking up.

"Something is wrong," says the Mother. "It looks like blood in his N-G tube."

"What?" The Husband gets out of bed. He, too, is wearing sweatpants.

The nurse—Valerie—pushes open the heavy door to the room and enters quietly. "Everything okay?"

"There's something wrong here. The tube is sucking blood out of his stomach. It looks like it may have perforated his stomach and that now he's bleeding internally. Look!"

Valerie is a saint, but her voice is the standard hospital saint voice: an infuriating, pharmaceutical calm. It says, Everything is normal here. Death is normal. Pain is normal. Nothing is abnormal. So there is nothing to get excited about. "Well now, let's see." She holds up the plastic tube and tries to see inside it. "Hmmm," she says. "I'll call the attending physician."

Because this is a research and teaching hospital, all the regular doctors are at home sleeping in their Mission-style beds. Tonight, as is apparently the case every weekend night, the attending physician is a medical student. He looks fifteen. The authority he attempts to convey, he cannot remotely inhabit. He is not even in the same building with it. He shakes everyone's hands, then strokes his chin, a gesture no doubt gleaned from some piece of dinner theater his parents took him to once. As if there were an actual beard on that chin! As if beard growth on that chin were even possible! *Our Town! Kiss Me Kate! Barefoot in the Park!* He is attempting to convince, if not to impress.

"We're in trouble," the Mother whispers to the Husband. She is tired, tired of young people grubbing for grades. "We've got Dr. 'Kiss Me Kate,' here."

The Husband looks at her blankly, a mix of disorientation and divorce.

The medical student holds the tubing in his hands. "I don't really see anything," he says.

He flunks! "You don't?" The Mother shoves her way in, holds the clear tubing in both hands. "That," she says. "Right here and here." Just this past semester, she said to one of her own students, "If you don't see how this essay is better than that one, then I want you just to go out into the hallway and stand there until you do." Is it important to keep one's voice down? The Baby stays asleep. He is drugged and dreaming, far away.

"Hmmm," says the medical student. "Perhaps there's a little irritation in the stomach."

"A little irritation?" The Mother grows furious. "This is

blood. These are clumps and clots. This stupid thing is sucking the life right out of him!" Life! She is starting to cry.

They turn off the suction and bring in antacids, which they feed into the Baby through the tube. Then they turn the suction on again. This time on low.

"What was it on before?" asks the Husband.

"High," says Valerie. "Doctor's orders, though I don't know why. I don't know why these doctors do a lot of the things they do."

"Maybe they're . . . not all that bright?" suggests the Mother. She is feeling relief and rage simultaneously: there is a feeling of prayer and litigation in the air. Yet essentially, she is grateful. Isn't she? She thinks she is. And still, and still: look at all the things you have to do to protect a child, a hospital merely an intensification of life's cruel obstacle course.

The Surgeon comes to visit on Saturday morning. He steps in and nods at the Baby, who is awake but glazed from the morphine, his eyes two dark unseeing grapes. "The boy looks fine," the Surgeon announces. He peeks under the Baby's bandage. "The stitches look good," he says. The Baby's abdomen is stitched all the way across like a baseball. "And the other kidney, when we looked at it yesterday face-to-face, looked fine. We'll try to wean him off the morphine a little, and see how he's doing on Monday." He clears his throat. "And now," he says, looking about the room at the nurses and medical students, "I would like to speak with the Mother, alone."

The Mother's heart gives a jolt. "Me?"

"Yes," he says, motioning, then turning.

She gets up and steps out into the empty hallway with him, closing the door behind her. What can this be about? She hears the Baby fretting a little in his crib. Her brain fills with pain and alarm. Her voice comes out as a hoarse whisper. "Is there something—"

"There is a particular thing I need from you," says the Surgeon, turning and standing there very seriously.

"Yes?" Her heart is pounding. She does not feel resilient enough for any more bad news.

"I need to ask a favor."

"Certainly," she says, attempting very hard to summon the strength and courage for this occasion, whatever it is; her throat has tightened to a fist.

From inside his white coat, the surgeon removes a thin paperback book and thrusts it toward her. "Will you sign my copy of your novel?"

The Mother looks down and sees that it is indeed a copy of a novel she has written, one about teenaged girls.

She looks up. A big, spirited grin is cutting across his face. "I read this last summer," he says, "and I still remember parts of it! Those girls got into such trouble!"

Of all the surreal moments of the last few days, this, she thinks, might be the most so.

"Okay," she says, and the Surgeon merrily hands her a pen.

"You can just write 'To Dr.— Oh, I don't need to tell you what to write."

The Mother sits down on a bench and shakes ink into the pen. A sigh of relief washes over and out of her. Oh, the pleasure of a sigh of relief, like the finest moments of love; has anyone properly sung the praises of sighs of relief? She opens the book to the title page. She breathes deeply. What is he doing reading novels about teenaged girls, anyway? And why didn't he buy the hardcover? She inscribes something grateful and true, then hands the book back to him.

"Is he going to be okay?"

"The boy? The boy is going to be fine," he says, then taps her stiffly on the shoulder. "Now you take care. It's Saturday. Drink a little wine."

·   ·   ·

Over the weekend, while the Baby sleeps, the Mother and Husband sit together in the Tiny Tim Lounge. The Husband is restless and makes cafeteria and sundry runs, running errands for everyone. In his absence, the other parents regale her further with their sagas. Pediatric cancer and chemo stories: the children's amputations, blood poisoning, teeth flaking like shale, the learning delays and disabilities caused by chemo frying the young, budding brain. But strangely optimistic codas are tacked on—endings as stiff and loopy as carpenter's lace, crisp and empty as lettuce, reticulate as a net—ah, words. "After all that business with the tutor, he's better now, and fitted with new incisors by my wife's cousin's husband, who did dental school in two and a half years, if you can believe that. We hope for the best. We take things as they come. Life is hard."

"Life's a big problem," agrees the Mother. Part of her welcomes and invites all their tales. In the few long days since this nightmare began, part of her has become addicted to disaster and war stories. She wants only to hear about the sadness and emergencies of others. They are the only situations that can join hands with her own; everything else bounces off her shiny shield of resentment and unsympathy. Nothing else can even stay in her brain. From this, no doubt, the philistine world is made, or should one say recruited? Together, the parents huddle all day in the Tiny Tim Lounge—no need to watch *Oprah*. They leave Oprah in the dust. Oprah has nothing on them. They chat matter-of-factly, then fall silent and watch *Dune* or *Star Wars*, in which there are bright and shiny robots, whom the Mother now sees not as robots at all but as human beings who have had terrible things happen to them.

Some of their friends visit with stuffed animals and soft greetings of "Looking good" for the dozing baby, though the room is

way past the stuffed-animal limit. The Mother arranges, once
more, a plateful of Mint Milano cookies and cups of take-out
coffee for guests. All her nutso pals stop by—the two on
Prozac, the one obsessed with the word *penis* in the word *happiness,* the one who recently had her hair foiled green. "Your
friends put the *de* in *fin de siècle,*" says the Husband. Overheard,
or recorded, all marital conversation sounds as if someone must
be joking, though usually no one is.

She loves her friends, especially loves them for coming,
since there are times they all fight and don't speak for weeks. Is
this friendship? For now and here, it must do and is, and is, she
swears it is. For one, they never offer impromptu spiritual lectures about death, how it is part of life, its natural ebb and flow,
how we all must accept that, or other such utterances that make
her want to scratch out some eyes. Like true friends, they take
no hardy or elegant stance loosely choreographed from some
broad perspective. They get right in there and mutter "Jesus
Christ!" and shake their heads. Plus, they are the only people
who not only will laugh at her stupid jokes but offer up stupid
ones of their own. *What do you get when you cross Tiny Tim with a
pit bull?* A child's illness is a strain on the mind. They know
how to laugh in a fluty, desperate way—unlike the people who
are more her husband's friends and who seem just to deepen
their sorrowful gazes, nodding their heads with Sympathy.
How exiling and estranging are everybody's Sympathetic
Expressions! When anyone laughs, she thinks, Okay! Hooray: a
buddy. In disaster as in show business.

Nurses come and go; their chirpy voices both startle and
soothe. Some of the other Peed Onk parents stick their heads in
to see how the Baby is and offer encouragement.

Green Hair scratches her head. "Everyone's so friendly here.
Is there someone in this place who isn't doing all this airy,
scripted optimism—or are people like that the only people
here?"

"It's Modern Middle Medicine meets the Modern Middle Family," says the Husband. "In the Modern Middle West."

Someone has brought in take-out lo mein, and they all eat it out in the hall by the elevators.

Parents are allowed use of the Courtesy Line.

"You've got to have a second child," says a different friend on the phone, a friend from out of town. "An heir and a spare. That's what we did. We had another child to ensure we wouldn't off ourselves if we lost our first."

"Really?"

"I'm serious."

"A formal suicide? Wouldn't you just drink yourself into a lifelong stupor and let it go at that?"

"Nope. I knew how I would do it even. For a while, until our second came along, I had it all planned."

"What did you plan?"

"I can't go into too much detail, because—Hi, honey!—the kids are here now in the room. But I'll spell out the general idea: R-O-P-E."

Sunday evening, she goes and sinks down on the sofa in the Tiny Tim Lounge next to Frank, Joey's father. He is a short, stocky man with the currentless, flatlined look behind the eyes that all the parents eventually get here. He has shaved his head bald in solidarity with his son. His little boy has been battling cancer for five years. It is now in the liver, and the rumor around the corridor is that Joey has three weeks to live. She knows that Joey's mother, Heather, left Frank years ago, two years into the cancer, and has remarried and had another child, a girl named Brittany. The Mother sees Heather here sometimes with her new life—the cute little girl and the new,

young, full-haired husband who will never be so mania-
cally and debilitatingly obsessed with Joey's illness the way
Frank, her first husband, was. Heather comes to visit Joey, to
say hello and now good-bye, but she is not Joey's main man.
Frank is.

Frank is full of stories—about the doctors, about the food,
about the nurses, about Joey. Joey, affectless from his meds,
sometimes leaves his room and comes out to watch TV in his
bathrobe. He is jaundiced and bald, and though he is nine, he
looks no older than six. Frank has devoted the last four and a
half years to saving Joey's life. When the cancer was first diagnosed, the doctors gave Joey a 20 percent chance of living six
more months. Now here it is, almost five years later, and Joey's
still here. It is all due to Frank, who, early on, quit his job as
vice president of a consulting firm in order to commit himself
totally to his son. He is proud of everything he's given up and
done, but he is tired. Part of him now really believes things are
coming to a close, that this is the end. He says this without
tears. There are no more tears.

"You have probably been through more than anyone else on
this corridor," says the Mother.

"I could tell you stories," he says. There is a sour odor
between them, and she realizes that neither of them has bathed
for days.

"Tell me one. Tell me the worst one." She knows he hates
his ex-wife and hates her new husband even more.

"The worst? They're all the worst. Here's one: one morning, I went out for breakfast with my buddy—it was the only
time I'd left Joey alone ever; left him for two hours is all—and
when I came back, his N-G tube was full of blood. They had
the suction on too high, and it was sucking the guts right out
of him."

"Oh my God. That just happened to us," said the Mother.
"It did?"

"Friday night."

"You're kidding. They let that happen again? I gave them such a chewing-out about that!"

"I guess our luck is not so good. We get your very worst story on the second night we're here."

"It's not a bad place, though."

"It's not?"

"Naw. I've seen worse. I've taken Joey everywhere."

"He seems very strong." Truth is, at this point, Joey seems like a zombie and frightens her.

"Joey's a fucking genius. A biological genius. They'd given him six months, remember."

The Mother nods.

"Six months is not very long," says Frank. "Six months is nothing. He was four and a half years old."

All the words are like blows. She feels flooded with affection and mourning for this man. She looks away, out the window, out past the hospital parking lot, up toward the black marbled sky and the electric eyelash of the moon. "And now he's nine," she says. "You're his hero."

"And he's mine," says Frank, though the fatigue in his voice seems to overwhelm him. "He'll be that forever. Excuse me," he says, "I've got to go check. His breathing hasn't been good. Excuse me."

"Good news and bad," says the Oncologist on Monday. He has knocked, entered the room, and now stands there. Their cots are unmade. One wastebasket is overflowing with coffee cups. "We've got the pathologist's report. The bad news is that the kidney they removed had certain lesions, called 'rests,' which are associated with a higher risk for disease in the other kidney. The good news is that the tumor is stage one, regular cell structure, and under five hundred grams, which qualifies you for a national experiment in which chemotherapy isn't done but your boy is monitored with ultrasound instead. It's not all that risky, given that the patient's watched closely, but here is the literature on it. There are forms to sign, if you decide to do that. Read all this and we can discuss it further. You have to decide within four days."

Lesions? Rests? They dry up and scatter like M&M's on the floor. All she hears is the part about no chemo. Another sigh of relief rises up in her and spills out. In a life where there is only the bearable and the unbearable, a sigh of relief is an ecstasy.

"No chemo?" says the Husband. "Do you recommend that?"

The Oncologist shrugs. What casual gestures these doctors are permitted! "I know chemo. I like chemo," says the Oncologist. "But this is for you to decide. It depends how you feel."

The Husband leans forward. "But don't you think that now that we have the upper hand with this thing, we should keep going? Shouldn't we stomp on it, beat it, smash it to death with the chemo?"

The Mother swats him angrily and hard. "Honey, you're delirious!" She whispers, but it comes out as a hiss. "This is our lucky break!" Then she adds gently, "We don't want the Baby to have chemo."

The Husband turns back to the Oncologist. "What do *you* think?"

"It could be," he says, shrugging. "It could be that this is your lucky break. But you won't know for sure for five years."

The Husband turns back to the Mother. "Okay," he says. "Okay."

The Baby grows happier and strong. He begins to move and sit and eat. Wednesday morning, they are allowed to leave, and leave without chemo. The Oncologist looks a little nervous. "Are you nervous about this?" asks the Mother.

"Of course I'm nervous." But he shrugs and doesn't look

that nervous. "See you in six weeks for the ultrasound," he says, waves and then leaves, looking at his big black shoes as he does.

The Baby smiles, even toddles around a little, the sun bursting through the clouds, an angel chorus crescendoing. Nurses arrive. The Hickman is taken out of the Baby's neck and chest; antibiotic lotion is dispensed. The Mother packs up their bags. The Baby sucks on a bottle of juice and does not cry.

"No chemo?" says one of the nurses. "Not even a *little* chemo?"

"We're doing watch and wait," says the Mother.

The other parents look envious but concerned. They have never seen any child get out of there with his hair and white blood cells intact.

"Will you be okay?" asks Ned's mother.

"The worry's going to kill us," says the Husband.

"But if all we have to do is worry," chides the Mother, "every day for a hundred years, it'll be easy. It'll be nothing. I'll take all the worry in the world, if it wards off the thing itself."

"That's right," says Ned's mother. "Compared to everything else, compared to all the actual events, the worry is nothing."

The Husband shakes his head. "I'm such an amateur," he moans.

"You're both doing admirably," says the other mother. "Your baby's lucky, and I wish you all the best."

The Husband shakes her hand warmly. "Thank you," he says. "You've been wonderful."

Another mother, the mother of Eric, comes up to them. "It's all very hard," she says, her head cocked to one side. "But there's a lot of collateral beauty along the way."

Collateral beauty? Who is entitled to such a thing? A child is ill. No one is entitled to any collateral beauty!

"Thank you," says the Husband.

Joey's father, Frank, comes up and embraces them both.

"It's a journey," he says. He chucks the Baby on the chin. "Good luck, little man."

"Yes, thank you so much," says the Mother. "We hope things go well with Joey." She knows that Joey had a hard, terrible night.

Frank shrugs and steps back. "Gotta go," he says. "Goodbye!"

"Bye," she says, and then he is gone. She bites the inside of her lip, a bit tearily, then bends down to pick up the diaper bag, which is now stuffed with little animals; helium balloons are tied to its zipper. Shouldering the thing, the Mother feels she has just won a prize. All the parents have now vanished down the hall in the opposite direction. The Husband moves close. With one arm, he takes the Baby from her; with the other, he rubs her back. He can see she is starting to get weepy.

"Aren't these people nice? Don't you feel better hearing about their lives?" he asks.

Why does he do this, form clubs all the time; why does even this society of suffering soothe him? When it comes to death and dying, perhaps someone in this family ought to be more of a snob.

"All these nice people with their brave stories," he continues as they make their way toward the elevator bank, waving good-bye to the nursing staff as they go, even the Baby waving shyly. *Bye-bye! Bye-bye!* "Don't you feel consoled, knowing we're all in the same boat, that we're all in this together?"

But who on earth would want to be in this boat? the Mother thinks. This boat is a nightmare boat. Look where it goes: to a silver-and-white room, where, just before your eyesight and hearing and your ability to touch or be touched disappear entirely, you must watch your child die.

Rope! Bring on the rope.

"Let's make our own way," says the Mother, "and not in this boat."

Woman Overboard! She takes the Baby back from the Husband, cups the Baby's cheek in her hand, kisses his brow and then, quickly, his flowery mouth. The Baby's heart—she can hear it—drums with life. "For as long as I live," says the Mother, pressing the elevator button—up or down, everyone in the end has to leave this way—"I never want to see any of these people again."

There are the notes.
Now where is the money?

TERRIFIC MOTHER

Although she had been around them her whole life, it was when she reached thirty-five that holding babies seemed to make her nervous—just at the beginning, a twinge of stage fright swinging up from the gut. "Adrienne, would you like to hold the baby? Would you mind?" Always these words from a woman her age looking kind and beseeching—a former friend, she was losing her friends to babble and beseech—and Adrienne would force herself to breathe deep. Holding a baby was no longer natural—she was no longer natural—but a test of womanliness and earthly skills. She was being observed. People looked to see how she would do it. She had entered a puritanical decade, a demographic moment—whatever it was—when the best compliment you could get was, "You would make a terrific mother." The wolf whistle of the nineties.

So when she was at the Spearsons' Labor Day picnic, and when Sally Spearson handed her the baby, Adrienne had burbled at it as she would a pet, had jostled the child gently, made clicking noises with her tongue, affectionately cooing, "Hello, punkinhead, hello, my little punkinhead," had reached to shoo a fly away and, amid the smells of old grass and the fatty crackle of the barbecue, lost her balance when the picnic bench, the dowels rotting in the joints, wobbled and began to topple her—the bench, the wobbly picnic bench, was toppling her! And when she fell backward, wrenching her spine—in the slowed quickness of this flipping world, she saw the clayey clouds, some frozen faces, one lone star like the nose of a jet— and when the baby's head hit the stone retaining wall of the Spearsons' newly terraced yard and bled fatally into the brain, Adrienne went home shortly thereafter, after the hospital and the police reports, and did not leave her attic apartment for seven months, and there were fears, deep fears for her, on the part of Martin Porter, the man she had been dating, and on the part of almost everyone, including Sally Spearson, who phoned tearfully to say that she forgave her, that Adrienne might never come out.

Martin Porter usually visited her bringing a pepper cheese or a Casbah couscous cup; he had become her only friend. He was divorced and worked as a research economist, though he looked more like a Scottish lumberjack—graying hair, red-flecked beard, a favorite flannel shirt in green and gold. He was getting ready to take a trip abroad. "We could get married," he suggested. That way, he said, Adrienne could accompany him to northern Italy, to a villa in the Alps set up for scholars and academic conferences. She could be a spouse. They gave spouses studios to work in. Some studios had pianos. Some had desks or potter's wheels. "You can do whatever you want." He was finishing the second draft of a study of First World imperialism's impact on Third World monetary systems. "You could paint. Or not. You could not paint."

She looked at him closely, hungrily, then turned away. She still felt clumsy and big, a beefy killer in a cage, in need of the thinning prison food. "You love me, don't you," she said. She had spent the better part of seven months napping in a leotard, an electric fan blowing at her, her left ear catching the wind, capturing it there in her head, like the sad sea in a shell. She felt clammy and doomed. "Or do you just feel sorry for me?" She swatted at a small swarm of gnats that had appeared suddenly out of an abandoned can of Coke.

"I don't feel sorry for you."

"You don't?"

"I *feel for* you. I've grown to love you. We're grown-ups here. One grows to do things." He was a practical man. He often referred to the annual departmental cocktail party as "Standing Around Getting Paid."

"I don't think, Martin, that we can get married."

"Of course we can get married." He unbuttoned his cuffs as if to roll up his sleeves.

"You don't understand," she said. "Normal life is no longer possible for me. I've stepped off all the normal paths and am living in the bushes. I'm a bushwoman now. I don't feel like I can have the normal things. Marriage is a normal thing. You need the normal courtship, the normal proposal." She couldn't think what else. Water burned her eyes. She waved a hand dismissively, and it passed through her field of vision like something murderous and huge.

"Normal courtship, normal proposal," Martin said. He took off his shirt and pants and shoes. He lay on the bed in just his socks and underwear and pressed the length of his body against her. "I'm going to marry you, whether you like it or not." He took her face into his hands and looked longingly at her mouth. "I'm going to marry you till you puke."

They were met at Malpensa by a driver who spoke little English but who held up a sign that said VILLA HIRSCHBORN, and when Adrienne and Martin approached him, he nodded and said, "Hello, *buongiorno*. Signor Porter?" The drive to the villa took two hours, uphill and down, through the countryside and several small villages, but it wasn't until the driver pulled up to the precipitous hill he called "La Madre Vertiginoso," and the villa's iron gates somehow opened automatically, then closed behind them, it wasn't until then, winding up the drive past the spectacular gardens and the sunny vineyard and the terraces of the stucco outbuildings, that it occurred to Adrienne that Martin's being invited here was a great honor. He had won this *thing,* and he got to live here for a month.

"Does this feel like a honeymoon?" she asked him.

"A what? Oh, a honeymoon. Yes." He turned and patted her thigh indifferently.

He was jet-lagged. That was it. She smoothed her skirt, which was wrinkled and damp. "Yes, I can see us growing old together," she said, squeezing his hand. "In the next few weeks, in fact." If she ever got married again, she would do it right: the awkward ceremony, the embarrassing relatives, the cumbersome, ecologically unsound gifts. She and Martin had simply gone to city hall, and then asked their family and friends not to send presents but to donate money to Greenpeace. Now, however, as they slowed before the squashed-nosed stone lions at the entrance of the villa, its perfect border of forget-me-nots and yews, its sparkling glass door, Adrienne gasped. Whales, she thought quickly. *Whales* got my crystal.

The upstairs "Principessa" room, which they were ushered into by a graceful bilingual butler named Carlo, was elegant and huge—a piano, a large bed, dressers stenciled with festooning fruits. There was maid service twice a day, said Carlo. There were sugar wafers, towels, mineral water, and mints. There was dinner at eight, breakfast until nine. When Carlo bowed and departed, Martin kicked off his shoes and sank into the ancient tapestried chaise. "I've heard these 'fake' Quattrocento paintings on the wall are fake for tax purposes only," he whispered. "If you know what I mean."

"Really," said Adrienne. She felt like one of the workers taking over the Winter Palace. Her own voice sounded booming. "You know, Mussolini was captured around here. Think about it."

Martin looked puzzled. "What do you mean?"

"That he was around here. That they captured him. I don't know. I was reading the little book on it. Leave me alone." She flopped down on the bed. Martin was changing already. He'd been better when they were just dating, with the pepper cheese. She let her face fall deep into the pillow, her mouth hanging open like a dog's, and then she slept until six, dreaming that a baby was in her arms but that it turned into a stack of plates, which she had to juggle, tossing them into the air.

A loud sound awoke her—a falling suitcase. Everyone had to dress for dinner, and Martin was yanking things out, groaning his way into a jacket and tie. Adrienne got up, bathed, and put on panty hose, which, because it had been months since she had done so, twisted around her leg like the stripe on a barber pole.

"You're walking as if you'd torn a ligament," said Martin, locking the door to their room as they were leaving.

Adrienne pulled at the knees of the hose but couldn't make them work. "Tell me you like my skirt, Martin, or I'm going to have to go back in and never come out again."

"I like your skirt. It's great. You're great. I'm great," he said, like a conjugation. He took her arm and they limped their way down the curved staircase—Was it sweeping? Yes! It was sweeping!—to the dining room, where Carlo ushered them in to find their places at the table. The seating arrangement at the tables would change nightly, Carlo said in a clipped Italian accent, "to assist the cross-pollination of ideas."

"Excuse me?" said Adrienne.

There were about thirty-five people, all of them middle-aged, with the academic's strange mixed expression of merriment and weariness. "A cross between flirtation and a fender bender," Martin had described it once. Adrienne's place was at the opposite side of the room from him, between a historian writing a book on a monk named Jaocim de Flore and a musicologist who had devoted his life to a quest for "the earnest andante." Everyone sat in elaborate wooden chairs, the backs of which were carved with gargoylish heads that poked up from behind either shoulder of the sitter, like a warning.

"De Flore," said Adrienne, at a loss, turning from her carpaccio to the monk man. "Doesn't that mean 'of the flower'?" She had recently learned that *disaster* meant "bad star," and she was looking for an opportunity to brandish and bronze this tidbit in conversation.

The monk man looked at her. "Are you one of the spouses?"

"Yes," she said. She looked down, then back up. "But then, so is my husband."

"You're not a screenwriter, are you?"

"No," she said. "I'm a painter. Actually, more of a printmaker. Actually, more of a—right now I'm in transition."

He nodded and dug back into his food. "I'm always afraid they're going to start letting *screenwriters* in here."

There was an arugula salad, and osso buco for the main course. She turned now to the musicologist. "So you usually find them insincere? The andantes?" She looked quickly out over the other heads to give Martin a fake and girlish wave.

"It's the use of the minor seventh," muttered the musicologist. "So fraudulent and replete."

"If the food wasn't so good, I'd leave now," she said to Martin. They were lying in bed, in their carpeted skating rink of a room. It could be weeks, she knew, before they'd have sex here. " '*So fraudulent and replete,*' " she said in a high nasal voice, the likes of which Martin had heard only once before, in a departmental meeting chaired by an embittered interim chair who did imitations of colleagues not in the room. "Can you even use the word *replete* like that?"

"As soon as you get settled in your studio, you'll feel better," said Martin, beginning to fade. He groped under the covers to find her hand and clasp it.

"I want a divorce," whispered Adrienne.

"I'm not giving you one," he said, bringing her hand up to his chest and placing it there, like a medallion, like a necklace of sleep, and then he began softly to snore, the quietest of radiators.

They were given bagged lunches and told to work well. Martin's studio was a modern glass cube in the middle of one of the gardens. Adrienne's was a musty stone hut twenty minutes farther up the hill and out onto the wooded headland, along a dirt path sunned on by small darting lizards. She unlocked the door with the key she had been given, went in, and immediately sat down and ate the entire bagged lunch—quickly, compulsively, though it was only 9:30 in the morning. Two apples, some cheese, and a jam sandwich. "A jelly bread," she said aloud, holding up the sandwich, scrutinizing it under the light.

She set her sketch pad on the worktable and began a morning full of killing spiders and drawing their squashed and tragic bodies. The spiders were star-shaped, hairy, and scuttling like crabs. They were fallen stars. Bad stars. They were earth's animal try at heaven. Often she had to step on them twice—they were large and ran fast. Stepping on them once usually just made them run faster.

It was the careless universe's work she was performing, death itchy and about like a cop. Her personal fund of mercy for the living was going to get used up in dinner conversation at the villa. She had no compassion to spare, only a pencil and a shoe.

"Art *trouvé*?" said Martin, toweling himself dry from his shower as they dressed for the evening cocktail hour.

"Spider *trouvé*," she said. "A delicate, aboriginal dish." Martin let out a howling laugh that alarmed her. She looked at him, then looked down at her shoes. He needed her. Tomorrow, she would have to go down into town and find a pair of sexy Italian sandals that showed the cleavage of her toes. She would have to take him dancing. They would have to hold each other and lead each other back to love or they'd go nuts here. They'd grow mocking and arch and violent. One of them would stick a foot out, and the other would trip. That sort of thing.

At dinner, she sat next to a medievalist who had just finished his sixth book on the *Canterbury Tales.*

"Sixth," repeated Adrienne.

"There's a lot there," he said defensively.

"I'm sure," she said.

"I read deep," he added. "I read hard."

"How nice for you."

He looked at her narrowly. "Of course, *you* probably think I should write a book about Cat Stevens." She nodded neutrally. "I see," he said.

For dessert, Carlo was bringing in a white chocolate torte, and she decided to spend most of the coffee and dessert time talking about it. Desserts like these are born, not made, she would say. She was already practicing, rehearsing for courses. "I mean," she said to the Swedish physicist on her left, "until today, my feeling about white chocolate was why? What was the point? You might as well have been eating goddamn *wax.*" She had her elbow on the table, her hand up near her face, and she looked anxiously past the physicist to smile at Martin at the other end of the long table. She waved her fingers in the air like bug legs.

"Yes, of course," said the physicist, frowning. "You must be . . . well, are you one of the *spouses*?"

. . .

She began in the mornings to gather with some of the other spouses—they were going to have little tank tops printed up—in the music room for exercise. This way, she could avoid hearing words like *Heideggerian* and *ideological* at breakfast; it always felt too early in the morning for those words. The women pushed back the damask sofas and cleared a space on the rug where all of them could do little hip and thigh exercises, led by the wife of the Swedish physicist. Up, down, up down.

"I guess this relaxes you," said the white-haired woman next to her.

"Bourbon relaxes you," said Adrienne. "This carves you."

"Bourbon carves you," said a redhead from Brazil.

"You have to go visit this person down in the village," whispered the white-haired woman. She wore a Spalding sporting-goods T-shirt.

"What person?"

"Yes, what person?" asked the blonde.

The white-haired woman stopped and handed both of them a card from the pocket of her shorts. "She's an American masseuse. A couple of us have started going. She takes lire or dollars, doesn't matter. You have to phone a couple days ahead."

Adrienne stuck the card in her waistband. "Thanks," she said, and resumed moving her leg up and down like a tollgate.

For dinner, there was *tacchino alla scala*. "I wonder how you make this?" Adrienne said aloud.

"My dear," said the French historian on her left. "You must never ask. Only wonder." He then went on to disparage subaltered intellectualism, dormant tropes, genealogical contingencies.

"Yes," said Adrienne, "dishes like these do have about them

a kind of omnihistorical reality. At least it seems like that to me." She turned quickly.

To her right sat a cultural anthropologist who had just come back from China, where she had studied the infanticide.

"Yes," said Adrienne. "The infanticide."

"They are on the edge of something horrific there. It is the whole future, our future as well, and something terrible is going to happen to them. One feels it."

"How awful," said Adrienne. She could not do the mechanical work of eating, of knife and fork, up and down. She let her knife and fork rest against each other on the plate.

"A woman has to apply for a license to have a baby. Everything is bribes and rations. We went for hikes up into the mountains, and we didn't see a single bird, a single animal. Everything, over the years, has been eaten."

Adrienne felt a light weight on the inside of her arm vanish and return, vanish and return, like the history of something, like the story of all things. "Where are you from ordinarily?" asked Adrienne. She couldn't place the accent.

"Munich," said the woman. "Land of Oktoberfest." She dug into her food in an exasperated way, then turned back toward Adrienne to smile a little formally. "I grew up watching all these grown people in green felt throw up in the street."

Adrienne smiled back. This now was how she would learn about the world, in sentences at meals; other people's distillations amid her own vague pain, dumb with itself. This, for her, would be knowledge—a shifting to hear, an emptying of her arms, other people's experiences walking through the bare rooms of her brain, looking for a place to sit.

"Me?" she too often said, "I'm just a dropout from Sue Bennet College." And people would nod politely and ask, "Where's that?"

·   ·   ·

The next morning in her room, she sat by the phone and stared. Martin had gone to his studio; his book was going fantastically well, he said, which gave Adrienne a sick, abandoned feeling—of being unhappy and unsupportive—which made her think she was not even one of the spouses. Who was she? The opposite of a mother. The opposite of a spouse.

She was Spider Woman.

She picked up the phone, got an outside line, dialed the number of the masseuse on the card.

"*Pronto!*" said the voice on the other end.

"Yes, hello, *per favore, parla inglese?*"

"Oh, yes," said the voice. "I'm from Minnesota."

"No kidding," said Adrienne. She lay back and searched the ceiling for talk. "I once subscribed to a haunted-house newsletter published in Minnesota," she said.

"Yes," said the voice a little impatiently. "Minnesota is full of haunted-house newsletters."

"I once lived in a haunted house," said Adrienne. "In college. Me and five roommates."

The masseuse cleared her throat confidentially. "Yes. I was once called on to cast the demons from a haunted house. But how can I help you today?"

"You were?"

"Were? Oh, the house, yes. When I got there, all the place needed was to be cleaned. So I cleaned it. Washed the dishes and dusted."

"Yup," said Adrienne. "Our house was haunted that way, too."

There was a strange silence, in which Adrienne, feeling something tense and moist in the room, began to fiddle with the bagged lunch on the bed, nervously pulling open the sandwiches, sensing that if she turned, just then, the phone cradled in her neck, the child would be there, behind her, a little older now, a toddler, walked toward her in a ghostly way by her own dead parents, a Nativity scene corrupted by error and dream.

"How can I help you today?" the masseuse asked again, firmly.

Help? Adrienne wondered abstractly, and remembered how in certain countries, instead of a tooth fairy, there were such things as tooth spiders. How the tooth spider could steal your children, mix them up, bring you a changeling child, a child that was changed.

"I'd like to make an appointment for Thursday," she said. "If possible. Please."

For dinner there was *vongole in umido,* the rubbery, wine-steamed meat prompting commentary about mollusk versus crustacean anatomy. Adrienne sighed and chewed. Over cocktails, there had been a long discussion of peptides and rabbit tests.

"Now lobsters, you know, have what is called a hemipenis," said the man next to her. He was a marine biologist, an epidemiologist, or an anthropologist. She'd forgotten.

"Hemipenis." Adrienne scanned the room a little frantically.

"Yes." He grinned. "Not a term one particularly wants to hear in an intimate moment, of course."

"No," said Adrienne, smiling back. She paused. "Are you one of the spouses?"

Someone on his right grabbed his arm, and he now turned in that direction to say why yes, he did know Professor so-and-so . . . and wasn't she in Brussels last year giving a paper at the hermeneutics conference?

There came *castagne al porto* and coffee. The woman to Adrienne's left finally turned to her, placing the cup down on the saucer with a sharp clink.

"You know, the chef has AIDS," said the woman.

Adrienne froze a little in her chair. "No, I didn't know."
Who was this woman?

"How does that make you feel?"

"Pardon me?"

"How does that make you feel?" She enunciated slowly, like a reading teacher.

"I'm not sure," said Adrienne, scowling at her chestnuts. "Certainly worried for us if we should lose him."

The woman smiled. "Very interesting." She reached underneath the table for her purse and said, "Actually, the chef doesn't have AIDS—at least not that I'm aware of. I'm just taking a kind of survey to test people's reactions to AIDS, homosexuality, and general notions of contagion. I'm a sociologist. It's part of my research. I just arrived this afternoon. My name is Marie-Claire."

Adrienne turned back to the hemipenis man. "Do you think the people here are mean?" she asked.

He smiled at her in a fatherly way. "Of course," he said. There was a long silence with some chewing in it. "But the place *is* pretty as a postcard."

"Yeah, well," said Adrienne, "I never send those kinds of postcards. No matter where I am, I always send the kind with the little cat jokes on them."

He placed his hand briefly on her shoulder. "We'll find you some cat jokes." He scanned the room in a bemused way and then looked at his watch.

She had bonded in a state of emergency, like an infant bird. But perhaps it would be soothing, this marriage. Perhaps it would be like a nice warm bath. A nice warm bath in a tub flying off a roof.

At night, she and Martin seemed almost like husband and wife, spooned against each other in a forgetful sort of love—a cold, still heaven through which a word or touch might explode like a moon, then disappear, unremembered. She moved her arms to place them around him and he felt so big there, huge, filling her arms.

The white-haired woman who had given her the masseuse card was named Kate Spalding, the wife of the monk man, and after breakfast she asked Adrienne to go jogging. They met by the lions, Kate once more sporting a Spalding T-shirt, and then they headed out over the gravel, toward the gardens. "It's pretty as a postcard here, isn't it?" said Kate. Out across the lake, the mountains seemed to preside over the minutiae of the terracotta villages nestled below. It was May and the Alps were losing their snowy caps, nurses letting their hair down. The air was warming. Anything could happen.

Adrienne sighed. "But do you think people have *sex* here?"

Kate smiled. "You mean casual sex? Among the guests?"

Adrienne felt annoyed. "*Casual* sex? No, I don't mean *casual* sex. I'm talking about difficult, randomly profound, Sears and Roebuck sex. I'm talking marital."

Kate laughed in a sharp, barking sort of way, which for some reason hurt Adrienne's feelings.

Adrienne tugged on her socks. "I don't believe in *casual* sex." She paused. "I believe in casual marriage."

"Don't look at me," said Kate. "I married my husband because I was deeply in love with him."

"Yeah, well," said Adrienne, "I married my husband because I thought it would be a great way to meet guys."

Kate smiled now in a real way. Her white hair was grandmotherly, but her face was youthful and tan, and her teeth shone generous and wet, the creamy incisors curved as cashews.

"I'd tried the whole single thing, but it just wasn't working," Adrienne added, running in place.

Kate stepped close and massaged Adrienne's neck. Her skin

was lined and papery. "You haven't been to see Ilke from Minnesota yet, have you?"

Adrienne feigned perturbance. "Do I seem that tense, that lost, that . . ." And here she let her arms splay spastically. "I'm going tomorrow."

He was a beautiful child, didn't you think? In bed, Martin held her until he rolled away, clasped her hand and fell asleep. At least there was that: a husband sleeping next to a wife, a nice husband sleeping close. It meant something to her. She could see how through the years marriage would gather power, its socially sanctioned animal comfort, its night life a dreamy dance about love. She lay awake and remembered when her father had at last grown so senile and ill that her mother could no longer sleep in the same bed with him—the mess, the smell—and had had to move him, diapered and rank, to the guest room next door. Her mother had cried, to say this farewell to a husband. To at last lose him like this, banished and set aside like a dead man, never to sleep with him again: she had wept like a baby. His actual death, she took less hard. At the funeral, she was grim and dry and invited everyone over for a quiet, elegant tea. By the time two years had passed, and she herself was diagnosed with cancer, her sense of humor had returned a little. "The silent killer," she would say, with a wink. "The *Silent Killer.*" She got a kick out of repeating it, though no one knew what to say in response, and at the very end, she kept clutching the nurses' hems to ask, "Why is no one visiting me?" No one lived that close, explained Adrienne. No one lived that close to anyone.

Adrienne set her spoon down. "Isn't this soup *interesting?*" she said to no one in particular. "*Zup-pa mari-ta-ta!*" Marriage soup. She decided it was perhaps a little like marriage itself: a good idea that, like all ideas, lived awkwardly on earth.

"You're not a poetess, I hope," said the English geologist next to her. "We had a poetess here last month, and things got a bit dodgy here for the rest of us."

"Really." After the soup, there was risotto with squid ink.

"Yes. She kept referring to insects as 'God's typos' and then she kept us all after dinner one evening so she could read from her poems, which seemed to consist primarily of the repeating line 'the hairy kiwi of his balls.' "

"Hairy kiwi," repeated Adrienne, searching the phrase for a sincere andante. She had written a poem once herself. It had been called "Garbage Night in the Fog" and was about a long, sad walk she'd taken once on garbage night.

The geologist smirked a little at the risotto, waiting for Adrienne to say something more, but she was now watching Martin at the other table. He was sitting next to the sociologist she'd sat next to the previous night, and as Adrienne watched, she saw Martin glance, in a sickened way, from the sociologist, back to his plate, then back to the sociologist. "The *cook*?" he said loudly, then dropped his fork and pushed his chair from the table.

The sociologist was frowning. "You flunk," she said.

"I'm going to see a masseuse tomorrow." Martin was on his back on the bed, and Adrienne was straddling his hips, usually one of their favorite ways to converse. One of the Mandy Patinkin tapes she'd brought was playing on the cassette player.

"The masseuse. Yes, I've heard."

"You have?"

"Sure, they were talking about it at dinner last night."

"Who was?" She was already feeling possessive, alone.

"Oh, one of them," said Martin, smiling and waving his hand dismissively.

"Them," said Adrienne coldly. "You mean one of the spouses, don't you? Why are all the spouses here women? Why don't the women scholars have spouses?"

"Some of them do, I think. They're just not here."

"Where are they?"

"Could you move?" he said irritably. "You're sitting on my groin."

"Fine," she said, and climbed off.

The next morning, she made her way down past the conical evergreens of the terraced hill—so like the grounds of a palace, the palace of a moody princess named Sophia or Giovanna—ten minutes down the winding path to the locked gate to the village. It had rained in the night, and snails, golden and mauve, decorated the stone steps, sometimes dead center, causing Adrienne an occasional quick turn of the ankle. A dance step, she thought. Modern and bent-kneed. Very Martha Graham. *Don't kill us. We'll kill you.* At the top of the final stairs to the gate, she pressed the buzzer that opened it electronically, and then dashed down to get out in time. YOU HAVE THIRTY SECONDS said the sign. TRENTA SECONDI USCIRE. PRESTO! One needed a key to get back in from the village, and she clutched it like a charm.

She had to follow the Via San Carlo to Corso Magenta, past a gelato shop and a bakery with wreaths of braided bread and muffins cut like birds. She pressed herself up against the buildings to let the cars pass. She looked at her card. The masseuse was above a *farmacìa,* she'd been told, and she saw it now, a little sign that said MASSAGGIO DELLA VITA. She pushed on the outer door and went up.

Upstairs, through an open doorway, she entered a room lined with books: books on vegetarianism, books on healing, books on juice. A cockatiel, white, with a red dot like a Hindu wife's, was perched atop a picture frame. The picture was of

Lake Como or Garda, though when you blinked, it could also be a skull, a fissure through the center like a reef.

"Adrienne," said a smiling woman in a purple peasant dress. She had big frosted hair and a wide, happy face that contained many shades of pink. She stepped forward and shook Adrienne's hand. "I'm Ilke."

"Yes," said Adrienne.

The cockatiel suddenly flew from its perch to land on Ilke's shoulder. It pecked at her big hair, then stared at Adrienne accusingly.

Ilke's eyes moved quickly between Adrienne's own, a quick read, a radar scan. She then looked at her watch. "You can go into the back room now, and I'll be with you shortly. You can take off all your clothes, also any jewelry—watches, or rings. But if you want, you can leave your underwear on. Whatever you prefer."

"What do most people do?" Adrienne swallowed in a difficult, conspicuous way.

Ilke smiled. "Some do it one way, some the other."

"All right," Adrienne said, and clutched her pocketbook. She stared at the cockatiel. "I just wouldn't want to rock the boat."

She stepped carefully toward the back room Ilke had indicated, and pushed past the heavy curtain. Inside was a large alcove—windowless and dark, with one small bluish light coming from the corner. In the center was a table with a newly creased flannel sheet. Speakers were built into the bottom of the table, and out of them came the sound of eerie choral music, wordless oohs and aahs in minor tones, with a percussive sibilant chant beneath it that sounded to Adrienne like "Jesus is best, Jesus is best," though perhaps it was "Cheese, I suspect." Overhead hung a mobile of white stars, crescent moons, and doves. On the blue walls were more clouds and snowflakes. It was a child's room, a baby's room, everything trying hard to be harmless and sweet.

Adrienne removed all her clothes, her earrings, her watch, her rings. She had already grown used to the ring Martin had given her, and so it saddened and exhilarated her to take it off, a quick glimpse into the landscape of adultery. Her other ring was a smoky quartz, which a palm reader in Milwaukee—a man dressed like a gym teacher and set up at a card table in a German restaurant—had told her to buy and wear on her right index finger for power.

"What kind of power?" she had asked.

"The kind that's real," he said. "What you've got here," he said, waving around her left hand, pointing at the thin silver and turquoise she was wearing, "is squat."

"I like a palm reader who dresses you," she said later to Martin in the car on their way home. This was before the incident at the Spearson picnic, and things seemed not impossible then; she had wanted Martin to fall in love with her. "A guy who looks like Mike Ditka, but who picks out jewelry for you."

"A guy who tells you you're sensitive and that you will soon receive cash from someone wearing glasses. Where does he come up with this stuff?"

"You don't think I'm sensitive."

"I mean the money and glasses thing," he said. "And that gloomy bit about how they'll think you're a goner, but you're going to come through and live to see the world go through a radical physical change."

"That was gloomy," she agreed. There was a lot of silence as they looked out at the night-lit highway lines, the fireflies hitting the windshield and smearing, all phosphorescent gold, as if the car were flying through stars. "It must be hard," she said, "for someone like you to go out on a date with someone like me."

"Why do you say that?" he'd asked.

She climbed up on the table, stripped of ornament and the power of ornament, and slipped between the flannel sheets. For a second, she felt numb and scared, naked in a strange room, more naked even than in a doctor's office, where you kept your jewelry on, like an odalisque. But it felt new to do this, to lead the body to this, the body with its dog's obedience, its dog's desire to please. She lay there waiting, watching the mobile moons turn slowly, half revolutions, while from the speakers beneath the table came a new sound, an electronic, synthesized version of Brahms's lullaby. An infant. She was to become an infant again. Perhaps she would become the Spearson boy. He had been a beautiful baby.

Ilke came in quietly, and appeared so suddenly behind Adrienne's head, it gave her a start.

"Move back toward me," whispered Ilke. *Move back toward me,* and Adrienne shifted until she could feel the crown of her head grazing Ilke's belly. The cockatiel whooshed in and perched on a nearby chair.

"Are you a little tense?" she said. She pressed both her thumbs at the center of Adrienne's forehead. Ilke's hands were strong, small, bony. Leathered claws. The harder she pressed, the better it felt to Adrienne, all of her difficult thoughts unknotting and traveling out, up into Ilke's thumbs.

"Breathe deeply," said Ilke. "You cannot breathe deeply without it relaxing you."

Adrienne pushed her stomach in and out.

"You are from the Villa Hirschborn, aren't you?" Ilke's voice was a knowing smile.

"Ehuh."

"I thought so," said Ilke. "People are very tense up there. Rigid as boards." Ilke's hands moved down off Adrienne's forehead, along her eyebrows to her cheeks, which she squeezed repeatedly, in little circles, as if to break the weaker capillaries. She took hold of Adrienne's head and pulled. There was a dull cracking sound. Then she pressed her knuckles along Adrienne's neck. "Do you know why?"

Adrienne grunted.

"It is because they are overeducated and can no longer converse with their own mothers. It makes them a little crazy. They have literally lost their mother tongue. So they come to me. I am their mother, and they don't have to speak at all."

"Of course they *pay* you."

"Of course."

Adrienne suddenly fell into a long falling—of pleasure, of surrender, of glazed-eyed dying, a piece of heat set free in a room. Ilke rubbed Adrienne's earlobes, knuckled her scalp like a hairdresser, pulled at her neck and fingers and arms, as if they were jammed things. Adrienne would become a baby, join all the babies, in heaven, where they lived.

Ilke began to massage sandalwood oil into Adrienne's arms, pressing down, polishing, ironing, looking, at a quick glimpse, like one of Degas's laundresses. Adrienne shut her eyes again and listened to the music, which had switched from synthetic lullabies to the contrapuntal sounds of a flute and a thunderstorm. With these hands upon her, she felt a little forgiven, and began to think generally of forgiveness, how much of it was required in life: to forgive everyone, yourself, the people you loved, and then wait to be forgiven by them. Where was all this forgiveness supposed to come from? Where was this great inexhaustible supply?

"Where are you?" whispered Ilke. "You are somewhere very far."

Adrienne wasn't sure. Where was she? In her own head, like a dream; in the bellows of her lungs. What was she? Perhaps a child. Perhaps a corpse. Perhaps a fern in the forest in the storm; a singing bird. The sheets were folded back. The hands were all over her now. Perhaps she was under the table with the music, or in a musty corner of her own hip. She felt Ilke rub oil into her chest, between her breasts, out along the ribs, and circularly on the abdomen. "There is something stuck here," Ilke said. "Something not working." Then she pulled the covers back up. "Are you cold?" she asked, and though Adrienne didn't answer, Ilke brought another blanket, mysteriously heated, and laid it across Adrienne. "There," said Ilke. She lifted the blanket so that only Adrienne's feet were exposed. She rubbed oil into her soles, the toes; something squeezed out of Adrienne, like an olive. She felt as if she would cry. She felt like the baby Jesus. The grown Jesus. *The poor will always be with us.* The dead Jesus. Cheese is the best. Cheese is the best.

At her desk in the outer room, Ilke wanted money. Thirty-five thousand lire. "I can give it to you for thirty thousand, if you decide to come on a regular basis. Would you like to come on a regular basis?" asked Ilke.

Adrienne was fumbling with her wallet. She sat down in the wicker rocker near the desk. "Yes," she said. "Of course."

Ilke had put on reading glasses and now opened up her appointment book to survey the upcoming weeks. She flipped a page, then flipped it back. She looked out over her glasses at Adrienne. "How often would you like to come?"

"Every day," said Adrienne.

"Every day?"

Ilke's hoot worried Adrienne. "Every *other* day?" Adrienne peeped hopefully. Perhaps the massage had bewitched her, ruined her. Perhaps she had fallen in love.

Ilke looked back at her book and shrugged. "Every other day," she repeated slowly, as a way of holding the conversation still while she checked her schedule. "How about at two o'clock?"

"Monday, Wednesday, and Friday?"

"Perhaps we can occasionally arrange a Saturday."

"Okay. Fine." Adrienne placed the money on the desk and stood up. Ilke walked her to the door and thrust her hand out formally. Her face had changed from its earlier pinks to a strange and shiny orange.

"Thank you," said Adrienne. She shook Ilke's hand, but

then leaned forward and kissed her cheek; she would kiss the business out of this. "Good-bye," she said. She stepped gingerly down the stairs; she had not entirely returned to her body yet. She had to go slowly. She felt a little like she had just seen God, but also a little like she had just seen a hooker. Outside, she walked carefully back toward the villa, but first stopped at the gelato shop for a small dish of hazelnut ice cream. It was smooth, toasty, buttery, like a beautiful liqueur, and she thought how different it was from America, where so much of the ice cream now looked like babies had attacked it with their cookies.

"Well, Martin, it's been nice knowing you," Adrienne said, smiling. She reached out to shake his hand with one of hers, and pat him on the back with the other. "You've been a good sport. I hope there will be no hard feelings."

"You've just come back from your massage," he said a little numbly. "How was it?"

"As you would say, 'Relaxing.' As I would say . . . well, I wouldn't say."

Martin led her to the bed. "Kiss and tell," he said.

"I'll just kiss," she said, kissing.

"I'll settle," he said. But then she stopped, and went into the bathroom to shower for dinner.

At dinner, there was *zuppa alla paesana* and then *salsiccia alla griglia con spinaci.* For the first time since they'd arrived, she was seated near Martin, who was kitty-corner to her left. He was seated next to another economist and was speaking heatedly with him about a book on labor division and economic policy. "But Wilkander ripped that theory off from Boyer!" Martin let his spoon splash violently into his *zuppa* before a waiter came and removed the bowl.

"Let us just say," said the other man calmly, "that it was a sort of homage."

"If that's 'homage,' " said Martin, fidgeting with his fork, "I'd like to perform a little 'homage' on the Chase Manhattan Bank."

"I think it was felt that there was sufficient looseness there to warrant further explication."

"Right. And one's twin sibling is simply an explication of the text."

"Why not?" The other economist smiled. He was calm, probably a supply-sider.

Poor Martin, thought Adrienne. Poor Keynesian Martin, poor Marxist Martin, perspiring and red. *"Left of Lenin?"* she had heard him exclaiming the other day to an agriculturalist. "Left of *Lenin?* Left of the Lennon Sisters, you mean!" Poor godless, raised-an-atheist-in-Ohio Martin. "On Christmas," he'd said to her once, "we used to go down to the Science Store and worship the Bunsen burners."

She would have to find just the right blouse, just the right perfume, greet him on the chaise longue with a bare shoulder and a purring *"Hello, Mr. Man."* Take him down by the lake near the Sfondrata chapel and get him laid. Hire somebody. She turned to the scholar next to her, who had just arrived that morning.

"Did you have a good flight?" she asked. Her own small talk at dinner no longer shamed her.

"Flight is the word," he said. "I needed to flee my department, my bills, my ailing car. Come to a place that would take care of me."

"This is it, I guess," she said. "Though they won't fix your car. Won't even discuss it, I've found."

"I'm on a Guggenheim," he said.

"How nice!" She thought of the museum in New York, and of a pair of earrings she had bought in the gift shop there but had never worn because they always looked broken, even though that was the way they were supposed to look.

"But I neglected to ask the foundation for enough money. I didn't realize what you could ask for. I didn't ask for the same amount everyone else did, and so I received substantially less."

Adrienne was sympathetic. "So instead of a regular Guggenheim, you got a little Guggenheim."

"Yes," he said.

"A Guggenheimy," she said.

He smiled in a troubled sort of way. "Right."

"So now you have to live in Guggenheimy town."

He stopped pushing at a sausage with his fork. "Yes. I heard there would be wit here."

She tried to make her lips curl, like his.

"Sorry," he said. "I was just kidding."

"Jet lag," she said.

"Yes."

"Jetty-laggy." She smiled at him. "Baby talk. We love it." She paused. "Last week, of course, we weren't like this. You've arrived a little late."

He was a beautiful baby. In the dark, there was thumping, like tom-toms, and a piccolo high above it. She couldn't look, because when she looked, it shocked her, another woman's hands all over her. She just kept her eyes closed, and concentrated on surrender, on the restful invalidity of it. Sometimes she concentrated on being where Ilke's hands were—at her feet, at the small of her back.

"Your parents are no longer living, are they?" Ilke said in the dark.

"No."

"Did they die young?"

"Medium. They died medium. I was a menopausal, after-thought child."

"Do you want to know what I feel in you?"

"All right."

"I feel a great and deep gentleness. But I also feel that you have been dishonored."

"Dishonored?" So Japanese. Adrienne liked the sound of it.

"Yes. You have a deeply held fear. Right here." Ilke's hand went just under Adrienne's rib cage.

Adrienne breathed deeply, in and out. "I killed a baby," she whispered.

"Yes, we have all killed a baby—there is a baby in all of us. That is why people come to me, to be reunited with it."

"No, I've killed a real one."

Ilke was very quiet and then she said, "You can do the side lying now. You can put this pillow under your head, this other one between your knees." Adrienne rolled awkwardly onto her side. Finally, Ilke said, "This country, its Pope, its church, makes murderers of women. You must not let it do that to you. Move back toward me. That's it."

That's *not* it, thought Adrienne, in this temporary dissolve, seeing death and birth, seeing the beginning and then the end, how they were the same quiet black, same nothing ever after: everyone's life appeared in the world like a movie in a room. First dark, then light, then dark again. But it was all staggered, so that somewhere there was always light.

That's not it. That's not it, she thought. But thank you.

When she left that afternoon, seeking sugar in one of the shops, she moved slowly, blinded by the angle of the afternoon light but also believing she saw Martin coming toward her in the narrow street, approaching like the lumbering logger he sometimes seemed to be. Her squinted gaze, however, failed to catch his, and he veered suddenly left into a *calle*. By the time she reached the corner, he had disappeared entirely. How strange, she thought. She had felt close to something, to him, and then suddenly not. She climbed the path back up toward the villa, and went and knocked on the door of his studio, but he wasn't there.

"You smell good," she greeted Martin. It was some time later and she had just returned to the room, to find him there. "Did you just take a bath?"

"A little while ago," he said.

She curled up to him, teasingly. "Not a shower? A bath? Did you put some scented bath salts in it?"

"I took a very masculine bath," said Martin.

She sniffed him again. "What scent did you use?"

"A manly scent," he said. "Rock. I took a rock-scented bath."

"Did you take a bubble bath?" She cocked her head to one side.

He smiled. "Yes, but I, uh, made my own bubbles."

"You did?" She squeezed his bicep.

"Yeah. I hammered the water with my fist."

She walked over to the cassette player and put a cassette in. She looked over at Martin, who looked suddenly unhappy. "This music annoys you, doesn't it?"

Martin squirmed. "It's just—why can't he sing any one song all the way through?"

She thought about this. "Because he's Mr. Medleyhead?"

"You didn't bring anything else?"

"No."

She went back and sat next to Martin, in silence, smelling the scent of him, as if it were odd.

For dinner there was *vitello alla salvia,* baby peas, and a pasta made with caviar. "Nipping it in the bud." Adrienne sighed.

"An early frost." A fat elderly man, arriving late, pulled his chair out onto her foot, then sat down on it. She shrieked.

"Oh, dear, I'm sorry," said the man, lifting himself up as best he could.

"It's okay," said Adrienne. "I'm sure it's okay."

But the next morning, at exercises, Adrienne studied her foot closely during the leg lifts. The big toe was swollen and blue, and the nail had been loosened and set back at an odd and unhinged angle. "You're going to lose your toenail," said Kate.

"Great," said Adrienne.

"That happened to me once, during my first marriage. My husband dropped a dictionary on my foot. One of those subconscious things. Rage as very large book."

"You were married before?"

"Oh, yes." She sighed. "I had one of those rehearsal marriages, you know, where you're a feminist and train a guy, and then some *other* feminist comes along and *gets* the guy."

"I don't know." Adrienne scowled. "I think there's something wrong with the words *feminist* and *gets the guy* being in the same sentence."

"Yes, well—"

"Were you upset?"

"Of course. But then, I'd been doing everything. I'd insisted on separate finances, on being totally self-supporting. I was working. I was doing the child care. I paid for the house; I cooked; I cleaned. I found myself shouting, "This is feminism? Thank you, Gloria and Betty!""

"But now you're with someone else."

"Pretaught. Self-cleaning. Batteries included."

"Someone else trained him, and you stole him."

Kate smiled. "Of course. What, am I crazy?"

"What happened to the toe?"

"The nail came off. And the one that grew back was wavy and dark and used to scare the children."

"Oh," said Adrienne.

. . .

"Why would someone publish six books on Chaucer?" Adrienne was watching Martin dress. She was also smoking a cigarette. One of the strange things about the villa was that the smokers had all quit smoking, and the nonsmokers had taken it up. People were getting in touch with their alternative selves. Bequeathed cigarettes abounded. Cartons were appearing outside people's doors.

"You have to understand academic publishing," said Martin. "No one reads these books. Everyone just agrees to publish everyone else's. It's one big circle jerk. It's a giant economic agreement. When you think about it, it probably violates the Sherman Act."

"A circle jerk?" she said uncertainly. The cigarette was making her dizzy.

"Yeah," said Martin, reknotting his tie.

"But six books on Chaucer? Why not, say, a Cat Stevens book?"

"Don't look at me," he said. "I'm in the circle."

She sighed. "Then I shall sing to you. Mood music." She made up a romantic Asian-sounding tune, and danced around the room with her cigarette, in a floating, wing-limbed way. "This is my Hopi dance," she said. "So full of hope."

Then it was time to go to dinner.

The cockatiel now seemed used to Adrienne and would whistle twice, then fly into the back room, perch quickly on the picture frame, and wait with her for Ilke. Adrienne closed her eyes and breathed deeply, the flannel sheet pulled up under her arms, tightly, like a sarong.

Ilke's face appeared overhead in the dark, as if she were a mother just checking, peering into a crib. "How are you today?"

Adrienne opened her eyes, to see that Ilke was wearing a T-shirt that said SAY A PRAYER. PET A ROCK.

Say a prayer. "Good," said Adrienne. "I'm good." *Pet a rock.*

Ilke ran her fingers through Adrienne's hair, humming faintly.

"What is this music today?" Adrienne asked. Like Martin, she, too, had grown weary of the Mandy Patinkin tapes, all that unshackled exuberance.

"Crickets and elk," Ilke whispered.

"Crickets and elk."

"Crickets and elk and a little harp."

Ilke began to move around the table, pulling on Adrienne's limbs and pressing deep into her tendons. "I'm doing choreographed massage today," Ilke said. "That's why I'm wearing this dress."

Adrienne hadn't noticed the dress. Instead, with the lights now low, except for the illuminated clouds on the side wall, she felt herself sinking into the pools of death deep in her bones, the dark wells of loneliness, failure, blame. "You may turn over now," she heard Ilke say. And she struggled a little in the flannel sheets to do so, twisting in them, until Ilke helped her, as if she were a nurse and Adrienne someone old and sick—a stroke victim, that's what she was. She had become a stroke victim. Then lowering her face into the toweled cheek plates the table brace offered up to her ("the cradle," Ilke called it), Adrienne began quietly to cry, the deep touching of her body melting her down to some equation of animal sadness, shoe leather, and brine. She began to understand why people would want to live in these dusky nether zones, the meltdown brought on by sleep or drink or this. It seemed truer, more familiar to the soul than was the busy, complicated flash that was normal life. Ilke's arms leaned into her, her breasts brushing softly against Adrienne's head, which now felt connected to the rest of her only by filaments and strands. The body suddenly seemed a tumor on the brain, a mere means of conveyance, a wagon; the mind's go-cart now taken apart, laid in pieces on this table. "You have a knot here in your trapezius," Ilke said, kneading Adrienne's shoulder. "I can feel the belly of the knot right here," she added, pressing hard, bruising her shoulder a little, and then easing up. "Let go," she said. "Let go all the way, of everything."

"I might die," said Adrienne. Something surged in the music and she missed what Ilke said in reply, though it sounded a little like "Changes are good." Though perhaps it was "Chances aren't good." Ilke pulled Adrienne's toes, milking even the injured one, with its loose nail and leaky underskin, and then she left Adrienne there in the dark, in the music, though Adrienne felt it was she who was leaving, like a person dying, like a train pulling away. She felt the rage loosened from her back, floating aimlessly around in her, the rage that did not know at what or whom to rage, though it continued to rage.

She awoke to Ilke's rocking her gently. "Adrienne, get up. I have another client soon."

"I must have fallen asleep," said Adrienne. "I'm sorry."

She got up slowly, got dressed, and went out into the outer room; the cockatiel whooshed out with her, grazing her head.

"I feel like I've just been strafed," she said, clutching her hair.

Ilke frowned.

"Your bird. I mean by your bird. In *there*"—she pointed back toward the massage room—"*that* was great." She reached into her purse to pay. Ilke had moved the wicker chair to the other side of the room, so that there was no longer any place to sit down or linger. "You want lire or dollars?" she asked, and was a little taken aback when Ilke said rather firmly, "I'd prefer lire."

Ilke was bored with her. That was it. Adrienne was having a religious experience, but Ilke—Ilke was just being social. Adrienne held out the money and Ilke plucked it from her hand, then opened the outside door and leaned to give Adrienne the rushed bum's kiss—left, right—and then closed the door behind her.

Adrienne was in a fog, her legs noodly, her eyes unaccustomed to the light. Outside, in front of the *farmacia*, if she wasn't careful, she was going to get hit by a car. How could Ilke just send people out into the busy street like that, all loose and dazed? Adrienne's body felt doughy, muddy. This was good, she supposed. Decomposition. She stepped slowly, carefully, her Martha Graham step, along the narrow walk between the street and the stores. And when she turned the corner to head back up toward the path to the Villa Hirschborn, there stood Martin, her husband, rounding a corner and heading her way.

"Hi!" she said, so pleased suddenly to meet him like this, away from what she now referred to as "the compound." "Are you going to the *farmacia*?" she asked.

"Uh, yes," said Martin. He leaned to kiss her cheek.

"Want some company?"

He looked a little blank, as if he needed to be alone. Perhaps he was going to buy condoms.

"Oh, never mind," she said gaily. "I'll see you later, up at the compound, before dinner."

"Great," he said, and took her hand, took two steps away, and then let her hand go, gently, midair.

She walked away, toward a small park—il Giardino Leonardo—out past the station for the vaporetti. Near a particularly exuberant rhododendron sat a short, dark woman with a bright turquoise bandanna knotted around her neck. She had set up a table with a sign: CHIROMANTE: TAROT E FACCIA. Adrienne sat down opposite her in the empty chair. "Americano," she said.

"I do faces, palms, or cards," the woman with the blue scarf said.

Adrienne looked at her own hands. She didn't want to have her face read. She lived like that already. It happened all the time at the villa, people trying to read your face—freezing your brain with stony looks and remarks made malicious with obscurity, so that you couldn't read *their* face, while they were busy reading yours. It all made her feel creepy, like a lonely head on a poster somewhere.

"The cards are the best," said the woman. "Ten thousand lire."

"Okay," said Adrienne. She was still looking at the netting of her open hands, the dried riverbed of life just sitting there. "The cards."

The woman swept up the cards, and dealt half of them out, every which way in a kind of swastika. Then, without glancing at them, she leaned forward boldly and said to Adrienne, "You are sexually unsatisfied. Am I right?"

"Is that what the cards say?"

"In a general way. You have to take the whole deck and interpret."

"What does this card say?" asked Adrienne, pointing to one with some naked corpses leaping from coffins.

"Any one card doesn't say anything. It's the whole feeling of them." She quickly dealt out the remainder of the deck on top of the other cards. "You are looking for a guide, some kind of guide, because the man you are with does not make you happy. Am I right?"

"Maybe," said Adrienne, who was already reaching for her purse to pay the ten thousand lire so that she could leave.

"I am right," said the woman, taking the money and handing Adrienne a small smudged business card. "Stop by tomorrow. Come to my shop. I have a powder."

Adrienne wandered back out of the park, past a group of tourists climbing out of a bus, back toward the Villa Hirschborn—through the gate, which she opened with her key, and up the long stone staircase to the top of the promontory. Instead of going back to the villa, she headed out through the woods toward her studio, toward the dead tufts of spiders she had memorialized in her grief. She decided to take a different path, not the one toward the studio, but one that led farther up the hill, a steeper grade, toward an open meadow at the top, with a small Roman ruin at its edge—a corner of the hill's original fortress still stood there. But in the middle of the meadow, something came over her—a balmy wind, or the heat from the uphill hike, and she took off all her clothes, lay down in the grass, and stared around at the dusky sky. To either side of her, the spokes of tree branches crisscrossed upward in a kind of cat's cradle. More directly overhead she studied the silver speck of a jet, the metallic head of its white stream like the tip of a thermometer. There were a hundred people inside this head of a pin, thought Adrienne. Or was it, perhaps, just the head of a pin? When was something truly small, and when was it a matter of distance? The branches of the trees seemed to encroach inward and rotate a little to the left, a little to the right, like something mechanical, and as she began to drift off, she saw the beautiful Spearson baby, cooing in a clown hat; she saw Martin furiously swimming in a pool; she saw the strewn beads of her own fertility, all the eggs within her, leap away like a box of tapioca off a cliff. It seemed to her that everything she had ever needed to know in her life she had known at one time or another, but she just hadn't known all those things at once, at the same time, at a single moment. They were scattered through and she had had to leave and forget one in order to get to another. A shadow fell across her, inside her, and she could feel herself retreat to that place in her bones where death was and you greeted it like an acquaintance in a room; you said hello and were then ready for whatever was next—which might be a guide, the guide that might be sent to you, the guide to lead you back out into your life again.

Someone was shaking her gently. She flickered slightly awake, to see the pale, ethereal face of a strange older woman peering down at her as if Adrienne were something odd in the bottom of a teacup. The woman was dressed all in white—white shorts, white cardigan, white scarf around her head. The guide.

"Are you . . . the *guide?*" whispered Adrienne.

"Yes, my dear," the woman said in a faintly English voice that sounded like the Good Witch of the North.

"You are?" Adrienne asked.

"Yes," said the woman. "And I've brought the group up here to view the old fort, but I was a little worried that you might not like all of us traipsing past here while you were, well—are you all right?"

Adrienne was more awake now and sat up, to see at the end of the meadow the group of tourists she'd previously seen below in the town, getting off the bus.

"Yes, thank you," mumbled Adrienne. She lay back down to think about this, hiding herself in the walls of grass, like a child hoping to trick the facts. "Oh my God," she finally said, and groped about to her left to find her clothes and clutch them, panicked, to her belly. She breathed deeply, then put them on, lying as flat to the ground as she could, hard to glimpse, a snake getting back inside its skin, a change, perhaps, of reptilian heart. Then she stood, zipped her pants, secured her belt buckle, and waved, squaring her shoulders and walking bravely past the bus and the tourists, who, though they tried not to stare at her, did stare.

By this time, everyone at the villa was privately doing imitations of everyone else. "Martin, you should announce who you're doing before you do it," said Adrienne, dressing for dinner. "I can't really tell."

"Cube-steak Yuppies!" Martin ranted at the ceiling. "Legends in their own mind! Rumors in their own room!"

"Yourself. You're doing yourself." She straightened his collar and tried to be wifely.

For dinner, there was *cioppino* and *insalata mista* and *pesce con pignoli,* a thin piece of fish like a leaf. From everywhere around the dining room, scraps of dialogue—rhetorical barbed wire, indignant and arcane—floated over toward her. "As an aesthetician, you can't not be interested in the sublime!" Or "Why, that's the most facile thing I've ever heard!" Or "Good grief, tell him about the Peasants' Revolt, would you?" But no one spoke to her directly. She had no subject, not really, not one she liked, except perhaps movies and movie stars. Martin was at a far table, his back toward her, listening to the monk man. At times like these, she thought, it was probably a good idea to carry a small hand puppet.

She made her fingers flap in her lap.

Finally, one of the people next to her turned and introduced himself. His face was poppy-seeded with whiskers, and he seemed to be looking down, watching his own mouth move. When she asked him how he liked it here so far, she received a fairly brief history of the Ottoman Empire. She nodded and smiled, and at the end, he rubbed his dark beard, looked at her compassionately, and said, "We are not good advertisements for this life. Are we?"

"There *are* a lot of dingdongs here," she admitted. He looked a little hurt, so she added, "But I like that about a place. I do."

When after dinner she went for an evening walk with Martin, she tried to strike up a conversation about celebrities and movie stars. "I keep thinking about Princess Caroline's husband being killed," she said.

Martin was silent.

"That poor family," said Adrienne. "There's been so much tragedy."

Martin glared at her. "Yes," he said facetiously. "That poor, cursed family. I keep thinking, What can I do to help? What can I do? And I think and I think, and I think so much, I'm helpless. I throw up my hands and end up doing nothing. I'm helpless!" He began to walk faster, ahead of her, down into the village. Adrienne began to run to keep up. She felt insane. Marriage, she thought, it's an institution all right.

Near the main piazza, under a streetlamp, the woman had

set up her table again under the CHIROMANTE: TAROT E FACCIA sign. When she saw Adrienne, she called out, "Give me your birthday, signora, and your husband's birthday, and I will do your charts to tell you whether the two of you are compatible! Or—" She paused to study Martin skeptically as he rushed past. "Or I can just tell you right now."

"Have you been to this woman before?" Martin asked, slowing down. Adrienne grabbed his arm and started to lead him away.

"I needed a change of scenery."

Now he stopped. "Well," he said sympathetically, calmer after some exercise, "who could blame you." Adrienne took his hand, feeling a grateful, marital love—alone, in Italy, at night, in May. Was there any love that wasn't at bottom a grateful one? The moonlight glittered off the lake like electric fish, like a school of ice.

"What are you doing?" Adrienne asked Ilke the next afternoon. The lamps were particularly low, though there was a spotlight directed onto a picture of Ilke's mother, which she had placed on an end table, for the month, in honor of Mother's Day. The mother looked ghostly, like a sacrifice. What if Ilke were truly a witch? What if fluids and hairs and nails were being collected as offerings in memory of her mother?

"I'm fluffing your aura," she said. "It is very dark today, burned down to a shadowy rim." She was manipulating Adrienne's toes, and Adrienne suddenly had a horror-movie vision of Ilke with jars of collected toe juice in a closet for Satan, who, it would be revealed, *was* Ilke's mother. Perhaps Ilke would lean over suddenly and bite Adrienne's shoulder, drink her blood. How could Adrienne control these thoughts? She felt her aura fluff like the fur of a screeching cat. She imagined herself, for the first time, never coming here again. *Good-bye. Farewell.* It would be a brief affair, a little nothing; a chat on the porch at a party.

Fortunately, there were other things to keep Adrienne busy.

She had begun spray-painting the spiders, and the results were interesting. She could see herself explaining to a dealer back home that the work represented the spider web of solitude—a vibration at the periphery reverberates inward (experiential, deafening) and the spider rushes out from the center to devour the gonger and the gong. Gone. She could see the dealer taking her phone number and writing it down on an extremely loose scrap of paper.

And there was the occasional after-dinner singsong, scholars and spouses gathered around the piano in various states of inebriation and forgetfulness. "Okay, that may be how you learned it, Harold, but that's *not* how it goes."

There was also the Asparagus Festival, which, at Carlo's suggestion, she and Kate Spalding, in one of her T-shirts—*all right, already with the T-shirts, Kate*—decided to attend. They took a hydrofoil across the lake and climbed a steep road up toward a church square. The road was long and tiring and Adrienne began to refer to it as the "Asparagus Death Walk."

"Maybe there isn't really a festival," she suggested, gasping for breath, but Kate kept walking, ahead of her.

"Go for the burn!" said Kate, who liked exercise too much.

Adrienne sighed. Up until last year, she had always thought people were saying "Go for the *bird*." Now off in the trees was the ratchety cheep of some, along with the competing hourly chimes of two churches, followed later by the single off-tone of the half hour. When she and Kate finally reached the Asparagus Festival, it turned out to be only a little ceremony where a few people bid very high prices for clutches of asparagus described as *"bello, bello,"* the proceeds from which went to the local church.

"I used to grow asparagus," said Kate on their walk back

down. They were taking a different route this time, and the lake and its ocher villages spread out before them, peaceful and far away. Along the road, wildflowers grew in a pallet of pastels, like soaps.

"I could never grow asparagus," said Adrienne. As a child, her favorite food had been "asparagus with holiday sauce." "I did grow a carrot once, though. But it was so small, I just put it in a scrapbook."

"Are you still seeing Ilke?"

"This week, at any rate. How about you?"

"She's booked solid. I couldn't get another appointment. All the scholars, you know, are paying her regular visits."

"Really?"

"Oh, yes," said Kate very knowingly. "They're tense as dimes." Already Adrienne could smell the fumes of the Fiats and the ferries and delivery vans, the Asparagus Festival far away.

"Tense as dimes?"

Back at the villa, Adrienne waited for Martin, and when he came in, smelling of sandalwood, all the little deaths in her bones told her this: he was seeing the masseuse.

She sniffed the sweet parabola of his neck and stepped back. "I want to know how long you've been getting massages. Don't lie to me," she said slowly, her voice hard as a spike. Anxiety shrank his face: his mouth caved in, his eyes grew beady and scared.

"What makes you think I've been getting—" he started to say. "Well, just once or twice."

She leapt away from him and began pacing furiously about the room, touching the furniture, not looking at him. "How could you?" she asked. "You know what my going there has meant to me! How could you not tell me?" She picked up a book on the dressing table—*Industrial Relations Systems*—and slammed it back down. "How could you horn in on this experience? How could you be so furtive and untruthful?"

"I am terribly sorry," he said.

"Yeah, well, so am I," said Adrienne. "And when we get home, I want a divorce." She could see it now, the empty apartment, the bad eggplant parmigiana, all the Halloweens she would answer the doorbell, a boozy divorcée frightening the little children with too much enthusiasm for their costumes. "I feel so fucking *dishonored*!" Nothing around her seemed able to hold steady; nothing held.

Martin was silent and she was silent and then he began to speak, in a beseeching way, there it was the beseech again, rumbling at the edge of her life like a truck. "We are both so lonely here," he said. "But I have only been waiting for you. That is all I have done for the last eight months. To try not to let things intrude, to let you take your time, to make sure you ate something, to buy the goddamn Spearsons a new picnic bench, to bring you to a place where anything at all might happen, where you might even leave me, but at least come back into life at last—"

"You did?"

"Did what?"

"You bought the Spearsons a new *picnic bench*?"

"Yes, I did."

She thought about this. "Didn't they think you were being hostile?"

"Oh . . . I think, yes, they probably thought it was hostile."

And the more Adrienne thought about it, about the poor bereaved Spearsons, and about Martin and all the ways he tried to show her he was on her side, whatever that meant, how it was both the hope and shame of him that he was always doing his best, the more she felt foolish, deprived of reasons. Her rage flapped awkwardly away like a duck. She felt as she had when her cold, fierce parents had at last grown sick and old, stick-boned and saggy, protected by infirmity the way cuteness protected a baby, or should, it should protect a baby, and she had been left with her rage—vestigial girlhood rage—inappropriate and intact. She would hug her parents good-bye, the gentle, emptied sacks of them, and think *Where did you go?*

Time, Adrienne thought. What a racket.

Martin had suddenly begun to cry. He sat at the bed's edge and curled inward, his soft, furry face in his great hard hands, his head falling downward into the bright plaid of his shirt.

She felt dizzy and turned away, toward the window. A fog had drifted in, and in the evening light the sky and the lake seemed a singular blue, like a Monet. "I've never seen you cry," she said.

"Well, I cry," he said. "I can even cry at the sports page if the games are too close. Look at me, Adrienne. You never really look at me."

But she could only continue to stare out the window, touching her fingers to the shutters and frame. She felt far away, as if she were back home, walking through the neighborhood at dinnertime: when the cats sounded like babies and the babies sounded like birds, and the fathers were home from work, their children in their arms gumming the language, air shaping their flowery throats into a park of singing. Through the windows wafted the smell of cooking food.

"We are with each other now," Martin was saying. "And in the different ways it means, we must try to make a life."

Out over the Sfondrata chapel tower, where the fog had broken, she thought she saw a single star, like the distant nose of a jet; there were people in the clayey clouds. She turned, and for a moment it seemed they were all there in Martin's eyes, all the absolving dead in residence in his face, the angel of the dead baby shining like a blazing creature, and she went to him, to protect and encircle him, seeking the heart's best trick, *oh, terrific heart.* "Please, forgive me," she said.

And he whispered, "Of course. It is the only thing. Of course."